Belle "Mendelssohn"

WILD SEED

By Paige Mitchell

A WILDERNESS OF MONKEYS
LOVE IS NOT A SAFE COUNTRY
THE COVENANT
ACT OF LOVE
WILD SEED

Paige Mitchell

WILD SEED

DOUBLEDAY & COMPANY, INC.

GARDEN CITY, NEW YORK 1982

Library of Congress Cataloging in Publication Data
Mitchell, Paige.
    Wild seed.
    I. Title.
PS3563.I79W5   813'.54
AACR1
ISBN 0-385-14368-0
Library of Congress Catalog Card Number: 79–8029

PROLOGUE

1

He had slept badly—not enough sleep for a man scheduled to perform a full day of heart surgery—he had tossed all night like a man running from himself.

Now, coming out onto the bedroom balcony, Tate saw the gunmetal shadows of night had thinned to a shroud and the first rays of dawn were branding the River Oaks estate—striking masses of roses and prize-winning azaleas, striking the stables and the swimming pool and the adobe-brick terrace that descended like the weathered treads of an Aztec temple. Light broke the next instant. Raising his eyes, he watched the sky spread like spilled silver. Then, like a threat and a promise, the Texas sun arched into view over the ancient oaks and exploded through the haze.

He remained motionless, troubled, aware of the wind from the Houston port, grit in the wind, and he could smell the refineries—Calder refineries—the acrid smell of petroleum and chemicals just underneath the sweet scent of yellow *huisache,* reminding him of the perfumed whores who had still worked the Calder oil-fields when he was a kid. Frowning, he watched the sun move swiftly, aware that his shadow crawled with it, a lean muscular shadow, massive hands falling empty without the scalpel that, in the last dozen years, had become an extension of himself. Often, he dreamed of stalking cancer like a hunter in some lush tropical jungle of malignancy; he dreamed of penetrating the pulsing cavern of the human chest as if the heart cavity were an Egyptian tomb and cardiac surgery had endowed him with an archaeological permit to disturb the ancient mysteries of love and death. Last night, his dreams had been nightmares. He had dreamed of a bloody sunrise, burning like Hell. And sex. And a terrifying instant when he looked into a hole deep in the heart of a nine-month-old child pronounced doomed by a hospital loudspeaker that invoked the dead as it paged the living: *Dr. Calder . . . Dr. Tate Calder . . .*

He went inside. He shut the french doors behind him and pulled the shutters half-closed. In the light and shadow of the bedroom, Joanna slept, face-down like a child, one slender arm trailing off the edge of the massive four-poster. He stood there a moment, staring at the bed. Joanna, too, had been plagued by dreams: *Other times, other places . . . trying to tell me something—I don't know what.* His great-grandfather, Ben Calder, had hewn the four-poster from cypress that grew on the edge of the Brazos. His father had been born in that bed; so had he. Four generations of Calders had been conceived there, including his own children.

"It's the bed." He crossed the room and stood over Joanna.

She turned, a disheveled mane of wheat-colored hair tumbling over her profile.

"The bed," he said. "It's more than a hundred years old. That's forty, fifty thousand nights. Even Scheherazade only had to deal with a thousand and one."

He watched her sit up, knees propped, forehead lowered, arms wrapped around her shins, creating a cocoon.

"It's all that Calder history," he said. "All those dreams and nightmares that don't belong to us." He lowered himself to the edge of the bed. "I don't want a divorce."

She looked up, gazing at him, trying to look into him, or through him. In the silence, he could hear the echo of their midnight discussion, crisp phrases: ritual had replaced intimacy; he could remember her saying that. Friendship had supplanted passion. The domestication of all wild impulses had taken place. "You can't legislate feelings," she said.

"What does that mean?"

"We should try to be mature."

"Man is a species that dies before it matures."

"Why are you making me say it?"

"The marriage isn't working." His tone was curt. He heard the truth in it. Fleetingly, he heard other truths underneath, like the chattering of insects just before a tornado.

"What do we do about it?"

"I don't know."

"You've already claimed your freedom," she said. "Other women—"

He had an image of both of them, like Texas tumbleweeds, rolling and thrashing and picking up whatever they encountered. He had an impulse to hold her. He didn't touch her. For an instant, he saw through the crack in their marriage and caught a glimpse of a deeper truth: it said they were heading toward events prescribed by forces beyond them; it said they were being carried by emotions that had originated before they were born and they were being propelled toward some inexorable cataclysm.

BOOK ONE

1844–48

2

That summer it rained.

Every day Ben Calder watched the clouds move in from Prussia over the rolling hills of the western Beskids to converge with the black drifts that traveled from eastern Russia across Poland. Every day the clouds hovered over the heart of Europe like old women in mourning. Then darkness would shroud the linen mill, and his best friend, Thomas, would light candles and they'd continue to work, block printing the linen with madder and indigo and quercitron—as the thunder cracked and roared through the Upper Silesian countryside and the heavens unleashed a raging black rain.

Then the mud turned the lowlands to marshes; and the potato tubers began to rot. That was July. It was August when Magda, the village crone, shuffled her cards and warned that the winter of 1844 would be the worst in twenty years.

Ben went to see Magda in August.

Magda claimed to be a hundred and twelve. Magda could remember when Upper Silesia belonged to the Empress Maria Theresa of Austria. She had no use for the Prussian Frederick the Great, and sometimes confused him with the Bavarian hunchback, King Ludwig. Ben wanted to know about Thomas' sister, Lilli—but when he asked about Lilli, Magda shook her head and her cheeks shriveled, revealing an absence of teeth.

"You will risk the unknown," she told him. *"You will change the nature of those you sire and those who come afterward. You will sow a wild seed."*

But he was only nineteen, and anything beyond the village of Brieg was remote to him.

He thought constantly of Lilli. Lilli glowed in his mind like a candle in the darkness. On Saturdays—through the open door of the dye room —he watched her appear with the others who brought in their linen to be weighed and examined. Lilli seemed fragile, ephemeral—pale silken curls that were gold in the sun and silver by moonlight; he'd never seen them by moonlight. On Saturdays Lilli turned into a wildcat if Vogel tried to cheat her.

"She's only sixteen," Thomas said. "and you're not a Catholic."

By autumn he had fallen in love with her anyway.

In autumn the wind came to blow through the range of the Sudeten Mountains and lift Ben's eyes toward the sky. From the lowlands he watched the men look up at the royal forests where patches of crimson and yellow appeared. Then the men vanished. Then only the smoke from the furnaces strained toward the thin rays of sunlight, and only the mills and the forges sent sparks flying heavenward long past dark, as the man-made arteries of the industrial giant throbbed without surcease. In autumn the heart of Europe always beat faster.

They cut his pay.

They cut Thomas' pay, too.

Thomas was half Ben's size. Thomas was squat and compact, compressed by the same poverty that had honed Lilli to a fragile perfection. Thomas threatened to hurl Vogel into the River Oder.

Mornings, Ben watched his mother rise two hours earlier to comb the scutched flax and work the handloom, and her own pay was two groschen less. Hannah Calder said nothing. What was left of last year's potatoes, she used sparingly—and Ben watched her dry the peelings and store them for days to come that might be worse.

Along the path to the mill, in the dull predawn light, he saw the torchweeds were dead, and the wind whipped the stunted willows. He came home in darkness, stooping as he entered the hut, and once inside, he stood hunched and bowed—and when Hannah spoke, he responded in a voice that boomed and echoed, like a man standing under a bridge, ankle-deep in rushing water.

He ate black bread and sauerkraut. After supper, he went out again and walked alone along the River Oder, which glittered with frost and reflected the cottages and set them trembling in the water. He walked slowly, thinking about Lilli. Looking up at the stars, he remembered old Magda who had predicted other kinds of lives to be lived—not meant for him now; perhaps later.

He veered away from the bank and trudged through mud until he reached the abandoned monastery that had served for a time as a school for the peasants until the Prussians had forbidden the use of the Polish language and closed it. Now empty, it was a refuge for screech owls. He pushed aside the loose boards at a rear window and entered as he always did, by crawling through. In the cloister, he stood quietly for a long time, listening to the silence that no longer echoed with the litany of ancient mass or the promise of heaven. Like most Germans, he had been reared as a Lutheran, but he thought about God in the same way he thought about his father and his three brothers: as absent. Not God, but a need for solitude drew him here. When anger threatened to seize him, he came here to bellow where no one could hear. Then it passed. When yearning overwhelmed him, images appeared in the diamondlike patches of moonlight, indecipherable. Then they, too, passed. Now, this night, he prowled along the stone corridor and through the old wine cellar, seeking equilibrium, waiting—until what came, finally, was old Magda's voice:

"You will go from the bowels of the earth to the stars."

It was only a fragment.

"So remember this—"

Hope stirred, irrational.

"Let those who would be gods first learn to be human."

The prophecy broke in midair, like glass cracking—and he was left with a premonition of danger, of something waiting for him.

3

Ben borrowed the mule and the potato cart from the peasant, Nicolai Lubeck. Ben promised Nicolai firewood.

The moon came up, obscured by clouds and the wind howled bitterly. Ben watched a half-dozen farms pass, a forge and a brandy distiller, fields and forests. He watched Thomas prod the mule into forbidden territory.

"How much farther?"

"Just through these woods." Thomas struck the mule. The moon slipped from the clouds. The twin towers of the Pless castle pierced the trees, and Thomas said, "We'll have to be careful now." Thomas' broad flat face was scarred and bruised from fights in the tavern. Thomas' yellow beard was scrubby. It struck Ben that he loved Thomas. The thought was strange to him.

The mule picked its way deeper into the forest. The wind wailed and whipped the stunted willows. Thomas leaned forward. "Listen—"

"What?"

"Dogs."

"It's the wind," Ben said.

A clearing appeared. The forester's house became visible—a low wooden structure of rough-hewn logs near the mouth of a churning brook. Thomas halted and called out, "Hello, Ott!"—and gave a low shrill whistle. From nearby, dogs answered, baying. Thomas cursed them.

"They're penned," Ben said.

Then the door creaked and a hulk of a man materialized, carrying a double-barreled shotgun and holding a big black dog on a leash. "Who calls Ott?"

"Thomas Hlasko—"

"The Pole?"

"*Da*—"

Ott leashed the dog to a stump and lit a small torch before he strode toward the cart—as tall as Ben, and broader, arms as thick as firs and an oxenlike torso under the leather apron. "Poverty turns women into whores and men into scavengers, eh?" Ott laughed. The torch lit his face. What was visible under the mane of grizzled hair and the bristly gray beard was as rusted as old iron. Thomas handed over the jug of vodka. Ott drank deeply, wiped his mouth on his shirtsleeve, then raised the torch to Ben's face. "And you? Who are you?"

"Ben Calder."

Ott moved closer, squinting. "The Frenchman's son?"

Ben nodded.

Ott shifted the torch and peered into Ben's face. "Which one of the four?"

Ben shielded his eyes. "The youngest," he said. "The last."

"The others gone?"

Ben nodded.

"How long since your father left? Twelve years? Fourteen?"

"*Ich weiss es nicht—*"

"Aye—so you're German then, like your mother," Ott said. He prodded the mule with his shotgun and sent the mule plunging forward. "Cut only the woods near the old gold mine," he called after them. "And get out before dawn. Do you hear my dogs? They're caged now." The wind carried his final warning. "At dawn, I have to set them loose, and they'll tear you apart!"

The mine had been boarded up. Now, the boards had been torn aside to reveal a gaping hole like the mouth of hell. Thomas yanked the mule to a halt and peered into it. "Do you think there's any gold left?"

"Not a nugget."

"What if there is—?"

Ben shivered. "I don't want to go down there."

Thomas produced two axes and a smaller jug. He swallowed some vodka and offered it. Ben shook his head, retrieving the French military saber that had belonged to his father and strapping it on before he climbed down. Thomas was squinting at him. "How much do you weigh?"

"I don't know."

"How long do you think it would take you to wrestle Schroeder to the mat?"

"Schroeder?"

"That Prussian corporal who's always swaggering about. The one with the missing earlobe." Thomas grinned. "They say a prostitute bit it off in Oppel when he refused to pay." Thomas swallowed more vodka. "The purse is two thalers."

"I've nothing against Schroeder." Still uneasy, Ben looked around— seeing nothing—only moonlight and shadows, only pine and fir and an occasional wild pear. He had made Hannah's handloom from wild pear. He thought about Lilli, in Thomas' cottage—three women sharing one loom; Lilli and her sister, Helma, and her mother, somebody sleeping, somebody always weaving. He thought about making Lilli a loom. The thought eased him.

Thomas lit a lantern. A family of jackrabbits took flight. Thomas lurched after them. From the shadows, Ben heard the thud of an ax. Then Thomas came back with the bloody carcass. Ben built a fire. Thomas skinned the animal and set it on a spit to roast. Then their axes rang out. Under their hands, trees fell, crashing through branches to lie at their feet. The smell of the roasting rabbit permeated the woods. Periodically, Thomas warmed himself with vodka. Regularly, Ben checked the sky.

"Ott keeps his word," Thomas said. They moved deeper into the forest. "How did he know your father?"

"I don't know." The wild pear fell.

"What happened to him? Is he dead?—like mine?"

"Yes," Ben said. "He's dead." It seemed true. He had buried the image of Anatole Calder who had carried him on his shoulders, singing French Revolutionary songs. Then Anatole Calder had left. Ott had stirred no memories—and even the weight of his father's sword summoned up nothing beyond the thought of his own protection.

Thomas chanted something in Polish and crossed himself. Who the prayer was for, Ben couldn't tell.

The moon sank. Darkness rolled in, gnawing at the small area of lamplight. Then the heavens rumbled and lightning flashed briefly. "We'd better go back now," Ben said. A few drops, big as hailstones, began to spatter.

Together, they retraced their steps, cutting the trees into logs, then stacking the logs in each other's arms and carrying them back. They were down to the last load when the thunder rolled like cannon fire and lightning seared the heavens, illuminating the woods around them. Nearby, a pine sizzled and burst into flames. Then the sky broke and the rain came down in torrents.

Thomas reached the cart first. Ben looked back. The burning pine had already been extinguished and had turned to char. "The rabbit—" Thomas shouted. The fire was wet ash. Thomas lunged at the spit and came back, carrying it.

Ben struck the mule. The cart rolled a few inches, then stopped. Ben lashed out with the whip. The mule strained forward in the rain, but the cart refused to budge. The earth, already mud, was quickly turning to bog. Beneath him, Ben felt the cart begin to sink. "We'll have to build a track—"

Working in sheets of rain, they laid a dozen logs in the mud, pushed the cart over the improvised track, then gathered the logs and laid them again. Boughs creaked in the storm, sending channels of water to earth. The cart moved at a snail's pace. Each time Ben looked back, he could still see the mine. Then the jackdaws started to chatter and the rain quit suddenly, leaving an eerie silence behind. A strange powdery light washed the mist and turned it iridescent. At the same instant that Ben realized he was looking at the first rays of dawn, he heard the dogs.

Ben leaped for a branch, caught it, then slung himself up and began to climb. When he looked down, he saw Thomas was standing on the cart, paralyzed, and the dogs were coming out of the woods. There were three of them, yellow-eyed, big as wolves. "Throw the rabbit and *jump*—" Ben ordered. Thomas hurled the carcass. The dogs pounced on it, fighting. Thomas sailed toward the branch, caught hold of it and swung back and forth a moment, legs dangling, before he hurtled to earth not ten yards from the dogs. He bolted then, racing across the bog until the mine swallowed him. An instant later, the dogs bounded after him, howling in pursuit, leaving only bleached bones behind.

Ben made no decision. There was no choice in it, no thought and no feeling. His legs carried him down the tree, without his volition. Running, he stumbled once and sank to his knees in the mud, but he raised himself and kept going. Then he made himself enter the gloom of the mine.

Thomas was crouched on a ledge, a pool of water separating him from the dogs. Bloodthirsty, they were whining and snarling, running back and forth. Then one of them turned and Ben looked directly into its crazed eyes before he fell, reeling. He felt the dog's slaver. Pain seared his cheek and he recognized the smell of blood as his own. Thrashing, he managed to pull out the saber and strike out, wildly. The monster roared, then fell back, writhing and screaming. The other two came at him now. The first sprang sideways. He caught it in the side, gashing the animal nearly in half. The second whirled madly in a series of frantic acrobats. He raised the blade again and brought it down on the animal's rump. Stunned, the dog howled and soared across the water, covering the distance between Thomas and itself.

The teeth fastened as it landed, tearing at Thomas' leg, exposing flesh and muscle and bone as white as chalk. For a split-second, Ben saw the fragility of life. Then Ben howled. The cry shuddered, wrenched from him. The cry filled the cavern, originating in some primal part of his being he had not known existed. The dog halted and turned slowly, as if he had called it, had cursed it, in its own language. Uncertain, it deferred. Thomas, silent, inert, slid into the water.

Ben dived in and brought Thomas up. When he reached the bank, he lay still, holding Thomas. For a long time, he couldn't move. Silence and darkness enveloped him. Then, from somewhere in the recesses of his mind, he heard his own voice, saying: *"I paid you a half groschen —can't you give me something for now?"* And he heard old Magda answer: *"In the forest is a cave. In the cave, there are three demons. If you slay the demons, you will set loose the Satan within."* Magda had crossed herself: *"This will be a month hence."*

A chill ran through him. He counted backward. It was exactly a month. Then he raised his head. There were three dogs. Two were slain. The third was mortally wounded.

He told himself Magda was a crazy old woman.

He knew now she wasn't. He knew there was more. What else had she said? What? He strained, listening, but only silence rang in his ears.

Slowly, he rose and lifted Thomas in his arms and carried him out. Lying quietly in a pool of its own blood, the animal watched them depart.

4

Lilli didn't ask why. She said the old monastery was fine and nine o'clock was fine. She looked tired.

Ben stood beside her outside the mill while the others filed past in a sluggish river of weary humanity. Their resignation disturbed him.

He hadn't seen Lilli since he had brought Thomas home. She seemed smaller to him now, less headstrong, subdued. The proud tilt of the chin was the same, but the feathery curls were finer than he remembered and her eyes, which were gray like the smoke from the furnaces, no longer burned like they were being stoked by the devil. He found himself thinking about her breasts.

She said, "Thomas has been asking for you."

"I'll come when I can."

"It's three weeks—"

"I know." He watched her go over his face, trying to see what was wrong.

"You're different, aren't you?"

"Yes."

"I'm not afraid of it," she said.

He had carried Thomas from the mine. He had emptied the cart of everything but the pear wood; he had kept the pear wood. Then he had harnessed himself alongside the mule and pulled the cart up to the main road.

He had brought Thomas home.

He had washed his father's saber in the River Oder and put it away.

Days, he dipped the wooden blocks into alum and mordant and moved the length of the linen and back again, and he tried not to think about Thomas; he immersed the cloth in the boiling vats and he watched the pinks and purples erupt, and he managed not to think about Thomas. After two weeks, they sent him someone to train, a pale thin boy of fifteen; he despised him.

Thomas' wound festered. They applied leeches. They brought in Father Wolchek to pray over Thomas in Polish. Then they cut off Thomas' leg.

He couldn't make himself go to see Thomas.

Nights, he worked on the loom. He set up a primitive shop in the cellar of the monastery. He worked by candlelight, splicing the pear wood and framing the outline and wrapping the wires in twine, painstakingly knotting each to form a small eye. He carved a treadle. He made a dozen pair of shafts. It was no longer for Lilli. It was for himself, to connect him to what had gone before, to what he had felt before. Feelings had once bubbled in him like water from an underground spring. Now they rushed in a torrent, threatening to drown him in physical desire.

He understood something was happening to him. He blamed *them*. The prince and the ministers, the judges and the constable and the tax collectors—even the soldiers—had been distant oppressors. Then they had sent dogs, killers. What was Thomas' crime? What was his? What was one cart of firewood from miles of forest? Was a life less to them than a cart of firewood? Were two lives less? Were hundreds?

He signed up to wrestle Schroeder.

On the second Saturday in October, they set up the ring in the tavern and lit the torches outside. The crowd gathered, filling the benches, bringing stools and barrels to sit on, or squatting on the sawdust floor. The Germans sat apart from the Poles, the millworkers from the peasants, and the peasants from the Prussian patrol—the tavern filled and the air grew heavy with a love of violence and a need for vengeance against those who could be named and those who could not. Ben knew what they wanted; they wanted to see a murder.

Schroeder was faceless to him, an anonymous enemy, no more than

a sack of potatoes to be heaved around for the price of two thalers.
Ben heard neither the voices of those who urged him on nor those
who cursed him. He heard only the thud of flesh against flesh, and a
buzzing in his head, and the dark silence of his own mindless anger.
Then he heard the bell—and he found Schroeder on the mat beneath
him, head half-turned to reveal a missing earlobe, veins bulging in his
throat; nearly strangled.

Afterward, it frightened him. Afterward, when he looked in the glass,
he saw his own scar, a half moon, three inches long, that curved beneath his left cheekbone. When he looked in the glass, he saw his eyes
were yellow and they had started to glitter like the eyes of the dogs.

Lilli came wearing Thomas' old sweater and Thomas' cap, as if she
meant to look like a small boy to him. It made him more conscious of
her womanhood. In the vaulted cloister, the ceiling was more than
twenty feet high, the beams eaten away by time and weather. Moonlight filtered through, shrouding her figure in an unearthly glow, giving
her the look of a medieval saint. It made him more conscious of his
physical desire. He turned his head, afraid she might see.

He led her along the stone corridor, past boarded-over windows and
a marble statue of the crucifixion broken in three places. He wondered
if she was thinking about the Polish monks who had once walked here,
counting their beads and praying. Now crows nestled in the belfry, and
the bell that had once announced mass had been stolen, melted down
in some blacksmith's forge. He wondered if she saw their presence as
the same kind of desecration. He wondered if it would be.

"Why haven't you been to see Thomas?" She hadn't spoken until
then.

He hesitated. "I can't."

He led her down the winding stone staircase into the cellar, past the
rows of deteriorating casks which still emitted a sweetish smell, a memory of ancient wine. The walls were whitewashed and streaked with
rust. The floor was covered with a fine layer of sand. He set the lantern
on a ledge. Through the window, he could see the graveyard, moonlight
on the headstones. From somewhere, a screech owl hooted.

She touched his arm, tentatively, asking him for something.

"Did you know that screech owls are Cracovite nuns who were false
to their vows?"

He shook his head.

"Are you superstitious?"

He thought about old Magda. He nodded. He remembered Magda had warned him. To slay the demons meant to release the Satan within. It struck him the Satan within was the one in himself.

"How is it at the mill?"

"The same."

"Do you miss Thomas?"

"Why are we always talking about Thomas?" He heard his own anger.

"You saved Thomas' life," she said.

He shook his head and turned away. Outside, a tree cast a shadow which kept changing shape. As he watched, it turned into unspeakable shapes. His groin began to throb. "I didn't save Thomas' life," he said. "I saved my own." His voice cracked. "I climbed a tree. I kept climbing. I didn't help Thomas up. I didn't go back for him."

He waited for her to answer. She didn't answer. He couldn't bear to look at her, so he strode to the far end of the cellar where he stooped and lit the remains of the candles. He watched the light flicker over the soft pile of sawdust until it encompassed the loom, making the tarred twine gleam like silver. In a minute, she followed him.

"I want to marry you," he said.

She gazed at the loom for a long time. She walked around it, examining it. Then she stroked the burnished wood tenderly, as if she were stroking a child. Without looking at him, she said, "I'm going into a convent. In Kolisz."

"No," he said.

"I'm going to take Thomas with me. Father Wolchek knows someone who can teach him to make gunstocks. There's going to be a Polish uprising." She looked at him directly. "We need a wagon. We need someone to take us across the border."

"No," he said again.

"I love you," she said. "I've loved you for a long time. Even before I knew what it was I felt."

"Then *why*—?"

She faced him, solemnly. "I've already been to all the places I'll never see. I've already loved all the men I'll never know and all the children I'll never bear. I have no destiny. Do you understand that?"

He shook his head. But he felt something stir in him, the memory of

Magda—a sense of worlds beyond this one, vague and incomprehensible. "I don't know anything about women," he said.

"They break our spirit," she said. "They starve us and they cripple us and they make our children slaves. The only men who survive are the servants and the animals. The only women who survive are the nuns and the prostitutes."

He saw she wasn't sixteen anymore. In the past three weeks, he had changed. He saw she had changed, too. She had catapulted into a terrible wisdom.

She looked past him into the darkness. "I want every word I say to be Grace," she said. "And every step I take to be Dance. I want to fear nothing in God's world. Not even my own death."

He closed his eyes. He refused to believe she was going away, though he sensed she had already gone—to a place he didn't recognize and so to a place where he could not follow. His own need overwhelmed him. He swore reprisal against those who had severed her from his life.

When he opened his eyes, she was sitting on the pile of shavings and she had taken off the cap and the sweater, and the candles surrounded her with an aureole of light. There was a tragic daring about her, like a moth dancing around a flame.

He reached in his pocket and took out the two thalers. "This is for Thomas."

"Where did you get it?"

"It doesn't matter," he said. "Take it. Use it to get a wagon and horses. I'll take you across the border."

She reached up and took his hand and pulled him down beside her. Gently, she touched the scar on his cheekbone. "I don't want to go without *knowing*," she said.

He wanted to strike her. He wanted to see her crack into pieces like the statue upstairs.

"Jesus loved Mary Magdalene better than He loved Martha," she said. She waited while he grasped the meaning of her words.

He fell on her, then. He threw himself on her the way the dogs had converged on the rabbit, the way he had hurled himself upon Schroeder, as if she were something to be devoured or defeated. A sound came from him, like the roar of a starved man or a cornered animal. He tore at her clothes. Her body shone. She smelled like sun and grass. Then he heard her cry out, "No—not like *that*."

He stopped. There were tears in her eyes. He saw she was trembling.

He buried his face in his hands. She cradled his head against her breast and held him. He was surprised by the authority of her body, by the warmth that emanated from something so fragile. He cursed his own need.

"I love you," she whispered.

He was aware of her mystery, of her alien being, the fact that she was a native of an unexplored land, part giver, part guide. His hands turned gentle of their own accord, finding their way. A wave of tenderness swept him. Then the river roared in his head, carrying both of them. She made him feel that death was in life, and life was in death, revolving like the sun and moon, timeless. Life seemed interchangeable with death, though he knew it was not—he knew that animals and men could go from life to death but never back again. She made him feel these things. When she cried out, he felt the cry in his own throat. She brought mortality.

5

The child was slow in coming. Lilli writhed and her brow was covered with beads of sweat, and the peasant, Nicolai Lubeck, stood near the door, wringing his hands. "The first always comes hard," Hannah said, knowing she was talking to herself, reassuring herself. It had been six hours; four o'clock when Nicolai came in the wagon for her, a cold sunset and now it was dark. Lilli had walked five miles to his cottage for a bit of buttermilk and a handful of eggs. Lilli had gone into premature labor.

The stove burned. Nicolai had lit lanterns and boiled water and brought clean rags. He had gone out once to slay a chicken, returning with a scrawny plucked bird, hardly worth killing, then standing there helplessly, not knowing what to do with it. Hannah had found a handful of turnips and put on soup. Lilli hadn't eaten. Nicolai hadn't eaten either. Nicolai was young, maybe twenty. He was Polish and Jewish. She had encouraged him to pray. The words that came from him were foreign to her. Now, he was watching her—something about him reminded her of Anatole, the thick chestnut hair that Ben had inherited and the huge hands. Hannah had been fifteen, waiting tables in the Black Bear Inn when she met Anatole who was twenty-two, a refugee from Napoleon's army on retreat from Moscow. Hannah had started to think about Anatole again, since the night Ben had taken the sword and gone off with Thomas, since the morning Ben had returned and she dressed his wound; since he had married Lilli. The fear had started then.

Lilli fell quiet. Hannah crossed to the window and looked out. In the cloudy glass, she saw her own reflection—a big woman with prominent bones and deeply etched lines of concern. Last night, Ben had said, "They're bringing in mechanical looms. Machines. One machine will do the work of six, ten, even a dozen." Lilli had said nothing, but Hannah had recognized the look of a man who had been searching for his enemy and had found it. She had recognized Anatole's old angers.

Outside, the stars were cold, like pieces of ice. She heard a faint rumbling, like a drum roll or the echo of thunder, except that the sound seemed to come, not from the sky, but from the earth. She listened. It was a strange sound, ominous. Then Lilli moaned and Hannah went back to her. But the contraction was short and violent and came to nothing.

"How much longer?" Nicolai asked.

"Soon." Hannah sat beside the bed and pressed a cold cloth to Lilli's forehead. The abdomen tightened again, rising hard and firm under her hand. Lilli cried out. Hannah pushed downward. Lilli shuddered, silent now, working. Ill the whole time, Lilli had grown more and more frail. Now, Hannah instructed her, crooning, as if Lilli were the child. She saw Lilli was painfully thin, no flesh on her beyond the distended womb where the infant flailed, then stopped, then set out again, stubbornly demanding its right to live. The struggle began in the womb, Hannah thought. Afterward, the struggle continued, through poverty and the flight of time and the inevitable partings. She thought about her own sons who were gone—to the ironworks at Gliwice, to the royal coal pits near Beuthen, the zinc furnace at Wesola. Ben was her last. Ben and Lilli and the child would keep her from loneliness.

Behind her, Nicolai opened the door and she heard the rumbling again, louder now, like the sound of men marching.

"Somebody's coming," he said.

Lilli screamed and reared forward.

"Help me hold her," Hannah ordered.

Nicolai slammed the door and hurried to pin Lilli's arms to the bed. Lilli's face blanched with pain. Her cries followed one another, unreconciled, whimpering as the abdomen heaved of its own accord, swifter and sharper. Then Lilli cried out, a loud piercing shriek and Hannah recognized the cry of triumph as the infant hurtled through the passage in one long, unrestrained thrust.

The top of the head appeared. Hannah plunged her hands into the cavity and drew the child out. A boy emerged, already yelling, withered and small but perfectly formed. In one deft motion, Hannah cut the cord, washed her grandchild and swaddled it. Lilli's eyes were closed. She lay perfectly still, her breathing heavy and she was bathed in sweat—but when Hannah laid the child on her breast Lilli smiled as Hannah knew she would; it was always so. The child quit yelling. In the silence, Hannah realized that the rumbling had ceased. In its place was a flurry of hoofbeats, a single horseman approaching.

The hoofbeats stopped outside the cottage. Somebody descended and started pounding on the door.

Nicolai froze. Lilli opened her eyes, pale and frightened, and clutched the child. Nicolai lifted an ax from the wall before he lumbered to the door.

A Prussian soldier stood in the wind, stamping mud and snow from his boots. "Captain Frederick Schmidt, Servant to the Crown," he said brusquely. His breath froze in the air. "You'll have to come. We're deputizing peasants."

Hannah hurried to the door. "What is it?"

Schmidt spat on the ground. "There's an incident."

"Where?"

"It's not women's business."

Behind Schmidt, Hannah saw a glow above the trees, as if the sun had turned defiant and had reversed its course and now fought bitterly to rise at night. Hannah's heart stopped, then began to beat again, fiercely. She knew it was a fire. She knew that Ben was at the center of the fire.

She clutched her shawl and moved past Schmidt. *"Halt!"* he shouted. Hannah ran. Schmidt fired. The bullet screamed past her. She kept running until she reached Nicolai's wagon. Climbing in, she struck the horses and headed toward the burning red sky.

Schroeder was drunk. He was lying in a room above the tavern, on a straw mattress, with the constable's wife—a woman of generous proportions and matching nature—when he heard a bell go off, jangling incessantly somewhere, and he vaguely understood he was being summoned to a crisis. At the same moment, he heard Hansen's voice shouting, "They've gone crazy!"—and a racket began at the door. Clara giggled and burrowed deeper under the blankets. Through a haze of brandy, Schroeder remembered Hansen was a sergeant, so he rose, reluctantly, and managed to get into his uniform with Clara's aid—and as he descended the stairs, he could smell the smoke.

The fire was in the distance, at least three miles off. In the street, the men were carrying lanterns and blazing torches and dogs were running in circles, yelping—and the horses were neighing and pawing the ground in wild confusion. He spied the constable with Captain Schmidt at the center of a group of peasants. The constable was administering an oath and Schmidt was arming them. The plowmen were taking the rifles with a half-hearted authority, uncertain of whom they were to fight. Schroeder glanced cautiously back at the upper window. There, Clara, as drunk as he, was waving gaily—whether at him or her husband, he couldn't be sure.

Hansen had to help him on his horse. Schmidt glowered at him. Schroeder became aware his beard was tangled and his cap was askew and he had buttoned his tunic in a crooked line. He wavered. Hansen settled him upright. There was a discrepancy in rank between them, but they were friends and companions. They had both been conscripted, and Hansen was no more patriotic than he. Except for men like Schmidt who relished killing—it was a dirty business, soldiering.

"Damn fools have set fire to the mill," Hansen said. "They're out to destroy the machines."

"Who?"

"They say it's Calder."

Schroeder remembered Calder. He remembered that moment on the wrestling mat when it crossed his mind that Calder meant to kill him.

The trumpet sounded. The troops gathered in a facsimile of military formation. Schroeder heard Schmidt's words of command and wielded his musket. Suddenly, a double-shot blazed from his rifle, accidentally fired. The flash of gunfire jolted him into a moment of sobriety. Schmidt cursed him. Then a fog settled around him again, clouding his vision. The mill was three miles away. He hoped the rogues would be gone by the time he got there. He hoped he wouldn't have to shoot.

The child cried.

Lilli heard it, but she couldn't move. She was no longer there.

In her dream, the stove was out and she dressed by the yellow light of a candle. Then, in the morning light, she walked to the river which gleamed and greeted her, singing. Reeds waved from the bank. She saw herself wearing bridal ribbons. She saw herself and Ben farming somewhere, the smell of plowed earth, rye, coming up. She saw herself laugh and scold children and lie beside Ben in the dark. Then she realized the hills had turned brown and now it was snowing; ice encased the bare branches and hoarfrost lay on the roofs and the windowsills.

She tried to call out to the sun, but the clouds shielded the sky from her gaze, reminding her she was no longer connected to the earth, or to her own nature or to the glory of living.

A deep sadness overwhelmed her.

Then she saw the monastery. It looked shabby, forlorn. She saw it as life's shadow. In the graveyard, she walked from one stone to another, studying the inscriptions. Then she found herself inside, moving through the cloister until she stopped in front of the broken statue of Christ.

"Forgive me," she heard herself say, crossing herself. "You're better off without me at the convent . . ."

Kneeling briefly, she asked for a blessing.

She emerged to a curious stillness. Through an afternoon haze, sunlight spread over the earth, gilding it. She walked back to the river and followed the bank until she found a secluded place. In a cluster of reeds, she removed her clothes. Then she bathed in the river. The stillness deepened. A profound sense of joy came over her, an overwhelming tenderness. The clouds parted like a curtain and sunlight flowed and the air turned crystal, crackling with life. Her flesh shimmered, translucent. Water dripped from her limbs like jewels. The birds sang—and the wind's breath rippled her hair and whispered, evoking a sweet shy bliss. She dived under the water and came up laughing, freed.

From a long way off, she heard her child cry. Then all sound ceased for her.

Ben had watched the first spark flare in the morning when the machines arrived and the men refused to unpack them. Then the constable had appeared, flanked by two deputies and a Prussian captain named Schmidt. Ben and the others had obeyed then, but the spark had smoldered.

Then, after work, when he found Hannah and Lilli both gone—the cottage empty and cold—he had strapped on his father's sword and gone to the tavern as if he had known the men would gather, though no one had called them together; they had been drawn by the momentum of their shared anger. Then the speeches had started, the talk of oppression and poverty, men talking in circles, impotence and outrage until someone had shouted, *"Goddamn their souls!"*—and he had recognized his own voice:

"To be oppressed by men—to be brought to heel by human will and human greed is unendurable."

He had meant to take no part in it:

"Men—even men of power—die, suffer accidents, grant reprieves, sometimes experience a change of heart."

He was a printer and dyer, not a weaver:

"But a machine is not human. A machine is heartless, bloodless. To be replaced by a machine is to be made less than human. It threatens our survival and it humiliates our souls."

Uncertain where the words had come from, or even if they had come from him, he had found himself marching . . .

Now, the fire raged. Now, he was one of a hundred dark figures, moving against the red glow of the sky. He grasped the pole, backed up, then hurtled forward with the others, ramming the pole against the final barricaded door. The door gave. From behind, somebody pushed in another wagon of burning straw and shouted, "Get back!" A moment later, the mill burst like an overripe melon.

Windows cracked and boards crashed. Around him, men with black faces and burned clothes cheered wildly as the bales of flax caught and blazed, sending the forked flames even higher. Then he heard the thud of hoofbeats and the drummer's warning.

He looked back. The mechanical looms rose against the flames, smoking skeletons. The drummer was closer now. The others heard it, but nobody moved to run. Instead, a strange silence descended—and he took his place with the others who were gathering into a circle, forming a human barrier around the mill. Their faces were grave. A few held rifles. Most had only sticks or clubs or pieces of burning debris. But Ben felt an electricity run through the circle, binding them, the miracle of divergent men unified by a common heartbeat.

The soldiers charged from the shadows. The constable came first, thin and nervous, his face liverish, firing his weapon with the kind of servant's indecision that had given him a reputation for indiscriminate violence. Near Ben, a laborer crumpled. Then the trumpet issued a clarion call and horsemen appeared, riding like savages into the eerie red light—Schmidt shouting orders, riding like a sentry, his aim as precise as his manicured moustache; murderous. Another man fell. The laborers closed ranks, maintaining an impenetrable barrier, refusing to let the patrol through. For a few moments, like waves in the sea, they swept back and forth, stubbornly, before they parted suddenly for the rampaging horses. The patrol swept through, brandishing pistols and sabers and rifles with saber points. The flames cast a strange glow on blood-streaked faces. From the village, the church bell tolled ominously, like a lament. Then a dull sound, like a hollow blast of wind, swept through the red clouds of smoke, punctuated by screams and a volley of gunfire.

The circle broke. Hand to hand combat began, a devil's dance in the firelight as men thrashed and tore at each other. Then more men emerged from the darkness, on foot, armed peasants, creating more chaos. On the periphery, women appeared, some with children, some carrying axes and knives, striking out at the soldiers' horses. A soldier was hurled to his death on the bonfire. Horses reared wildly, burned by torches, trampling over fallen bodies. The final remnants of the mill crashed to earth in a flaming explosion.

Someone began to sing. The women on the sidelines and the children and the wounded began to sing:

> "Say not for bread, but freedom
> Do we fight with soul and heart,
> And if we be torn apart,
> Say we were men . . ."

Ben heard the hymn of freedom rise over the combat and the bloodshed. It warned him. He whirled suddenly to find Schmidt riding down upon him. Crouching, he struck out at Schmidt's horse. Schmidt clung there, cursing, as the horse screamed and reared, threatening to dismount him.

Then he saw Hannah.

The wagon was careening toward the burning mill like a dark bird soaring into a dying sunset. In it, his mother leaned forward, straining to stop the horses which were out of control.

He called her. Hannah turned. He began to run. The wagon trembled as he reached it, then rolled over and Hannah was thrown to earth. A soldier swept past on horseback. There was a flash of gunfire. Hannah lay still.

He bent over her, numbly.

She said, "You have a son . . ."

He saw her chest had been split open by the musket.

Grief swept through him, soundless, paralyzing him. Tears refused to come. They welled in him, solid, a mass of tears as thick and powerful as thunderclouds. Then his body convulsed and he cradled Hannah and watched her die, while his heart wrestled with the pain and his spirit hovered, searching the chaos, seeking out the man who had done this.

He rose. Slowly, blindly, he moved through the bloody crowd which no longer existed for him, feeling nothing, cold as metal, following a powerful instinct, led by an indefinable but utterly trustworthy conviction that he would know him, the man who had done this. And he knew him. The soldier sat quietly on horseback, waiting, like a stunned man, a man already dead even before Ben plunged the sword again and again into his chest.

The tears came then—as the soldier fell, his head turned slightly sideways, revealing Schroeder's missing earlobe.

6

Unmoving, he traveled in search of numbness, in a half sleep where it never grew darker than an eternal twilight where he wrestled with despair. He descended into oblivion, into an accidental universe where Lilli and his mother were no more than reflections in a pool of light that had been extinguished as easily as blowing out a candle. Once, he heard himself cry out in anguish. Then he heard nothing, not even the sound of the icy wind that blew through him as if he didn't exist.

Then he woke, his body bruised and aching and still attached to the idea of existence like a slug to its shell. He woke trembling, seeing death everywhere, waiting—a shadow in the woods beyond the grimy window, a shaggy figure reflected in a battered kettle.

He saw old Magda's image:

She had worn a piece of yellowed spidery lace on her head. Her hands had looked like eagle's claws. She had laid out a deck of withered cards with strange markings. Then she had closed her eyes and all her bones rattled.

Ott brought him whiskey.

The cottage was filled with caged birds. A shrill call, like the ghost of the mill whistle, summoned him back to the living. A wounded raven eyed him.

"It's two days," Ott said.

The whiskey burned and fanned out through his veins. He lay under a fur rug, smelling of ashes, smelling of sweat and dried tears. He had a vague memory of being grazed by gunfire, of being carried through darkness. "Who brought me here?"

"Nicolai Lubeck."

"Lilli—?" He knew Lilli was dead. How had he known Lilli was dead? How had he known to cry in his sleep?

"They're burying her this afternoon."

Ben sat up. Pain gripped his shoulder with iron fingers. "I have to go—"

Ott raised a restraining hand. "Schmidt's dead. They're combing the woods for you."

"I didn't kill Schmidt."

"They think you did."

Ben slung his legs over the mattress and swam through dizziness until Ott's figure emerged again. "I loved her." Ott didn't respond. "And my mother? Are they burying her too?"

"Yes."

"I can't leave without saying good-bye—"

Ott shrugged. He moved to the stove and began to stir something.

Ben rose. The room blurred again. For a moment, it became his own cottage, skeins of flax hanging from the rafters, Hannah bent over the loom. Then Hannah faded, and he saw Lilli—in the monastery, holding out her arms. Loss swept him, obliterating all feeling.

Ott was still at the stove, his back turned. A tin kerosene lamp shed a golden light on a planked table. A tawny dog slept by a roaring wood fire. Ben could smell coffee and sauerkraut. "It was *Schroeder*—" he shouted.

Ott turned. "They're coming for you in an hour."

"Who?"

"His name's Mursa. He's a gypsy."

There was meat in the sauerkraut. The coffee was thick and strong. Ott didn't eat. Ott set out black bread and cheese, then sat across the table in silence, watching Ben's face.

Finally, Ben spoke. "I have a brother in Gliwice."

Ott shook his head. "There was a strike there last month." He hesitated. "Your brother, George, fought with the Duke's soldiers—against the ironworkers. They sent him to the Krupp ironworks in Essen."

"Why should I believe you?"

"Because I'm a coward," Ott said quietly. "Because I guard land that isn't mine and woods that aren't mine. I'm never cold and I'm never hungry and, for that, I'm tied to the Prince for the rest of my life. That's my destiny—to be like the dogs, to be penned in the forest like the dogs." He shook his head. "Even if I had known you were still there, I wouldn't have had the courage to hold the dogs back for a half hour."

"I don't understand."

"Even if a man cannot get himself out of the mud," Ott said, "he can help to lift another."

Ott rose with an air of weariness and lumbered out. The door closed behind him. In front of the fire, the dog stretched in its sleep. The raven beat its one good wing helplessly against the bars of the cage, then settled down and fastened its eyes on Ben. Ben picked up his fork and ate quickly, ashamed of the hunger that betrayed his longing to live. Tears welled in his throat, making it difficult to swallow. The memory of old Magda returned. Three times, he had asked Magda about Lilli. Three times, Magda had shaken her head. He looked down. His tin plate was empty. It gleamed and blinded him, and he heard nothing.

Ott came back, carrying two pails of creek water, which he hung over the fire. Then he pulled a copper tub from the wall. "The gypsies will take you as far as Berlin."

"After that?"

"I don't know." Carefully, Ott packed a short thick pipe. "There's talk of people going to America."

"Where's my son?"

"Nicolai has your son." Ott lit the pipe and sucked on it until it glowed in his overgrown beard. "Your son will be a man of spirit. A renegade." Ott's eyes burned for a moment, brighter than the pipe. "Like you," he said. "Like your father."

"I don't remember my father."

"He came to me. He said: *'It's like having wild horses in me.'* He said: *'If I don't let them take me, they're going to turn and trample me to death.'*" Ott laid down the pipe, then lifted the pails from the fire and emptied the steaming water into the tub. "Your father went to Alsace. He planned to cross the border and join the French Communards." Ott gestured at the bath. "You don't have much time."

Ott brought him soap. The lye stung Ben's skin and sent the blood coursing through his veins again. He watched Ott, moving around, clearing the plates, setting out food for the birds. Ott took a needle and thread from a cupboard and a few dull-colored stones. "There're still nuggets buried in the mine," Ott said, sewing them into the lining of a ragged cap. "They're not worth much, enough for a bowl of soup or a night's shelter—"

Ben dried himself in front of the fire. The scar beneath his left cheekbone burned, calling him back to life.

Ott brought him a bundle of clothes—layers of linen and wool, a red kerchief for his neck, the ragged cap. Ott stained his face. Then Ben crossed to the window and looked out. Sunset bathed the trees. The birds chirped and the brook gurgled.

He closed his eyes. He said good-bye to Lilli. It took a long time.

He said good-bye to Hannah, then. He said good-bye to his childhood, to the boy he had been, to those who had loved him and protected him and to those who had taught him the will to survive. He said good-bye to his son.

Then he stood quietly, knowing it wasn't finished. He cursed old Magda as if she had taken away his choice and thrust him into a life that was already out there, waiting for him.

When he opened his eyes, the sunset struck the cloudy windowpane and burst into a prism of color. In the flashing center, Magda's image returned to complete the prophecy:

"The land is dry," Magda said. *"The trees grow knives instead of leaves, and there are dragons in them. Four hundred will wear your crown. Then you will see the face of God."*

The image vanished. The voice ceased. He knew that was all of it.

He understood none of it.

A roar came out of him, filling the room, part bellow, part sob, an anguished war cry that carried the knowledge of his own defeat.

He turned around. He saw Ott was sitting at the table, smoking again. "Did my father make it?"

"I don't know."

"Who will raise my son?"

"Nicolai."

"Nicolai is a Jew."

"God loved the Jews first." Ott tapped out the pipe. He rose and opened a trunk and brought out a small linen bag, no bigger than his thumb. He tied it with string. Then he crossed to the window and hung it around Ben's neck. "When you're ready to eat what's inside, you must fast for twenty-four hours. Then you'll see . . ."

A whistle sounded outside. "What?"

Ott opened his arms and held Ben. "God's face," he said.

The whistle sounded again. Ott turned away and bent over the trunk again and retrieved Anatole Calder's sword.

Ben shook his head. "You keep it."

Ott nodded. He touched the linen bag. "Go with God," he said.

7

At twilight, the wind swept Berlin from the east.

Beyond the city, the wind ruffled the sandy plains where the gypsies were camped. The women closed up the wagons and the dogs howled and the children began chasing each other in circles around the fire where the men crouched, eating with their fingers from a common plate.

Inside the walls of Berlin, in the Stralau Quarter and on the Alexanderplatz, grit stifled the nostrils of laborers on their way home; and, in the Tiergarten and on the Friedrichstrasse, the wind rocked the carriages of the rich and puffed the skirts of nursemaids from the Spreewald, stirring the mire in the open drains and sending the new spring leaves from the lime trees scudding along the Unter den Linten. There, the wind joined the last rays of the sun to salute the statue of Victory over the Brandenburg Gate before it whirled in vain against the arched windows of the Grand Ballroom in the Von Wahlstadt Palace.

Inside, two massive fireplaces burned, each rose-colored marble, intricately carved with the family crest. Over one, a tilted gold mirror reflected the gleaming expanse of parquetry as yet unmarred by Hessian boots and dancing slippers—hand-polished only a few hours earlier by an army of servants wearing sheepskin mitts. Over the other, a portrait of Frederick Wilhelm IV on horseback was surrounded by tapers and potted palms. Overhead, a dozen chandeliers blazed—five hundred tiny flames in crystal prisms which shone as brightly as the diamonds that adorned the necks of the Berlin matrons and the earlobes of their virginal charges.

Roped off by crimson twists of velvet, the orchestra waited for the signal to begin. Waiting, murmuring, spreading their skirts like flower petals, the girls cast tremulous glances at the uniformed young men— White Cuirassiers and Hussars.

Only Anna Bellinger failed to take part in the covert surveillance.

"He's handsome, isn't he?" Iris bent over Anna like a goose fluttering on a winter pond.

"Who?"

"Eduard von Lanz."

"Impeccable bloodline," Katrin pronounced, "but they say the fortune's been considerably dissipated."

"He had Caroline von Kessler *hypnotized* before her family moved to Frankfurt." Iris giggled. "He keeps looking at *you*, Anna."

"Pay attention, Anna," Tante Henriette said.

Anna studied him critically. His crimson tunic was a bit too scanty, too well-cut—she noticed that—and his dark green pantaloons were too skin-tight as if his tailor had dipped his elegant body in paint pots; her brother, Alfred, would have despised him on sight.

Behind her, Tante Henriette had returned to her confidential exchange with Frau Weber.

Anna's sea-green gown was too costly, Rudolph Bellinger had said. Worth it, Tante Henriette had told him. Didn't Frau Weber agree that the green matched Anna's eyes and framed her ivory shoulders? Rudolph sometimes forgot he was only a barrister, untitled. Tante Henriette lowered her voice. She had had to remind Rudolph that his only son, Alfred, had been threatened with expulsion from medical school; revolutionary activities. What, then, was the price of green silk when weighed against his only daughter's happiness?

Tante Henriette sighed, then leaned forward to whisper to Anna. "Lieutenant von Lanz has just returned from maneuvers in Spandau where he was commended by the king himself."

Anna nodded. Hands folded and eyes lowered, she ignored the young officers who responded to the orchestra's first notes by swooping like birds in brilliant plumage across the field of waiting girls. Only a month ago, she had gone with Tante Henriette to select a servant girl from those who displayed themselves on the Friedrichstrasse, hoping to attract a mistress. Was she any different? Since the season began, Tante Henriette had displayed her at tea dances and suppers and opening nights at the Wallner Theatre and calculated four-o'clock strolls through the Zoological Gardens—for the sole purpose of attracting a suitable husband.

Servitude, Alfred had called it.

"It's what your mother would have wished," Tante Henriette had insisted.

Anna had acquiesced. She had acquired enough pretensions to appear cultured and enough domestic skills to seem admirable. She had rouged her cheeks and suppressed her fawn-colored hair into a braid at the crown and three foolish *Braunschweiger* curls over each ear, and cinched her waist until it disappeared beneath her rib cage. Now, surrounded by the aura of a considerable dowry to be siphoned off from the Bellinger assets, all that remained was a candidate.

She had turned down a half dozen.

At night, she woke and walked about the house in darkness while forbidden thoughts and only vaguely understood wishes crept from the shadows. At night, she longed for a destiny beyond a life of boredom and confinement.

Tante Henriette nudged her.

Lieutenant von Lanz was surfacing from a precise military bow. His heels clicked. His teeth gleamed as if he were posing for a daguerreotype. A skilled hypocrite, Anna thought. Too much pride in the sculptured jaw, too much vanity in the hair that sprang into ringlets like gold coins. But she felt something stir in her like a restless wind.

"Anna Bellinger?"

Anna nodded. Obediently, she rose and took Eduard von Lanz's arm and joined the parade of girls, wearing mulberry and citron, floating like swimmers on the arms of their partners through green-leaved arbors on the floor.

"Anna's an extraordinary name." His eyes trailed over her with impropriety.

"Oh?"

He led her onto the floor to the strains of the waltz. "Spelled backward and forward, it's the same," he said.

Anna smiled. Deliberately, she planted her dancing slipper in the way of his polished boot. Eduard tripped. She made a pretense of being startled and forgave him. Then, in a moment, she tripped him again.

Eduard reddened. "Sorry—"

Anna lowered her eyes. "It's a difficult piece," she said, patronizingly. A puzzled look crossed his face. She smiled demurely, squeezed his hand and sent him stumbling again. He stared at her. Feigning innocence, she tossed her head in a caricature of flirtation. "I understand you were commended at Spandau."

"For marksmanship," he said. "Twelve shots a minute at fourteen hundred yards without a miss."

"Admirable." She found herself watching his mouth. He had a passionate mouth. She reminded herself Alfred would have found him pointless and planted her foot strategically again. He avoided it. She smiled. He returned her smile. Then, without warning, he flipped her foot out from under her. She gasped and toppled forward, weaving a moment before he caught her.

"You dance beautifully," he said, in a voice like honey.

"You're too kind," she answered, and undercut his heel. He pitched sideways. When he regained his balance, he took a deep breath. In the next instant, she felt his foot snake around her ankle. Plunging forward, she sent him an incredulous look. He gazed at her with comic adoration. She retaliated with a series of loops and sidesteps that sent him teetering like a drunken Guardsman. Then the floor wavered and slipped beneath her and, feet tangled, they went sprawling together.

He landed on his back. She fell across him in an awkward imprudent embrace.

Heads turned. A rush of whispers competed with the violins.

Stone-faced, Eduard extracted himself and helped her up with a gallant gesture. He bowed. She composed her expression and curtsied. He offered her his arm. She nodded, took it and sailed past the sea of raised eyebrows into the adjoining reception room where they stared at each other for a long moment before they burst into unrestrained laughter.

The waltz ended. Other couples appeared. A servant in livery delivered glasses of champagne. Anna sipped silently, aware he was watching her, his eyes dark-blue like the falling darkness outside.

"You *did* declare war," he said.

She looked at him over the rim of her glass. "Don't all Prussian officers believe wars are necessary for the good of mankind?" She thought about Alfred again. Tonight Alfred was holding another one of his meetings in a Molkenmart cellar—students and laborers who wanted constitutional reform, freedom of the press, the emancipation of the Jews and the liberation of women.

"We could call a truce then," he said.

"On what terms?"

"Three questions. The rule is—absolute truth."

"Is that military protocol?"

"Ladies first."

"Did you seduce Caroline von Kessler?"

He flushed. Then he nodded. "Yes."

"When the revolution starts, on whose side will you fight?"

"My own."

"What do you think about at two o'clock in the morning?"

He hesitated. "I think about breasts like yours," he said. "Flesh like yours. Only it never had a face before."

She lowered her eyes. She remembered being twelve and being taken by her father on the first Berlin-to-Potsdam train. She remembered watching the sand hills pass and the gypsy wagons and the tiny windmills perched on stones—and the feeling of vertigo when she finally descended, the sense for days afterward that she was still traveling. She had the same feeling now. "It's your turn," she said.

"My driver's waiting in a *droschke* downstairs," he said. "Will you go with me?"

"No."

"Do you *want* to go with me?"

"Yes."

"Why not, then?"

"That's your third question," she said.

"I'm leaving for Frankfurt in a day or two—"

"Frankfurt?"

"A meeting of the *Verein*. We're forming a society to sponsor emigration to America."

She thought about Caroline von Kessler who now lived in Frankfurt. She thought about Alfred. "Sending the discontents to America won't avoid a revolution here," she said. She quoted Alfred. "We'll have a Bastille Day here in Berlin. You'll see—"

Eduard frowned. "Are you aware that kind of talk can endanger your brother?" He shook his head. "The Crown keeps track of its adversaries."

"I'm your adversary, not Alfred."

"Oh?"

"I serve in the hospital." It was a lie. "Charity Hospital," she said, compounding it. Alfred had begged her to take training, she'd been afraid. "The wards are filled with those you oppress and exploit."

He was smiling again. "I'm afraid your beauty is more compelling than your politics."

She handed him her champagne glass and gathered her skirts. "I'd appreciate it if you'd return me to Tante Henriette."

"You haven't answered my third question."

"What was it?"

"Why won't you go with me?'

She smiled. "I can't think of a good reason," she said.

The city prison abutted the River Spree. A steamy fog hung low on the water, absorbing the stench of the sewerage which drained there and carrying it on ghostlike streams of mist to dissolve in the streets. Inside, the damp walls trapped the smell and magnified it.

"It's not an easy thing to be me, you know," Leopold said. The iron bars cast craterlike shadows across his face. "Not that I want pity, not that. But a bit of respect, decency. You can understand that?"

"Yes." Alfred nodded, trying to hide his concern. Leopold had always been gaunt. Now his skin seemed threadbare.

"At first, they put me in a spiked cell," Leopold said. "Spikes everywhere—floors, walls, no place to lie down. That was three days. I'd be there now except they needed the cell for a slanderous poet." He managed to smile. "The only thing worse than a Jew is a poet."

"We're trying to get you out." Alfred heard his own lack of conviction.

Leopold shook his head. "They're going to execute me on the wheel, you know. Because I have no rights. I'd rather be crucified. I'd rather be set up in front of a squad. But they're not going to ask me what I'd rather. So if you could slip me a bit of rat poison or morphine, anything to make it a bit easier."

"Don't talk like that."

"Ah, we're realists, aren't we. Doers. Life reformers. Men of practical vision with a commitment to truth. Are you going to turn sentimental on me now?"

Alfred shook his head. "No."

"The printing press is in a warehouse in the Stralau Quarter. There's a gypsy named Bendejo who works as a packer—he'll contact you when it's safe to move it."

"All right."

"I'm twenty-three, you know. And I don't regret anything except perhaps that I don't have a son. Leopold's not a bad name, you know. Perhaps if someone in the group should have a son and no particular name in mind—" Leopold grimaced. "Ah, look at me now, turning sentimental on myself." He wriggled his fingers through the bars and clasped Alfred's hand. "You'll see I get morphine?"

Alfred nodded.

"And watch the streets on your way back, because one of those poor devils we've been fighting for would just as soon club you as thank you."

He was being followed.

He became aware of it after he entered the Molkenmart where his comrades who had gathered earlier without him were waiting for news of Leopold. He was preoccupied, wondering what he might say to them to give them hope. Then slowly he began to feel the presence of a shadow, another pair of footsteps keeping pace with his own through the narrow cobblestone streets.

Twice, he stopped and looked back. He saw no one.

He passed a number of poor lodgings and innyards, a country wagon parked outside, an occasional beer dray. Few ventured out on the streets after midnight. He told himself he was imagining pursuers; he knew he was not.

When he reached the Krugelhof, the buildings grew shabbier. Spring had not touched the Krugelhof; in every season, peeling stucco exposed rotting brick and, everywhere, moisture dripped on slime-washed walls. Scarred doors were boarded over and first-floor windows were sealed with iron bars where the poor had imprisoned themselves in fear of each other. In the narrow alleyways which led to dead ends, drunks slept and rats fought over garbage which had already been picked clean by men.

Once more, he turned and looked back. "Who's there?" he shouted.

Then he heard something rustle and a figure stepped out of the gloom—a head taller than he, large and burly, holding out his hands to show he carried no weapon. "Bendejo," he said. "A friend of Leopold's."

"The gypsy?"

"What about Leopold?"

"He's going to die," Alfred said.

The gypsy pressed Alfred suddenly against the wall. "There's a carriage coming. Listen—"

Alfred heard the echo of the cobblestones. Almost at once, it grew louder and more insistent, ringing out in the darkness.

"In here—" The gypsy pushed Alfred into the alley in front of him just as the carriage plunged out of the mist and stopped a few yards away.

"Are you sure you saw him?" A young Hussar leaped from the carriage to peer up and down the empty street.

The gypsy inched deeper into the shadows, beckoning to Alfred. Alfred moved backward. His boot struck a sleeping mongrel. Howling, it nipped at his leg. Alfred kicked it. The dog fell back, whining.

The soldier appeared at the entrance to the alley and shouted, "Bellinger!"

Alfred was silent.

A few feet away, a rat crawled up a rusted drainpipe. Carefully, the soldier drew his weapon, aimed and fired. The rat fell.

Alfred stepped over it as he emerged from the alley, smiling. "Target practice, Lieutenant?"

"Are you Bellinger?"

"Yes."

The pistol disappeared. A silver cigarette case took its place. Alfred shook his head. Then he struck a match and held it to the soldier's face. It was a face from the head of a coin.

"Don't go to the meeting tonight," the soldier said.

Alfred extinguished the match. "Have you been drinking French champagne, Lieutenant?"

"The meeting will be raided."

"You're mistaken."

"No."

The lieutenant's back was to the alley. Behind him, Alfred saw the gypsy's shadow take shape, crouched and waiting. "Who do I thank for this message, Lieutenant?"

"You could say that I'm a friend of a friend."

"If I have friends in such high places," Alfred said quietly, "tell them I'm free and able to take care of myself. Tell them to concern themselves with my friend Leopold for whom the wheel is waiting."

The blow was delivered silently, a dull thud to the back of the neck.

The lieutenant crumpled.

The driver shouted from the *droschke*. The gypsy stooped, pulled out the lieutenant's pistol and fired a shot directly over the horses' heads. The animals reared and neighed before they galloped off, carrying the *droschke* and driver into the mist.

Effortlessly, the gypsy hoisted the lieutenant onto his shoulders and carried him deep into the alley. When he came out, he handed Alfred the cigarette case along with the soldier's money, pistol and identification papers. "They'll only be stolen," he said, grinning. "We can use the papers and the pistol. The rest"—he shrugged—"that's up to you."

Alfred struck another match. It flared, illuminating the gypsy's face. For a long moment, Alfred scrutinized him—the tattered cap, the unruly beard, a crescent-shaped scar that gleamed high on one cheek. The eyes that looked back at him were startlingly blue.

"You're not a gypsy."

"No."

"Who are you?"

"A revolutionary—like you."

"Bendejo?"

"Ben Calder," the gypsy said.

The parlor clock struck two.

Anna came down the stairs carrying a lighted candle.

At the bottom, she stopped to study her own image in the pier glass. The eyes that looked back were different from the eyes of the girl who had dressed in sea-green silk for the ball. A new knowledge burned in them.

The door to her father's study was ajar. She crossed the reception hall and stopped outside to peer in. A fire burned in the porcelain stove, casting a rosy glow over the papers that were scattered on a mahogany writing table. She could see her father's profile in the carved armchair—the bristly side-whiskers, the neat smoking jacket and tartan vest and silk foulard; a pair of battered crimson slippers protruded from under his lap robe, like a mark of vulnerability. But Rudolph Bellinger's expression was solemn, a mixture of sternness and apprehension as he watched Alfred pacing back and forth, in and out of her view.

"I was too late," Alfred was saying. "By the time I got there, a crowd had gathered and they were bringing Schiller out on a stretcher —his head had been split. They carried Malvina, screaming and cursing, into a police wagon. It took three soldiers to do that. The rest, they herded with pistols and clubs." Alfred pulled a pair of broken spectacles from his pocket. "These belong to the chemist, Stahl. He was shot."

"How badly?"

"A shoulder wound. At the hospital, they say he'll recover." Alfred quit pacing. He poured a glass of brandy from a crystal decanter and drank it down. "Can you help Leopold?"

Rudolph Bellinger shuffled the papers on the writing table. "I suppose you've read these?" He donned his spectacles. *"Justice is the whore of German Princes . . ."* he read aloud. *"Soldiers are legal murderers protecting legal thieves . . . The power of the German Princes is based on treason and perjury . . ."* He removed the spectacles. "I suppose you agree with that?"

Alfred nodded.

"Your friend, Leopold—is he the author?"

"The author's dead. His name was Buchner."

"How many copies did Leopold print and distribute?"

"A thousand."

Rudolph Bellinger poured a glass of brandy for himself. "You thrive on this turbulence, don't you?"

Alfred shook his head. "Tonight, after the raid, I walked for a long time through those awful streets. Not a sprig of grass anywhere. The foul smell of the sewers. Poverty has its own smell, you know. It drives even the mudlarks away." Alfred's voice dropped. "After a while, I began to wish I had no feeling for any of it. But it didn't happen. I know what I know—and there's no way to turn my back on it."

Rudolph Bellinger sighed deeply. "Sometimes I see myself through your eyes, and I know, to you, I seem hypocritical. Cowardly. I've always lived by the rules. A certain buying and selling of influence, favors. I want Anna to marry well . . ." His voice trailed off.

"And Leopold?"

"I could use my influence to keep you in medical school in spite of your activities. You're my son."

"And Leopold?" Alfred repeated.

Anna watched her father turn away from Alfred's gaze. "I can't help Leopold."

The candle burned beside her bed.

Anna waited.

Her father came up first. She heard his footsteps move heavily down the hallway. Then his bedroom door closed. Carrying the candle, she came out into the hall and waited at the top of the stairs. A few minutes went by before Alfred appeared, carrying a half-filled glass of brandy, looking pale and defeated.

"I couldn't sleep," she said. "I heard you and father—downstairs."

He shook his head. "It's a bad night."

She took his hand and led him into her bedroom. Wearily, he lowered himself into a chair and looked around like a sleepwalker. The last of her childhood dolls lay sprawled on the canopied bed. The green silk ball gown was hanging on the armoire. He frowned at it. The shadows turned his face ancient.

She knelt beside his chair. "What will happen to Leopold?"

"They'll execute him."

"Oh, Alfred—"

He stroked her hair. She took the glass of brandy from him and swallowed deeply.

"Metternich set the pattern in Austria," Alfred said. "The persecution in Prussia will soon be as bad. It'll stir more anger. Perhaps it'll accelerate the revolution."

"I'm afraid for you," she whispered.

"We're all afraid," Alfred said quietly.

Anna swallowed more brandy. "Do you remember—right before Mother died—when she took us to the aquarium?"

"Yes."

"She didn't say a word, remember? She just held our hands and took us through those underground grottoes, past all that silence behind glass—those tanks swarming with life that didn't make a sound. Coral and sea urchins and fish made out of silver—do you remember?"

Alfred nodded.

"And if we started to speak, she put a finger to our lips. Until I had the feeling that we weren't in an aquarium at all. That she had taken us inside her head, inside her thoughts." She laid her head on Alfred's knee. "Then suddenly we came out into the aviary—into all that screeching and flapping of wings and she started to chatter like the birds, like she'd been set *free*. She knew all the names. The scarlet ibis, do you remember that? And we walked around and around until we were running and laughing and completely out of breath." Anna looked up. "That's all I can remember about her. No matter how hard I try, I can't remember anything else."

Alfred peered into her face. "What is it, Anna?"

"Am I like her?"

"You're as beautiful as she was."

"I think she died from—not living."

Alfred touched her cheek. "Who is he?"

"His name is Eduard von Lanz. He's a lieutenant. He's a member of the inner circle of the Court." She bit her lip. "They know who you are. They know every move."

"You sent him to warn me?"

"Yes."

"You shouldn't have done that, Anna."

She shook her head. "Tonight, while I was with him, I had the feeling that everything I knew was disappearing. That my life was strange to me. That I was strange to myself." She rose and crossed to the armoire and put the green silk ball gown away. With her back to him, she asked, "Have you ever made love to anyone?"

"Yes."

"What was it like for you?"

"It was like the aquarium. And the aviary. Only without glass and without bars."

"Yes." She turned around. "Do you believe in erotic freedom?"

"Each kind of freedom has its own risks," he said.

"I want to go to work in the hospital. I want to start as soon as possible."

Alfred drained the brandy. Then he pulled himself out of the chair slowly and came over to where she stood. Holding her, he stroked her hair. "I'll talk to Dr. Kruger tomorrow."

8

"Typhus fever," Dr. Kruger said.

He frowned, stroking a small pointed beard.

The girl was Anna's age, eighteen. She complained of shivering, great debility and headache. Yesterday, she had been bled, purged and given an emetic. Today, her pulse was a hundred, her skin was hot, her lips dry. Today, her abdomen was covered with red spots.

Kruger ordered cups to the abdomen to draw off another eight ounces of blood.

"I have three babies at home," the girl told Anna, counting them off on her fingers like religious beads.

Anna tried to smile. She was afraid. She had grown afraid.

In the next bed, the old woman's jaw was distended. A tumor the size of a man's fist had been taken from the region of the parotid gland. Two months ago, Anna had never heard of the parotid gland. Now, as she changed the bandage under Kruger's gaze, she recognized as well as he did the signs of infection.

"Erysipelas of an atonic character on face and neck," Kruger told her to write. He prescribed meat broth and a little wine. Then he left.

The old woman's wrist was cold and her pulse feeble. The old woman wandered occasionally in her talk. Anna fed her slowly and patiently. In between spoonfuls, the old woman dozed.

Crossing to the window, Anna traced Eduard's initials in the moisture on the pane. She yearned for a breath of fresh air, but open windows were *verboten* except for a scant ten minutes midmorning and midafternoon. For a moment, the smell of illness threatened to overpower her in spite of the vinegar and herbs she had burned less than an hour ago in a vain attempt to deodorize the ward. Then the nausea passed. With a fierce gesture, she rubbed out Eduard's initials and peered through the circle of pale light. Directly below was the street. There were no grounds around the three-story hospital. Even the hundred and fifty patients who occupied the entire second-floor Department for the Insane received no exercise. Periodically, she heard them screaming—sometimes a high shrill cry like a frightened child and sometimes a growling like that of a wounded animal. Kruger had assured her it was nothing more dangerous than a high state of cerebral excitement. The common varieties of alienation in Berlin—Kruger had told her—were melancholia and monomania, especially those morbid thoughts relating to religion. She could see how that kind of madness happened. Her own obsession had become not God but Eduard.

He had gone to Frankfurt. Two months had passed. It was already June and she knew he had returned three days ago and still no word. At night, distraught and impatient, she crouched in her own bed and stroked her own face, cradled her sore breasts, weeping helplessly. She told herself he loved her. She told herself he had mocked her—he had accepted her body as an unexpected gift, and now if he made love to her ever again, it would be absentmindedly, as if she reminded him of someone else.

Now she pressed her forehead against the windowpane. Outside, a summer rain began, spattering on the cobblestones below and flushing the yawning gutters.

The old woman called her. By the time she reached the bed, the old woman had dozed off again. Anna waited. After a moment, the old woman opened her eyes. The old woman's forehead was pale and clammy, but her eyes were bright and feverish. "Can you hear the river?"

"It's the rain," Anna answered.

Anna held the old woman's wrist. The pulse had grown weaker, more erratic.

"There are all kinds of love," the old woman said. "The love of a man. The love of a child. The love of a friend. The love, even, of an enemy." A shudder overtook the old woman's frail frame. She seemed to surrender to it. "Everything passes," the old woman said, "—except love."

The old woman's eyes closed. The pulse under Anna's fingers fell silent. Anna looked up. The rain had quit.

Anna crossed the old woman's lifeless hands on her chest. She removed the old woman's nightcap and stuffed it in her apron pocket before she pulled the sheet up. Then she turned quickly, scratched out a brief note which she sealed, and left the ward. In the corridor, she found a servant-nurse. The girl listened sullenly. At Elizabeth Hospital, the women had patterned themselves after the Sisters of Mercy—but here, at Charity, there were only servant-nurses, untrained, poorly paid, working long and inhuman hours.

"I want this message delivered to Alfred Bellinger at the Medical School as quick as your legs can carry you—"

The girl paled. "What if Dr. Kruger finds me gone, miss?"

Anna added a coin to the note. The girl's face brightened. She scurried off. "And when you get back, I want to see you in a clean apron and your hands scrubbed," Anna called after her.

She found Kruger in the men's ward, attending a fourteen-year-old boy with pleuropneumonia. Kruger had extracted ten ounces of blood by means of leeches. He had prescribed a decoction of sweetened rice, an aromatic potion containing twelve grains of tartarized antimony and an ounce of syrup of poppies. He had applied a burgundy pitch plaster on the left side of the thorax. The boy seemed no better.

"Ward Three, bed number twelve—the old woman died," Anna said, close to his ear.

"I can't tend to both the dead and the living," Kruger answered in a tired voice.

"There're no relatives."

"You can take care of it then, can't you?"

"Yes."

"Is that all?"

"There's a gypsy in one of the men's wards. He's called Bendejo."

Kruger sent her a sharp look. "He's under detention."

"Is he?" Anna met Kruger's gaze directly.

"He was working as a packer in a commercial house. The police raided it. They found a printing press. He wounded one of them with a grappling hook. Got his head bashed in for his trouble. He'll go straight from here to jail."

"When?"

"When I release him."

"We need twenty-four hours," Anna said.

Gently, Kruger laid his hands on Anna's shoulders and scrutinized her. "He's in the ward next door, bed eight," he said finally. "And I'll take no responsibility."

"Thank you."

Kruger shook his head. "Take some time off," he said. "You don't look well to me."

Ben had lost track of the days. He had been thrown back in time, wrapped in the shadows of a failing sunset—he had left Ott's cottage behind, traveling with Mursa, the gypsy, slender and mobile with brooding eyes; the two horses had been as silent as midnight, hooves padded with straw and wrapped in rags, moving like thieves away from everything he had known.

"It is our ancestors who refused lodging to the virgin when she sought refuge to bear the child Jesus," Mursa had told him. "We were compelled to make a journey of repentance. And so we journey . . ."

Later, he had learned from old Phuro it was a lie for the *gadjos*.

He, Ben, was called a *gadjo*, a stranger, rolling along with the gypsy wagons under clouds like curdled milk in a stone-gray sky, past flocks of sheep heavy with wool, bells tinkling and the barking of sheep dogs.

Mursa owned a caged bear, a trio of trained monkeys and a parrot that had been taught to pluck cards from a deck held by the old woman Biba. One eye rolled up in Biba's head, always looking inward and one side of her mouth turned down disapprovingly, and she carried a snow-white dog with black rings around its eyes, a lucky dog that frightened away evil spirits.

The wagons were made out of wood with iron bands and hand-hammered bolts. All day pots and pans had creaked and rattled against hammers, a cobbler's awl, tongs, a smoking stove. At night, shrieking children slept six abreast in a bedstead piled with rag quilts and eiderdowns. Led by twelve-year-old Yerko, they disappeared at daylight to steal or beg, returning to empty their pockets with glee and pride, scrutinizing Ben openly with calculating eyes. "Are you going to America?"

"Why?"

"All murderers go to America," Yerko told him.

He woke on and off. Under the bandage, his head throbbed mercilessly.

In the next hospital bed was a fellow his own age, seized by rigors. An army of leeches sucked at his left thigh. Barely sensible, the fellow's breathing sounded like metal scraping on stone; Ben could feel the heat emanating from him.

At the end of the world, there was a hole through which one descended into the underworld. The journey was made on two cocks harnessed together and took the direction of the setting sun. The dead walked in silence and darkness for two months, and if the dead spoke there, they remained there forever. At the end of the darkness was a mountain that housed the world of the dead. It was guarded by nine white dogs. This was the Kingdom of the Spirits.

Old Phuro—imperturbable, unblinking, sucking on a thick brass pipe—had told him this.

This was where Lilli had gone.

And his mother.

That was nine months ago.

The windows of the hospital ward weren't barred—but he was three stories up, and he knew that guards had been posted somewhere; he didn't know where.

He slept again.

In his sleep, he sat next to Yakori on the wagon seat, behind a pair of gray Belgium plow horses. Yakori was swarthy, with a powerful torso and brawny arms and never without his horsewhip. Yakori brought horses that were old and ill, incorrigible, some with festering sores and foot thrush. Yakori taught him to prepare them for sale: to groom and currycomb them, to talk to them softly, to bleed them, to perform worming operations. A small dose of arsenic put life in the horses' eyes, lameness was concealed by shoeing, holes were bored in the horses' teeth with a cobbler's awl and filled with birchwood. Old horses appeared young; ill horses appeared healthy; Yakori sold or traded them.

Yakori taught him to forge horseshoes, using a stone anvil driven halfway into the earth, a goatskin bellows, a fire protected by a clay mound. Yakori taught him to make nails, hatchets, knives, knitting needles, to forge locks and bolts which the women would sell in Berlin.

It took seven weeks to reach Berlin. In seven weeks, what had seemed restless and unstable became normal. He acquired a piercing gaze, the ability to concentrate on an object or person until he fathomed its depths. He acquired a fire in his eyes and he grew to love the flash of gold and silver and ornaments. He learned to shake his head when he meant yes and to click his tongue when he meant no, and to draw his thumbnail down across his upper front teeth to say "nothing," meaning he had nothing to eat and not a penny in the world. He learned Romany and Spanish; he learned to walk with soft steps, inaudible footsteps, supple and light-footed and to sit lightly poised on his heels, ready to leap into action at the slightest hint of danger. He learned to read the gypsy signs at the crossroads: a rag dangling from a tree branch indicated the safest direction, a feather on the road left word there was a barnyard nearby, a set of crossed sticks meant water up ahead. He slept wrapped in an eiderdown by the failing fire under the ominous black night and woke to old Phuro making coffee from water that had frozen in the bucket. *"First the heart changes,"* old Phuro told him, *"then the man changes."*

He became less and less *gadjo.*

Everything in him that was German, that was solid and pragmatic and pious shifted to absorb the ways of wanderers, thieves, fortune-tellers, minstrels, conjurers, tinkers.

Now, as he slept, he saw and heard and felt these things with a premonition of having already left them, with a sense of looking back from a great distance.

All winter they had camped on the outskirts of Berlin, the wagons in a circle to protect them from the wind. The men had dug holes in the ground ten feet deep and laid rafters halfway across, covering those with straw and sod to create half-cave structures as shelter. In an oven made of dried cow-dung built around a sunken fire, the women had baked bread in round flat pieces.

Looking back, he saw himself at twilight, squatting with the men around a low circular table filled with bowls of maize pudding or stolen chicken—sometimes a platter of hedgehog which had been wrapped in leaves and stewed among the cinders with vinegar and onions, sometimes only a gruel of turnips and garlic and pork fat—always accompanied by laughter and music: the lute and the violin and the gypsy bagpipes. He had come from a place where a man worked and married and drank and died—the gypsies had taught him to live in a world with no walls and no ceilings and no windows that separated yearning from truth; the gypsies had taught his mind and his body to roam free.

Now, a stillness descended, telling Ben he was reliving a moment trapped in its journey through time while time had already moved on.

He heard something rustle. His skin prickled, suddenly alert. His senses moved into the present. Sharp and menacing, a straight razor glinted inches from his throat. He roared and thrust forward, grabbing at the wrist of the hand that held it.

The razor dropped to the bed.

A bowl of steaming water by his bedside tumbled, sending scalding vapors into the air.

A figure sprawled headlong across the bedcovers: his attacker was no more than a girl, half his size, a few bold curved strokes under a servant-nurse's apron.

"Don't move." He pressed the side of the razor to the nape of her neck exactly at the place her hair parted to be caught into braids over each ear. He looked quickly around. On one side of him, the young boy was still breathing with difficulty. On the other, an old man lay with his eyes closed, his face drugged and withdrawn. "Now sit up slowly," he said, "and don't make a sound."

"You're a *madman.*" She lifted herself to a sitting position and fixed him with a penetrating gaze. Her cheeks were flushed, patches of bright color, angry. Momentarily—he attributed it to the dizziness in his head—he saw her surrounded by pink and mauve and turquoise, colors shimmering with passion.

"It's not polite to cut a man's throat while he's asleep."

"And a fool," she added. She smoothed her apron. It was an aristocratic gesture and, at the same time, bold and sensuous. She was an odd girl, unafraid.

He pointed the razor at her. "Under the bed," he said, "there are some things tied in a kerchief. I want you to get them. Then I want you to take my arm and pretend you're supporting me. Then I want you to walk me out of here."

"There's a guard in the corridor. There are three more posted at the exits downstairs."

"Four guards for one poor gypsy?"

"You're not a gypsy."

He stared at her. He saw she was accustomed to being stared at. "And you're not a nurse, are you?"

"I'm going to get up in a moment." She reached down and picked the pan up from the floor. "And I'm going to fill this pan with hot water. After that, I'm going to come back and shave you."

His hand went inadvertently to his beard. Chestnut, untrimmed, it sprang out from his jaw like a live animal. "I'm afraid I'm attached to it."

She took a roll of gauze from her apron pocket. Then she pulled out the old woman's nightcap. "After you're shaved, I'm going to bandage your throat. Then you'll put on this cap. Then I'll cover you and roll you down the corridor. An old woman has just died. You'll take her place. I've made arrangements for her body to be taken over to the Medical School. It's your body that'll be carried out in her coffin."

"Why go to so much trouble for a madman?"

"It's not for you."

"For who, then?"

"Alfred Bellinger."

"Is he your lover?"

She stiffened. "He's my brother."

He gestured at the nightcap. "I won't be womanized."

"Better to be imprisoned," she answered curtly. "Better to be executed."

"You talk with somebody else's fire. Do you make love that way also?"

Her nostrils widened. Sparks flared in her eyes. "I can't strike a wounded man."

"A gentlewoman's code?"

"What would you know of that?"

His eyes narrowed. He flipped his thumbnail across the razor, engrossed in it for a moment. When he looked up, he saw her the way the gypsies had taught him to see. He saw her essence: a naked will.

"My best friend lost his leg to Prince Pless' dogs," he said quietly. "We were stealing firewood. My wife was his sister. She was sixteen. They say she died in childbirth. I say she died from poverty. My mother was killed by a soldier's bullet during a weaver's strike." He slashed an X on the bedcovers in front of her. "You and I—we meet only at this point where these lines cross." He looked up into her face. A hidden source of light flickered over it, about to break through. He watched her resist it.

She rose. He kept his eyes on her as she left the ward, carrying the empty pan. After a few minutes, she came back with hot water and set it beside the bed. She stroked the razor efficiently across a leather strop. Her gestures were neat, unsparing. Her face was composed. Silently, she began to shave him.

Beads of sweat rolled down Otto Steuben's face as he stacked the last of two dozen barrels of tallow from Poland which had arrived on the dock at dawn. He worked alone, using his good left hand and the metal hook which was attached to his right wrist where the hand was missing. In the last four hours, he had unloaded bark mats from Haiti, painted chests from China, palm oil from Africa and six dozen bales of dried codfish—a minimum load for Lasvogel's commercial house which purchased goods from all around the world.

The goods were stored, then resold—loaded and unloaded by men who were called giants.

Otto was a giant. Otto had lost his hand as a penalty for theft and now in its place was the permanently attached grasping hook which he wielded with a terrible efficiency and a peculiar grace.

In the Stralau Quarter, in the commercial houses that lined the River Spree, a packer who had lost one hand for thievery was traditionally given a chance afterward to prove himself a trustworthy employee. The principle was sound. No man wanted to lose two hands. Now Otto—he was called "Hook"—lived in the warehouse and also served as night watchman, having come in this strange manner to represent the epitome of honesty and a living example to those around him who might at times be tempted to succumb to the whisperings of greed.

Otto seldom spoke. When he worked with a partner, it was most often with the foreman, Goliath. Only Goliath—foreman by virtue of his size, taller and broader than the rest—understood that Otto had not been a thief, nor was Otto now a repentant and honorable servant.

It was Goliath who had severed Otto's hand.

It was his job.

The punishment had been performed in front of the other packers, illegally, dispensed in lieu of official imprisonment under a barbaric kangaroo system of justice which preserved the integrity of merchandising.

They had remained friends.

Only Goliath knew that the items stolen by Otto Steuben—coffee beans, tobacco and sugar, smuggled out in African baskets—had found their way into the gypsies' black market in return for a share of the profits to be used for revolutionary activities.

Only Goliath was aware that Leopold Blum's printing press had been installed by the gypsy Bendejo in a storeroom directly adjacent to Otto's quarters, with Otto's full knowledge and cooperation.

And Goliath, also, was the only man other than Otto who knew that the *gendarme* who had been carried away from the raid on a stretcher, a gash in his side as long and deep and wide as a child's forearm, had been wounded not by Bendejo's grappling hook but by Otto's metal apparatus.

So when the medical student who called himself Alfred Bellinger appeared and spoke to Goliath hurriedly—Goliath simply folded his burly arms across his leather apron and nodded.

Alfred departed. Goliath mixed himself a glass of the only brew he ever drank—half beer, half olive oil and a bit of sugar. Water made a man weak. So did wine and brandy. He swallowed the brew which he believed was the source of his strength and which, according to legend, would kill him. All packers died at fifty. None lived longer. Most drank forty pints a day, and in the end the spirit of the beer would kill them.

When he had drained the glass, he went looking for Otto.

"The *gendarme* died," he said.

Otto wiped his brow. "When?"

"Today."

Otto pulled off his cap and ran his good hand through a mass of bushy black hair. He frowned. His face creased like old leather and his eyes darted about like small black beads. Finally, he asked, "Bendejo?"

"Put on a black arm-band," Goliath said. "Our poor old mother just died and we're going to pick up her body."

Eduard wasn't at home.

Anna walked past his flat and saw that the shutters were closed in the upper window. That meant he was gone—though not to the Officers' Club; it was too early for that.

He was not at the neighborhood *Konditorei,* reading his newspaper over coffee and pastry.

He was not at the nearby beer garden either.

She walked briskly, paying no attention to the shop windows which held the latest Paris combinations of organdy and taffeta executed by Berlin dressmakers. Instead, she scanned the faces of the passers-by— helmeted officers and young lieutenants, none as handsome as Eduard —women carrying baskets of cake and fruit, ragged urchins and Berlin toughs and street vendors.

In the Alexanderplatz, the Wednesday marketplace thronged with people. Still looking for Eduard, she moved past booths of flowers, cheese stalls, a stand stocked with hundreds of different kinds of caged birds. Carcasses hung in butcher stalls, freshly killed calves, pigs, scraggy sheep, tons of sausages and joints of purple beef. The sight made her queasy.

She kept walking, past booths piled with black bread, with apples and honey, dried fish, looking glasses, combs and pins and needles. A country lad with spangles on his hat cracked a newly purchased whip. A woman passed, wheeling geese in a wheelbarrow, followed by another with two baskets of live ducks suspended from her shoulders. The faces merged—old enemies out looking for a quarrel, old friends in search of each other, everyone shouting and bargaining—one face indistinguishable from another; none of them Eduard.

Banners fluttered from the wine-merchant's shop. She searched the back room where dice games and card games and champagne were available for the rich. Eduard wasn't there either.

When she came out, she felt faint and weak. Momentarily overcome by the heat and confusion, she leaned against the wall.

Near a stall of potted plants where women sat weaving wreaths of oak and laurel and ivy, a young gypsy woman lowered her smudged hooded eyes and continued casting shells to tell a *hausfrau's* fortune. The shells were cowries, Anna heard her say, smooth and glossy, shaped like a pig's back, symbols of birth and creation—the young gypsy smoothed her bright skirts across her abdomen in a gesture that revealed she was with child. Then the gypsy raised her eyes suddenly and met Anna's in a strangely intimate look. Her gaze implied a shared secret, a recognition of the truth which Anna had stubbornly resisted. Now it surfaced to demand its due: she, Anna, was also with child. She, Anna, was carrying Eduard's child.

"*I'll tell the child's fortune,*" the gypsy said.

Anna turned and ran through the crowd.

Shrouded, Ben lay tense and motionless, waiting, hardly daring to breathe.

He heard the voices of women. None of the voices belonged to the girl; she had vanished.

He cursed her—a girl weighing no more than a hundred-weight whose name he didn't know. He had taken her word. He had submitted to being shaved—and to the indignity of the nightcap. She had rolled him into the women's ward without incident. Where the devil had she gone after that?—leaving him with a full bladder, bedeviled by questions.

He crossed his hands over his chest. Under them was the small linen bag he had worn since the day Ott had hung it around his neck. The bag contained the face of God, Ott had said. As if the thought had summoned it, Ben heard a murmuring: last rites being said over his body by the priest who came every evening like an arthritic black vulture who crept through the ward collecting souls. The old woman had been a Catholic. The priest mumbled in Latin, consigning body and spirit to heaven and earth in that dry tone that promised only purgatory.

The voice ceased.

"Over here—" another voice said.

Ben recognized the voice as Hook's. Then he was being heaved into the air by a pair of arms that handled him as easily as a sack of meal, and lowered unceremoniously into what he took to be a hastily constructed coffin. It smelled of codfish.

"Rest in peace," a second voice growled.

Ben recognized Goliath. He imagined Goliath crossing himself for the benefit of the priest. From the far corner of the ward, a woman wailed a blessing. Then the coffin swung into motion.

"What of the guard in the corridor?" Hook whispered.

"The girl slipped a bit of morphine in his tea," Goliath answered.

The girl was around then, somewhere. Ben wondered where. He was being swung down the corridor. He could hear the noises of servant-nurses carrying evening trays; the girl's voice wasn't among them.

The box tilted suddenly, as Hook and Goliath began to descend the stairway. Each step jarred him. There was a landing, then another set

of stairs, then another landing and yet another set of stairs, the last—
only a few steps from freedom, Ben thought, when a voice shouted,
"Halt!"—when Ben heard boots, two pair of them thumping toward
him. The coffin stopped in midair. "Set it down," a voice ordered.

A second voice asked, "What have you got there?"

The coffin struck the ground. Ben froze. "It's my poor old mother,"
he heard Goliath say.

"My mother, too," Hook said.

A moment passed. "It's your mother and not a tear between you
being shed?"

"It's a pauper's grave we're carrying her to," Goliath said. "Enough
crying in life—"

"We'll just have a look at her."

"It's a sin to disturb the dead."

"Aye—well, perhaps I'll poke around with this sword a bit just to
make certain. If it's your dead mother after all, I'll confess my sin
directly afterward."

The bolt grated, metal scraping against wood. Then the hinge
creaked as somebody began to lift the lid. Light pierced the darkness.
Ben ceased breathing. For a split-second, time stopped.

In that instant, the girl's voice filled the stairwell. "It's the gypsy!"
she shouted. "He's knocked out the guard upstairs and now he's trying
to escape! Come quickly—the third floor!"

The lid dropped shut.

The boots pounded up the stairway.

The coffin swung into the air, moving as fast as a train, moving toward freedom.

9

The shutters were open now.

Anna went through the portico to the inner courtyard and climbed the stairs. She could hear Eduard whistling inside.

He was startled to see her. She had led herself to believe he expected her. Instead, a light flush colored his face and his greeting was awkward. She saw he hadn't expected her at all. She suspected he had somewhere to go.

When the door closed behind her, she said without preliminaries, "I'm with child."

Disbelief crossed his face, followed by a flicker of vanity—a pride in his own virility—instantly replaced by a search for a response that would relieve him of obligation. Unable to find this, he lay down on the divan and closed his eyes. She stood quietly, watching him, feeling strangely dispassionate, knowing she should leave but unable to move. Through the double windows a dull gray light illumined polished parquetry, a Persian rug, arabesque-patterned wallpaper. In a pier glass, she could see her own figure and, behind it, a table adorned with complicated embroidery and beadwork and family photographs in oval frames. The massive white porcelain stove had not been lit. In spite of the fact that it was June, the room was cold. She shivered.

He got up abruptly and laid his hands on her shoulders and cleared his throat. "Oh Anna—" he said. His tone was exasperated.

She saw him as a perfectly ordinary man, stripped of the qualities with which she had endowed him. He had a weak chin. "Does Caroline von Kessler have more money?" she asked quietly. "A better family?"

"Both," he said. A long time went by. Neither of them spoke. Finally, he broke the silence. "I didn't mean for that to happen."

"It happened."

"God," he said.

"I'll arrange something," she said.

She felt his gaze. It burned her. She felt his shock and consternation. She knew he was wrestling with it. She knew he would lose. She would lose. Loss was inevitable. She touched a wisdom that was way beyond her, a sense of the motion of life. She had followed her heart. She felt a pride in that. She knew the pride would vanish. Pain and desperation hovered at the periphery of her small circle of wisdom. Yet, for a brief moment, she felt a supreme calm that told her she was stronger than he; she had a strange need to spare him pain.

"Is she prettier than I am?"

He shook his head.

She made a gesture of acceptance. She managed to smile.

"Revolution's inevitable," he said. They were her own words, Alfred's words. "There'll be bloodshed. Power built over centuries doesn't topple easily. I was born to power. I have to defend it. Not because I believe in it—I don't. If I believed the revolution would succeed, I'd abandon my position in a minute. But the revolution will fail. There'll be retaliation, a period of oppression, a tightening of authority. There'll be a counterrevolution and more fighting after that. It'll seesaw back and forth for years. I'll be an old man before Germany is free." He took a deep breath. "Until Germany is free, I'm not free."

She turned away and crossed to the desk at the end of the room. She looked down at the papers that had claimed his attention before she knocked. A heading read: SOCIETY FOR THE PROTECTION OF GERMAN IMMIGRANTS IN TEXAS. "So you'll marry a title," she said. "And money."

"My superior officers would never approve a marriage to you. I'd lose my commission, my status—I'd be disowned by my family. I'd be on the side of the intellectuals and the oppressed. To marry you would be to lose my position, to become a victim of history."

She was still staring at the papers. The words swam before her eyes:

A society has been organized whose sole purpose is to direct German emigration to one single, favorably located point, to protect the emigrants on their long journey and to employ every means to secure for them their new home across the sea . . .

She placed her palm over the print, blotting out the words. "And the *Verein*," she said. "The *Verein* would certainly abandon you."

"The *Verein* met in Frankfurt. Count Castell, Prince Leiningen—" He spoke quickly, making an attempt to change the nature of their discussion. "The *Verein* has acquired six million acres in Texas on the condition that we colonize it. If we succeed, we'll have another Germany across the seas."

"And Caroline? Will you take Caroline to America?"

"I don't love Caroline," Eduard said softly. "But love has nothing to do with marriage. Eventually, I'll have a series of mistresses. Caroline will be less to me than you. My mistresses will be less to me than you. But I'll rise in the ranks to become a Colonel or perhaps even a General. I'll have no power over my own destiny, but I'll have power over the destiny of Germany." He hesitated. She heard another deep intake of breath. "Everyone will think of me as strong and brave," he said. "Only you and I will know that I was weak and cowardly."

He had moved quietly across the room and now he was standing directly behind her. She turned and looked up into his face. His eyes glistened. She could smell brandy on his breath. She raised her hands slowly and began to unbutton his tunic, feeling a strange fatalism, as if all decisions—his and her own—had been made by some cry of the mind as yet unheard. He shook his head, telling her he was powerless to stop her. "As long as it's done—" she said.

He shook his head again. Then he lifted her into his arms and carried her into the bedroom.

The following week, the notice of betrothal appeared in the Berlin newspaper:

We herewith, respectfully, have the honor to announce the betrothal of our eldest daughter, Caroline, to Eduard von Lanz, Lieutenant of Reserve, First-Dragoon Regiment, Berlin, eighth March, 1845. . . . Carl von Kessler and Marie von Kessler . . .

Anna read it at breakfast, dispassionately, under Tante Henriette's eye and pretended that it concerned her not at all.

Alone, afterward, in her own room, she paced in a circle, quietly and stubbornly. No tears came, only waves of indecision.

In search of a sign, she went to the armoire and took out the red kerchief which held the gypsy's belongings. She had taken it from under the bed, stored it in a cupboard in the hospital, then brought it home. Now, she went through it. Buried in the clothes—a shirt and trousers, a woolen vest—was a small leather packet which held a lock of yellow hair. *"They say she died in childbirth,"* he had said. *"I say she died from poverty."* There was a cap with what felt like rocks sewed into the lining. She opened the lining. A handful of gold nuggets fell into her lap, glittering.

At the bottom of the kerchief was a letter which she opened and read:

Dear Ben,

I was not able to find the Jew, Nicolai Lubeck. They say he has crossed into Poland with your son.

I grieve for that.

This year, there are no potatoes in the fields and many have died of starvation. Now the typhus has come and the spotted fever. Ott died alone. I buried him in secret with no coffin and no money to pay the gravedigger.

Only this morning, Prince Pless posted a notice that says if a man has two legs and three hundred florins, he can go to America. If I had two legs and even ten florins, I would go to a brothel in Poznania.

Your friend,
Thomas Hlasko

The letter had no meaning for her. The names and references were strange to her. Yet, it touched her. It made her want to weep.

Ben Calder, Alfred had said his name was. He had killed a soldier in a weavers' strike in Silesia. She compared him to Eduard; physical strength without grace, raw and untamed; Ben Calder had watched her the way one watches a child about to burn a finger on a candle flame, letting it happen, waiting for her to feel pain. He had made her aware that she had never been cold, had never been hungry, had never been without protection.

She returned everything to the kerchief, knotted it and put it back in the armoire.

Outside, it was raining again. A few rivulets made their way silently down the glass like tears. Then a jangling sound made her turn and she saw Tante Henriette, her larder keys dangling from a cord around her waist. "Your eyes are too bright," Tante Henriette said. "You're pale as an Easter lily." She crossed the room, picked a hand mirror off the dresser and held it in front of Anna's face.

Anna turned her head away.

Tante Henriette sighed. "I saw all the signs, but I didn't want to believe them." She reached out and laid a hand on Anna's abdomen. "It's so, isn't it?"

Anna dropped her head in acquiescence.

Tante Henriette's skirts rustled. Anna saw she was drawing her hands along her apron; it was a nervous gesture she used when firing servant girls or contemplating the rising cost of eggs. *"Liebchen, Liebchen,"* Tante Henriette murmured, but she made no gesture of affection.

"You never married," Anna said. "Have you ever been with a man? How could you spend your life caring for children that are not your own?—a brother instead of a husband?"

Like a match struck in a high wind, a light flared and went instantly dead in Tante Henriette's eyes. "I did my duty."

"What did you do with them?—with your feelings? Your needs?"

"It wasn't suitable." Tante Henriette's voice wavered slightly. Then her shoulders straightened. "We must do what's suitable."

The young gypsy woman was in the same place, her shells laid out. Her hair was jet-black, her eyebrows thick and full like fur frames over dark expressive eyes. On her right hand, she wore a ring of two large pearls, one black and one white. Her gestures were striking and dramatic; bracelets clanked at her wrists. She motioned for Anna to take a seat on a barrel.

"I'm looking for Bendejo," Anna said.

A cloud passed over the gypsy's face. "I don't know Bendejo."

"I have some things that belong to him. I took them from the hospital. Charity—" Anna revealed a gold nugget.

"Who are you?"

"Anna Bellinger."

"I don't know Bendejo," the gypsy repeated. Anna returned the nugget to her purse. "Wait—" the gypsy said. She held the cowrie to Anna's ear, then to her own. "Your wish is to be free," she said.

Anna said nothing.

"To be free to follow your own nature," the gypsy said.

Anna remained silent.

"To bow to the demands of flesh the way the willow bows to the river, the way the stars cluster around the moon and the clouds around the sun." The gypsy's voice was hypnotic. "To hear the harmony in the wind, to feel the blessing of the rain, to let the night wrap you and take you. To dance to the rhythm of the seasons. To assert nothing, to believe nothing, to trust everything. To listen to the music of your own heart."

Anna lowered her eyes.

"I can't tell you more—" the gypsy said.

Anna looked up. A curtain had fallen over the gypsy's eyes. "And my child?"

The gypsy shook her head. Anna rose slowly.

The gypsy's eyes followed her. "Why come to me to find Bendejo?"

"I don't know."

"One week from today," the gypsy said. "Three o'clock. At the fish market near Kurfürstenbrücke."

The courtyard was separated from the street by an iron railing. The courtyard was empty. Through the windows on the ground floor of the university, she could see the heads of the students in the lecture rooms.

She took a seat on a stone bench to wait. Inside, Alfred was in the midst of his public examination. He had passed the examination by the dean and the *rigorosum* before the faculty. He had written his thesis in Latin. For the past two weeks, he had been undergoing his surgical examination: Somewhere inside the building, he was performing an operation on a cadaver and describing the steps of the procedure to a panel of judges.

She wondered if he was performing his surgery on the body of the old woman they had stolen from the hospital.

A half hour passed before Alfred came out, his eyes glazed and red-rimmed. It had started to drizzle again. He had only an hour before he was due at the hospital where he was in charge of the treatment of two patients for a fortnight. The daily notes of these patients would be read as his final examination.

"I've made the arrangements," he said.

She didn't answer. Instead, she took his arm. They walked in silence.

On the Friedrichstrasse, a flight of stone steps led down beneath the street level to the Weinstube. Inside, the rooms were small and dark, lion and tiger skins scattered over a few divans, the walls hung with scenes from the Cape of Good Hope. They took a wooden table. Nearby, a grave gentleman with a gold-headed cane eyed them with envy—Anna saw he believed they were lovers.

She let Alfred talk.

His friend, Dreyfus, would do it. Dreyfus had been the finest student in obstetrics. Dreyfus believed a woman should have the right to determine how she used her body. Dreyfus had once been a Jew; he was now an agnostic. There would be no question of moral judgment or financial blackmail. Dreyfus would perform the abortion because of his own beliefs and be forever silent afterward.

Alfred reached out and stroked her hand. There was a physical risk. That would be minimized as much as possible. Unless she objected, he would attend the procedure himself. They were emancipated, weren't they? He would take care of her afterward.

Her own wine remained untouched. She listened, watching Alfred's face, moved by the bond between them that went back to their childhood.

They were no longer children.

When she answered Alfred, her voice was calm. No tears came. She trembled only slightly. "There are three thousand people in Berlin," she said. "I chose the one lieutenant who would bring me pain. I keep asking myself why? There are eighteen gates in Berlin and no escape for me. Why? Because Eduard can trace his descent back to the free knights of the Middle Ages? How can my life be determined by such things?" She paused a moment, speaking slowly, struggling with the words. "I'm going to have the baby," she said.

Alfred searched her face. "Why?"

"I kept thinking of it as Eduard's child," she said "—as if it had nothing to do with me. I kept thinking of what was moral or acceptable. Now, I know it's none of that. There's something more important—"

"I don't understand," Alfred said.

"This child that I'm carrying—it was conceived by *me*—out of the most daring part of myself. If I kill the child, I'll kill that part of myself. Don't you see? That Anna"—she shook her head—"I couldn't live as that Anna."

10

The place was in the old quarter near the river. On the ground floor was a spirit shop where the police drank without payment. On the floors above were lodgings for those who had cash to pay for the landlord's discretion, those who happened to be without passports or were otherwise tarnished. The landlord asked no questions. Ben had been told to arrive after dark and leave before daylight and pay cash. He had been told there were prostitutes available.

The stairs were dark, the walls were dirty. At the end of the hall was a heavy oak door. Inside, the room was as desolate as the others had been—he had changed quarters every night since Goliath and Hook had carried him out of Charity Hospital.

An oil lamp cast a yellow glow on a table surrounded by a half-dozen wooden stools. Walls partitioned the rest into narrow compartments, each with a small window and a cot with a straw mattress. Outside, the muddy canal ran along the edge of the street where three-story houses, sprouting balconies, perched on stilts over the canal. Ben marked his route of escape if he should need it: He could climb down the series of balconies, wade through the canal and make his way beneath the houses.

The only other occupant was a squat burly Turk wearing a soiled fez, full trousers and a tattered fur vest. The Turk took his measure surreptitiously, pretending to be absorbed in the contents of a trunk—

taking inventory. Ben saw himself through the Turk's eyes: he was wearing Goliath's castoffs, he hadn't bathed in five days and his newly shaved jaw was covered with coarse bristles.

"I won't harm you," he said.

The Turk pretended not to hear.

The landlord came in, carrying a candle, counted his guests, put a jug of water on the table and turned down the lamp. "Who wants a woman?"

The Turk looked up from his trunk. "What kind?"

The landlord cackled viciously, waving a hand at the Turk's trunk. "A gypsy. They're hot-blooded, but they'll steal you blind." He turned to Ben. "It's you she wants. The big one, she told me. Bad thinking, I'd say. You don't look like you've got much worth stealing." His hands arched in the air over his stomach. "She's with child. Some men like that. Two for the price of one, you might say." He cackled again.

"How much?" the Turk asked.

Ben spoke quickly. "I'll take her."

"We'll have a bidding, then." The landlord rubbed his palms together. He was small and slightly bent, with a narrow thrusting chin that gave him the look of a hungry bird.

The Turk pawed through the trunk. "A fine piece of wool from Tibet." He was moon-faced, small black eyes and teeth like seed pearls. There was a bluish cast to his dark skin that could have been menace or illness.

"One florin," Ben countered. Two were all he had.

"Three yards of embroidered Chinese silk. Stitches so fine, the women go blind sewing." The Turk brought the fabric over to the oil lamp. An embroidered dragon of spun silver glittered in a field of poppies.

Ben addressed the Turk. "One and a half florins for the gypsy *and* the silk."

The Turk showed his tiny teeth. "Three," he bargained.

"Two."

"Agreed."

"I have to be paid for the whore," the landlord said. "How much for the whore?"

"Two thalers," the Turk said.

"Robbery—"

"Trade," the Turk corrected.

The money changed hands. The landlord pocketed his share and left, locking the door from the outside. The Turk strapped his trunk shut, pulled it into one of the cubbyholes, shifted the straw mattress from the cot to the trunk, then lay down on top and closed his eyes. Ben took a seat on one of the stools to wait, trying not to think about those who engaged in the buying and selling of flesh and goods as if they were the same. *"The world is a pasture,"* old Phuro had said. *"There are no boundaries, no nations, no states, no property. These exist only in the minds of those who create them."* As if in response to Ben's thought, the Turk turned over, groaning.

Eventually, Ben heard footsteps. A key rasped in the lock. The door cracked open and the figure of a woman was cast unceremoniously inside. She landed on all fours, like a bundle of rags. As the door shut and the key scraped in the lock again, she shouted, "May your children make the nails for the second crucifixion!" Then she turned her head slowly toward Ben. "How much did you pay for me?"

"Two florins."

"I'm worth more."

"It was all I had." Ben picked up the Chinese silk and stooped beside her and draped it around her shoulders. She looked down at the gleaming dragon, then stroked it in amazement. He took her face in his hands. "Why didn't you tell him you were my wife?"

"It would have cost double," she said.

Rudolph Bellinger was propped up in bed, several pillows behind him, a flannel nightcap on his head. Anna saw his face was the color of the tallow candle that burned on the nightstand and, periodically, he wheezed, setting off a rattling in his chest. The bed was strewn with legal documents. He had taken to bed reluctantly, protesting it was only a mild summer cold, continuing to work in spite of the fact that his condition had grown steadily worse. He needed a month in a dry climate, Alfred had told him. He had snorted at that. A month away from Berlin would kill him, Berlin was his life.

He peered at Anna through his spectacles. "Tante Henriette tells me you're determined to bear this child. I don't understand. Help me to understand."

"I have to," she said.

"Have to?"

"Yes."

He took off his spectacles and wiped them. "Then you must let me arrange a marriage as soon as possible. There's a clerk in my office. He's bright. He could rise to be a barrister—"

"I can't give myself to a man I don't love."

He put on his spectacles and scrutinized her again. "Love?"

"Yes."

"Then you must go to Munich. Under another name, of course. The child will be placed in an orphanage—"

"No," Anna said quietly.

Her father's glasses clouded. "Your mother was stubborn."

"I have no real memories of my mother," Anna said softly. "Only a wish. I know what that wish feels like, Papa. It can take over your very being. Think what it would do to a child whose mother was taken away not by death, but by her own cowardice."

He shook his head sadly. "There's no place for your kind of courage in Berlin." He paused to remove his glasses once more. "There's no place in Munich or Frankfurt or anywhere in Europe. Perhaps in some uncivilized place—" he leaned back and closed his eyes. His chest heaved.

Anna reached for his hand. Her fingers found his pulse. His heart was beating rapidly. "You should rest, Papa."

"Thirty years ago, when I was a law student," he said, "I joined a group called the *Burchenschaft*. We expressed the unity of students all over Germany. We were dedicated to Germany, but scornful of our parents' money values. In private meetings, we sang the 'Marseillaise' to remind us that Germany's true goal was no different from France— liberty, fraternity, equality." His eyes fluttered open. "I believed those things then just as Alfred does now. It's part of being young to be idealistic, to be unforgiving of the older generation. I'm afraid it's also part of being young to be unforgiving of yourself."

"I've forgiven myself, Papa," Anna said in a hushed voice.

"I'm not a demonstrative man, Anna. I never married again, so I don't know a great deal about women. I imagine I'm saying all the wrong things to you now. I'm talking to you as an equal when we both know that women in Germany will never have equality—not in my lifetime or in yours. Yet, I know if you take this mistake and turn it into a principle—if you try to make a life from that—you'll destroy everything I've built."

"I'm sorry, Papa. I love you, Papa. But I also love this child. It's mine. It came into being from a true part of my own nature. The mistake is Eduard's, not mine. The principle is Alfred's, not mine. Only the child is mine. If I can't be true to myself in Germany, then I'll have to go to a place where I can."

"I don't want to lose you, Anna."

"America," she said.

Tears sprang to her father's eyes. He wiped them away. His hand quivered. Blinking, he leaned back against the pillows wheezing heavily.

Old Phuro had married them.

Biba had disapproved; Biba disapproved of everything.

Selinda had been a widow—married six years and childless when her husband was killed in a knife fight in Barcelona. When a gypsy died, everything he owned was burned; the tribe took care of widows and orphans.

Ben was a *gadjo,* Biba had said. Better a *gadjo* than no man at all, old Phuro had answered.

The ceremony had been simple: the bridal pair had stepped over a broom. They had broken a loaf of bread, sprinkled it with salt, exchanged halves, taken a few bites and then washed them down with wine. *O Deloro,* the gypsy god was not invoked. That they were blessed was celebrated with music and dancing. *Beng,* the gypsy devil, was appeased by the ringing of bells and the lighting of candles. Afterward, sugar was sprinkled on the floor of the wagon and incense burned. Afterward, in the darkness of the wagon, Selinda had released his hands, his mouth, the boundaries of his flesh, bringing him to near delirium. Afterward, he had understood it had been less a consummation than an initiation.

Now she rose from the floor of the dingy quarters over the tavern and, caressing the Chinese silk, she moved slowly into a dance laced with sadness and sensuality. Watching her, Ben had the feeling as he often did that spirits moved through her—not the *mulos,* which were the spirits of the dead, but the life spirits, which brought self-forgetfulness.

Softly, in Spanish, she sang: *"Listen to your heartbeat, listen to your*

*breath—we are sound. See the night fall, watch the sun rise—we are
sight. What we hear, we will become. What we see, we will become.
What we become, we live . . ."*

She had brought him money. She had brought him a change of
clothes, a piece of roasted pork and the last wild blueberries of summer. These things she carried in a sack tied around her waist, nestled
over his unborn child.

She brought him the full richness of her body, her awesome capacity
to lose herself in the moment of lovemaking. Her hands caressed him.
Her hands bewitched him, astonished him. "We are alive," she whispered.

Lying next to her, he imagined himself under the stars again. Lying
next to her, he seemed free, no longer imprisoned, in hiding—the noise
of the drinkers below and even the groans of the Turk ceased to exist.

She was older than he. Yet, afterward, she lay curled like a child in
his arms. He felt a need to protect her. She had protected him. She had
taught him to pay attention to every sound that struck his ears, to the
leaves and the wind and the spattering of the rain, the cry of a wolf, a
stranger's silent footsteps. She had taught him to improvise, to make
life his ally, to trust his own strength and the irrationality of his own
thoughts. He stroked her hair.

"Anna Bellinger," Selinda said.

"What?" He felt a flash of apprehension.

"That's her name. The girl in the hospital. She came to see me."

"How did she find you?"

"She's filled with ambition, self-deception. She's surrounded by
phantoms who pull her this way and that way. Still, fate guides her."
She looked deeply into Ben's eyes. "She has your gold nuggets. She'll
return them to you at the fish market near Kurfürstenbrücke. One week
from today."

"What does she want?"

"I don't know."

He felt she was lying. The lie fell like a shadow across the cot. It fell
dark and wide, obliterating the thin rays of moonlight that illumined
their intimacy. Ben watched it fall like a sign of things to come. In the
same instant, suddenly warned, he raised his head. The Turk stood at
the foot of the cot, rigid with urgency, like an animal in heat. "I'll have
my turn at her now."

Ben cursed him.

A knife appeared from the voluminous trousers, glinting. The Turk advanced on the cot with harsh, panting noises. Ben sprang, sending him reeling backward. The Turk struck the edge of the table, made a strange sound like the whinny of a horse, then staggered to regain his balance. Ben crouched, then dove again. Wrestling furiously, they rolled across the floor, the knife airborne, searching for a place to plunge. Ben struck out with his fist. Blood trickled from the Turk's mouth. He spat two seed-pearl teeth into the air. Ben struck a blunt fierce blow to the abdomen. The Turk howled. The knife sailed upward, then dropped a few feet away. Ben palmed it quickly and bent over the Turk, holding the knife to his throat.

"Don't kill him," Selinda said quietly. She crossed the room and cast a cold gaze at the Turk. "Among the gypsies, when a man commits rape, they cut off his testicles and serve them to the dogs."

A shudder convulsed the Turk. His eyes bulged with fear. Then the lids dropped over them.

Ben bent over his chest. "His heart's beating."

"He's only fainted." Selinda knelt beside Ben. "Remove his clothes," she said. "We'll tear them into strips and bind and gag him. We'll take his trunk and leave him here, stripped of everything, naked. That's fit enough revenge."

Quickly, Ben began to remove the layers of clothes. A passport and money purse was strapped around the Turk's waist. The Turk groaned as Ben took them.

"Hurry," Selinda said.

The Turk's eyes popped open, rolling around in terror as he became aware of his nakedness. Selinda pressed the knife to his throat. "It's done," she told him.

The Turk fainted once more.

The pier glass had been moved to the foot of Eduard's bed. In it, Anna watched their limbs undulate like stalks of jungle foliage. The glass wavered, flawed—at one angle, it multiplied their image; at another, it splintered them into pieces; at yet another, they seemed a pair of sea anemones, formless merging.

The oil lamp cast a dull phosphorescent glow. Shadows nestled in the curve of Anna's breasts which had grown firm and round. Her flesh glistened. She took note of these things, a portion of her mind standing apart, watching, distilling the act of lovemaking to flesh and groin, a body to serve her, a vehicle through which she could monitor her own experience.

Like an acrobat who had slung a rope across the street from house to house, Eduard was giving a show of his skill.

That served her.

She told herself she no longer came to him as a loving trusting girl. She believed the power that had erupted in her own body could no longer take her by surprise, overwhelming her, obsessing her dreams and leaving her prey to a hungry dependency. Now, she crept from her father's house in darkness to be carried by Eduard's *droschke* through the sleeping streets in order to test herself, in order to gain dominion over her own flesh.

He was her first lover. He had seduced her. She had been caught in life's endless perpetuation of itself—she had accepted the consequences as a guide to her own destiny. Now, she vowed to diminish her own vulnerability, to gain the strength she would need for what she had chosen to do: bear and rear her own child.

She watched Eduard's body glow in the lamplight, watched his hand trace the curve of her thigh. She permitted herself to respond, then willed herself to withhold. Eduard's breathing altered. His face flushed, the texture of his skin changed. She felt a sense of satisfaction at her own power.

Breathing deeply, she allowed him to penetrate her, acquiescing to the entry of this alien force which hurled itself at the gates of her being, moving relentlessly, searching. Underneath were veins and ducts and tiny canals, the explosion of semen that could engender new life. Beneath her own inner walls was a network of nerves, an excruciating sensitivity, an involuntary demand that would accept and foster and nurture that new life. A man and a woman were nature's puppets, she thought. Desire was nature's bully, ecstasy was nature's bribe.

Eduard's eyes were closed. She kept her own open, watching, measuring her response, refusing to yield except of her own volition. An involuntary wave of desire rippled through her spinal cord. Her hands grasped his buttocks. Her own eyes closed as a fissure cracked her hard-won resolve. The darkness blazed in silence.

Eduard fell upon her, insensate. His body continued to quake. In that instant, she loved and hated him and he mattered not at all.

The church clock bonged three times, reverberating through the empty streets.

The house blazed with lights.

Anna drew her skirts up and emerged from Eduard's carriage, running.

In the reception hall, the chandelier brimmed with crystal tears, weeping. It cast no light. The room was washed by shadows.

Then she saw Tante Henriette at the top of the stairs, her silhouette sharp as a knife, her face a dull smear as if someone had bruised it. Tante Henriette took the steps slowly. Her feet made no sound. At the bottom, she stopped, clutching the bannister, and regarded Anna with stricken eyes. "Dr. Kruger just left."

"Papa—?"

"He won't last the night."

Anna swept past Tante Henriette. The upstairs corridor, too, was lit. Alfred was coming out of her father's room. His face was drawn, lined with grief. "He wants to see us together," he said.

She nodded and followed Alfred inside.

The shadows that had filled the house had converged in her father's room, waiting, blurring the outlines of the bed where Rudolph Bellinger's face stood out in sharp relief against the pillows. His skin seemed transparent, the thinnest of shields, as if its purpose was no longer to contain the life force but to reveal the essence of the man beneath. Anna was shocked by the look of flesh already being transformed into spirit; it gave him a terrible beauty.

"You're going to be fine, Papa." She heard her own fear.

He shook his head. "It's not a time for lies," he answered.

Alfred moved forward, carrying a chair close to the bed so that Anna might perch on the edge of it. Then Alfred stood beside her, as if he meant to guard her from the mixture of pain and pride and regret which Rudolph Bellinger emanated. These emotions had a kinetic quality; they seemed to charge the air in a final attempt at reconciliation.

"A week ago, I cursed Kruger," Rudolph Bellinger said. He spoke with difficulty, a rasp of breath accompanying each word. "What kind of doctor are you, I asked him, without the power to save a man's life?" He heaved a deep sigh. "Then I cursed your mother. What kind of a woman are you, I asked her, to have left me years ago so that I must die without your hand upon my brow? I even cursed Tante Henriette. What kind of sister are you, I asked her, not to stand between me and death and bargain for a few more days?" An ironic smile crossed his face. "After that," he said, "I accepted it. And so I made arrangements—"

"Don't, Papa—" Anna said.

He held up a hand, silencing her. "You must listen, Anna. Both of you." His eyes moved slowly from Anna to Alfred. "I wanted you to become a doctor," he said to Alfred. "I wanted you to carry on my position in Berlin. And you, Anna"—his eyes darted to Anna again—"I wanted you to marry well, to take your place in society. These things were important to me, I can't deny that. But I'm a barrister, and I pride myself on my ability to face reality even when that reality is death—" His voice wavered. He paused to gather strength. Then his gaze settled on Alfred again. "Soon, any day now, there's going to be a siege of mass arrests. You will not be given your medical license. Your activities have made you vulnerable. Alive, I might have been able to protect you. Now, you're going to have to go underground."

"Yes, Papa," Alfred said quietly.

"Death holds a mirror to the truth," Rudolph said.

Alfred tried to speak. His voice broke. Tears sprang to his eyes. Anna wept silently.

"I've made arrangements to liquidate everything," Rudolph said. "This house, most of the furnishings, all my assets, everything." His chest rose and fell painfully. "The creditors will take most of it," he said. "What's left I've divided equally between you." He shook his head. "I'm afraid that my pride demanded a style of living beyond my means—" He reached out and took Alfred's hand. "I've opened a bank account for you in Amsterdam. It's only a small sum, three thousand gulden. I'm sorry—"

Alfred knelt and kissed his father's hand. Anna watched a silent exchange take place between them, like the passing of a torch.

Then her father raised his head and his eyes swept her face. His voice trembled. "I know you must go to America, Anna. I had to come to that, too." A peculiar strength burned in his eyes. Anna saw it was not his own strength, it had been given to him and soon it would be taken away. "Your bit of money, I've deposited here in Berlin," he said. "Perhaps it will be enough for you to start a new life in a new world. You'll have Tante Henriette." The ironic smile crossed his face once more. "Perhaps Tante Henriette will marry an Indian," he said.

Anna sobbed. "No, Papa. No—"

"Do you know the first thought I had—after the anger passed? Do you know what that was?"

Anna shook her head.

"I thought—I shall leave a grandchild."

"Oh, Papa—" she closed her eyes. "I love you, Papa."

He took her hand and pressed her palm against his mouth. Anna felt an impulse move through her arm to still her hammering heart. Then she felt her heart beat, slowly, rhythmically, in time with his. Between them, she felt the blood connection that had been transmitted from his veins to hers to those of his grandchild, the passing on of his spirit.

Then her heart stopped suddenly; there was silence where the beating of life had been. She looked up. Her father's eyes were closed. His fingers loosened. Her own hand fell back.

She didn't take his pulse. She ceased weeping. She sat silently, watching the light recede from his face with a feeling of being suspended in time. The air that had been charged with parting wrapped her, as if he were giving her a final caress with velvet gloves.

When she became aware that her own heart was beating in her chest again, the sound surprised her.

Alfred bent over the bed and removed all but one of the pillows from behind her father's head. She watched Alfred press his lips to his father's forehead with great tenderness before he pulled the sheet over her father's face. Then he stooped over the lamp and blew out the flame. The last remnants of an odd bright glow faded.

Alfred crossed to the windows and opened the drapes. "The sun's coming up," he said.

Anna stared at his figure sheathed in the first rays of dawn. "What?"

"It's daylight," he said.

"When will you leave?"

"I'll help you pack," he said.

"When will you leave?" she repeated.

"Tonight," he said.

11

"There'll be three of us going," Anna said. "Tante Henriette, myself" —she laid a gloved hand on her abdomen—"and the child."

"The land's not surveyed," Eduard said. "It's wilderness."

Anna waved a hand in dismissal. "According to the *Verein's* announcement, the parcels are six hundred and forty acres each. The required capital is six hundred gulden per parcel. I have a bank draft here for eighteen hundred gulden. That entitles me to three parcels of land—nineteen hundred and twenty acres to be exact."

Eduard crossed to the desk and turned his back to her. "Brandy?"

"No thank you."

He poured a glass for himself and drained it quickly. "An emigrant's entitled to only one parcel of land."

"I'm not your ordinary emigrant."

Eduard turned. "Of the six hundred and forty acres in a parcel, three hundred and twenty belong to the *Verein.*"

"I have no intention of turning over half of my land to the *Verein.*"

"For God's sake, Anna, you can't make your own rules."

"Would you prefer that I make a formal request of Baron von Kessler in Frankfurt?"

"That's coercion."

"Yes."

Eduard set his empty glass down and began to pace. "I'll have to go before the *Verein*."

"Remind them of my father's services to the Court."

"You want three parcels of land. You want the aid and protection of the Society. And you want passage to America—"

"First class."

He halted. "There are no traveling classes for emigrants."

"You'll arrange that too, then—won't you?" She sent him a serene smile.

He bent over the desk and shuffled through the papers. "There's a final stipulation," he said. "The land grants are for men—for a single man, or a man with a family. The title can't be registered in the name of an unmarried woman."

"What does the *Verein* require?"

"A marriage document."

"You mean a husband?"

Eduard didn't look at her. "Yes."

"I'll need a few days."

He looked up then. "I'll miss you," he said. A morose look crossed his face. "Other women will seem dull to me, unexciting."

"I won't even think about you," she said quietly.

Ben lowered himself through the rear window of the packing house, dropped to the sawdust-littered floor and crouched among the barrels.

Hook handed him a letter and set the wick of a lamp. He turned the flame down. "You can't stay here," he said. "They're still searching for you. They come every day, different ones every day, asking for the gypsy, Bendejo."

The letter was from Essen. Weeks ago, Ben had sent word to his brother, George, of Hannah's death and his own exile. Now, squatting in the shadows, he read George's response:

Essen was a small town, George wrote, in the coal basin between Dusseldorf and Dortmund. Essen was like Upper Silesia, filled with foundries, a forest of chimneys, huge black hillocks of coal where the heavy locomotives came and went like giant ants. The Krupp works was one of the smaller forges, hardly more than a dozen workmen. They could use Ben, George wrote. Herr Krupp was working on a secret process, a steel with a power of resistance that could be greater than Bessemer steel. Herr Krupp would one day be an emperor of steel.

It was a strange letter. There was no sound of grief in it, only a ring of power and obsession as if George had applied Herr Krupp's secret process to his own nature.

A wave of homesickness swept Ben.

He folded the letter and put it away.

"You can't stay—" Hook repeated, handing him a pistol.

Ben turned the weapon over in his hand. It was new, never fired. "Where'd this come from?"

"Alfred Bellinger," Hook said.

"Kurfürstenbrücke," Anna said.

Her father's carriage was waiting outside of Eduard's lodgings. The driver sent her a watery glance meant to chastise her; he had driven her father only to fine places.

The horses moved into a steady clop. The streets swept past, crowded in midafternoon.

Her father was buried.

Alfred was gone.

Soon the carriage, too, would be gone, she thought—and the streets of Berlin.

When they reached the Kurfürstenbrücke district, she told the driver to stop beside the Spree.

"Wait here," she said.

She removed her mourning veil and, gathering the folds of her dove-gray cape, strode purposefully toward the bridge which led to the fish market.

In the stream below, floating tanks covered with wire grating stored the freshwater fish. On either side of the bridge, men in slickers and peaked caps and high fishing boots waded, stocking tin pails. Anna stopped, halfway across, to scan the crowd, her eyes moving quickly over the fishwives bundled into thick jackets and broad-brimmed hats and long waterproof aprons, armed with hand nets filled with fresh carp. In front of the fishmongers' shops, housewives examined salmon and mackerel, eels writhing on marble slabs, tubs swarming with live fish and straw boxes which overflowed with crawfish, young lobster, prawns and crab. Anna's eyes darted, searching each face, searching for a figure that would tower over everyone else—cap pulled low on his forehead, collar hunched around his neck—she expected Ben Calder to be burrowing into his clothes by way of camouflage. She expected Ben Calder to be waiting for her.

She didn't see him.

She saw no one like that.

For an instant, what she saw instead was her own precarious position, a slight figure standing on a bridge—carried by the momentum of her own action, carried by a courage that now eluded her. For an instant, she felt frail, vulnerable, a girl on a foolish errand born of an impulse that now seemed remote to her.

She asked the time. Half-past three, she was told.

Slowly, she turned and began to walk back to the carriage.

Ben had always had them—glimpses that parted the curtain of the future, swift revelations like arrows of sunlight piercing the clouds of ordinary perception—when the mystery of who he was and what he was to become was unveiled for a tantalizing instant. These glimpses took place in that flicker of infinity between the instants of time, when he saw the arc of his life like a dazzling rainbow, as iridescent and insubstantial, as promise filled.

Now, waiting in the carriage—the pistol trained on the driver—he watched Anna Bellinger approach and he saw his life like that: as a bridge between two worlds.

He watched her come closer. Instinct told him she lived as a blind person, shielded from the knowledge of her own blindness by the impact of her will. It told him she had given names to life and laws to herself in a failed attempt to coax equity from nature and order from the opposing currents of her own desires. It told him she was brave and gentle, dark and destructive and consuming. It told him she did not know these things about herself.

Twice, he saw her stop and look back at the bridge, a regal shift of her head as if she meant to summon a servant. There was a fine strength about her, the authority of breeding, a stubborn belief in her own immunity. She had a full mouth, greed in it, and her cheeks were flushed from the wind, but a shadow fell across her eyes and he could see a hint of fear that shimmered there like quicksilver. Then she squared her shoulders and moved forward again, intently, as if her mind were racing ahead of her.

He reached out and opened the door of the carriage for her.

She froze, staring at him, trying not to betray her surprise as she took in the sight of the pistol. Then she smiled suddenly, a swift relieved smile that mystified him.

"It's all right," she said calmly to the driver. "We'll go home, now."

She held out her hand and let Ben help her in. She settled her skirts around her, sent Ben a slightly disdainful look and asked quietly, "Do you always confront a woman with a weapon?"

He slid the pistol beneath his jacket. The horses started to move.

"Draw the curtains," she said, assuming charge.

He obeyed her again, amused by her. The carriage darkened. She leaned back in the shadows and fixed him with a steady gaze, assessing him, the way Yakori appraised a plow horse.

"Alfred's gone underground," she said.

Ben nodded. "I know."

"You've seen him?"

Ben shook his nead. "No."

"We're all fugitivies now," she said. A sigh escaped her. "Alfred taught me that those who believe in freedom must help each other. Do you agree with that?"

"Yes," Ben said. "I agree with that."

"My father's dead," she said abruptly, without emotion.

"I'm sorry."

"I'm going to have a baby." She said that too without emotion.

An odd sensation lurched in his chest. He looked away, no longer amused, seized by a strange rush of anger.

"I've made arrangements to acquire nearly two thousand acres of land in America," she said. "In Texas. Have you heard of Texas?"

He kept his eyes averted. He felt a flash of desire for her, a complex yearning which seemed roused to life by her inaccessibility. Someone had subdued her; he had a need to subdue her. "I've heard of Texas."

"Six million unclaimed acres," she said quietly, as if she understood that it was an old dream, land—a dream that had always been as powerful for him as it was remote.

He didn't respond.

"Texas is the new fatherland for Germans who want to be free," she said.

When he turned to face her, she was opening her bag and shaking the nuggets out. Ott's nuggets glowed in the shadows against her gloved palm. He took the gold from her. The weight of the stones in his own hand inducted him through one of those cracks in time where the past merged with the present, but the future escaped him. The brush of Anna's fingers revealed to him only the size of his own hungers.

"It's not enough gold to buy land," she said softly. "Not enough to buy freedom."

"Whose child is it?"

"That's not important."

"Why tell me, then?"

"Those who believe in freedom—" she stopped. The same odd smile crossed her face again, making him aware of the unknown man in him, making him aware that unfulfilled wishes still burned in him. "I need a legal father for my child," she said. "I need a legal husband in order to claim title to the land in Texas. I need protection there until I'm settled in some civilized fashion. The marriage will be in name only—" she broke off with a sharp intake of breath.

It took him a moment to absorb what she was saying. A broad grin creased his face. Then he put his head back and emitted a bull-like roar. "You're *amazing*—"

"After the child is born and the land is established, you'll be completely free and well compensated."

"*Arrogant*—"

"Emancipated."

"You want to buy a husband?"

"Without conjugal rights."

"What kind of compensation?"

"Land. Three hundred and twenty acres of the original tract."

"That's not enough," he said.

"That's a standard emigrant's parcel."

"I don't see this as standard—"

"—plus half of all Texas land over and above my two thousand acres. The land's there, waiting to be claimed." Her eyes narrowed. "And you're free to fill your bed any way you like."

"Discreetly—" he restrained the impulse to smile.

"Of course."

"Let me see if I understand the terms. You provide the capital, I provide the legitimacy. In addition, I'm to assume responsibility for the safety and well-being of yourself and your child—"

"And Tante Henriette," Anna interjected.

"Three of you, then? Two women and a child?"

Anna bit her lip. "A partnership," she said. "Half and half."

"Nothing," he said.

Anna's brows rose. "Nothing?"

"Not a florin," he said. "Not a hair on your head. Not a foot of your two thousand acres. But all land beyond that—every acre that I claim through my own labor—is mine alone."

Anna's eyes narrowed. Ben watched tiny glints of greed flit across her pupils. "I can't agree to that," she said.

He leaned toward her, close enough to notice she smelled of spice, cardamon and mace. "If you'll be kind enough to ask the driver to stop—"

"I agree," she said.

He met her eyes. "Why?"

"I have no choice—"

"Why *me?*"

She hesitated. She brushed back a tendril of hair that whispered against her cheek and scrutinized him again. The sharp thrust of her jaw softened. "Because I don't love you," she said quietly. "Because I'll never love you."

He nodded gravely.

"I can have the marriage arrangements settled by day after tomorrow," she said.

The smile he sent her was entirely without malice. "I'll have to ask my wife," he answered.

Old Biba had told him: *"The gypsies have a warning. No one escapes their law."*

He had not returned because of that.

He hadn't come back out of fear. He had come back out of respect, out of gratitude. He had come back for guidance, for punishment or absolution, for release. Two women had hold of him, two worlds, each tugging at him with equal force.

He reached the camp at dusk. A girl of eight named Bena, dark as a berry, was the first of the children to shriek at the sight of him. He tugged at her braids and kept going.

The gypsy law was called *Kris.*

The gypsy tribunal which was presided over by old Phuro decided all matters.

Smoke curled from the cooking fires. Old Biba poured cornmeal into boiling water, then stirred the maize pudding, adding pieces of garlic and pork fat. Around her, a group of women soaked rags in lard and placed them in hollowed out potato halves, making candles for the Spring Feast which would soon mark the parting of families—the time when each would go their separate ways until the reunion of the Feast of Kettles next autumn.

When Biba saw him, she spat into the fire.

Squatting, old Phuro sucked silently on his worn brass pipe.

Beyond the circle of wagons, Yakori was watering the horses in the falling darkness, a twilight that was still more purple than black but already as cold as it would be at midnight.

"Te trais," Ben said, greeting him in Romany. *Long life to you.*

Yakori looked up. "The tribunal is arranged." Yakori's eyes swept Ben, like those of a prowling wolf. "Are you certain?"

Ben nodded.

"You're not a gypsy."

"Nor a *gadjo,"* Ben said.

One of the horses lifted its head and whinnied. Yakori patted its flank. "Once you submit to the *Kris,* you cannot go against the tribunal's decision. The penalty is death."

"Bater," Ben said. *May it be so.*

Downstairs, the packing crates were sealed. The paintings would be taken away in the morning. After that, the furniture would go.

Anna's own trunks were packed, stored in a separate room, twenty-three trunks.

Downstairs in the kitchen, Tante Henriette was weeping.

Upstairs in her room, Anna padded back and forth, distraught and impatient.

Ben Calder had listened to her offer as if it had not come from her at all, as if it were an unexpected gift from fate, as if she were simply a vehicle of destiny.

"Is it a legal marriage?"

"No."

"Then there's no problem, is there?"

"Yes, there is."

"I don't understand."

"You wouldn't," he had said. *"It's a problem of the heart."*

She threw herself across the bed. Her plan had gone awry. She had tested her powers and found them lacking. It seemed something to examine, to think about later. For the moment, she felt only impatience. Her old life was going, being crated and taken away, piece by piece. She had already let go of it. She could feel the emptiness where her life had been; a void ready to be filled with the new.

He was delaying her. Ben Calder.

She said his name in her mind with a mixture of contempt and imperiousness. Telling herself:

She would go with or without him. Ben Calder.

"Thirty-six hours," he had said. "Midnight," he had said. "I'll bring you an answer."

She buried her face in her arms and wept.

Ben stood before the tribunal.

The five men sat cross-legged on the ground in a semicircle. In front of them, flames clawed at the darkness from a fire which had been built in a three-foot pit. Old Phuro motioned for Ben to sit. Ben nodded and lowered himself slowly to the ground, peering through the flames at faces which seemed suddenly alien to him.

There was Mursa. It was Mursa—Ben reminded himself—who had taken him from Ott's cottage. It was Mursa who had taught him the notes of the violin while the bear, Ivan, leashed to a pole, hopped in narrowing circles. To the *gadjos,* Ivan appeared to keep time to the music when, in truth, it was the violin that kept time to Ivan's angers: Mursa had taught him that.

There was Anaro. Anaro wore his trousers tucked into leather boots which he polished each night in front of the fire. Anaro was a gambler. Anaro had perfected a false shuffle, and a system of marking cards by pricking them with a fine needle. Anaro could make a card slip by rubbing it with soap or make it cling by rubbing it with resin. Anaro had taught him these things.

Anaro and Mursa sat on the left of old Phuro.

Anaro and Mursa seemed strangers.

On the right of old Phuro were Yakori and Opi. Opi was a Spanish gypsy, an expert at shearing the back, ears and tail of a mule; Opi could silence the wind with his *Cante Jondo,* the Andalusian *"deep song";* Opi claimed a friendship with Tom Smith, the gypsy winner of the featherweight boxing championship in England the year before. Opi, too, seemed a stranger—and even Yakori who had been closest to him seemed remote and forbidding.

Old Phuro raised his right hand and moved it clockwise in an arc over the flames.

"We come from Egypt," old Phuro said, "from a district in Eperus."

He spoke in a hushed tone. He turned his creased face heavenward, paused, then spoke again.

"From the priests of Egypt, we learned Sanscrit from which Romany comes. From the priests of Egypt, we gained our secret knowledge of metals, the magic of bronze and iron. From the priests of Egypt, we gained our love of gold and jewels and our knowledge of their spiritual and healing properties." Old Phuro's eyes rolled up into his head. "The wisdom of Egypt is in our hearts. May it guide us tonight."

"Bater," the others murmured. *May it be so.*

"When Abraham left Ur for Canaan, he was accompanied by gypsies," old Phuro said. "We had already traveled around the world twice before the Christ, as far as Mexico where we built the second pyramids. We unraveled the riddles of Greece. We witnessed the revelations of Crete. We were given the secrets of the Orient. The wisdom of all nations is in our hearts. May it guide us tonight."

"Bater," the others murmured. *May it be so.*

Old Phuro's hand retraced its path across the flames. The pupils of his eyes dropped back into place; his eyeballs bulged like a lizard's, unblinking. "Truth must call before wisdom can answer," he said.

Ben bowed his head. A profound loneliness swept him, a deep apprehension.

"You may speak," old Phuro said.

Ben raised his eyes, looking through the flames at the fire-burnished faces which glowed like mended copper. He saw them through the eyes of a twenty-year-old facing his fathers, through the eyes of an equal facing his peers, through the eyes of both stranger and brother, supplicant and warrior—eyes that canceled and contradicted his own vision until he closed them because they showed him nothing.

He began to speak. At first, he could not hear himself speak. He could not hear the words or even the sound of his own voice, as if his ears, too, had been closed. The thoughts spoke themselves, blunt and stubborn, with the ring of earth in them and a crude power:

He talked of himself, of the poverty from which he had come, of the hungers which had been the harvest of that poverty. He talked of his French father, Anatole, who had left him with nothing but a dream of freedom. He talked of Hannah, his German mother, who had imbued him with a love of land and a sense of self, saying to him all through his childhood: *"You did not come into this world for anyone's sake but your own."* He talked of the village crone, Magda, and of the voices that had spoken to him from the deep silence of the monastery, wondrous and terrible voices that had promised him a new world.

He had killed a soldier. Then Mursa had brought him to the gypsies and he had married Selinda, believing that the new world was the gypsy world.

Selinda carried his child. He had already lost a wife and a child; he did not want to lose another. But Anna had offered him the true new world. Texas, she had said. Six million acres, she had said. And more, he said—the hunger throbbing in his voice. All the land a man could seize.

"A man can only ride one horse at a time," Yakori said.

"Not enough," Ben answered.

"A man can only eat one pig at a time," Opi said.

"Not enough—"

"A man can only make love to one woman at a time," Anaro said.

"The only piece of land that a man ever owns is the earth that buries him," Mursa said.

"Not enough—" Ben thundered. "Not enough!"

Old Phuro raised both hands. "And one lifetime, Bendejo? Is that not enough for you either?"

"No," Ben cried out. "Not enough. I want—" He halted. Then he shouted, *"I want!"* —less a shout than a howl, a cry like the one that had been torn from his bowels in the cave, that demonic cry from which even the murderous dog had recoiled and bowed in recognition of man's supremacy. "I want land," he bellowed "—and power," he roared "—and—" he hesitated "—and immortality," he whispered.

A silence fell.

In the silence, Ben's eyes opened. In the silence, his ears opened. In that long moment of silence, he looked at the faces in the firelight and he saw the hidden places in himself. He saw his own rapaciousness, and he saw he had already left these gentle people.

Then a strange event occurred. He saw old Phuro's face crease and shrivel and change before his eyes into the face of the old crone, Magda; and from Phuro's mouth came Magda's voice . . . *"You will go from the bowels of the earth to the stars. So remember this: Those who would be gods must first learn to be human."*

The image vanished in the woodsmoke.

"—to Texas," old Phuro was saying, in his own voice, solemn and severe. "You will take Anna. You will take Selinda. You will go to Texas, but you must take them both."

Ben bowed his head. *"Bater,"* he said. *May it be so.*

12

The Bremen coast was bleak. The sea was gray and angry. From the deck of the *Armenius,* Anna could no longer see the dike-protected lowlands along the Weser River. Shrouds of fog obscured her last glimpse of Germany. Standing at the rail, she felt the first stirrings of Eduard's child. Standing at the rail, she took a vow not to look back.

August 19, 1845
Our quarters consist of two rooms on the upper deck. They are small and cramped, less than adequate for Tante Henriette and myself.

Selinda occupies the gangway outside; her gypsy nature chafes at confinement. She appears to harbor no ill will for the fact that I bear the title "Frau Calder" while she has been registered as my servant.

At all hours, Ben stalks the deck as guardian. He is an angry leviathan aboard ship; his voice thunders over the roar of the sea, and what seemed crude and coarse in cultured Berlin now constitutes the entire source of our much-needed protection.

In steerage, a hundred and twenty-four emigrants have been packed into suffocating layers of bunks, sharing one toilet. They escape these conditions by remaining constantly on deck where they engage in their personal ablutions or in wild bouts

of brawling and debauchery. The rumor is the town of Hesse-
Darmstadt has emptied its prison and other German cities
have purged themselves of the indigent and the poverty-
stricken to populate the new world. I fear cholera or small-
pox. There are no medicines on board.
  Tomorrow, Tante Henriette says, we must start to learn
English from her books.

The Atlantic gales were treacherous. Mean and icy winds lashed the
ship for days.
Only Selinda was free from seasickness.
Anna witnessed several knifings; one death.
"Stay in your cabin," Ben told her. "Women are being molested."
The leader of the ruffians was an ironworker from the Rhine named
Mueller—a burly man with powerful arms and Simian features and a
vicious temper—Ben deliberately and methodically thrashed him on
deck in plain view of all.

September 11, 1845
Yesterday, I was summoned below to tend a woman who
had been stricken with severe diarrhea and vomiting during
the night. She was in the throes of a high fever and was suffer-
ing from a desperate loss of body fluid and spasmodic con-
tractions of the limbs. I ordered her clothing and bed linen
thrown overboard, her body scrubbed with lye and the inges-
tion of liquids. Ben and two others hastily constructed a shed
on deck for quarantine. By morning, she was dead.

Over Anna's protests, Tante Henriette started regular English classes
—a few illiterate men, one or two peasant women and a number of
incorrigible children—she laced her lessons with moral precepts.
Standing at the rail, it seemed to Anna the sea was less alien than
the space, the immense sky that pressed down upon her and then receded to such vast distances that it left her dizzy and disoriented.
"Keep your eyes beyond the sea," Ben told her.
"Perhaps it wasn't cholera," she answered.

September 20, 1845
Four more are dead.
  All able-bodied passengers must now assist in scrubbing
down the deck and the gangways, emptying the chamber pots

and washing the bedclothing. Ben has assigned Mueller to supervise the work detail.

Another murderous gale is visible on the horizon. The first mate predicts that when it strikes, it will be worse than the others.

Tonight, I lie curled up, exhausted, in the same foetuslike position as my child, as if to protect us both in sleep from blows I fear might come. A few moments ago, Tante Henriette said, "I never had a life. In Texas, I will have a life."

Today, we passed the halfway mark.

Seventeen were dead.

More than a fourth of the survivors were so weakened, they could not leave their berths. Anna counted victims of scurvy, malnutrition, broken limbs, venereal disease, pneumonia. Others were severely debilitated by cholera. There were eight orphans.

In spite of the cold, cholera remained a threat. Under Anna's orders, more sheds were built on deck for quarantine and those who died in agony, without morphine, filled the deck with their screams.

Anna held their heads and watched them die.

They were buried at sea.

There were two Annas. There was the young Anna who, overtaken by exhaustion, wept and prayed to be miraculously returned to civilized Germany. There was another. She swore to survive.

Three days off the Texas coast, the torrential winds of a "blue norther" struck without warning. Icy blasts from northern seas sent the temperature down to freezing at the rate of a degree a minute and rain turned instantly to hail.

Already battered by previous storms, the ship was frail. It strained under the seizure. Anna lashed Tante Henriette and herself with leather straps to their cabin berths. Below, she could hear those who were not tied to their bunks being flayed and dashed about until their bones were broken.

On deck, ninety-mile-an-hour winds cracked the masts and tore the sails and hurled the ship about, the gale whistling like the wrathful breath of some sea monster whose appetite had been only whetted by seventeen pitiful corpses.

Ben ordered all extra weight thrown overboard to lighten the ship and preserve its fragile hulk.

Defying the perilous winds and the icy deck, Anna beat at him vainly with her fists as he hurled the trunks overboard. Silver and china, treasured mementoes, her father's books, her mother's portrait, every vestige of the life she had known sank to the bottom of the sea while she poured scalding curses on him.

October 25, 1845
There is no time to mourn . . .

Selinda was in labor when they washed upon the shore.

The ship limped painfully in, no more than a mass of floating debris, as wounded as the creatures who Anna ordered to be carried from their berths.

There were no trees.

The land was not land, but a strip of crushed and powdered shell washed up by years of waves—an island separated from the Texas mainland by a series of lakes which, by evening, threatened to overflow.

The rain came down in sheets. The few barracks which existed were filled. Shelter was a camp of tents erected along the beach, barely a shield from the rain and the ice-cold winds. The temperature was close to zero. The wind howled.

One trunk survived. Ben brought it in from the ship. When Tante Henriette opened it, Anna wept for the first time.

Selinda gave birth by the light of an oil lamp that flickered, casting an illusory glow of safety over mother and son. Selinda crooned softly to the son she called Bendejo.

"A *Tejano*," Ben called him in Spanish, the first Calder to be born on Texas soil.

Mueller brought a jug of corn brandy.

Anna sat quietly, rereading the letter Tante Henriette had discovered attached to the lid of the trunk which had been packed by Alfred. In it were medicines—morphine and quinine and bandages—Anna had not known they were there. The trunk also had weapons—short carbine rifles and sidearms, cartridges and gunpowder. The letter said:

My dear Anna,

I don't know where you will be when you read this. I don't know where I will be. Leopold was executed today. That we all expected. It has not lessened the anguish. For you, my brave sister, and for myself, there is no turning back. We have each embarked in our own way upon journeys that will lead to a new world where men and women will be free. You have followed your heart. That was, and is, a revolutionary act. I have taken the liberty of packing one of your trunks with the necessities of a revolution. New worlds are built with arms and with medicines. The heart is not enough. Leopold has taught us that. If your child should be a boy, and if you should endow him with the freedom-loving name of Leopold, I should feel honored and remembered . . . Your brother, Alfred.

December 24, 1845

My son was born three days ago. I have named him Leopold.

He is extraordinarily beautiful, a fair-skinned child with sea-blue eyes and aristocratic features. When I hold him to my breast, I am awed. How can one so tiny have been the reason for my journey and the reward for my endurance? How can all hardships have suddenly become blessings? I feel indescribable joy.

Two days ago, a ship was wrecked on the coast. The immigrants were saved, but the ship had been carrying badly needed provisions supplied by the Verein, *and those were lost. There are not enough tents. Pneumonia is rampant. It is destined to be a melancholy Christmas, cold and bitter, except that the rain has ceased—miraculously—permitting Ben and Mueller to cross the forbidding streams and bring back a stunted oak from the swampy flatlands. Tante Henriette has gathered the children to decorate it with prunes and strings of barley beads. Tomorrow morning, the Catholics and the Lutherans will put away their differences and gather for a Holy Communion service.*

Tante Henriette claims it is the affirmation of God's spirit that eased Leopold's birth and has now provided the newest miracle; today, a schooner arrived from New Orleans, carry-

ing lumber and provisions and medicines. Faith is for Tante Henriette. For me, as midnight creeps in to signal Christmas, my thoughts are concerned not with Heaven, but with this earth. I have my son. The will to prevail is stronger than trust in God.

13

Tante Henriette ignored the guard.

Breeding showed, Tante Henriette thought, as Conrad Ahrenbach rose. She nodded brusquely for him to return to his desk.

"There are four blacksmith shops in New Braunfels," she said, tartly. "I see no need for four blacksmith shops. You might order two of them to merge. Or the cigar manufacturers—three are too many for a town of fifteen hundred—women and children have no use for cigars."

Ahrenbach's brows went up. "I'm afraid I don't quite—"

"I've brought fourteen orphans from Indianola. Who'll pay for them at the inn? The *Verein* promised schools. The Evangelical Church serves as the school and the pastor serves as schoolteacher. Texas is now a state. In America, we're bound to separate Church and State. And the hospital, it's shameful—primitive. How can you call this a German colony? Shall these children remain *Einwanderers?*" She halted to take a breath. "I'm told the owners of the tavern are in the employ of the *Verein*. The tavern can be rebuilt elsewhere. Is a tavern more important than an orphanage?"

"As you pointed out, this is America," Ahrenbach said. He looked amused. "I'm the Director of the colony, not its Sovereign."

Tante Henriette sent him a biting look. Thirty-two, they said, and unmarried. Wed to his work, they said. Rumors were the *Verein's* funds were short. Rumors were he was keeping the colony going on credit and ingenuity. "Two of the children died on the trip from Indianola," she said, quietly.

"It grieves me to hear that," he said. Tante Henriette watched concern etch sudden lines in his forehead.

"Three hundred miles," she said. "Every step, the prairies were soaked by rain. The wagons sunk to their axles. The men harnessed themselves alongside the animals. The rivers were at the flood stage. Rafts had to be built. One of the children drowned. The other succumbed to pneumonia."

"You were with the Calder party?"

"By God's grace." She saw Ahrenbach's eyes narrow slightly. His thoughts seemed to shift elsewhere.

He brought himself back. "I'll speak to Donnersmark at the inn. He came with the first settlers."

"And my building?"

"I'll make some kind of arrangement."

"We'll need sustenance. Fifteen dollars a barrel for flour, thirty-seven cents for a chicken—it's thievery."

Ahrenbach smiled. "Some might say you have the makings of a fine thief yourself."

"I'm a Christian," Tante Henriette said.

It rained all week. The rain had turned Sequin Street into a swamp, and a sharp April wind was rattling the metal sign that said: KELLER'S MERCANTILE.

Inside, Ben tracked mud down an aisle lined with barrels of flour and beans and rice, striding past farm implements, past boxes of nails and bolts of calico; his head grazed a number of hanging cooking utensils and set them banging as he went by. At the rear, a deputy was posted. Ben identified himself and climbed a wooden stairway. Upstairs, one end of the storage area had been cleared. Lit by the glow of a oil lamp, Ahrenbach was seated on a stool at an accountant's table, making entries in a ledger. "Calder?" He spoke loudly. The rain was beating on the tin roof.

Ben nodded.

"Excuse my temporary predicament—" Ahrenbach climbed down from the stool and shook Ben's hand. In a corner, Ben could see a cot made up in military fashion. Behind Ahrenbach was an arrangement of files and a map of the Texas territory tacked to the wall. A large portion had been colored in red. "Does Tante Henriette find my quarters adequate for her orphanage?"

"Did you send for me to discuss Tante Henriette?"

"I'm prepared to offer you employment with the *Verein.*"

"I don't work for German princes."

A brief smile crossed Ahrenbach's face. "I'd heard you were something of a revolutionary."

"A man running from the gallows finds allies where he can."

"My records show you killed a captain in Upper Silesia—"

"A corporal."

Ahrenbach rose, approached the map and swept his palm across the area that had been colored in red. "Here—between the Llano and Colorado rivers—is the Fisher-Miller land grant. It extends all the way out there into western Texas." He stopped. "Can you read a map?"

"Yes."

"Fisher's out of it now, but no matter. We inherited the terms of his original contract. Fisher never set foot on the grant. That didn't keep him from presenting the *Verein* with glowing descriptions and false promises. Then Prince Solms came here. His reports were a bit overenthusiastic. Unenlightened, some might say."

"Shortsighted," Ben said, rising and pushing the chair aside. "Only fools have come to Texas to create another Germany. And only women are content with a half-acre town plot and a ten-acre vegetable garden." He joined Ahrenbach and studied the map. Then he reached out and pressed his thumb against it, leaving a smudged print. "Right here," he said. "Mark it Calder. Eighteen hundred acres."

"Comanche territory," Ahrenbach said. "They've killed every surveyor we've sent in." Ahrenbach's forefinger hovered over the map, then rested on a spot outside the grant. "This is New Braunfels, here, on the Comal and Guadalupe rivers. Over here—sixty miles northwest, on the Pedernales River—I've obtained another tract to be called Fredericksburg. Only four miles away, there's a group of Mormons already established. That means it's reasonably safe. Day after tomorrow, I start moving the first group of three hundred to start a second community there. Once that's done, we'll move from Fredericksburg to the north bank of the Llano River—here—just inside the bounds of the grant. It's the only way to advance on the Comanches—in stages."

Ahrenbach regarded Ben with a grim expression. "By the terms of the contract, we have to settle two hundred immigrants inside the grant by next autumn or we forfeit all rights to the land." He hesitated. "Your land," he said.

"Why give me such inflammatory information?"

"You don't strike me as a man to be convinced by lies." Ahrenbach crossed to a bolted window, released the wood shutters and surveyed the pouring rain. "Two thousand immigrants are still stranded at Indianola," he said, "and more arrive every week. The teamsters I hired to transport them inland have broken their contract—the Government's offered them twice as much to move General Taylor's forces from Corpus Christi to the Rio Grande. War's certain to be declared—they won't be back." He bolted the window shut again and turned. "You know the inland route. You know how to deal with swamps and swollen rivers—and, if necessary, Mexican bandidos."

"I want to be paid in land."

"That's not possible."

"To transport settlers to Fredericksburg, twenty acres a head. To bring the immigrants in from Indianola, forty acres a head. You provide the horses and wagons and defray all other expenses." Ben waited.

"Indianola," Ahrenbach said. "By five o'clock tomorrow, I'll have a dozen teams for you."

"That's not enough."

"It'll have to be enough."

"Fifty acres a head, then."

Ahrenbach scrutinized Ben. When he spoke, his voice was grave. "Seventy years ago, the King of England purchased twenty-nine thousand soldiers from German feudal lords. He sent them to fight the American Revolution. Some deserted and became Americans. Others came back to Germany with stories of liberty and opportunity. They talked of human dignity . . ."

"Those are your reasons," Ben said. "I came for my own."

"I'll have the contract ready by two," Ahrenbach said.

It was still raining outside.

He found Mueller at the inn. Mueller was drinking with a group of men and taking wagers on how long it would be before Polk declared war on Mexico. Ben led him to a private table in a corner. It took the better part of an hour to explain the arrangements to Mueller and to come to terms on a deal.

On his way out, he purchased a jug of brandy.

The rain had quit, but the sun was still buried in clouds.

At exactly two o'clock, he entered the General Store and purchased two glasses from Keller before he nodded at the guard and climbed the stairs to Ahrenbach's quarters again.

He set the jug and the glasses on Ahrenbach's desk.

The contract was prepared. He watched Ahrenbach scratch his name on it. Holding the contract under the light, he read it through twice before he signed his own name.

He waited for Ahrenbach to blot the signatures before he poured the brandy.

Then he waited, again, for Ahrenbach to stand and raise his glass.

"To Fredericksburg," Ben said.

"Indianola," Ahrenbach corrected.

"I've leased the contract," Ben said. He smiled.

Ahrenbach set his glass down. "You can't do that."

"Does it say there"—Ben laid his hand on the contract—"that I can't?" He continued smiling.

The beginning of an irate frown started across Ahrenbach's face. Then, half-formed, the scowl halted, fluttering for an instant, uncertain, before it was suddenly and completely vanquished by a spontaneous burst of laughter. Shaking his head, Ahrenbach let the laughter overtake him until he was roaring aloud. "How much did you give him?"

"Ten acres a head—" Ben's own laughter erupted to merge with Ahrenbach's. Roaring appreciatively in an impulsive bonding, Ben heard their laughter rising in unison and resounding through the warehouse.

Ahrenbach sobered first. "Who is he?"

"Mueller."

"Is he capable?"

"Yes."

Reclaiming his glass, Ahrenbach raised it once more. "The French are dedicated to honor," he said, "the Americans to liberty—" he paused, smiling. "It used to be said that the German flaw was obedience."

"To the new German," Ben said.

"To the new American." Saluting Ben with his glass, Ahrenbach drained the brandy. A moment of awkward silence fell. The rain started to beat on the tin roof again. Ahrenbach shook his head. "I'm trying to grow accustomed to being addressed as Conrad . . ." he said. "It seems a difficult thing for people to do—"

"Done," Ben said.

"We'll leave Friday at sunrise."

"These Mormons"—Ben refilled his glass—"is it true what I hear about them?—that a man can have two wives?"

"I've seen your Anna in town," Ahrenbach said, reaching for the brandy. "With a woman like that, what would a man want with two wives?"

14

"No," Anna said. "I'll not be uprooted again."

The days had grown longer. But the wind still followed the rain at night, bringing a damp bitter chill. At night, a false peace burned in the firelight.

Ben was pacing. The pacing had started directly after supper, though he never ceased watching Anna as she rocked Leopold's cradle. The gesture seemed natural to her, a perfect rhythm that wrapped the two of them—herself and her child—not his child; he was always aware of that.

"The second caravan to Fredericksburg leaves next week." He stated it now as a command.

"I'll not go," Anna answered firmly. He was aware of Selinda sitting apart, nursing Bendejo and watching them in silence. "We have a roof now," Anna said. "We have walls around us."

He scowled. He pulled at his beard which was full again and ragged. He saw the two women, suddenly, as parts of his nature which were at war with each other. "I'm master of this house."

"No more ships," Anna said, her voice rising. "No more tents, no more open wagons. It's seven months," she said, "living on the move, under pitiless conditions."

"Fredericksburg is sixty miles closer to our land."

"*My* land," she answered. "Mine."

He quit pacing. He stood over her, glowering. He saw she was watching his hands. He was aware of the blunt power of his hands. He knew she could feel them resisting an impulse to strike her.

"I'll not be intimidated," she said.

"It's the disease of the *gadjo*," Selinda said quietly. "Land hunger."

"He's your husband," Anna said.

"He's your husband," Selinda answered.

"He's the father of your child," Anna said.

"They all believe he's the father of your child," Selinda answered.

"What does it matter what they believe?" Ben bellowed.

"It matters to you," Selinda told him. Her eyes blazed. "Once it didn't matter, but now it does."

"No," he said. He watched Selinda rise. She was holding Bendejo. At six months, Bendejo was dark and sturdy. It struck him Bendejo was too large to be clinging yet to his mother's breast.

"You lie," Selinda said sharply. She turned and disappeared into their quarters.

He stalked to the doorway. "They're Germans!" he shouted. "They'll remain Germans! They'll run their *Bäckereien* and their *Apotheke* and they'll live by the old ways—and a hundred years from now, people will point out this town and say: *'That's where the Germans live.'* I'll not be among them!" he shouted. "Call it land hunger. Call it any name you like—"

From the other room, Selinda set loose a stream of Romany curses.

"Remain a savage if you like—" he said, "but know that no law here makes my son a gypsy!"

No response came back, only a soft low crooning as she tended Bendejo.

Turning on his heel, he glared at Anna. "And you"—he heard his voice turn suddenly quiet—"your arrogance will do you no good here. Here, a Baron is my friend and equal. Here, your land—eighteen hundred acres—is a peasant's parcel. Before I'm finished, I'll have thousands of acres. Hundreds of thousands of acres—" He halted suddenly. He felt his face flame. A strange rigidity overtook him. He strode to the fire and turned his back to her. "I'll not serve your aristocratic ways," he said.

Leopold started to cry.

When he turned, she was gathering Leopold in her arms. "I'll not move again until Leopold is a year old," she said.

"You're a fool."

A moment of tension bound them. "I've no use for crude opinions," Anna said. "I live by my own—"

"—greed," he said.

She managed a smile. "Call it any name you like," she said.

Perhaps an hour went by. He knew, upstairs, Anna was listening to his pacing in the common room. He knew his footsteps jarred the house, still indignant. Periodically he stopped and then paced again, wrestling, with a new reluctance—an inner turmoil—that kept him from Selinda's bed.

Then he climbed the stairs.

He appeared in the doorway.

"These are my quarters," she said. Her lamp was burning. She was writing in a journal.

"I brought Leopold's cradle," he answered. He carried it in and set it beside her bed. When he stood, his head grazed the rafters. He watched her catch the sweetish smell of brandy. He knew the brandy had made his eyes hard. He knew a rush of desire emanated from him.

Leopold was sleeping on Anna's bed. When she lifted him up, he heard the corn-husk mattress rustle. She laid Leopold in his cradle.

"You don't belong here," she said, rising.

"I built every inch of this house," he replied.

"We made a bargain," she said icily.

"In Germany," he answered. "This is Texas. Near Fredericksburg, there are Mormons who believe a chaste woman is denied salvation. It's a man's duty to grant grace to her."

"You've been drinking—"

"Not enough." He moved toward her. Sharply outlined in the lamplight, he could see himself in her looking glass. He looked battered. The winds and storms had whipped his face; it had grown craggy and rocklike—the old scar cut his cheek like a thin white crescent path.

"No," Anna was saying, shaking her head. She was wearing a muslin dressing gown. He was aware of her body.

He halted for an instant, unsure. Then a sudden meeting took place, not of eyes, but of hidden need, an ancient attraction of opposites, of opposing forces. It was a hunger for conflict, a need for violence; he saw Texas had engendered that in both of them.

He grasped her shoulders, gently; he made an effort to be gentle. Under the muslin, her flesh was warm. She shook her head again, saying no—but he took her in his arms and bent his head and silenced her with his mouth. Her fists beat at his back, but he could feel her heart hammering. He could feel carnal memories press against her own resistance. An urgent hunger engulfed him, fierce and demanding.

With enormous force, she pushed him away.

"If you touch me again, I'll kill you," she said quietly.

He felt a strange expression pass over his face. He felt suddenly imperious and lordly, the way he had felt astride the restless stallion just before he left for Fredericksburg.

"You'll come to me," he answered.

"Never," she said.

"Never is a long time," he said.

"Der Grass ist grun, die See ist blau," Tante Henriette said, chalking the phrase on a piece of slate.

"The grass is green, the sea is blue," the children translated in unison. Only one was silent, a scrawny flaxen-haired boy of fourteen slouched at the rear of the classroom in a patch of brutal sunlight.

"Der Sand ist gelb, die Maus ist grau—"

"The sand is yellow, the mouse is gray." The children's voices rose, all but Josef's; he continued to stare savagely out of the window.

Ben was passing. Through the window, Tante Henriette watched him pass walking the length and breadth of New Braunfels again, like an animal pacing off his cage. Lately, Ben had been as restless as the wind that whirled eddies of dust in the glare-ridden streets. Lately, Ben had been caught by inner furies; they had started the first week in June, when Mueller returned from Indianola, unrecognizable and driven half-mad.

"Der Baer ist braun, die Rose rot—" she said.

"The bear is brown, the rose is red," the children recited.

"Josef—" she said softly.

Josef sent her a furious look. In his eyes, she could read Mueller's ravings—stories of malaria and typhoid and spinal meningitis—

polluted drinking water and no sanitation, mass graves filled with blanket-wrapped bodies, entire families wiped out. Josef Bremer had come from Indianola. Those who had survived there had turned on each other. Mueller had lost an eye, gouged out in a fight by a twist of a vicious thumb; Mueller carried the eye in his pocket. Mueller had killed three men. The animals had been slaughtered—sixty had abandoned all belongings and had set out from Indianola on foot. They had left a trail of dead for the coyotes which had followed them and the vultures which had continually circled overhead. The dying had prayed to be buried. Fewer than a dozen had survived; Josef was the only child.

"*Die Kohle ist schwarz, und weiss das Brot—*"

"The coal is black, and white the bread," the children responded.

Josef sprang from his seat and bolted from the classroom.

"The bread is white," Tante Henriette corrected. The children echoed her, then waited. But she was looking out the window, watching Josef sprint down the street to accost Ben. Gesturing, Josef seemed to be making an impassioned plea. Tante Henriette watched Ben listen, his face grim. After a moment, Josef quieted. They stood talking then, like two men, poised for danger. She saw there was no carelessness left in Ben, no boy left in him—nor in Josef. She saw Ben nod, finally. Then, taking Josef by the shoulder, Ben started to lead him back.

"Fifteen-minute recess," Tante Henriette said.

Leaping from their chairs and shouting, the children evacuated the classroom.

Ben brought Josef inside.

They stood together in front of her—the boy, skinny and tense and painfully defiant—the man towering over him; Ben looked weary of heroism.

"He's been hanging around the old blockhouse restaurant," Ben said, "listening to all the talk there of the war." His hand still rested protectively on Josef's shoulder; it was a hand big enough to crack bones. "He dreams of killing," Ben said.

"Is this true, Josef?" Tante Henriette's eyes scanned Josef's face. The boy's jaw was pitted with scars from the smallpox that had brutalized him, but spared him. A few stray golden hairs glittered on his upper lip.

"I'm fourteen," Josef said. "I'm a man."

"You're a boy. You have to go to school." She reached out to touch him. "What do you know of killing Mexicans?"

Josef pulled back from her. "I *know*," he said. His eyes, blue and cloudy, lit with a momentary flash of pure hatred.

"Go and pack your things," Ben told him.

Tante Henriette watched him leave. "He's a *child*—"

"He buried twenty-four, including his parents and a brother. He has to confront his own death so he can find courage."

"That's barbaric." She turned away, rubbing the German phrases from the slate with a ferocious motion.

"You want to teach them English and literature," Ben said. "You want to civilize them. It's the civilized who'll die in Texas. Only the barbaric will survive."

Tante Henriette's hands fell to her sides. When she faced Ben again, she asked quietly, "Has your soul grown so hard?"

"My soul wants land," he answered. "Now, the Mexicans say it's their land." He picked up the chalk and drew a rough map of the territory between the Nueces River and the Rio Grande. "Right here," he said, marking a spot on the north side of the Rio Grande, "we join Zachary Taylor's forces at Port Isabel on the twenty-fourth of June."

"Must you take Josef?"

"If I don't, he'll go on his own."

Tante Henriette nodded slowly. Her eye fell on the small muslin bag Ben wore nestled against his chest. She reached out and touched it. "Is it a talisman? Will it keep you safe?"

"A woodsman gave it to me in Silesia." Ben's eyes clouded. "He told me I was like my father. He said—it's like having wild horses in you. He said—you must let them take you or they'll turn on you and trample you to death." He shook his head. "I'll miss you," he said.

"What will we do without you—Anna and Selinda and I?"

"It's only six months. You have Ahrenbach's protection."

"You know," she said, with an answering smile, "all three of us are in love with you in different ways."

"War is easier," he said.

15

Ben Calder
The Rio Grande

Blood and thunder, Josef says.

The fifers and the drummers play the march of the dead. We are burying men at night in gunboxes and cracker barrels. Some are dead from smallpox, measles, the cholerina. Some from homesickness and murder. We came for land, for patriotism, for other reasons. Now, men die from loneliness and kill from boredom.

Josef grows thinner every day. The biscuits crawl with brown bugs. We use the bugs as pieces of gunflint. From the Gulf, black storms strike daily. Our muskets rust in the rain, blister in the sun. Men kill for a Mexican sombrero.

When will we fight? Josef asks.

These Mexicans are not fighters, I say. They are peasants taken from the land.

The Mexicans are calling us conquistadores. *To them, German miners and Irish hay cutters and Indiana farmers are* conquistadores.

We travel across the river on a Mexican barge. We are ferried across by a naked boatman. In Matamoros, in front of the flat-roofed houses, the amputees are lying in the dusty streets on cowhides. They are begging for opium pills. In his tent, General Taylor gives interviews to reporters. Two French artists have come to sketch him. He holds military exhibition drills in the Plaza. Only the whores come to watch.

Last night, I dreamed of Nicolai Lubeck and my first-born son. I went back to Silesia. Thomas was lying there with one leg. Then the bugle woke me. I woke with a terrible desire to live. It was born from the memory of living.

Lilli's son is two years old now. My son. In the Church, they are saying that war is a crossroads of the soul.

Horgan and Ryan have disappeared, both Irishmen. Deserters, they say—gone over to the Mexican side. At The Resaca House saloon, the Scotsman McWhorter says the Mexican priests are serving God by soliciting Catholics for the Mexican forces.

The Scotsman says, "War is man's refuge from women."

Outside, a regimental band is playing after evening mess. At the grilled windows whores are smoking cigarittos. Josef is staring. I pass money to one of them. Take him, I say. Teach him about flesh so his life will not be ruled by women.

New Braunfels

"As you know, my husband failed to plant in the spring before he went to Fredericksburg," Anna said. "Then he left for Port Isabel and, by late summer, I had turned my attention to more profitable undertakings."

"Cattle, I understand." The Baron was standing near the fire-oven in the common room. He had appeared unexpectedly. Refusing tea, he had expressed a preference to stand, and had formally requested that she not address him as Baron. *Conrad,* he had said.

"Thirty-five head," she said, "plus a dozen milk cows and nine calves. We get a hundred liters of milk a day. Fifty are sold and the rest goes to market as butter and cheese. Six cattle will be slaughtered on the fifteenth of October—the calves will replace them and add three more to the herd."

She was seated at a table. Open in front of her was her journal which had become a bookkeeping ledger. She looked sideways at him, speaking more softly now, with a deliberate seductiveness. "I left Germany with twelve hundred gulden," she said, "—a thousand American dollars. By the time my husband went to war in June, my resources had dwindled to less than eight hundred dollars. I couldn't afford to continue to buy provisions. Nor could I afford to use my ten acres to raise kohlrabi and sweet potatoes."

"Your enterprise is beyond question."

"Thank you."

"I'm afraid your practices are not."

She sent him a bewildered look. "Oh?"

"You own two pigs, I believe. They're being allowed to run loose in the bottomland near the creek. The law requires them to be penned."

Anna rose and crossed in front of him to light the lamp. It was not yet six o'clock. In September the days darkened earlier. In September today's sudden bout of blue northern cold would give way again tomorrow to blistering heat. "The pigs will be butchered as soon as the weather cools in November." She looked up at him over the lamp. "I'll see that you receive sausage."

"I'd prefer a meatless plate and an obedience to the law," he answered.

She sent him a flirtatious smile. Without rancor, she said, "Those who are still dependent on the *Verein* for support have grown accustomed to meatless plates."

The Baron's shoulders stiffened. His bearing was aristocratic like Eduard's, but his eyes were more like Alfred's, the clear direct gaze of an idealist. She found him attractive. She practiced his name to herself: *Conrad.*

"The *Verein* has been overwhelmed by problems in Germany," he said.

"Has the revolution begun?"

"Not yet."

The fire had been laid. Anna turned the lamp down and, crossing again in front of him, she stooped and set the kindling aflame. In the silence the norther howled. She was aware of Conrad's eyes on the curve of her back. "My brother is Alfred Bellinger," she said. "When the revolution begins, you'll hear his name."

"I've heard his name. I respect it," he said quietly. He paused. "Your brother's wish has been to give land to the peasants," he said. "How is it that yours is to take it away?"

She straightened slowly. She sent him a composed look. "Those without funds trade their land to me at market value—a dollar and a half an acre. Should I refuse them milk and butter and beef? Should I let them starve? Or do you define democracy as charity?"

He emitted a sound of exasperation. "I'm told you have two gentlemen working for you. I believe they're called Hook and Goliath?"

"They're friends of my husband's from Berlin."

"They're here without sponsorship."

"Temporarily. They'll be leaving to join General Taylor's forces."

"They've cut ten miles of prairie grass around New Braunfels—land used for common grazing. Now, I understand you plan to market it as livestock feed this winter."

"You'll have to discuss that with Tante Henriette," she said. "That enterprise will subsidize the orphanage which the *Verein* can no longer support."

He frowned. Striding to the table she had vacated, he picked up her bookkeeping ledger and studied it. "You have an unorthodox way even with figures."

"It's my own method."

He looked at her. "How old are you?"

"Nineteen."

"You know you're using the *Verein's* failure to justify your own—" he broke off in midsentence.

"Greed?" She tossed her head. "Is that the word you had in mind?"

"When I was your age, I dreamed of peach orchards," he said.

"When I was your age, I dreamed of democracy and freedom."

"You have no wife, no children," she answered. "You can indulge in such dreams." Gathering her skirts, she crossed to where he stood and took the ledger out of his hands. "Land is power," she said quietly. "I have a son. My son will have land, and my son will have power."

"Your son will have his own destiny," he said. "It will not be determined by you."

Their eyes locked in silent combat. She broke the tension with a provocative laugh. "You assume authority over matters not within your domain."

"My apologies."

She hugged the ledger to her breast. Head lowered, she regarded him through thick lashes. "You'll forgive me if I find it difficult to believe you came here to discuss pigs and prairie grass."

"You're a beautiful woman—"

"Thank you."

"—but you count too much on your powers as a woman."

"Do I?"

"It's come to my attention that you've purchased two slaves," he said. "You cannot own slaves in this colony."

She shrugged helplessly. "Do you expect one poor girl to engage in the physical labor of herding cattle and milking cows?"

"We're abolitionists," he said.

"President Polk is a slaveholder—"

"The citizens of this colony are not."

"What does that mean—abolitionist? Whigs, Democrats, Abolitionists—politics mean nothing to me." She set the ledger down and appraised him openly for a moment. "I paid six hundred dollars for those slaves."

"I can't permit you to remain here, then."

"You're not serious?"

"I'm afraid I am."

"Where shall I go?"

"You seem quite capable of making some arrangement." He smiled. "Perhaps you could relocate east of the ninety-eighth meridian where the cotton plantations begin."

Anna whirled. She paced for a few moments. He stood waiting, quietly. When she stopped, her eyes narrowed sharply. "I'm a nurse," she said. "Your hospital is overrun with malaria and spinal meningitis. Your quinine is gone, the rest of your medicine supply is dangerously low, and you have only one doctor. I have a large supply of medicines which I brought from Germany. I have a knowledge of these plagues. I'll exchange the quinine and my services—"

His sudden laughter interrupted her. He was shaking his head. "I'm amazed by your incorrigibility."

She sent him her most enchanting smile. "Those are *my* politics."

"You'll have to pay the Negroes wages."

"I can't afford wages."

"You pay a gypsy woman as a house servant."

"You have no understanding of my circumstances."

He sighed. "I presume they're like your bookkeeping."

"You're an honorable man"—Anna hesitated, gazing down at her wedding ring and toying with it a moment before she looked up with sudden candor—"but your unyielding ways force me to take you into my confidence."

"No more bargains," he said.

"The gypsy woman is not my servant," she said. "She's my husband's wife."

16

Ben Calder
The Rio Grande

Monterrey is a hundred and seventy miles west by south. The regulars are taken upstream to Camargo by steamboat. We volunteers are ordered to march.

The river roads are flooded. We trudge thigh-deep in snake-infested waters. Inland, the mountain roads grow parched, arid. Our feet are burned through our boots. Past Reynosa, we move at night. We pass a fresh graveyard of thirty crosses. Murder victims of Mexican bandidos, McKay says. I have seen no bandidos. Only women fleeing by moonlight, carrying babies and fowl and leading goats.

Another Irishman and a German-Catholic have deserted to join the Mexicans. Our orders are to shoot them on sight.

We move on.

The packmules carry three hundred pounds apiece. Mexican arrieros tend the mules. Dark-skinned, they keep to themselves. They share private jokes and invent lewd songs about the camp women who follow us. One of them is caught with copies of a proclamation. It calls this war a godless aggression for the sake of acquiring more slave territory. The arriero is staked alive to the ground and left for the sun and the rattlers.

Death is at home in the valley of the Rio Grande.

At Ceralvo, we make camp. I can see the mountains of Monterrey in the distance. We wait for orders. Nights, inside the tent, cards are dealt on a poncho. McWhorter cheats. The gypsies taught me cards.

McWhorter has rubbed the high cards with soap to make them slip.
The low cards have been treated with resin to make them cling. The
suits have been marked by pricking them with a fine needle.

Outside, I find Josef staring at the midnight sky. Look, he says.
There is a rainbow around the moon. He is watching it with wonder.
How far is it from here to the moon?—he asks.

Come and count my winnings, I answer. We'll go home as rich men.

New Braunfels

She knew Conrad Ahrenbach wanted her.

She had known it since September when they bargained for the
slaves.

Since then, the epidemic of spinal meningitis had swept Tante
Henriette's orphanage, and the cholera had taken a quarter of her cattle, and the icy winds and winter days had each brought a new crisis;
and she had left all girlish pretensions behind. Time had made her a
woman. Time had burned away all coquettishness.

In November she invited him into her bed with a full knowledge of
what she needed.

Her body tingled. His hands woke it from its long sleep, sending demanding messages to that part of her which had locked off her heart.
He stirred in her a memory of her first awakening. It had never left
her. She felt the pain and power and delight of each pore opening, each
with its own pulse, each with its own heartbeat. She withheld nothing.
She took everything.

Afterward, she felt a fullness inside, a sweet heaviness; she awoke
drenched in her own perfume, as if on a summer night, as if in a fever.

Then she rose and bent over Leopold's crib with a fierce burst of
love and anxiety that took her breath away; and she renewed her vow
to guard him, to stand between Leopold and this place, this Texas,
where vastness and barbarism decreed that a single life was in-
significant and not a moment was free of danger.

"Part of you has never taken root here," he told her. He was staring
at the ceiling in the darkness.

She knew he was right. Old dreams still floated—memories of Berlin
and Eduard—like puddles of oil on the surface of a pail of water, cap-
turing her attention with false rainbows.

She had tried to skim them painfully, discarding old images of herself. She had tried to see New Braunfels through Conrad's eyes.

The landscape was sparse. Berlin had been a city, masses of people, a stratified life, one class cordoned off from another by visible criteria, by elegance or the absence of elegance.

"In Berlin, what was gross and coarse was kept at a distance," he said. "That's over," he said.

He had taken it upon himself to humanize her. She knew he wanted her to see each man and woman singly, to see each as singular, to sense the hidden nature of people, the crude and the beautiful, the dangerous and the unexpected.

Suddenly, she laughed. "In your heart, you're more of an aristocrat than I am," she said.

She felt herself thrive.

Now that Conrad was her lover, Selinda was easier with her; they were almost friends.

She strode through the muddy streets of the village; she gave orders to the Negro woman, Beatrice; she severed the head of a rattler, and stroked the warm solid haunches of the milk cows, and rode herd with the Negro man, Samuel.

She counted the bales of prairie grass as Goliath tied and bound them, and Hook loaded them into wagons with the metal clasp that served as his hand.

She moved through the smell of death in the hospital, tending to the ill and the doomed with the authority of a new-found strength.

As the days passed she began to understand that she had undertaken a journey in ignorance and youthful rebellion—she had come as a reluctant pioneer, able to endure hardship but not to accept it. Now, she watched her hands grow rough and her nails grow brittle with a sense of satisfaction, a knowledge that what was being prepared was not a new land, but a new Anna growing inside the old, whispering to her that all mysteries were rooted in the body, that all secrets of self were to be discovered in the flesh.

She wondered if she might be falling in love.

She knew she wasn't. She felt she was moving beyond him.

She felt Selinda watching her, carefully.

Conrad had moved from Keller's warehouse into a small limestone house. The common room served as his public headquarters where, all day, troubled colonists laid insoluble problems on the desk in front of him. His bedroom was separate, private. She came to him late at night, carrying a rifle; he had insisted she begin carrying a rifle.

"The *Verein* is collasping," he told her. "We're operating on borrowed funds and diminishing credit. Supplies are low. We can't fulfill our promises."

"What will you do?"

Instead of answering, he began to curse those who had grown accustomed to the *Verein's* support. "They're indolent and demanding," he said. "They're becoming thugs and drunks and insurgents," he complained.

"They only want their land," she said quietly. "They were promised land." He answered with a stream of abuse heaped onto the very colonists he had ennobled. In a cold voice, she asked, "How dare you teach me democracy? How dare you teach me what you haven't learned yourself?"

His face turned pale as the moonlight. "I'm sorry," he said.

"My concern is the hospital. The cemetery is being called the *Verein's Plantation*. Dr. Burger is incompetent. I don't believe he's a doctor at all."

"He was appointed personally by Prince Solms."

"He's an ignorant man. Perhaps a fraud. How can you let him supervise the hospital while people die like flies around him?"

He didn't respond to that. Instead, he damned the epidemics and the erratic weather that fed them. "Here, the desert floods and the sun shines during a hailstorm," he lamented. "I was reared as a scholar, an intellectual. But Texas destroys the mind." He shook his head. "Solutions will come from the heart," he said, "from my own pledge to the common man and from the grace of God."

She knew he believed that. She knew he needed to believe that.

His body was lean and hard. His body was resistant, steeped in the day's burdens and uneasy with his own need for what his conscience considered illicit and clandestine. Each time she came to him, she blew out the lamp and enveloped him in darkness. Each time, she led him, until he lost himself in her flesh, until she felt his tension wash away in the stream of passion which she created. Then, in that split-second before consummation, she always saw Ben's image flash suddenly before her, taunting her with his boldness and the clear thrust of his desire; and when her body blazed with release, what she saw consumed by light was Ben's mocking smile.

"Anna, Anna," Conrad moaned. Her name seemed torn from him.

On Thanksgiving, Conrad arrived with a military flute for Leopold. Holding Leopold on his lap, he tried vainly to teach him to press his baby fingers in the proper places.

Samuel brought hams from the smokehouse. Beatrice pulled chickens from the oven, dishes of corn pudding and a twelve-egg cake. In Conrad's old headquarters, which now overflowed with Tante Henriette's orphans, the tables had been laid with sauerkraut and apples. Hook and Goliath brought three cowhide drums; Bendejo beat the longest and the loudest with a fierce rhythm that set Beatrice to melodic chanting, and set all hands and feet moving.

Conrad said grace.

Anna watched him, feeling remote from him.

Then, rattling under a cold blast of wind, the door flew open and Mueller's disheveled figure plunged inside.

A wounded roar rose from Mueller's throat.

"Damn you!" Mueller shouted, his one eye darting around until it fastened on Conrad. "Damn your lies and your promises!" Mueller's raised fist gripped a sheaf of land certificates. "Damn the *Verein*— thieves and whoremasters and murderers!" Breathing heavily, Mueller was weaving unsteadily on his feet.

"You're drunk," Conrad said, rising.

Mueller cursed him, lunging forward suddenly. Anna saw he was wielding a knife.

Tante Henriette screamed.

Goliath threw himself onto Mueller's back. In seconds, Goliath had picked him up bodily and, holding Mueller thrashing over his head, Goliath carried him out.

A silence fell. Anna saw lines of anguish cross Conrad's face. It struck her she had lost her need to comfort him. It struck her she wanted to be taken, without guilt or ceremony.

Conrad returned to the table and folded his hands. "Preserve us in the name of the Father, the Son and the Holy Ghost," he said. "Amen."

It was dark when Goliath came back carrying a liter of whiskey. Dinner was finished and the children had been put to bed. "This is the demon," he said. "I told Mueller we'd tame it for him." He poured glasses all around for the adults and, raising his own, he looked at Hook and asked, "Well? Do we celebrate?"

Hook stammered a moment. His eyes bulged slightly in his ravaged face before he turned helplessly toward Tante Henriette.

Puzzled, Anna watched Tante Henriette bend her head and turn crimson.

"We're going to war in a week," Goliath said. "In the name of the Virgin Mary, are you waiting to get younger?" He crossed himself, said three swift Hail Marys and swallowed his whiskey.

Tante Henriette raised her head. Anna saw her face was still burning. "I was hoping for a courtship," she said, with a shy smile. She looked across the room at Hook. "A few sprigs of morning glories—"

Leopold started to cry. Anna picked him up and shushed him, burying her face in his neck while she tried to still a quickening of joy and envy and inexplicable mourning. Then she looked up and saw that Hook had moved to Tante Henriette's side. An awkward air of manhood cloaked his squat burly figure. He thrust painfully around for the words. "I love her," he said. Anna saw a lovely girlish smile cross Tante Henriette's face. "I want to marry her," he said. "I want to take care of her—and all her children."

"Glory Hallelujah," Goliath roared. He refilled his whiskey glass and drained it. "May God protect lovers and fools!"

Tante Henriette met Anna's eyes. "You once asked me what I did with my feelings—"

Anna nodded. "I remember."

"It wasn't the day Hook came to the orphanage and offered his services," Tante Henriette said. "Or the day he brought the money from the bales of prairie grass—it wasn't then either. It was the day he made a pair of crutches for four-year-old Heinrich who had broken his leg."

Tears welled in Anna's eyes.

"I'm a woman who's known only duty," Tante Henriette said, speaking softly to Anna as if they were alone in the room. "I used to tell myself—you can't have everything. Now I no longer believe that's true. If you can bear the pain, you can have the joy. Texas has taught me that." Tante Henriette's eyes glistened. "If you can take the risk of losing everything, you can have a chance to gain everything. You taught me that, Anna."

Anna's tears spilled onto her cheeks. A trembling passed through her, a resurgence of sexual longing and lost innocence.

Tante Henriette shook her head. "I'm fifty-two years old," she said, looking up at Hook, "and I've come to know that the parts of myself I've saved—those are the parts I've never owned. It's time," she said. "I'd be honored to be your wife."

Anna rushed to Tante Henriette and threw her arms around her. "Conrad can perform the ceremony," she said, half-laughing, half-crying. "Why not now? What better time than now?"

Anna watched Conrad position the bride and groom in front of the fire.

Selinda had vanished. Now, she returned carrying a Chinese shawl—poppies intricately embroidered on a field of silver—and, in a wordless loving gesture, draped it around Tante Henriette's shoulders.

Anna felt strangely numb as she took her place beside Tante Henriette.

The children had been roused from their beds. Still wearing nightgowns, they had gathered; now they fell quiet. Some of them grasped each other's hands. Heinrich leaned on his crutches. Several held candles.

In a solemn voice, Conrad administered the vows. Hook repeated the vows loudly, stammering over the words. Tante Henriette's response was reverent and gentle. Anna watched in silence. Then, removing the wedding ring that had symbolized her false marriage to Ben, she gave it to Hook who placed it on Tante Henriette's finger.

". . . by the authority vested in me as Director of the colony of New Braunfels," Conrad said, "I now pronounce you man and wife."

Goliath crossed himself as Hook kissed Tante Henriette shyly on the cheek. Tante Henriette blushed.

Suddenly tears streamed down Anna's face. Wiping them away, her eyes met Selinda's. Impulsively, she found herself opening her arms.

Selinda threw her head back and laughed, and the two women embraced.

Samuel pulled a mouth organ from his pocket and filled the orphanage with music.

17

"*Man is part spirit. The more of him that becomes spirit, the more he becomes one with the grace of the earth. He becomes caretaker to the birds and to the singing of the wind. He becomes custodian to his brother. He becomes a vehicle for the mercy of Jesus Christ.*

"*Grace is not a natural state. It is not gained by the strivings of will or the cravings of greed. It is granted to most only in Heaven.*

"*Heaven recognizes the bravery of those men who have fought nobly for God and country, men whose names we may never know. Heaven perceives the valiance of those women who have given birth in the darkness of war, while waiting for the dawn of victory. Heaven rewards the courage of children.*

"*To Heaven, we commit the soul of Josef Bremer, age fourteen, wounded September twenty-first in the battle of Independence Hill, now joined the gallant dead.*

"*Amen.*"

18

In her dream, Anna saw him at a strange angle; she was holding the rifle and looking up from the floor. The door was open. A mutilated figure was standing on the threshold in a pool of blood. Raising his arms to her, he said, *"Help me."* Then the rifle exploded and he fell. She opened her mouth to scream, but no sound issued from it.

She woke with a start, filled with foreboding.

"The year's like a bad snake," Beatrice told her at breakfast. "The sting's in the tail."

"You keep Leopold inside today," Anna said. A shiver of prescience told her Beatrice was right.

The New Year's Eve brawls began before noon and grew worse as the day wore on. Three times during the day, Anna left the hospital to check on Leopold. Each time, listening to the increasing sound of indiscriminate gunfire, she wondered if time's hand hadn't shaken the snake called 1846 so that all its lurking venom had amassed in the final lashing of its tail.

The hospital drew a stream of casualties. She enclosed a fractured thigh in splints, bound several broken arms and tended to a queue of smashed jaws, bruises and lacerations. By seven o'clock in the evening, she had dressed a half-dozen ugly injuries from knife slashings and more than twice as many gunshot wounds.

The waste angered her. Her tolerance had grown as low as the medical supplies which she inventoried nightly: Today had seen the last of the camphor; the emetics were low, the carbonate of ammonia had been gone for weeks and she had administered the final dose of mercury yesterday to a syphilitic. Her own trunkful of medicines had long been depleted except for enough prussic acid to treat the current pneumonia and bronchial infections. Reporting it to Dr. Burger was useless. Burger's treatment for everything, whatever the symptoms, was venesection—the bleeding of veins—the application of cups, leeches and the surgeon's knife.

She was making a list anyway when an aide came to summon her. Anna shook her head. "Tell Dr. Burger I've gone home."

"It's a bad case," the girl said.

Dr. Burger was waiting in the operating room. He looked strangely jubilant. A small balding man, his nostrils flared with inordinate pride and spatters of crumbs clung to his untrimmed moustache. He was wearing a smock which hadn't been changed for three days; Anna recognized the pattern of blood and pus and soup stains.

The patient, a young tannery worker, was already on the table, bleeding badly but still conscious.

"A ricocheting bullet has lodged between the fourth and fifth ribs," Burger said. "Prepare him for heart surgery." He spoke crisply, with a military authority.

Anna stared at him. "You can't open the chest cavity. It's forbidden."

"By whom?"

"By every leading surgeon in Germany—"

"This is Texas," Burger said.

There was no opium. Burger's opening surgical assault rendered the patient unconscious. He used a vistoury to make an incision on the patient's left side. Periodically, he wiped the vistoury on his smock. Then, using a Richter's fistula knife, he incised the pericardium. A fountain of blood obscured the wounded organ. Burger stuffed the cavity with rags and continued to work.

It took more than an hour for the tannery worker to die. Pulling the sheet over the corpse, Anna swore to herself to have Burger removed.

It was after nine o'clock when she layered herself in woolen shawls and a cloak and, slinging the rifle over her shoulder, stepped outside, welcoming the blast of cold air and the short walk to Conrad's quarters where she was determined to demand Burger's dismissal. She'd accept no more of Conrad's evasions, she told herself. She'd assist at no more deaths by mutilation.

Briefly, the thought of Ben crossed her mind, a swift yearning for his strength. A small voice whispered her longing was for more than that. Angrily, she stilled it.

Sequin Street was crowded with drunks and revelers. From the Meeting Hall, she could hear the noises of celebration, a dissonant clarinet being played by the local gravedigger and the kind of wild raucous laughter that presaged more carnage which she would not be around to tend. She meant to threaten Conrad: Unless Burger was dismissed, she'd not return to the hospital.

So engrossed was she in her wrath at Burger that she failed to register the significance of the scene in front of her, the group of men who were gathering—fists raised and shouting—in front of Conrad's quarters. Not until she was almost upon them did she see them as a mob.

The urge to flee gave way to anger.

Heart pounding, she pressed close enough to make out the discordant chorus of shouts, loud demands for land, a torrent of obscenities. She saw Mueller was wielding a coil of rope, urging them on, inciting them. Then she heard Mueller yell, *"What are we waiting for?"*

Conrad's guard had placed himself in front of the door. Three men hurled him aside. The mob plummeted forward.

Anna hesitated only a second before she threw herself into the crowd, moving with them.

Inside, Conrad was being pressed against the wall. Holding himself rigid and controlled, he was trying vainly to reason with them. Somebody brandished a whip. She saw Conrad shut his eyes. Then Mueller shouted over the roar of the crowd, *"Hang him!"*

Somebody turned to her and snarled, "No women here!"

She responded with an icy stare. A calmness overtook her. She felt a sudden pool of quiet spread around her. Heads turned threateningly and a wave of angry protests rippled through the crowd. She stood quietly, waiting while the crowd's anger subsided, then rose again, uncertain.

With a deliberately dramatic gesture, she gathered her skirts and climbed onto Conrad's desk where she faced the men, composed and silent, until the threats and objections diminished into an uneasy quiet.

"You all know me," she said. "I'm Ben Calder's wife." She spoke calmly. "Ben Calder has gone to war," she said, repeating Ben's name like an incantation. "Because my husband is not here to represent me, I must claim the right to represent myself."

"No women," somebody called out. "We don't need any women—"
A rash of derisive cries erupted from the crowd.

"I, too, have been promised land," Anna said quietly. From the corner of her eye, she was aware that Conrad had been temporarily released. "My husband, Ben Calder, fought at Monterrey for the promise of land," she said. "I am as aggrieved as you. I have been as betrayed as you."

"She's lying," Mueller shouted. "She's Ahrenbach's whore!"

Anna's brows rose, quizzically scanning the crowd, she asked, "Who presumes to make such accusations to Ben Calder's wife?"

Mueller stepped forward. He was carrying the rope coiled around his upper arm. "I do," he said with contempt. She saw he was drunk.

Fastening her gaze on Mueller's one grotesque eye, she spoke with firm authority. "Give me the rope," she said. "I'll be the first to hang it around the Baron's neck. Or better still—" she raised her rifle slowly and, swinging it in an arc over the heads of the crowd, she leveled it at Conrad—"why bother with a rope? Why not a bullet in his chest?"

Conrad stared at her. A moment of shock rumbled through the men like the shadow of thunder. Then silence fell.

"We owe the Society nothing!" Eyes narrowed, she addressed Conrad. "It's only by our presence that the *Verein* has any claim to the land at all. It's the *Verein* who owes us. And with what do they pay us? With cowardice!"

A spatter of cheers rose from the crowd.

"Last month, your surveyors set forth from Fredericksburg armed with a cannon," she said accusingly. "But when scouts reported two hundred Comanches lying in wait—they turned like cowards. They came back without firing a shot!"

A larger wave of cheers engulfed her.

"Kill him!" Mueller shouted.

She kept the rifle trained on Conrad. Turning only her head, she looked down on Mueller with disdain. "Will *you* survey the land, then —with one eye? Will *you* face the Comanches, then—armed with a knife?—with a rope?" Her eyes moved over the crowd, gauging them. "I propose that we sentence the Baron," she said. "I propose that we sentence him to a personal meeting with the Comanches. If, within three months, he succeeds in making a treaty that permits a survey and the settlement of our land, we return his life to him."

A murmur of arguments moved through the crowd. "What if he fails?" someone shouted.

Anna let a deliberately rueful smile cross her face. "If he fails," she said, "the Comanches will kill him for us."

She was upstairs when the cuckoo clock struck twelve. The first notes of the bells chimed and then its mechanical chirping floated to her ears up the stairwell.

She was sitting alone.

Beatrice and Samuel had gone to bed and Selinda had gone out, leaving Bendejo asleep in the crib next to Leopold. Lying side by side in the lamplight—the dark child and the light one—they looked to Anna like a Botticelli angel and his shadow.

Conrad had not appeared.

She was still dressed. Sitting by the flickering lamp, she had been trying to sort out her feelings, but she seemed unable to distinguish fear from yearning, or anger from triumph. Ben's image continued to haunt her, and this morning's dark dream kept merging with the night's events. She felt strangely stimulated. Her pulse was racing. Her own earlier daring had exhilarated her. Yet, as she rose and picked up her rifle along with the lamp, she could feel the foreboding still lying coiled within her, like the sleeping snake of the New Year, only waiting for its time to come.

She took the stairs slowly. She was midway down when the clock's last note rang. Then the foolish cuckoo quit and, in the silence, she heard a peculiar sound like the rustle of silk. With it, came a swift memory of the strains of a waltz, blazing chandeliers and soldiers in white tunics. The trick of a tired mind, she told herself, banishing Eduard's ghost. But she held the lamp out in front of her to illumine the rest of the stairs and before she entered the common room, she called out, "Who's there?"

No one answered. She heard the rustling sound again. Moving forward cautiously, holding the lamp in her left hand and the rifle in her right, she called out again. Then she gasped as the circle of light fell on Selinda's figure.

Selinda seemed an apparition. Her face looked haunted. Her eyes looked mad. Bending over the open trunk, she was filling an unrolled blanket with guns. It took Anna a moment to realize she was wearing the green silk ball gown: it had been savagely torn and there were fresh bloodstains on it.

A sound escaped Anna. Selinda's head jerked up. Like an animal clawing at herself, she dug into her bodice and pulled out a sheaf of land certificates. "Here—" she said, holding them out. Her hand was shaking. "I'll leave them for the guns."

Quickly, Anna set the lamp and the rifle on the floor and knelt beside her. "What happened? What is it? Where did you get these?"

"I took them from Mueller. After—" Selinda broke off.

"After what? What did they do to you?"

Selinda shook her head violently. She was trembling. "I went to the Hall—" She threw up her hands in a baleful gesture that sent the certificates fluttering around her. "Andalusian, Spanish—they don't know those things. To them, I'm a hated Mexican!" She laughed bitterly. Anna saw the bitterness was thin like an old disguise. "I was trying to be a *gadjo*—trying to be like you." Selinda's words came out in an angry rush, but Anna saw the anger, too, was threadbare, a refuge from terror, from whatever had happened; Selinda was thrashing, trying to escape it. "Why should I be like *you?*" Selinda said. "To you, even children are property. Bendejo is *mine*. Leopoldo is *yours*. With the gypsies life is the opposite. A child belongs to everyone and a man belongs to his own woman!"

Anna wanted to hold her. Something stopped her. Something told her it would be like touching fire; it would be like embracing a dark side of herself that frightened her. Instead, she reached out gently and touched a bruise on Selinda's cheek. "Let me tend to that."

Selinda pulled away. She rolled the blanket around the firearms. "I'm leaving tonight," she said. "I'm taking Bendejo. I'm taking a horse. And I'm taking these—"

"Why?"

"I'm a gypsy. I know how to sell guns."

"What are you talking about? Where will you go?"

"I don't know," Selinda said. She tied the blanket. "Fate will lead me."

"No—" Anna protested.

Selinda looked deeply into Anna's eyes. "I saw the way Ben looked at you," she said, her voice suddenly quiet. The anger was gone. The trembling had ceased. In Selinda's eyes, Anna saw sorrow and pain and a strange prescience. "I heard the way you and Ben talked about land," Selinda said. "I *saw*," she said. "Right now, you've taken the Baron for a lover. It won't make any difference. Fate has its own ways." Selinda's eyes were dark, without pupils. They shone like ebony. "Sometimes, fate is cruel," she said. "Tonight, fate was cruel to me. Fate used its cruelty to remind me that I'm a gypsy, that this life is a prison to me."

"I want to help you," Anna said. "Let me help you."

Reaching out, Selinda held Anna in a long terrible embrace. "Fate sent us the same man," she said against Anna's ear. "Fate sent us the same hardships." She gripped Anna tightly. "You and I, we're women. We know what that means. We're capable of anything. Anything." She let Anna go. "For every passion, there's a price," she said.

"Don't leave me," Anna whispered.

"There's no choice." Selinda rose.

"Why?" Anna cried. "In the name of Heaven—you have to tell me *why.*"

"Mueller tried to rape me. I slit his throat with his own knife."

She sat up all night, holding Leopold and rocking him in front of the dying fire.

Dawn slipped in with a dusty yellow light. She took no notice. A numbness had taken her over. The soft rapping at the door seemed to come from a long way off. It stirred no feeling in her. Then a brightness streamed in for a moment as the door opened and closed, returning the room to its morning twilight.

"I had to think about it," Conrad said. "I had to go over and over it."

She looked up, puzzled. "I want Dr. Burger dismissed," she said.

"Burger?"

"Today," she said.

He nodded. "Last night—" he began. He hesitated. "You're a brave woman," he said.

"No, I'm afraid."

He came closer. He peered down at Leopold sleeping in her arms. "Who was his father?"

"He has no father." She continued rocking Leopold. "He's mine," she said. "Only mine."

"He has light hair, light eyes. He could be mine."

She shook her head.

"I want to marry you," he said.

"I'm already married," she answered.

"I still have friends in power in Germany. An annulment can be arranged—a divorce."

She closed her eyes briefly. "Why?"

He pulled a letter from his pocket. She saw the letter was bordered in black. "There was a young woman in Germany," he said. "Our families were old friends." He hesitated. "She wove silk tapestry. She sent me poems about what she imagined life to be like in Texas." He paused again. "I received this yesterday. She died of petechial fever."

"Why tell me this, now?"

"I don't know."

"Where are your passions?"

"That's why I need you."

"No," she said.

"I've never been any good with women," he said. "But you came to me. You wanted me"—he averted his eyes—"physically," he said. "You're not like any woman I've ever known. You're more like"—he searched for the word—"I don't know."

"A whore?"

"I didn't mean that."

"Yes," she said, "you did."

"Not in that way."

"In what way, then?"

"For God's sake, whores are *paid*—" he said.

"How much do you owe me, then? How will you pay me?" She wondered why she was torturing him.

"I want to marry you." He knelt beside her. "I want to buy land—anywhere you want—where it's safe, and beautiful. We can build a stone house, a grand house. I'll do some writing, practice botany—"

"My life is devoted to Leopold."

"I'll arrange for legal adoption. Leopold will be my heir."

"What if there are other children?" She knew she was torturing him because he wasn't Ben.

"They'll share equally."

Leopold stirred in her arms. She drew Leopold closer to her. "No," she said.

"On the day of our wedding, I'll assign half of my estate to Leopold," he said.

She looked up. "I don't love you," she said.

A stricken look crossed his face. "I don't understand."

"My body makes demands," she said. "My heart has never followed my body. Never."

He stood up. Turning away, he walked slowly across the room and parted the curtains. The rays of dawn streamed past his figure. He stood there for a long time before he turned and went to the door. Opening it, he hesitated. Then he turned around once more. "I accept that," he said.

The door shut behind him.

She put Leopold back in his crib.

Then she came downstairs again and crossed to the trunk which Selinda had left open, and closed the lid. The lamp, extinguished now, was still on the floor. She set in on the trunk. Her rifle lay nearby and, around it, were the scattered land certificates Selinda had taken from Mueller. She began to gather them up.

Then she heard a sound and, grasping the rifle, she turned.

She saw him at a strange angle; she was holding the rifle and looking up from the floor. The door was open. Mueller's mutilated figure was standing on the threshold in a pool of blood. Raising his arms to her, he said, *"Help me."* Then the rifle exploded and he fell.

She opened her mouth to scream, but no sound issued from it.

19

Buena Vista
February 24

My dear wife, Henriette,

This letter is being written by a professional scribe. He has assured me that all that I say will fall on his ears in the strictest confidence.

I have been gathering the Mexican wounded and bringing them here to this field hospital in the mouth of the big north ravine. Santa Anna withdrew, leaving his wounded on the field. He was defeated after two days of bloody battle. I cannot describe the battle more than to say victory came as a surprise, we believed we were doomed.

The scribe has read this back to me. It does not sound like me. I am a simple man. It says none of the things I wish to say. It says none of the things I regret to say.

Ben was cited by Captain Lambert for heroism. Let me say that. He was given the rank of corporal.

This is the hardest thing to say. I do not know how to say it. Goliath is dead.

I do not know where Ben is now. He attacked the two privates who were ordered to build the gallows for Goliath. He rode them down in a drunken rage and left them beaten in a gully.

They shaved Goliath's head. They branded him on the cheek with a red-hot iron, with the letter D for Deserter. Then they lashed him with a whip in full view of all, two hundred lashes across his back and with each one, Goliath thundered curses at them. For a blindfold, they used the captured flag from the San Patrice Battery.

I do not know why he joined the San Patrice. A man's reasons are a man's reasons.

Goliath was given a Mexican funeral. Ben was not present. I am told he has been arrested. I am told he attacked Lieutenant Hamilton in his tent and bludgeoned him into unconsciousness with his fists.

I will do what I can.

The scribe has read this again to me. I have said none of the things I wanted to say. I have said nothing that is in my heart. When this is over, I would be grateful if you will teach me to read and write.

> *Your husband,*
> *Otto ("Hook") Steuben*

20

A gray daylight, sunless, filtered into the prison courtyard. It vanished early. Then an indigo blanket fell across Ben's barred window, and the rats came out to nibble at his boots and stir around in the mattress where the corn husks had long ago been eaten.

A stub of a candle had been burning in the corridor. It was out, now. He had saved a fist-sized piece of dry bread which he cast through the small square of bars in the metal door. In a minute, he heard the rats scrambling and clawing their way up the door and through the bars after it. They would battle for hours over it. Even the victors would wound each other. In the morning, rats would be found lying in the corridor like dead soldiers on the battlefield.

He had been drunk when they brought him in. He had meant to drink himself into senselessness, but he had reached only a state of violence and, afterward, a strange clarity had come over him, an odd sharpened vision.

The acuity persisted. It kept him from sleep. He could see in the dark. He could hear his own heartbeat. Inside of him, his spirit struggled, as if he held it captive the way his captors held him, in the same blind state. For a moment, he saw it like that: His body imprisoned in a cell, and his spirit imprisoned in a body.

Grasping the thought, he turned it over and over, spinning it until it left him; he could see it sending out sparks, shining in the dark. He was aware of his own breathing, the air moving in and out, involuntarily, asking: Who was master of his breath? The meager dinner of beans he had eaten earlier—what was hunger? And this war—why had he come to this war? What need in him did bloodshed fill?

In the corridor, the rats fell silent. Dawn would rise soon. There was a meaning in the dawn that escaped him. Slowly, he counted up the date on his fingers and that much came to him: it was his twenty-first birthday. Half a man's life. Few men lived past fifty. An urgency accompanied the recognition. They had taken his freedom. For how long, he didn't know.

Moving around the cell, he pawed the walls, as if they might open for him. He halted at the window and grasped the bars and peered out, searching the darkness. He could smell the defeat out there, and the poverty. It made him remember Silesia. It made him remember the son he had never seen. Then a noise outside startled him. Pressing his back against the wall next to the window, he froze. A hand thrust a knife through the bars.

"Who is it?" he hissed.

The answer came in a whisper, in Spanish. "It doesn't matter." The whisper belonged to a girl.

"Por que?"

"Por Goliath," she answered.

He reached out and took the knife. He examined it, looking for the trick in it. Then he pressed his face against the bars, but she was gone and when he looked up, he saw in the square patch of sky over the courtyard, a gray-violet dawn was rising.

A rope held up his trousers. Quickly, he cut a piece of the rope and, pushing up his sleeve, tied the knife to his left forearm. The sleeve fell over it. He moved back to his bunk and lay down to wait, for daylight, for the clanking of the metal doors to echo from the end of the corridor.

The sound came early. The light was still muddy outside his window. Feigning sleep, he waited as boots tramped toward him. Then a guard entered, carrying a corn-husk torch and ordered, "Get up, Captain Lambert's here to see you."

He had expected only the guard. Now, Lambert appeared, piercing eyes in a sharp-featured face, a stub of a man, but wiry, a streak of lightning on the battlefield, as dazzling and as ruthless. It was Lambert who had given him the ribbon for bravery and the rank of corporal.

He rolled from the bunk like someone roused from sleep and stood at attention.

"I'll speak to the prisoner privately," Lambert said.

The cell door closed. The guard set the torch in a ring and left without turning the lock. Ben could feel the metal knife blade pressing against his forearm.

"You exhibit strange behavior for a man newly commended," Lambert said crisply.

"Yes, sir."

"Your friend with the metal hand—he tells me there was a boy for whom you had some attachment. Josef Bremer, I believe. He was killed at Monterrey?"

"Yes, sir." Ben tensed, ready to spring. Something held him back.

"You might take solace from the fact that Josef Bremer won't travel the painful journey on this earth," Lambert was saying. "The boy won't commit the sins of this world." Lambert paused. A strange note in Lambert's voice rang in Ben's ears, a warning. "Perhaps if grief for the boy were the explanation for your unprovoked attack on Lieutenant Hamilton—" Lambert left the sentence hanging. "I'm told Goliath was your friend?"

"Yes, sir."

"According to your record," Lambert continued, "your six months was completed on the day you were cited for valor here in Buena Vista. That means your military arrest is invalid—we have to turn the matter over to civilian authorities." Lambert paused again. "The problem is—there are no civilian authorities here as yet, and I can't spare a patrol to return you to New Braunfels. So I have a proposition to put to you—" Once more, he left the sentence hanging. "At ease," he said.

Ben folded his arms. His hand slid up his sleeve and grasped the knife.

"You're a valuable soldier," Lambert was saying. "We're going on to take Mexico City. We've got plenty of volunteers—more than we need —but they're green. We need trained men. If you agree to sign up for the duration, we might be able to waive charges."

"I can't do that, sir."

"Why not?"

Ben's hands dropped to his sides. "For right now—I'm tired of killing, sir."

Lambert nodded slowly. "I see."

"Give me fifty volunteers and ten days," Ben said, "and I'll give you a company of trained soldiers."

Lambert scrutinized him. "Agreed," he answered. He scowled. "If you had pulled that knife, you'd be a dead man."

Ben watched him cross to the cell door.

"When this is over, I'm going to settle in Houston," Lambert said. "Houston's going to be the biggest city in Texas. You're an interesting man. If you ever get to Houston City—" He smiled. "One more thing," he said. "The girl who brought you the knife. Her name is Josefina Juarez."

The crumbling stone house was set back on a dirt street, seven blocks north of the main Plaza, where Lambert told him it would be. Ben recognized it by the rawhide stretched in the yard between posts that were nailed with jerked beef to dry in the winter sun, and by the tattered palm-leaf braids at the windows, the kind sold by the church as protection from harm. It was a compound of women, Lambert had said, a nest of insurgents.

A crop-eared cur, skinny and ferocious, part coyote, dashed into the street to circle him, howling. An old woman was on her knees in the yard at a metal-stone, grinding corn and making it into cakes. Looking up, she surveyed him with eyes that had long ago worn out their need for a man.

"I'm looking for Josefina Juarez," he said, in Spanish. He saw a slight contempt cross her face, a belief that he had come because he needed a woman. Then she snapped her head in the direction of the house.

Inside, three beds were filled with girls, sitting cross-legged, sewing. A couple of them giggled as he entered. Another old woman, centuries older than the one outside, was spinning yarn with a hand spindle. He addressed himself to her, asking again for Josefina Juarez.

"She's deaf," one of the girls said—the youngest, extracting herself from the others. She was wrapped in a *rebozo*. She stood on thin legs, shifting her weight from one foot to the other, her black eyes opaque and unreadable. "I'm Josefina." She motioned for him to follow her.

She led him through a littered courtyard, shooing a half-dozen mangy chickens scratching in the dirt, past a figure sleeping in a rolled-up blanket, to a dilapidated building, without a door, only a curtain to shield it from the wind outside.

There was a dirt floor and a bed piled with blankets, nothing else. She pulled the curtain shut, undressed quickly and climbed under the blankets. "Seven dollars," she said.

"That's a month's pay."

"I'm worth it. You'll see." She shut her eyes and waited. "The San Patrice would pay you more than that to desert," she said softly. "You'd be a captain."

He came over to the bed and pulled the blankets back and looked at her. Her hands were crossed on her abdomen. Her limbs were bone-thin and her breasts were small, new breasts, hardly born. He felt no passion. "How old are you?"

"Nineteen."

"You're lying."

"Seventeen."

He shook his head. "No."

"Fifteen," she said.

He drew the covers up over her. Then he sat on the edge of the bed and took out the knife and showed it to her. He watched her recognize it. She grabbed for it. He pulled it back and hurled it so that it landed upright, quivering in the dirt. "You were followed. Did you know that?"

"No!" She shook her head violently. "By the virgin of Guadalupe—" She crossed herself. "I came to help you. For Goliath," she said.

"What about Goliath? How did you know him?"

She turned her head away. "My brother stole from him. Goliath came here one day—he was carrying my brother under his arm. Goliath liked me. He was good to me—" She started to shiver under the blankets. "My brother is eight years old." She raised her head. "I need seven dollars," she said.

"Why did Goliath desert? Because of you?"

"My brother stole from Goliath. My brother steals clothes from both armies and he sells them for Ramirez. When he's caught, he cries and he says he was told they were rags." She sat up, wrapping the blankets around her, and crossed herself again. "My mother and father were murdered by the Comanches. That was three years ago, in September, at the rise of the full moon—the Comanches call it the Mexican moon. They come every year. They took our horses. They took my brother—"

He grasped her by the shoulders. "*Goliath—*" he said. "Not the Comanches. Not Ramirez."

"Ramirez is a trader. Ramirez is old and mean—" Her eyes filled with angry tears. "Ramirez paid the Comanches four dollars for my brother. Now, he wants seven dollars." She made a pleading gesture. "Goliath promised to buy my brother back from Ramirez."

"When? When did he promise you that?"

"Before he joined the San Patrice—"

"You brought him together with the San Patrice soldiers here?"

She glowered at him. Her eyes shone. Her head jerked in a sharp nod. "Yes." She spat the word.

"How did they get him to join them? What did they say to him?"

"I don't know."

His grasp tightened on her shoulders. "You're lying."

"I need seven dollars," she said, starting to weep.

He knew he should kill her. He knew Lambert had meant for him to kill her. She was a plucked sparrow, but her passion for her cause ignited her, gave her power over men who were ripe for conversion, made her dangerous. To leave her alive would be like leaving a wildfire burning, one that might cremate some of the very men he was training.

He laid the seven dollars on the bed. Then he plunged through the curtain without looking back.

He taught the men to kill.

He taught them to kill, and to survive, and to kill again.

He set up a training base outside of town at Ariste's Cotton Mill, now an ammunition depot.

The volunteers didn't know left foot from straw foot. Cannon fodder, Lambert had said. They were plowmen. They were tinkers and blacksmiths. He felt the weight of their ignorance.

Every rifle was different. He ordered each man to know his own rifle, to love it better than his wife or child, to treat it like a saint or a savior. What better object to worship than one's own rifle?—God was far away.

He had not realized he believed these things.

He had been put in command. He was driven by a goal larger than a single man, or a single life. He saw himself as a master of war, teaching men how not to be victims of war.

He discovered the power he exercised was not over their physical bodies. The use of arms, the drilling, the punishments, he saw these were the least of it. His real power was the claiming of their minds.

At the end of ten days, when it was time to turn them over to Lambert, they were—as he had promised—a company of men.

At dusk he walked back through the village of Buena Vista, wondering why a man's choices when a job was finished were always a tavern, a church or a whorehouse; he wanted none of these.

He wanted to leave.

He wanted to flee. He understood the hairline that had separated him from Josef and Goliath, the thing that was called luck, or fate.

There was a light in his tent. He hadn't lit the lamp.

He saw smoke was trailing from under the flap of the tent.

He ducked inside and came upright into clouds of smoke. Stamping and flailing his hands, he cleared the air enough to make out the shape of someone sitting at his table, puffing like a steamboat on one of the Mexican cigars.

"Me llaman Garras," the creature said. "They call me Garras. Rags."

It was a boy, a wiry devilish creature with the limbs of a cricket, so grimy his features were indistinguishable. *"Vamos!"* Ben snatched the cigar away. *"Vamos!"*

The boy didn't move. He fixed his eyes on Ben. They were strange implacable eyes, as if trapped inside the child was an animal, or trapped inside an animal was a child. Cursing in Spanish, Ben pulled him from the chair by his bony shoulders and pushed him outside. *"Vamos!"* he repeated.

Again, the boy didn't move. Instead, he reached under his shirt and held out a handful of small gleaming objects. "Solid gold teeth," he said in Spanish, "from the dead on the battlefield."

Ben smacked his hand and sent the teeth flying. The boy howled like a stuck pig and scrambled in the dirt looking for them.

Ben left him there. Inside the tent, he ground the cigar out with his heel and started to pack. Then he felt the boy standing behind him. "What do you want?"

"I stole the teeth from Ramirez. You tell me what you want," he said, "I'll steal it for you."

"Nothing," Ben said. "I don't want anything."

"I can get you clothes, horses. I can get you women. You tell me what you want." Garras tapped his shoulder. "My sister said you don't like women. She said maybe you like boys. I can get you boys."

Ben delivered a blow that sent him flying backward.

Garras yelled, rolling over and over in the dirt.

Ben planted his boot in the center of Garras' back, pinning him firmly to the earth. "Who's your sister?"

"She's gone," Garras howled, "with the San Patrice soldiers."

"Josefina Juarez?"

"*Si.*"

Ben removed his foot. Garras sat up, hugging himself. Then, coyote-swift, he pounced and sank his teeth into Ben's shin. Ben yelled and kicked him away. Swooping after him, he yanked Garras to his feet and clasped him from behind, pinioning him with his arms. "Why did she send you here?" Ben could feel his bones, frail and brittle as chicken bones. "*Why?*" he shouted.

Garras glared at him. "She said you bought me."

"What?"

"*Si—*" Garras spat out the word.

"*Que me ayude Dios!*" Ben roared.

"*Si,*" Garras said. "She said you bought me from Ramirez for seven dollars."

21

They crossed the Rio Grande at San Carlos.

The horses climbed slowly, picking their way along the curved lime-stone walls of the canyon. At Ben's back, the burning afternoon sun descended slowly, shimmering on the rocks and erupting in sharp blinding rays.

At nightfall, the whine of the wind turned shrill and the air grew thinner. They kept going. When they reached two thousand feet, the limestone canyon leveled off. Garras halted. Below, Ben could see the Rio Grande as it cut a jagged silver path in the moonlight. Ahead, the rugged peaks of the Chisos rose like the irregular points of a crown, climbing against the night sky to eight thousand feet.

Ben made camp.

They lay close together, wrapped in bedrolls, looking up at the stars.

"Casa," Ben said. "House."

"No more English," Garras said.

"You have to learn."

"Why?"

"Do you want to be stupid? *Tonto?*"

"Who taught you?"

"Women," Ben said.

"To make love?"

"That's not your business," Ben said.

"I know more than you about it," Garras said. Turning over, he crouched on his hands and knees. *"Te gusta mi verga?"* he said to his bedroll: Do you like my cock? *"Si! Si! Grande. Grande!"* He began to rock up and down. "I watched them all the time," he said. "I watched the soldiers and my sister." He was laughing uproariously. *"Primero como caballo!"* He yelled: Let's do it like horses. *"Me vengo, me vengo!"* he shouted: I'm coming, I'm coming. *"Ai, ai, ai!"*

Ben whacked him soundly.

"What'd you hit me for?"

"You're only eight years old," Ben said. "Shut up and go to sleep."

Ben awoke to the sun and the sight of a turkey buzzard perched on a rock. They dug for mesquite. Garras selected the greenest smallest twigs so that there would be no odor of fire or trail of smoke for the Comanches to detect. Then he whirled the point of the yucca in the pith of its stalk until it caught flame. Then he whittled several shafts, grinding the stones into arrow points and binding vulture plumes to the ends. "Up ahead are cimarron, the big-horned sheep, and deer," Garras said. "A rifle shot is loud. Hunting with a silent bow and arrow is safer."

It occurred to Ben that the more uncivilized the landscape became, the more civilized Garras seemed.

Again, they traveled at night.

The limestone vanished. The temperature dropped. The mountains were barren, burned rock, dark and somber. At the end of fifteen miles, the canyon ended in a pass of vertical rock. The walls soared a thousand feet overhead. Patches of mesquite twitched in the wind. The trail, hard and flat, packed by hooves, gleamed white as chalk in the darkness. Shafts of moonlight struck piles of bleached animal bones, corroding, turning to powder; the wind blew death everywhere like a fine white dust.

The Comanches had taught Garras to hunt.

When dawn shot the sky with streaks of purple and crimson, Ben halted to look back.

The square mesalike top of Santiago Peak towered over everything. By night, they had moved foot by foot over tilted rock to the highest point of the Chisos. Now, they were surrounded by mountain ranges, intersecting each other, mountain rising from mountain, peak on peak, falling into valleys and deep canyons and ravines, perhaps a thousand mountains, impassable except for the gift of nature which had opened the pass and the canyon through which the Great Trail ran.

A shudder passed through him. A few feet away, the dead carcass of a coyote was covered with burying beetles.

"It's not a bad sign," Garras said.

Ben knew it was. They moved forward anyway.

Garras chose the camping spot.

The clearing was surrounded by bluffs. In the early morning light, outcropping rocks protruded, forming ledges which had been piled with cone-shaped structures of smaller rocks. Indian burial places, Garras said. Abandoned, Garras said. The spring had been sealed up.

A natural orchard of wild crabapple trees writhed in the sunlight. Ben tethered the horses there. At the edge of the spring, semicircular walls of rock had been terraced to rise up the gradual slope of the hill. Through the Indian dam, enough water trickled to wash themselves and to water the horses.

Ben laid a fire without lighting it. Then he slept. When he woke, the sun was high and Garras was grinding cornmeal by scraping it across a flat-topped stone. Garras added water and shaped tortillas and laid them to dry. Then he picked up his bow and motioned for Ben to follow him.

Past the crabapple trees was a circular mound of rocks, hollow in the center and rimmed by another wall of rocks to protect it from the wind. Ben recognized it as a mescal pit, where the Indians had roasted their mescal before they stored it to ferment. Garras wet his finger and held it up. Then—so the deer wouldn't pick up their scent—he trotted into the wind.

They climbed the slope easily, then scrambled onto the bluff, pulling themselves up rock by rock. Garras climbed like a monkey. Twice, he stopped to wait for Ben. On the other side, the land sloped gently into an oblong valley. Garras pointed silently. Rising from a clump of bush were the antlers of a lone wild buck. The antlers didn't move. The stag had halted, motionless. Ben could almost hear him sniffing the air.

Garras took aim. The arrow zinged through the air, piercing the buck's haunch, crippling him. The stag froze for a moment. The eyes widened, in disbelief. But he didn't fall. Instead, he hurtled in the opposite direction, crashing through the bush in a lopsided three-legged gait.

"We'll run him down—" Garras said.

The stag was easy to track. He left a mangled path through the bush. He left the scent of pain and alarm.

When they found the buck, he had traveled almost a mile. When they found him, in a clearing, he was trapped by an army of coyotes.

The buck was still standing.

One of the coyotes was already at his muzzle, chewing, and three more were snapping at his flanks. Underneath, a pair were tearing at his stomach.

The buck trembled visibly in the sun. The stomach ripped. The entrails dragged the ground before the buck dropped suddenly to his knees still alive, patient, waiting for death.

Ben stared, spellbound, as if he were watching a fate from which he had been saved but which, he knew, would return again—in this very place; a voice told him that.

He watched the coyotes turn the buck over. He saw the stag's legs quiver in the air as the sharp teeth tore at his stomach, jaws snapping, feeding on the entrails. The crimson blood dried instantly in the sun, turning a rusty black. Then a silence fell. In the silence, he heard the grinding of teeth as the coyotes dismembered the buck and dragged the pieces through the dust. Ben couldn't tear his eyes away.

He saw it as nature's law, the law of predator and prey. The word that came to him was *loveless.* It was a strange word, a foreign word; but he heard a voice speak it silently, and he knew the word had been given to him by some wiser part of his being which he would not meet again for many years.

The coyotes departed. They left the mangled carcass for the ants and the beetles and the vultures. It was nature's law. The wind would dry the bones to dust.

Then he heard Garras' voice say softly, *"Vamonos—"* as if waking him from a dream.

He turned too slowly. They were surrounded by Comanches.

22

They took his rifle.

They bound his hands, loosely enough to handle a horse.

He counted nine captors. They sat upright on their horses, the muscles of their backs and shoulders rippling, their color ranging from copper to the last burned rays of the falling sunset. The ears of their horses were split. One of the braves carried a rifle, an old Spanish *escopeta*. The others carried four-foot bows and wore lynx-hide quivers slung over their shoulders. Ben could imagine anyone of them committing the atrocities that had kept the white settlers at bay.

They rode all night.

Morning brought rain. The wind blew sheets of water across the great limestone plateaus, flooding the expanse of barren rock as they traveled, land where not even thistles grew and no game had ever grazed. At noon, the sky lightened and the sun came out to gleam through another hour of steady drizzle. Then the rain quit and the stony land dried instantly in a searing wind that turned it to dust, as dry and parched as before. The rain left no trace. They forded the Pecos under a late afternoon sun that shone pitilessly down from an endless blue sky.

On the other side, the plains stretched out like a billowing sea. They rode past herds of buffalo grazing in the distance. Spurring the horses, the braves picked up speed, driving them faster and faster in a race with the descending sun.

Ben's first sight of the camp were the streamers of rawhide fluttering from tent poles against a streaked pink sky. The tepees rose in a semi-circle.

Alongside a patch of woods, women squatted in groups—some twisting horsehair ropes or plaiting lassoes; others working the buffalo hides, tearing the fat from the skin and mixing a tanning-paste from the buffalo's own brains and liver. A young boy was crossing the dirt, pulling a piece of buffalo meat attached to a string and several other boys were following, shooting arrows at it. No one looked up as they passed.

They rode past a tent which rose like a tabernacle over the village. A lance rose in front, topped by a menacing headdress of buffalo, its horns pointing skyward. They passed a group of Indians wearing white blankets, heads bowed like mourners.

At the rear of the camp their horses were led away and two warriors were posted outside a tepee. They were prodded inside and left.

The sun went down. An old woman brought them roasted buffalo meat and a mixture of maize and buffalo fat which they ate from a common vessel with their fingers. Garras slept. After a while, Ben slept, too.

A storm rose, raging outside, roaring through the open country when three braves appeared and roused him. Head bent against the lashing rain, he was taken through the camp to a painted wigwam on the edge of the woods.

He went in alone. The wind was whistling eerily through the fissures of the tent. Dancing firelight cast a reddish glow on the cone-shaped walls. An Indian with a ravaged face, entirely wrapped in a majestic fur cloak, was sitting cross-legged by the fire. In the shadows, a woman sat with her head bowed; Ben couldn't see her face. Nearby, a child slept in a hammock under a buffalo robe; periodically, the woman reached out and rocked it gently.

The old Indian scrutinized Ben. Then, as if satisfied by something, he took a drum from the wall and began to thump it with a slight rolling beat. He kept his eyes fixed on Ben. A crooning sound came from his throat, strange and hypnotic. Then he raised his voice to imitate the whistling of the wind and the cracking of the branches, his pitch rising and the drumbeat moving faster until the sounds inside

matched the storm outside. Finally, he put the drum aside. He spoke to
the woman in Shoshone. Then he rose and left.

Ben remained standing, waiting.

"I asked the *shaman* to find you in a vision," the woman said, rising
from the shadows. "The braves captured you at the place he described." She spoke to him in Romany, moving into the firelight so he
could see her face.

He stared at her. The rain quit as he spoke her name. His voice
echoed in the sudden silence. He heard it rise through the smokehole
and disappear into the night.

Selinda nodded.

Ben didn't move. He watched her bend over the fire and stir it. She
was wearing a tunic of deer leather adorned with embroidery and metal
pieces. Her gypsy braids were bound with rawhide.

"I have Bendejo with me," she said, softly. "We had to leave the settlement." She hesitated. "Mueller tried to rape me. I slit his throat."
Looking up, she searched his face as the old Indian had done, as if he
were foreign to her. "The Comanches found us at dawn on a sacred
mesa," she said. "I had guns. They had prayed for guns." She met his
eyes. "We are honored here."

"You're my *wife*." Again, his words disappeared.

"You have a wife."

From far away, he could hear the neighing of horses. A dog barked.
The sounds might have been the sounds of a gypsy camp. "I'll take you
back with me."

She shook her head. "We have different ways." She spoke in the
same soft voice. "When we touch each other, there's a strangeness, an
excitement. Your flesh misses me. I can feel that. But, between us, has
always been a question. Which way is better—yours, or mine? Who
should give up his birthright? Which one of us should change his
heart?" She smiled sadly. "I can't. You can't. So it's done. There are
more important things."

"No." He felt a powerful desire for her. At the same time, he felt
rooted to the ground. It struck him the old Indian had cast a spell on
him.

"Ahrenbach and his men are waiting on the lower San Saba," she
said. "Chief Ketemoczy has been gathering the head chiefs of the western Comanches to meet him. A council will be held here tomorrow."

In the hammock, the child stirred. Realizing the child was Bendejo, Ben strained against the invisible shackles. "I don't give a damn about Mueller—" he shouted.

She bent over Bendejo and adjusted the buffalo robe. "When you hear me out, you'll be free," she said, so softly Ben couldn't be sure of her words. She rose. "Did you see the mourners when you came in?"

"Yes."

"On the way to the San Saba, one of Ahrenbach's men killed a Comanche scout. Tomorrow morning, the mourners will burn the dead man's tepee. Some will lacerate themselves. Some will cut off the tips of their fingers. When Ahrenbach arrives, the mood of the camp will be hostile."

"Conrad can take care of himself—"

"He's changed," she said. "He has no judgment. His word is useless and his actions are erratic. They say he drinks too much. They say he's unsound." Selinda's hands cut the firelight in a pleading gesture. "If a treaty can't be reached, there'll be bloodshed." Her voice dropped to a whisper. "Years of bloodshed." She met his eyes again over the fire. "I asked the *shaman* to find you because you're the only one I know who can guarantee the terms of a treaty."

He felt the unseen bonds loosen. Slowly, he moved around the fire and stood over Selinda. On the wall of the tepee, their shadows flickered, merging and parting. "Do you have another husband?"

"Yes."

"If there were no Anna?"

"I belong here now."

"If there were no Anna?" he repeated.

"For you, there will always be an Anna," she said. "You must have an Anna the way a gypsy must have gold or a Comanche must have bright beads or pieces of mirror." She paused, her eyes moving over his face with an odd pride. "If something gleams, if it catches the light, if it's difficult to find and more difficult to keep—if it can cost you your life because others want it—then it has the power to let you see yourself as you wish to be."

"I've lost one son," he said. "I will not lose another—"

She turned to where the child slept. Leaning over him again, she pulled back the buffalo robe. Bendejo slept on his stomach, his head turned sideways, his profile lit by the fire.

It was six months. Bendejo had changed.

Ben searched his son's face for signs of his own ancestry, French-German; he found none. No longer did Bendejo bear the characteristics of Selinda's line, the Andalusian gypsy—nor did he look like a German child. He saw Bendejo was neither bronze nor white, neither Spaniard nor European. The word that came back to him was the one he had spoken when Bendejo was born: *Tejano*. The phrase that came back to him had been spoken by old Magda: *"You will sow a wild seed."* He heard it through a terrible sound, like the howling protest of an angry wolf; the sound came from his own throat.

"It's too late," Selinda whispered. Lifting the fur robe, she pointed to a place on the sole of Bendejo's left foot. Ben saw two overlapping circles had been tattooed there. "From this spot on his foot, the blood flows directly to the heart," she said. "The sun and the moon have been inscribed on his heart." She covered Bendejo. "He's been marked as a ceremonial runner. His name is Black Wing now. He belongs to them. If you take him, they'll kill you both."

Ben closed his eyes. A terrible shudder racked his frame. He recognized it as rage. He recognized it as the severing of a primal bond, a wrenching of soul.

He strode to the place where the old Indian had hung the drum. Striking out, he pounded on the drum viciously at first, then more slowly, like a man in search of the rhythm of his own heart. Finally, he stopped. When he turned, he looked across the fire again, into Selinda's eyes. "Why should I guarantee the treaty?"

"To gain safe access to your land."

"And if not for land?"

"So your son will not be killed by white men," she said.

He struck the drum once more. The sound died slowly. *"Bater,"* he said, finally. *May it be so.*

A chill wind blew across the plains. The sky was cloudless. The sun moved in a semicircle over the heads of the men, bronze and white, sitting cross-legged around the council fire.

Ben was seated next to Conrad. Conrad's face was pale and distraught. Conrad was lying. When Conrad spoke, his voice quavered. Ben frowned at the sound of it. Earlier, he had been greeted with an odd reticence; something like anger or shame had crossed Conrad's face at finding him here. Conrad had taken Ben's handshake swiftly, averting his eyes.

Now, Conrad spoke in Spanish while Chief Ketemoczy translated and interpreted for the other chiefs. The sandstone pipes, filled by the *shaman,* remained lying on the ground, still unlit.

Conrad had brought gifts, three thousand dollars' worth—blankets and beads and trinkets, metal and glass, European clothing and cooking utensils—the white man's medicine bundle—magic symbols of civilization. The last of it was being unloaded from five wagons and presented to Ketemoczy.

Then, from the horizon, a procession of a hundred young horsemen filed slowly into view.

The braves' faces were fiercely painted and they wore headdresses of buffalo horns. Sunlight glittered on crimson lances and shields of buffalo hide adorned with sacred symbols and surrounded by feathers that fluttered in the cold wind. The horses' manes and tails had been dipped in fiery red paint so that, necks arched and flanks gleaming, horse seemed one with rider, each a magnificent primeval creature, a foreboding creature.

Mounted in silence, the braves passed around the council, three abreast, forming circles that moved in alternating directions, weaving in an eerie and menacing rhythm. Then they reared as abruptly as they had come, in startling unison, and galloped off, leaving clouds of dust in an arrow-straight line.

Ketemoczy signaled his acceptance of Conrad's gifts. Then he motioned for Ocol to speak.

Ocol was squat and wrinkled, the only chief not dressed in Comanche fashion; he wore a soiled cotton jacket, the kind worn by Mexican peasants. "I have asked for guidance from the Great Spirit," Ocol said. "The eagle has carried my question. The thunder has returned with my answer. The thunder has warned me the white man will destroy our buffalo."

"We promise to preserve the buffalo," Conrad answered.

Buffalo Hump shook his head. The upper part of his body was naked; buffalo skin wrapped his hips and brass rings encircled his arms. "Our ancestors live in the Heavens," he said. "The stars are the footprints of our departed warriors. The sun is the eye of Heaven which watches over them. The sun has revealed to the spirit of our ancestors that the white man will drive us from our lands."

"We are a small band of people," Conrad replied. "We wish to farm. We wish to enrich the land. We wish to share the land and the fruits of the land with our Comanche brothers."

It was Santa Anna's turn. He touched his great necklace of bear claws before he spoke. "You wish us to put aside our war shirts and our eagle feathers," he said in a powerful voice. "You wish us to bury our coup sticks and break our arrows. You wish our fires to die. You wish our drums to be silent and our ceremonial runners to clip the wings from their mocassins. I understand what you wish. You wish to strangle our spirit until we cease to exist."

"We promise to honor the red man," Conrad answered. "We promise peace."

Ben watched Ketemoczy. A silent anger flared in the old chief's eyes as Conrad's false reassurances multiplied.

"My friend is a liar," Ben said quietly.

Ketemoczy's head turned. From under fierce brows, he narrowed his eyes at Ben.

"My friend believes his lies," Ben said. "But belief in a lie will not make it the truth."

Conrad flushed. "You have no authority—"

Ketemoczy raised his hand and silenced Conrad. "Speak," he ordered.

Grasping the small muslin bag he wore around his own neck—the bag Ott had said contained the face of God—Ben spoke slowly. "In this bag, I wear the spirit of my ancestors," Ben said. "It's like the medicine of the red man, but it's not like the medicine of the red man. The white man has a different nature. The white man has a different truth."

Beside him, Ben could feel Conrad stiffen with anger.

"The nature of the white man is greed," Ben said. "This is our truth." He paused. His eyes swept the chiefs. "I have lived with people of other natures," he said. "I understand your nature is different." Again, he paused while Ketemoczy translated his word into Shoshone. "To you, the earth is your mother, to be praised and honored," Ben said. "To us, the earth is our enemy, to be conquered and subdued. You are guided by your signs and your visions. We are driven by our needs and our desires." Ben shook his head. "I don't know why this is so. I don't know what has made us this way. But this is our truth."

Conrad moved to protest. Ketemoczy's raised hand silenced him again. Nodding, the chiefs murmured to each other.

"There is another truth," Ben said quietly. "We are here. This is also the truth. We are small in number. You can kill us. You can attack our settlements and kill everyone in our settlements. But others will come." He paused once more, as Ketemoczy translated his words. "They will come with more tongues," he said, "tongues that will dance with better lies. They will come with more guns—guns with more power than your strongest medicine." He was looking directly at Ketemoczy now. "I have reason to want to live in peace with you," he said quietly. "And so I promise you this. I will never lie to you." He touched the bag around his neck. "I will never lie to you," he repeated. "By the spirit of my ancestors—if I intend to seize your wife, or your horses, or your land, I will tell you first." His hand dropped. "This is all I ask from you. Then we can live together."

A silence fell.

Slowly, Ketemoczy translated Ben's final words.

Another silence fell.

Then Ketemoczy reached for the peace pipe and lit it with ceremony, puffing quietly for a moment before he passed it from his hand to Ben's.

Ben was mounted to leave when Conrad rode up and put out his hand.

Ben accepted the handshake silently.

"I wasn't lying to them, you know," Conrad said. "You were right. It was what I wished was so." The words came hard to him. "You accept your own passions," Conrad said. "The best I can do is struggle with mine." He hesitated. "I'm talking about Anna—"

"Anna?"

Conrad shook his head. "It would be another lie to say that I'm sorry—" He whirled on his horse and rode off, leaving the sentence hanging in the dust.

23

The Easter fires were being lit.

They sprang up on every rise of ground around the colony, blazing in the darkness. Jackrabbits scattered, shadows enlarged, looming against the firelight, then dancing away like drunken demons.

The Easter fires were a peasant tradition; the German farmers believed that as far as the firelight reached, the fields would be fruitful and the soil over which the ashes were blown would increase in fertility, and the houses on which the firelight shone would be free from illness. Watching, Anna believed it was so. Watching, she felt pagan ghosts stir within her. Then a pang of guilt pierced her secret longings; since New Year's Eve, Mueller's one eye had haunted her.

She held Leopold's hand more tightly. The flames crackled. The flashing shadows of the jackrabbits frightened the children. Clinging to Tante Henriette, several of them began to cry.

"Hush," Tante Henriette said, soothingly. "The rabbits are your friends. They're Easter rabbits, that's what they are. Isn't that right, Anna?"

"Yes," Anna agreed, lifting an anxious Leopold into her arms.

"They're going to hide the eggs in the fields," Tante Henriette said, embellishing her story. "Tomorrow, you'll see. If you wish hard enough, there'll be colored eggs for you to find everywhere!"

From a distance, the town looked on fire.

It was the promise of Hell, Garras said. Tomorrow was Passion Sunday. In Buena Vista, even Ramirez would go to confession. Crossing himself, he reeled off a list of appalling sins, finishing with, "Hail Mary, refuge of sinners, I repent and desire to make amends." Then he turned to Ben, grinning, "Maybe I'll become a priest."

Ben looked askance at him.

Garras responded with a string of obscenities.

The streets had been swept by the rain. The houses were luminous in the firelight. Not a garden was unkempt. Ben tried to imagine the life that had gone on here while he was away. It felt alien to him. He had seen too much, he thought. Too many barren Mexican villages, too many black-robed women; he had heard too many church bells toll the passing of the dead. Even Conrad's confession had failed to move him. He had waited for the anger. It had not come. Anna had served her purpose in his life, and he in hers. Nothing bound them.

The house was dark. He led Garras to the rear where they tethered the horses. Then he came back to the front door and raised his fist to knock. His hand halted in midair. Instead, he let himself in, quietly, motioning for Garras to follow.

Lighting a lamp, he looked around. The common room seemed different, smaller, more pristine. There was a reserved air about it, something at odds with his memory of a spoiled and willful Anna; the room had the strained celibate aura of a woman living alone, finding comfort in ritual. He wondered if she prayed now. It was a strange idea —Anna, praying.

There was no one home. The ticking of the cuckoo clock echoed through the empty house. A crude wooden rocking horse sat by the fireplace. He set it going with his foot. A hooded cloak hung on a hook, dangling like a hanged black bird. When he touched it, it rustled. A slight perfume emanated from it. The chairs were pushed neatly under the table. A basket of grain sat on the floor, waiting to be ground. The floors were polished. Colored glass shone in a corner cupboard, reflecting a flickering orange light being cast by the fires through the window.

He found brandy and drank directly from the jug. Then, carrying the lamp, he led Garras to the quarters he had shared with Selinda. The bed had been pushed against the wall. The room looked cold, monastic. "You sleep in here."

"Are you a rich man?"

"No."

"I never slept alone."

"The Madonna watches over penitents," Ben said, blowing out the lamp and closing the door.

He went upstairs. Light from the fires illuminated Anna's neatly made bed. Here, he could feel her fears and desires; this was where she kept them, stored privately. He had an image of her sleeping fitfully, beset by turbulent dreams. He could see her fingers clenching the sheets while dream figures threatened her, shouting imprecations; he heard her waking in the night with an incomprehensible cry. The images seemed to have nothing to do with the Anna he had known.

He tried to imagine Conrad in her bed. The idea had no substance; it flitted swiftly across his mind, provoking no passion or jealousy. War had numbed him, he thought. He remembered corpses were often found on the battlefield clinging to each other like lovers.

He went back downstairs. He looked at the brandy, but didn't touch it. Instead, he focused on where he was going and what he meant to do. He had seen enough of the land now to know what it would be—hill country, brush country—ash-colored brush that turned silver under the moon, gnarled shrubs and cacti thrusting through naked rock and clinging like thorny spiders to the sides of deep gullies. In his mind's eye, he could see himself riding alone over the bald summits of the flat-topped hills, surrounded by barren ridge rising from barren ridge, the silence broken only by the dwarf mesquite rattling in pockets of whirlwind. It drew him. It was ugly land, threatening land, bleak and ragged country, unfit for a woman—a woman like Anna—he knew it would not be tamed easily; it would test the marrow of his bone and the most desperate longings of his soul.

Outside the window, the fires continued to burn, casting light and shadows across the common room. He blew out the lamp. Choosing a spot, he sat down to wait for Anna.

She left Leopold asleep at the orphanage.

It was a short walk down Sequin Street, through patches of firelight and muffled shadows. Since New Year's Eve, she had ceased carrying a rifle. Since then—pursued by the memory of Mueller—she had courted protection by forbidding herself to think of unknowable things. It had left her with the ancient loneliness of all women who tried to still their hungers and grew famished; then spring had wakened a premonitory sense and, tonight, she had been swept again by a sense of mystery, by waves of expectancy and yearning.

She walked briskly, not certain what she meant to leave behind, or what she hoped to meet.

The garden was dappled with firelight. The walls of the house looked naked, like exposed flesh. The wind wailed, blowing her skirts. She hesitated on the threshold, as if listening to a voice. Then she knew, suddenly, that Ben was waiting inside.

A fire burned in the hearth. He had built it. He was standing in front of it, silhouetted, like a phantom from her imagination. He was standing in his own shadow; it rippled around his boots like a pool of dark water. Her eyes began there and traveled slowly over him, moving upward over the dusty trousers and the soiled rawhide jacket to the blunt square jaw that was beardless again, to the white half-moon scar on his cheekbone, halting—her heart hammering—to search out his eyes. Then she saw the absence of light in his face, as if his heart had grown rough and hard, closed.

"Hello, Anna," he said.

She watched him examine her, knowing intuitively that he didn't see her as she was. He was looking for signs to confirm his contempt—she could feel that—an anger he hadn't acknowledged, a violence humming in him.

She caught her breath under his inspection, feeling a chasm open between them: She was more separate from him than she had been when he was away—when the possibility of losing him had permitted her to need him. They had been alike, allies and enemies, caught in a common rhythm. Now, coming together had sundered them.

"Selinda's gone," she said quietly. "She took Bendejo."

"I know," he answered, unmoved.

"Have you seen her? Is she alive?"

"They're living in an Indian village. It's finished." His mouth tightened. "It was Mueller—"

"Mueller's dead," she said. "He came here that night, bleeding. I shot him."

He reacted with a long silence. Finally, he said, "I wouldn't have expected that."

She turned away and lit a lamp. They were talking like partners whose business had failed; they were talking like strangers. She took refuge in the motions of striking the match, giving the wick her attention. "We're both different," she said softly.

"You seem the same."

"I've changed."

He didn't answer.

Over the lamp, she saw the door to his former quarters was closed. She had a sense of someone in there, sleeping, or waiting. "Is there a woman with you?"

"A boy." A brief light gleamed in his eyes for the first time. "A savage," he said.

She set the lamp down. "I'm glad you're safe."

He shook his head. "I'm leaving tomorrow—for the land. We made a truce with the Comanches."

"We?"

"Conrad." He moved toward his quarters.

"Take me with you," she said quietly.

"No." He kept walking.

"I never loved Conrad."

He opened the door and closed it behind him.

The Easter fires cast specters on her wall, undulating shadows, seductive and erotic. She turned her head away, but the firelight sputtered on her pillow, tantalizing her: In the morning, he'd ride off. He wouldn't be back. The land would claim him. His own life would claim him.

She kept seeing him standing in front of the fire, cold and indifferent. What had happened between them downstairs? Nothing had happened. How could nothing cause such pain?

Thrashing, her body tried to rid itself of the feeling for him that had lived in her, had grown in her, like an ill-conceived child. He had penetrated and seeded her heart against her firmest resolve; the steady and inexorable growth of her need had taken place within her, impervious to her will. She had not known it until tonight when they met like adversaries, like tired veterans, still wary and on guard, still brandishing their arms.

He had been in a war.

She had been in her own kind of war. She went over it again, hearing the echo of battle between them, and the weariness of personal hardship that had torn apart what had once been their dream of Texas. Each of them—in different ways—had seen too much, had lived too much; the seeing had blinded them to each other and the living had deadened their hearts.

Now he would leave tomorrow. The thought was intolerable.

She lay still. In the stillness, she could see him here, in this room, before he left for Port Isabel. *"You'll come to me,"* he had said.

She rose slowly. She removed her nightgown and stood in front of the mirror, looking at her body as if with his eyes, cupping her breasts as if with his hands. Spasms of desire shot through her, ordering her to yield. Then a terrible uncertainty swept her. How did one yield? What did one do?

She thought about Selinda, how easily and naturally sensuality came to Selinda; that seemed lost to her. She thought about Alfred and the powerful passions that had made him risk his own life; that, too, seemed lost to her. What came to her, instead, was an image of Eduard; she remembered Eduard.

She remembered the exact moment when she had built a breakwater against her own desire; she had taken a vow to control her own erotic fate. She saw herself in Eduard's bed, splitting from herself, withholding, giving only a part of herself and that, at her own command.

She heard herself say to Conrad, *"My heart has never followed my body. Never."*

Tears sprang to her eyes.

She ran her hands along her body, feeling the smooth surface of it, knowing it would refuse to feel what she did not will, and knowing that her will with Ben was powerless. Her own flesh had bowed to her will. Ben would not.

Her hands dropped to her sides. Meeting her own eyes in the mirror, she saw she had imprisoned herself.

She returned to bed. The sheets felt cold to her naked body, alien and punishing. She thought briefly once more of Ben, lying in the same darkness. Then she turned her face to the pillow and wept until, spent and exhausted, she fell asleep.

He heard the thunder of cannons and the crack of gunfire.
He heard Josef's cry as he fell.
Goliath's shadow, hanging from a noose, blotted out the sky.

Another cannon roared and the ghosts of the dead passed before
him: Lilli and his mother, Ott and Thomas, Leopold stretched on the
wheel, the cholera victims on the *Armenius*, those who had died on
the way from Indianola, the men who had fallen in battle. They jour-
neyed silently, across a silent plain, flickering figures, lost to him.

Another explosion came. He lay, face down on his belly, his arms
clutching his head. Then he rolled over slowly and opened his eyes to
the sound of an electrical storm splitting the sky, dry without rain,
rending the night beyond his window with split-second flashes of brilliant light. The thunder rolled again. He sat up cautiously, with a sense
of danger.

Garras was asleep. Ben rose and put on his trousers. A dry wind
moaned, without tears, whipping the brush against the house and rattling the windows. His senses were strangely alert, like a man who had
not been wakened but summoned.

Then he heard a noise in the common room. Crossing to the door,
he threw it open. There was no one there. The front door had blown
open and the rocking horse was creaking in the wind.

He crossed the common room and shut the door. The fire had turned
to embers in the grate. In front of it, the rocking horse slowed and
came to a halt. He was suddenly aware of what it must be for a woman
to live alone with a child, listening to noises in the night.

The heavens split again. A hundred horses galloped across the sky.
The sound of the wind singed his flesh and made his scalp tingle.
Crossing the room, he stopped at the foot of the stairs. In the flashes of
lightning, the stairs lit in front of him, rising to Anna's room. It crossed
his mind that the wind hadn't blown the door open, that someone had
entered and had climbed these stairs.

He moved up them cautiously. Anna's door was open. From the
threshold, he could see the curtains had been pulled back at the window, and the remains of the Easter fire were visible under the splintering sky. He came into the room and stood over the bed. She slept on
her back, one arm flung upward in an attitude of abandon or despair.
Asleep, she looked open and vulnerable, not like the Anna he carried

in his mind. She stirred in her sleep, oblivious to the storm, like a cat stretching, the curves of her body steeped in sensuality. Then the sheet fell away, revealing the curve of her shoulder and the perfectly shaped mound of her breast. In the self-forgetfulness of sleep, the curves of her flesh seemed to invite his touch, promising to yield.

He saw she had lied to him. He saw every word of dismissal and every gesture of cold pride had been a lie. He saw who she was as her body opened to him in sleep.

When he touched her, her flesh burned his hand.

Roused by her compliance and fed by months of unendurable need, the anger rose in him.

"*Texas,*" she had said. "*Three million acres,*" she had said. She needed a man who was strong and brave and alert; she needed an animal to guard her. For these services, he would take her.

The storm rolled across the heavens. He plunged into her, like plunging to the center of the earth, mindless, rising and thrusting from the pain of his childhood, and the loss of his youth, and the deaths of those he had loved, and the relinquishment of his sons, and the severing from Selinda, and the war that had taken place on the battlefield and in his own heart. She no longer existed as Anna, but as the sum of all he had hated and all he had wanted, dream and nightmare made inextricable in flesh, to be subdued and conquered, to be made his.

The storm ceased. Anna heard it cease.

The sudden silence rang through her body.

Ben stopped. The thrusting ceased. The angry plunging that had filled her halted. Above her, Ben's figure froze, as if stricken by a bolt of lightning.

His eyes searched her, dazed. He shook his head slowly.

She reached up and pressed her fingers to his lips, tenderly, in a gesture that released him from remorse. Then she pulled his face to hers and explored his mouth, hungrily. Freed from months of wanting, her hands caressed the hard firm contours of his body, whispering to his flesh in the ancient language of pleasure.

He entered her again. She could hear the beating of his heart. She drew him to her, drawing him inside, more deeply than before. She felt him pass each boundary she had constructed, each barrier she had built, each vow she had taken. She felt him pierce every shadow that had concealed her from herself.

She breathed deeply, feeling his breath as her own. His breath penetrated the hidden places of her body, rocking her gently back and forth to meet him, and part from him, and meet him again. With each stroke, his breath rushed through her like a desert wind, quickening every nerve, igniting trembling fires in what had been a private darkness.

He smelled of sage and sun-parched rock. He smelled of earth and unknown dangers.

She held him closer. The inner fires licked at her spine. Surrendering to waves of crystalline heat, she felt her flesh turn liquid, like thick and golden honey. A sweet terror engulfed her. A succession of tremors passed from him to her as she hurtled blindly toward the mystery of his maleness and felt her form dissolve.

He was lying beside her, awake.

Past the window, there were threads of light in the sky. Below, the Easter fires were dark smudges on the hillsides.

His hands were clasped behind his neck and he was staring out the window, unaware she was watching him. She could hear his thoughts: He had meant to love no more women; he had meant to sire no more sons.

She closed her eyes. After a moment, she felt his mouth against the curve of her throat. "Pack your things," he said.

"What shall we call him?"

"Alfred."

"And the land?"

"Eden," he answered.

BOOK TWO

1861–65

24

"Who are they?" Anna asked in the darkness.

"Neighboring ranchers."

Anna reached out and turned up the lamp. Filtered by a rose-painted globe, the light cast a dusty glow over the massive four-poster which Ben had carved fourteen years ago from cypress that grew near Horsehead Crossing. In fourteen years, she had given birth to six children in it. Then she had wept and shouted, *"No more!"*

"What time is it?"

"Twenty past midnight." Ben wasn't looking at her. His face was taut, preoccupied. Anna could feel the tension in him.

She shivered, reaching for the down comforter which had slipped away, lace-edged, ordered from France, symbol of the comfort and riches she and Ben had wrested from the naked land. She would forever carry her first sight of Eden: vast and bleak and scorched by sun, fit only for savages and rattlers.

"There are no neighbors for a hundred and fifty miles."

"Germans," he said, "from Galveston and Houston City." Ben was seated, pulling off mud-caked boots. It had been raining on and off since New Year's, more than thirty days of it, filling the gullies and crags. Tonight, the rain had turned to sleet; more than a dozen men had arrived, soaked to the bone like animals.

"I know. I heard you talking German."

"Then you know what it's about." Ben's voice was impatient. There was no affection in it. It crossed Anna's mind he had taken a Mexican mistress, or a Negro, in spite of his high and mighty antislavery talk. Behind the closed doors of his library where the men had tracked ice and mud, she had heard their voices rise and fall in fear and defiance.

"South Carolina's seceded—"

Ben nodded. "Mobs are loose in the streets of Galveston—vigilante groups—looking for Unionists. They broke into the newspaper office and destroyed the *Die Union*'s presses."

Rising, Anna wrapped herself in a warm dressing gown and crossed to the window. The storm shutters were bolted. She could hear the wind shrieking outside, whirling full force across the flatland and heading toward the mountains. If she unbolted the window, the wind would sweep through the bedroom—like the winds of war, she thought; the wind that could destroy everything. "The men who came here tonight —they're abolitionists?"

"Yes."

"What did they want?"

"They don't want to fight for the Confederacy."

She turned. "Are we in it, then?"

"There was a special convention of the legislature in Austin. They went over Sam Houston's head. The vote was for secession."

"It's a fever. It'll pass."

Ben shook his head. "The cotton planters have fired the poorest Texan into believing the economy of the state depends on slaves." Ben removed his shirt. Underneath, he wore a cotton duster unbuttoned to the waist. The small muslin bag—the old German forester's last gift to Ben—nestled against his chest where the hair grew as thick as buffalo hide. Seeing it took Anna back to Germany when her own fate had been decided by the men who had divided her country—Eduard, her lover, on one side and her brother, Alfred, on the other. In the 1848 German Revolution, Alfred had been murdered.

"You're thirty-six," she said. "You can't go back to war at thirty-six."

"Sam Houston's almost seventy. When he took Santa Anna at San Jacinto he was older than I am now." Ben's face softened for an instant. Anna knew he wasn't talking about the war anymore; it was common knowledge Sam Houston's wife had just given birth to another child.

She shook her head and turned away. From outside, she could hear the unmistakable thud of horses' hooves plodding through the mud. Above the wind, a hoarse voice called out in German. Quickly unbolting the shutter, she cracked it to peer out.

Below, lanterns swung in the freezing rain, casting an unearthly light. A group of riders had halted, horses neighing and lurching in the fierce wind. As she watched, others joined them. One of the men were distributing rifles; she realized it was Garras. Heads bent, hunched on their animals, the others accepted the arms, rain pounding on the brims of leather hats which obscured their faces. Then Garras signaled with a sputtering lantern and the horsemen moved forward like a ghost party setting out on a trek to Hell.

Ben came up beside her and reached out to close the shutter and bolt it again. "I gave them fresh horses and provisions."

"And rifles—"

"Garras is going to guide them into Mexico."

"Why?"

"To avoid conscription."

"Oh, my God—"

"They're peasant farmers and craftsmen, free-soilers. They own little beyond their beliefs."

"Damn your war," she said. "Damn your beliefs."

"I'm a rancher," he said. "A cattleman. It's not my war. But the country's determined to split like an egg, and we'll have to deal with it."

She was shivering again. "It's cold," she said. She recognized fear. For women, war meant loss. A dark ambiguous foreknowledge chilled her.

Embers glowed in the fireplace. Ben added logs and stirred the coals. After a moment, the flames sprang to life; firelight and shadow played across Ben's face catching the white scar and revealing the strength in it and the pain. "I still want you," he said. "The way I wanted you the night of the Easter fires—the night Elizabeth was conceived."

Anna stiffened against her own need. Ben could always stir desire in her. "I was alone when Elizabeth was born," she said brusquely. "You were in New Braunfels. The *Verein* had gone bankrupt, and you were buying up land certificates for ten dollars each."

"Thirty thousand acres." Ben was staring into the fire. "Water. Grassland for the cattle. Timber for our second house."

"When Alfred was born, you were bringing in Mexican cattle, illegally, across the Rio Grande." Anna's voice rose. She knew what she was doing, deliberately driving him away, with anger. "It took you and Garras weeks to brand them before you could set them loose. Alfred was two months old before you ever saw him."

"Those cattle extended our holdings into the northern mountain range." Ben turned to face her. His eyes had turned hard.

"Then Hannah. The spring she was born, you bought that old steamboat from the Mexican-American War and you were pioneering a water route to market the cattle in New Orleans." Anna marched up and down, counting off on her fingers. "And the next autumn—you never saw Rudolph at all, only his tiny grave—it was Samuel who built Rudolph's coffin and delivered the Lord's Prayer when we buried him. That was the railroad deal, wasn't it? And Elijah—that was the fire in Houston City—when Lambert summoned you, and you mortgaged everything so the two of you could buy up the ashes." She shook a forefinger at him. "I know what you're thinking. You were here for Daniel's birth, that's what you're thinking. And so you were—but only because you had a rustler's bullet in your thigh which struck you with a fever for weeks—" She halted, suddenly weary of her own game. Her hands fluttered in a brief, helpless gesture. "I'm sorry," she murmured.

"It's late," Ben said. She saw she had done it. She had lost him. A part of him—his heart or his conscience—had gone off with the German farmers. Another part of him was already assessing the impact of civil war, calculating the risks and the opportunities.

"I still dream about how it was," she said softly. "That first log cabin. One windmill. A handful of cattle and a parcel of stony earth and runt mesquite. All we had were two Negroes and Garras and our bare hands."

She was watching Ben. His eyes remained cold. He didn't respond.

"We had each other," she said. "And Leopold. That was all. How did we do it? How did we survive the Comanches?—and the rattlesnakes?—the twisters and the droughts and then the floods?" She approached Ben and looked into his face. Her eyes brimmed with tears. "Do you remember when you had the blacksmith make the first Calder brand? *'It's your crown,'* you said. *'I'm going to build an empire and you're going to be the queen of it.'*"

"We'll survive the war, too," he said quietly.

"I'm afraid." Her voice dropped to a whisper.

"Tomorrow, you'll start packing. I want you to take the children to the house in Houston City. Take Samuel and Beatrice with you. The cities will be safer. Leopold's already there in school. You'll all be together."

"Leopold's sixteen. What if it lasts—?"

"I'll see he doesn't serve."

"And you? What about you?"

"It's going to be a war for fools and idealists and profiteers." He studied her a moment, coldly, the way he appraised cattle. Then he strode to the lamp and bent over it and blew it out. "I'm not a fool," he said.

By the light of the fire, she watched him pick up his shirt and his boots. Without looking at her, he moved toward the door.

She called after him. "Ben—" He didn't pause. "You have a woman," she cried. "That's why you're sending me to Houston City. I won't go. I won't go without you!"

The door closed behind him.

The silence woke her.

The wind had stopped. So had the rain. The air was ominously still. An eerie silver light came through the cracks in the storm shutters. The room was cold. The fire was dead, a pile of white ash.

Anna rang for Samuel to stoke the fire. He didn't appear. When Beatrice didn't arrive with her breakfast either, she rose and dressed hurriedly in warm clothing, pinning her hair up in one bold stroke and pausing only for a swift glance in the pier glass—long enough to remember that war made a man young again, but a woman old.

She was thirty-four. Why was she frightening herself?

Her reflection reassured her. Nothing more than a few faint lines around a mouth that was still sensuous betrayed her age. In spite of childbearing, her breasts were still firm and high and—with a bit of cinching—her waist was as small as a girl's. The bloom of womanhood was evident only in her eyes, in the revealing depths of living and experience and loss of innocence that had become strength. Turning away from the glass, she felt certain of her power to rouse Ben and bend him to her will.

Intent on her own thoughts, she was walking briskly through the upstairs hallway before she became aware of the commotion. The noise floated up the stairs, as if to defy her, even before she hurried down to be confronted by the crates and boxes, by the house servants scurrying and bustling and Samuel shouting orders. The front door was ajar. She could see the carriage was already outside and the children's baggage was being loaded.

Samuel was knotting a rope around a tin trunk. "Who told you to pack?" Anna demanded.

"Mr. Calder," he answered, not meeting her eyes.

"Where's Mr. Calder?"

Samuel shook his head. "Ain't seen him since sunup."

Beatrice was hurrying down the stairs carrying a pile of linen. "Not me neither," she said, as she passed.

The library was empty.

Except for Elizabeth, the children were eating breakfast at the dining-room table. "We're going to Houston City," Elijah called out. Alfred was staring morosely at an untouched plate. Giggling, Hannah wiped Daniel's mouth.

"We're not going," Anna said sharply. Looking up, Alfred brightened as she stalked past.

In the kitchen, the Mexican cook was heating tortillas on an iron griddle, the scullery boy was mopping around the pine worktable where Garras was hunched, dipping a tortilla into a bowl of *frijoles* and eating with clenched hands, staring into space with red-rimmed eyes. Anna stopped at the sight of him. It had been past midnight when she watched Garras ride off with the abolitionists. The border was a ten hour ride. What was he doing back?—looking dazed and exhausted, gripped by a peculiar rigidity as though, at twenty-one, he'd been frozen by a vision of his own death?

"Garras?" Anna could feel the undercurrent of anger and fear in him. Bending over the table, she touched his shoulder gently. "What happened?"

He jumped at her touch. With effort, he focused on her. "I had the fastest horse," he said in a strained voice. She caught a glimpse of the half-wild child Ben had brought back fourteen years ago.

"What are you talking about?"

Garras' mouth tightened. His head swung back and forth in a mute refusal.

"*Diablos,*" the cook muttered, turning to look out of the window. From far off, Anna could hear the hunting dogs barking, louder and louder as they bounded in toward the kennel. *"Señor* Calder," the cook said.

Anna swung out through the back porch without stopping for a wrap.

She found him in the kennel feeding the hounds. He was wearing last night's shirt under his rawhide jacket, and his eyes were dark and bloodshot. He stood in the middle of the dogs, looking blunt and stubborn; he smelled of earth and rage and a crude power, and she knew to tread carefully.

"Where've you been?" Her breath frosted the air. She was hugging her shoulders to keep herself warm.

"Hunting."

"Man or beast?"

His eyes traveled over her with a look that took her back fourteen years, to those first months in a tent when they had lived on deer and wild turkey and pigeons which had roared past in great clouds. There had been no rabbits; the wolves had devoured the rabbits. After the Mexican War, he had killed without relish, he said.

"They were easy to track." His words cut the air like knives. "There were ten of them. Two had been wounded. They had made a campfire and they were cooking bacon. I recognized most of them. Lone Star Minutemen, they call themselves." He pulled a piece of paper from his pocket. "When you get to Houston City, take these names to Lambert—"

"I'm not going to Houston City."

"The Germans were ambushed," he said quietly.

Anna stiffened in horror. "Oh, my God!"

"Not two hours from here. They were still on Calder land. Garras got the two who were wounded. He was the only one who got away." Ben's eyes narrowed. "Garras woke me before dawn. I went out with the dogs. I found the place. The sun was just coming up." His mouth tightened. "The Germans were hanging from trees."

She started to tremble. "Bastards—"

He took a deep breath. "The frontier's going to get the worst of it. Out here, killing's like breathing. Give them a difference and they'll go at each other like prairie dogs." He reached out and stroked her hair. "At least the cities have their pretenses to civilization."

"I don't want to go without you."

"But you will."

She stared at him. "Yes," she said finally.

He took off his jacket and wrapped it around her. "You were right," he said softly. "I do have a woman." Holding the lapels of the jacket, he managed a solemn grin. "When I met her, she was a spoiled and willful girl. Now she's a magnificent creature"—he bent and kissed her —"with a very sharp tongue."

25

Galveston hummed with violence.

Ben moved through clusters of minutemen bearing Lone Star flags aloft, and boys as young as thirteen wearing Lone Star hats and carrying bayonet-muskets purchased anywhere for ten dollars, and groups of businessmen arguing about the fall of eastern security prices and the closing of the boot factories and the rising value of gold. Men damned Lincoln with closed fists, ready to strike a blow.

In front of the Courthouse, the street throbbed with anger. Voices rose. There were four million slaves in the south—somebody shouted —fifteen hundred in Galveston alone. Texas was dependent on slaves. The illicit slave trade from Africa, unregulated, was far more heinous than legalized slavery; and drove the price of a fit black male as high as two thousand dollars—and drove up the price of cotton.

"They've locked the Courthouse." Lambert's face was pale.

Ben motioned for the small party of Rangers who shielded Sam Houston to turn around. "We'll have to use the Tremont Hotel," he called over the shouts of the crowd.

Curtly, Houston turned into the crowd again. Swinging briskly, wrapped in a military cape with a blood-red lining, the old soldier-statesman strode through the mob with no sign of fear, as tall and erect as Ben, silver locks glimmering in the April sunlight, his sculptured eaglelike profile oblivious to the sea of derisive cries surging around him.

"Hang Sam Houston!" a young man shouted, breaking from the crowd and stumbling after them up the back stairway of the Tremont. Lambert lunged and missed. Ben turned and delivered a swift blow that sent the hooligan rolling to the bottom. Without pause, Sam Houston kept climbing.

Ben's suite of rooms was at the end of the corridor on the second floor. Houston entered first. Outside, a wooden balcony ran the width of the building. Without hesitation, Houston stepped out and stood there silently, eyes burning under fierce brows, confident of the power of his presence to silence the mob below. Standing behind him, Ben scanned the crowd. It was a strange pastiche, menace laced with a carnival air. There was a sprinkling of women, dressed as if for church. Slaves, set loose from household duties and bent on celebration as though it were May Day, were decked out in the traditional manner of Galveston: Dressed in their masters' castoffs, wearing velvet frock coats, wearing silks and satins and crinolines and sporting hats with feathers and lace mantles, they testified to the affluence and gentility of their owners and to the joys of oppression. Then there were the men: merchants and plantation owners, cotton brokers and businessmen, indistinguishable, all with flushed expressions, coalesced by a rabid patriotism.

The war was in their faces, Ben could see that. Fort Sumter had been fired upon. Fear was there, too. Sam Houston had been deposed as governor for refusing to take the oath of allegiance to the Confederacy —the crowd was aware of that. Against all warnings, he had come to Galveston to make his final declaration.

"He's a courageous old bird," Lambert muttered.

Ben nodded. "They know that."

Nearly seventy, Houston could still subdue a mob. Man and legend, hero and villain, ex-President of the Republic and governor of Texas through every major crisis, the old warrior spoke quietly, and the crowd listened.

"I fear your fathers and husbands, your sons and brothers, will be herded at the point of bayonet . . ." Houston's words were deliberate, his voice deep and even, like a man half his age restraining his power. "The North is determined to preserve this Union," he said. "They are not a fiery impulsive people as you are for they live in cooler climates.

But when they begin to move . . . they move with the steady momentum and perseverance of a mighty avalanche . . ." Ben heard something uncivilized beneath the oratorical skill, threatening to erupt. He could feel the conflict churning in Houston, the bitterness of personal betrayal struggling with a deep love of Texas. As he continued to speak, Ben could feel him searching for a reconciliation. Unable to find it, Houston ended with a gesture meant to embrace those who had threatened him only minutes ago. "Whatever course my state shall determine," he declared, "I say"—he paused, his emotion apparent—"my state right or wrong." Then he turned abruptly and left the balcony.

Ben brought him a shot of brandy. Outside, the crowd had burst into wild applause.

"They're shouting for you," Lambert said.

Houston shook his head. "In an hour, they'll want to hang me again." He downed the brandy and looked directly at Ben. "It's going to be long and it's going to be bloody," he said. "So don't try to walk on both sides of the river."

It was a restless night. Unable to entertain even the thought of sleep, Ben found himself stalking the suite like a man caged by elusive demons. Twice, he paused to part the french doors and scan the cloud-ridden tropical sky. Then, with an effort, he made himself return to the desk where he poured and swallowed another shot of brandy before dipping a quill pen and continuing his letter to Anna.

"April 19 . . . more than two months since you took the children to Houston City . . ."

Writing came hard to him. His thoughts had always careened faster than he could capture them. He laid the pen down. Anna's image was fleeting, without substance. This afternoon, Lambert had boarded the steamer for Houston City. It was only a ten-hour cruise. He could have gone with Lambert. He hadn't. It told him something: It wasn't his need for Anna that drove him tonight.

Again he rose and crossed the room, this time stepping out onto the balcony where Sam Houston had spoken twelve hours earlier. Below him, the street was quiet. The crowd had long ago dispersed, returning the city to a semblance of order. At eight o'clock, the theater had run up its curtain as usual, a New Orleans company production of *Soldier's Daughter* which had vied for the attention of the cultured populace with the Third Presbyterian Church where Professor Hale had delivered the final lecture of a series on Electrobiology: "The Wonders of Human Electricity." Now a post-midnight hush had descended, deceptive, like a velvet curtain discreetly drawn to mask a rich and teeming night life.

In Zita Garrison's salon, the men would be smoking cigars and gambling. Women would be milling about, a Negro servant would be serving peach brandy and somebody would be playing the piano.

He needed a woman, he thought, a woman who wasn't Anna.

The thought caught him unawares. It struck him that the chaos that had filled the street had retreated inward, to take other forms. He could feel it rumbling in him like a boiler being stoked, demanding to carry him; he told himself he wasn't certain where.

Leaving the hotel, he told himself he only needed to walk, as long and far as he could, until he was tired, until he could sleep, or until dawn broke over the tree-lined streets and the high-ceilinged houses surrounded by their walled gardens and their oleander hedges, and over the narrow alleys and the shacks where the Negroes lived.

The moon sputtered dimly through a curtain of clouds. Palm fronds rustled. He could smell night jasmine. War heightened the senses, he thought; war made everything sharp and compelling.

When he reached the harbor, he halted and let his gaze wander over the Bay, which lay still and peaceful as the sabbath. Moored at the wharfs on the landward side, only tenuously protected from inevitable storms, a half-dozen sea-going vessels loomed like guardian specters. The wind shifted. A few ripples fanned outward toward the Trinity River which would carry the interior traffic to the sea. Standing motionless on the wharf, he felt his soul quiet briefly, long enough to tell him that the country had split, and Texas had split, and now the split was taking place inside of him; opposing forces of himself had squared off, ready to engage in bloody battle.

Staring out at the Galveston Bay, he was transported back seventeen years:

He saw the village of Brieg and smelled the smoke from the smelters and the stench of poverty and German royal oppression. He saw the blazing mill, and heard the cries of uprising, and felt his sword pierce Schroeder. He felt the loss of his mother, and Lilli, and his first-born son whom the Jewish peasant, Nicolai Lubeck, had taken to Poland.

The memories tumbled over one another like the items of an indictment. Hadn't he once been a slave himself? What had happened to his commitment to freedom?

Another voice within him rose in defense:

If a man was strong, he survived and prevailed. He had done that. He had fled oppression. He had clawed his way out and up, becoming American royalty, a Texas land baron and a power in the Southwest. Integrity was the privilege of the poor. Integrity was the solace of those with nothing to lose.

He found himself walking again.

He told himself the real issue of the war wasn't slavery. The issue was economics: The industrialized North—as dependent on labor as the southern planter—had to pay wages. The issue was a Union split by opposing economies.

He began to stride rapidly.

He left the Bay behind. As the distance widened, he could feel the harbor pulling at his back, as if he'd left something unfinished there; but he continued to walk, faster and faster.

The streets, paved with crushed oyster shells, crunched under his boots. The moon came out and sent slivers of light through the palm trees. A lone carriage passed. He could hear a woman's high shrill laugh.

When he halted again, he found himself in front of a cast-iron gate, looking past a gnarled pattern of fruit and flower garlands into a walled garden. Screened by tropical plants and climbing bougainvillea vines, the three-story house rose far enough off the street to be indiscernible except to those who knew it existed. There was a bell above the gate. He pulled at the chain. After a moment, a Negro in a white linen coat appeared. He gave him his card and waited. The Negro disappeared through the shrubbery, returning almost immediately to open the gate and vanish again; they exchanged no words.

As he came up the walk, the house emerged from the shadows, one of the few red-brick structures on the island. Cast-iron colonnades, twisted into the same motif as the gate, thrust a gingerbread veranda over the entrance. Long narrow windows, designed to capture the day-time breeze, were shuttered closed. Only a faint glimmer of light and the muted sound of a piano hinted at the diversions inside.

The Negro who let him in wore purple livery, brass buttons blazing under the fractured light of a tiered chandelier. A winged cherub was poised on the balustrade of a curved stairway that snaked up three floors where, on the second landing, a mongrel dog groomed to perfection was asleep on a window seat.

Ben glanced at the carved doors of the gambling salon which were discreetly shut against the smoke-filled tension where fortunes hung on the turn of a card; no women were allowed there. In a small parlor to his right, he saw a monkey outfitted in a red vest and a Lone Star hat and chained to the piano where, head cocked and wearing a puzzled expression, the animal was observing the mating rituals of the civilized. Turning away, he moved through a columned archway into the Blue Room, a grand salon that ran the length of the house, opulently furnished in shades of marine blue and cerulean, and adorned by girls who were gliding about as though swimming in an aquarium filled with brightly colored tropical fish. He recognized most of the men; several greeted him warmly, exuding the comradeship of those bonded by power, of men who had earned and who shared the privileges of catered passions and organized pleasure. With a cry of delight, Zita Garrison came sailing across the room, hands sprayed with diamonds and darting like swallows through her frizzed red hair, before her embrace enveloped him in oversweet perfume.

She stepped back and scrutinized him. "What do you need?"

"Everything."

"Start with a brandy," she said, lifting a glass from a passing tray.

He swallowed it down, his eyes drifting over the room. His gaze halted on a slender mulatto girl wearing amethyst satin. "That one— who's she?"

"Violet."

He studied her for a moment. The girl's eyes met his coldly—mouth slightly parted, practiced and unforgiving; her neck and shoulders glistened like liquor in a crystal bottle.

"Her," he said.

She bolted the door.

There was a porcelain washstand with a clean towel draped over it. Beads hung over a mirror, garnets and amber and pearls, framing a dressing table cluttered with cut-glass perfume flasks and silver-capped powder jars, a tray of combs and hair ornaments. A beaded bag was half open, its contents spilling out.

Her hair had been ironed. It fell from a center part, caught with ivory combs, revealing her ears. She removed the combs and laid them on the tray. She didn't look at him.

There was a dressing chamber. She didn't use it. She went about undressing as though he weren't there. Then she climbed into bed and drew the covers about her shoulders. She wore no expression, no crease in her high broad forehead, only a slight jut to her delicate chin. Her eyes, painted, were cold and blank. He knew if he touched her, she wouldn't feel it.

"Do you want the lamp off?"

"On," he said.

"Do you have a wife?"

"Yes."

A curt nod said: I thought so.

He took his boots off first. "Where are you from?"

"The West Indies."

He knew the run. The African slave trade was routed through the islands where only the most gullible or the most desperate were enticed aboard. He imagined her on the Galveston auction block, too fragile for a field hand, too light-skinned and pretty for a house servant.

"What did Zita pay for you?"

She shrugged. "Twelve hundred dollars."

It was less than the going rate for a field hand which was eighteen hundred. Rented out at three hundred a year, a Negro field hand would pay for himself in six years; after that, his labor was profit for his owner. Ben knew Zita's version: Zita would apply a percentage of whatever a girl earned against her purchase price, minus her keep. By the time a girl was no longer desirable, Zita's bookkeeping would show the girl had earned her freedom which was equivalent to the right to starve.

"How much do you owe her?"

"Eleven hundred and fifty-three dollars and twenty-five cents." Her reply was toneless. She was watching him shed his clothes, without interest. When he climbed into bed, she made no response.

"What's your real name?"

"You didn't pay for that."

"How much?"

"Twenty dollars."

"Why would it be worth that?"

Again, she shrugged. "What a man doesn't know, he'll pay for," she said. "After he knows it, it loses its value."

He left the bed, removed twenty dollars from his money clip, and laid it on the dressing table.

"Martinique," she said.

"How do I know that's so?"

"You don't."

He came back to bed and drew the covers away. His hand strayed over her body. It was smooth and unyielding, as if she had claimed the only freedom she could, the right to be indifferent. He felt a powerful need to make her respond to him. The need told him she was right; he'd come to *know* something.

"I don't own slaves," he said. The lie thickened his voice. He told himself Anna had purchased Beatrice and Samuel, and their children had been born into slavery; he hadn't bought and paid for any of them.

She didn't answer.

She drew him inside of her. It was like entering a cold dark tunnel. Her gestures were automatically wanton, no feeling behind them. She didn't close her eyes. Her gaze remained distant. His need surged into her, driving him. He found himself thrusting harder and harder in an effort to rouse her.

Her flesh was like stone. The deeper he penetrated, the more removed she became, as though she were determined to make him know he was using her. Then he felt a strange thing happening, a reversal of roles—she, becoming the mistress and he, the supplicant—searching for a way to please her. Anger rushed through him. For the first time, he felt her respond, not with desire but triumph. Instinct told him she was fueling his anger, provoking him, turning him into a scavenger and revealing his own cruelty to himself. Then, suddenly, she reared beneath him and her inner walls gripped him, contracting, making a savage demand for his release. Resisting, he plunged past her demand. She raised and lowered her pelvis, viciously, clamping him like a vise and oscillating until he was on the verge of explosion.

In that instant, she moved, without warning.

His seed erupted outside of her.

A roar escaped his throat. He flung himself at her and grasped her by the shoulders, hurling her backward off the bed. She fell like a cat, rolling in midair and landing on all fours.

Breathing heavily, he lay still. He watched her rise slowly. He watched her cross the room and pour water from a pitcher into the porcelain washstand and dip the towel. When she came back, he let her clean his thighs.

Her gaze was dispassionate.

He could hear music wailing downstairs and the echo of forced mirth.

He had wanted to kill her. He knew she had felt that. Now, he *knew*. He knew that would have constituted her final revenge.

Dawn broke through tattered clouds. The sun slashed at the Bay, leaving bloody wounds on the rippling water.

Drawn back to the same vantage point he had occupied earlier, Ben had the impression of looking out at a battlefield, a sense of having returned here to be given a glimpse of what was coming.

He was exhausted. He had had too much brandy and no sleep, and the mulatto whore had set a knowledge loose in him, a recognition of the meaning of slavery that had gone beyond the evocation of cruelty and the inevitability of violence. Yet, he had been impelled back here by that part of himself which had always whispered to him what things were and where Texas was going.

Now it told him it was imperative—more than that—crucial, to formulate a view of the consequences of the war and the course it might take.

He stood poised, watching the bitter sunrise reflected against the Bay, and what he began to see was the obvious:

Galveston, an island isolated from the mainland, would be tenuous in time of war. Galveston was no more than an appendage to Texas, an outpost, constantly threatened by storms and militarily indefensible.

Galveston would be abandoned before the war was done.

An excitement stirred in him.

The practical side of his mind took inventory, counting the ships in the harbor: four steamers and eleven barks, six brigs and eight schooners and two sloops. They were already being loaded or unloaded from the warehouses that were packed with cotton and wool, with coffee and animal hides and tobacco, with manufactured goods and pig iron.

He translated the scene into figures: two hundred thousand bales of cotton were compressed and exported yearly through Galveston at a tariff of fifty cents a bale; port fees for cotton alone were a million dollars.

Then he leap-frogged ahead.

Wasn't Houston City—at the junction of Buffalo and White Oaks Bayou—the natural point on the river to establish a major port? Wasn't Houston City already the railroad terminal of the Texas Empire? Why wouldn't the war—and the inevitable abandonment of Galveston when it occurred—provide the ideal moment to shift the center of shipping there also?

The question he posed to himself took a more direct form:

Why not pirate Galveston's port?

He walked back to town.

He rang the bell over the gate.

The same Negro came out. By daylight, his linen coat looked dingy and rumpled.

He asked for Violet. The Negro went away. In a few minutes, Violet appeared wearing a flowered wrapper and grease on her face. The sun turned her skin bronze. She looked at him as if she didn't know who he was. She didn't open the gate.

He counted out the money: eleven hundred and fifty-three dollars and twenty-five cents. Then he held the money out through the bars of the gate.

She stared at him, quizzically.

"Take the money," he said. "It's wages."

She kept staring at him, looking for the trick in it.

"Take it," he said.

Her hand darted out like an animal from hiding. The money vanished into a clutched fist. A small pinpoint of light appeared in each dark pupil like a harbinger of mirth, or tears. Her eyelids quivered. Her mouth parted. For a fraction of a second, she looked as if he'd struck her. Then the impassivity slid over her face like an old mask and she began to back away.

Eyes fixed on him, she took a few tentative backward steps. Then she spun around and started to run. Halfway up the walk, she halted suddenly and looked back at him once more, her eyes brilliant in the sunlight, brimming with either pain or scorn, he couldn't tell which. Then she disappeared through the shrubbery.

He watched her vanish. He wondered if she believed he had freed her in order to free himself of the issue of conscience. He knew that was so. But there was more. Wages, he had said. For a knowledge he could not have received in any other way.

Because of her, he knew how the war would come out.

For the South, it would be like last night's war with her: A war of spilled seed, a war of manhood wasted, unable to perpetuate itself.

The South would lose.

Wages, he had said. For that knowledge and for the foresight which had been born from it.

The South would lose. But he would win.

26

Fredericksburg, Virginia
December 16, 1862

Dear Papa Nicolai,

The rain is coming down. Tonight, even your Jehovah weeps. A terrible rumor says Fredericksburg has cost us twelve thousand dead and wounded.

Lee has reduced us to an army of stragglers. I write this from our original camp on the bank of the river. Through the rain the flames rise from the devastated city; the Secesh still occupy the other side of the Rappahannock.

The dead are not yet buried. But the sound of bursting shells and screaming shot is gone and the volleys of musketry have died away. In the silence, I hear the trot and rumble of your peddler's wagon, and I am struck with homesickness. I was eight when we left Konin in such a wagon, remember? Do you remember the talk of California gold fever in the streets of Warsaw? You dreamed of taking a ship across the Atlantic, over the Isthmus of Panama and up the coast to California. "We'll open a store, Jacob," you said, "for all those fools who think they'll find gold." How strange fate is. If we had gone to California instead of New York, how far we would be from this war!

I can hear your answer to that. Jacob—I can hear you say—whatever name they call it, and whether it is practiced by the feudal lords of Prussia, or the Czar's Cossacks in Poland, or the plantation owners in Georgia, any form of slavery enslaves the human heart.

So I am here. And I imagine you reading this in your market stall

*near the old hanging grounds in Washington Square, and I am filled
with a need to say what need not be said. You are not my natural father. I love you more for that. I was not born a Jew. I am more a Jew
for that. The gifts of living are far greater than the circumstances of
one's birth. Perhaps, when this is over, we will open a store as grand as
the new Lord & Taylor's on Broadway and Grand Street. Perhaps we
will call it Lubeck & Lubeck.*

*Your loving son,
Jacob*

27

"_. . . urgent,_" Lambert wrote from Houston. "_Anna appears to be acting without regard to consequences . . ._"

The letter, dated March 2, 1864, had arrived at the beginning of spring round-up.

"_. . . a touchy issue,_" Lambert wrote. "_. . . a flagrant disregard of propriety. I cannot convey the details by letter except to say that in any civilized society, the sexual aspects of human nature have always been, and should remain, a private matter. . . ._"

Around Ben, the wagons with their contraband cargo formed a protective circle against the night. Except for the hired band of ex-Rangers who patrolled the darkness, the men slept. Ben read by the light of the dying campfire, reading the letter through twice, then reading it again, as if he hadn't committed every word to memory.

"_. . . a committee of matrons has approached me regarding Anna's arrest . . . I advise you to come at once._"

Ben crumpled the letter. Then he rose, frowning, and made his way through scattered bedrolls, striding past men who were snoring like freight trains and men as still as corpses until he came out beyond the wagons. Cold desert air rushed through his nostrils. Stars, close enough to pluck, traveled toward a horizon without end; Calder land, stretched as far as he could see.

Anna had always been fiery and stubborn. Intractable, he thought, and unpredictable. He didn't want to go beyond that. How far had Anna gone beyond that?

Anna had always been *his*. He hadn't questioned that. Why not? He'd been a fool not to question what might happen to a woman as beautiful as Anna who—except for his occasional visits—had been left alone in Houston for three years.

He had been battling the Longhorns when Samuel brought the mail out on horseback; he had been riding the range like a madman through dark herds of half-wild cattle.

He should have been in Houston. He had promised Anna he'd be there in January for Leopold's birthday.

He hadn't gone.

The Longhorns were out of control, he'd written her that.

No beef had been slaughtered since the beginning of the war when the Union blockaded the Gulf and cut off the export market. Cotton was a silent cargo, easily smuggled across the Rio Grande to Mexican ports; beef bawled on the hoof, loud as foghorns across guarded waters.

He hadn't written that.

Had she started an affair?

He went through the men he knew, trying to figure out who: His attorney? One of his friends? A business associate? Why would the women in town be up in arms—unless Anna was flaunting it? Why would she flaunt it? To bring him back? To take revenge because she knew damned well he hadn't been celibate?

It was three years. *"No more children,"* she had said. He had finally accepted it. Had she lied? Was she having an affair with a man who was sterile? How would she know that? The bastard was impotent, he thought.

Her last letter had said Leopold had been threatened with expulsion from Houston Academy for drinking. The letter had said she was making arrangements for Elizabeth's debut.

He should have gone then.

He hadn't. The conscript law had taken most of his cowhands, leaving too few men to brand and castrate the calves and nobody to ride the far-away ranges. He was a cattleman, wasn't he?

He had written her that. It was a lie. It hadn't been the Longhorns. Since the war, his real occupation had been running the blockade. He was the one who saw that the cotton wagons loaded by Lambert in

Houston were moved swiftly and safely through miles of Calder territory to the banks of the Rio Grande. He was the one who loaded the
lion-colored low-built steamers and sent them off with the bales to Matamoros. He was the one who had sent Garras to deal with the Mexican agents—shipping the cotton to Europe and the West Indies and
the northern textile mills. It was Garras who reloaded the steamers
with precious ammunition and supplies, but he was the one who met
the ships when they returned, and he was the one who packed up the
cotton wagons and saw that the ammunition was safely transported
back to Houston where Lambert was in charge of the southwestern
Confederate Headquarters.

It was for Anna, wasn't it? To preserve and finance a way of life that
included sons and daughters who must be provided with debuts.

Had she fallen victim to an aberration—one of those seizures that
happened to women? Was it more than one affair?—two or three at the
same time? Houston wasn't that big—they were stumbling over one
another—all married men. The women had banded together against
her.

That was ludicrous.

It was one man. An important man. So important, it had upset the
whole community. The minister, he thought. Who else but the minister
would upset everybody?

The minister was five feet tall and sixty-three years old. The minister
was crazy. Anna had driven him crazy.

He was still clutching the letter. Straightening it out, he struck a
match and read it over until an image of the man appeared.

It was a stranger. An aristocrat. Somebody from Berlin. A stranger
who looked like Eduard had looked, or von Ahrenbach. It was one of
those civilized strangers who'd never touched a gun. It would be easy.
No duels. One bullet.

The match burned his fingers. He struck another and set the letter
aflame. The wind carried the ashes toward the first streaks of light in
the east.

Turning abruptly, he strode back through the circle of ammunition-
laden wagons and, standing in the center, hands cupped around his
mouth, he shouted, *"Move 'em out! Let's move 'em to Houston!"*

According to Garras' count, less than half of the cotton bales had
been unloaded. Covered with tarpaulins, they were piled on the Ma-

tamoros wharf waiting for the Mexican agents whose offices were closed. It was the beginning of the Holy Week festival, the Friday of Dolores, two days before Palm Sunday, and even the workers had abandoned the wharf. Garras found them on the street corners and in front of the church, buying candles for the *incendios,* the altars laid with flaming tapers which would be set up at twilight in the poorest homes. All day, he watched the processions that filled the streets, men and women carrying potted palms, and cages filled with doves and nightingales, and a life-sized statue of the Virgin of Solitude which had once wept real tears for the death of Christ. The processions moved him. He perceived a strange light around everything, and he wondered if he might be going mad.

He waited until dusk. At dusk, the church was dark and silent, a place of shadows and closed doors. As he entered, he felt enormous relief, a surcease from the anger burning in him. Still, his temples pounded and something sprang up in the pit of his stomach like a gush of water in the desert.

Hundreds of candles flickered at the altar, casting eerie shadows on the sculpture of the crucifixion and emanating a peculiar smell of sorrow. A lone old woman knelt, head covered, gnarled hands clutching a rosary and lips moving silently in penitential prayer.

He came down the side aisle and entered the Confessional and pulled the cord that rang a bell in the old priest's quarters. After a while, he heard the rustling of cassock skirts and the clanking of the huge silver cross which the old priest wore, and then it grew quiet except for the cadence of the familiar murmured blessing.

"I had a dream," Garras said, speaking in Spanish.

The old priest was silent.

"I dreamed it was the first day of the world," Garras said. "And when the sun started to go down, no one could tell me where the sun was going. So I mounted a horse and started to chase the sun. But the darkness kept rising at my back, no matter how hard I rode or how fast."

The old priest remained silent.

"I want to be a priest," Garras said.

"The *Tejano* refused you the land, then?"

"He offered me money. To buy land wherever I wanted."

"That seems honorable enough."

"You don't understand. It's not any land I want. It's that one parcel.

Didn't I help him clear a thousand times that? Haven't I been the one closest to him?—the one who's always done anything he ever asked?"

"He's a *gringo.*" The old priest sighed heavily. "You're not his son."

"Who am I, then?"

"You'll have to ask God," the old priest said.

Huge oaks lined the street, sheltering the imposing residences from the glare and the sun. Riding underneath, Ben spurred his horse. A fine veil of sweat covered the animal. At dawn, he had left the wagons behind; he had pushed the horse without mercy.

An iron fence surrounded the house. Dismounting, he tethered the bay. There was no carriage outside, no saddled horse waiting, no sign of the stranger who had invaded what had once seemed to him the most magnificent house he'd ever seen.

He had built it for Anna.

He had ordered a high and wide and handsome house; he'd had it designed by a European architect who had worked only in hand-hewn stone. He had hired only European craftsmen: French artisans had carved the walnut paneling inside, and had decorated the ceilings and walls in delicate friezes and panels ornamented in twenty-two-carat gold.

He had carried Anna across the threshold. Now, he'd pull it down on Anna's head.

He went through the gate, heels rapping on the stone walk. He let himself into the massive entrance hall that ran the length of the house. Nobody greeted him. There were no calling cards in the silver tray. The house was strangely quiet. The drawing-room doors were open; there was no one inside. The formal sitting room was empty. So was the dining room, which could seat forty, and behind it, the immense ballroom had been emptied and an army of Negroes were cleaning the crystals of the chandeliers and polishing the inlaid floor.

He took the wide curved stairway two treads at a time. The second floor held the massive library, the spacious bedroom he shared with Anna, and an informal sitting room. The doors were all shut. He tried the bedroom door first, opening it cautiously to find only sunlight streaming across a pristine bed. The library held nothing but books. When he reached the doors of the sitting room, he halted outside.

Coming from within, muted but unmistakable, was the sound of Anna's voice.

One hand rested on his holster. He cracked the door slowly.

Anna was at the far end of the room. Her back was turned to him. She was sketching with chalk on a blackboard and talking in the tone of a lecturer.

Surrounding Anna—their backs also turned to him—clustered in groups on the horsehair sofas and overstuffed chairs, a dozen girls were engrossed in whatever Anna was saying. Among the girls was Elizabeth; he recognized her long auburn hair.

He could hear Anna's voice, clearly now, but the words made no sense to him.

". . . and this is the scrotum," she was saying. He was sure his ears were mistaken. One of the girls giggled. "Ignorance is not preparation for womanhood," he heard Anna say firmly.

He watched Anna's hand move swiftly across the blackboard. "Sexual arousal causes an erection of the male penis because a network of blood vessels runs along here—" Anna said. He recognized what she had sketched. He didn't believe his eyes. "Ducts pump the sperm to the penis which ejects it into the vaginal canal," she continued. "The sperm then travels to fertilize the ovarian egg. The result is pregnancy." She turned around to face the girls, still unaware of him. "Any questions?"

"How does the sperm travel?"

"Magnetism," Anna answered.

He could feel the blood rush to his temples. He could feel himself being torn between relief and rage.

"What makes people *want* to do that?"

"The same thing that makes *you* want a debut." Anna answered. "Handsome soldiers in uniform," she said briskly. "A debut is an attempt to civilize an uncivilized impulse. Nature isn't civilized. It has one drive—to procreate. Those of you whose mothers are enlightened enough to permit you to obtain an understanding of nature—" She stopped, as if she might have sensed his presence. He saw a slight frown crease her forehead. "What we're talking about is courage," she said. "The boldness to understand our sexual instincts so we don't relinquish our destiny to nature from misunderstanding or ignorance."

She looked up then. Their eyes locked. Then she turned back to the blackboard and started to sketch again rapidly.

"There are nerve endings in the vagina," she said. "These cause the inner walls to contract around the male sex organ. This friction results in the release of sperm—"

He emitted a sound, like a bull bellowing. The noise came roaring from his throat and sent the girls scurrying and squealing. Bolting across the room, Elizabeth threw herself into his arms. Still roaring, he whirled his daughter around twice, then set her down gently. She was tall and lithe, with the eyes of a deer, soft and frightened and amazed. Leaning down to kiss her forehead, he said quietly, "Why don't you take the girls down to the kitchen and have Beatrice make you some tea?"

He stood in the doorway while the girls hurried past him, making swift half-curtsies with averted eyes.

Anna hadn't moved. She was still standing beside the blackboard, chalk in hand, watching him with a defiant expression. Behind her, the obscene drawings mocked every suspicion. He wanted to laugh. He wanted to thrash her. The conflict immobilized him.

"What in the *devil* do you think you're doing?"

"Educating them for womanhood."

"Have you lost your senses?"

"Women have rights."

"Rights?"

"If women had the vote, we wouldn't be in this war."

"If women had the vote, they'd put you in *jail*," he shouted.

A hint of a smile glimmered behind her stern expression. "I was attacked by the best families," she said. "The Hollanders, the Conroys, the Andersons, all of them. Forty women withdrew their daughters." Her eyes gleamed wickedly. "It occurs to me that most of the men are in your debt. It occurs to me they might be persuaded—" she left the sentence unfinished.

He crossed the threshold and stopped. "You're incorrigible."

She took a matching step. "Enlightened."

He narrowed his eyes and advanced another step. "Perverse—"

"If our ball is attended by only eleven girls, the Calder name will be the laughingstock of Houston—"

"Corrupt." He continued moving forward.

"Advanced." She was keeping pace with him.

"Libertine—"

"Sexual ignorance for women belongs to the dark ages—"

"How can you teach something you've *forgotten?*" he bellowed. Her hand flew to her mouth. A laugh bubbled through her fingers. He stared at her. Then a slow grin broke through his anger. His own laughter erupted, spilling out in a great roar that filled the room. He held out his arms. She threw herself into them, pressing her face against his chest. He could feel her trembling. When she looked up, tears were streaming down her cheeks.

"Leopold's joined the Confederacy—" she said.

28

The splendor began at the gate.

A procession of Negroes in white satin livery lined the iron fence and the walkway, each holding a beveled hurricane lamp, so that the guests descended from their carriages into a tableau of dazzling light.

The stone house glistened. Radiating from hundreds of faceted windowpanes, light pierced the trees and fractured the air, a cold sparkling light as though Anna had ordered the mansion encased in ice.

The girls wore white. Virginal in fragile lace and clouds of organdy, they lifted their voluminous skirts, revealing hoops and hem-stitched petticoats, to tiptoe in satin slippers across the threshold. Their eyes shone. Flushed, smelling of hyacinth, eager to be released from the shelter of guardians who had arrived on command, they fluttered like moths down the spacious entrance hall to be cloistered until the moment of presentation.

Inside the ballroom, Anna was told the first guests were being relieved of their wraps. Crossing to the french doors, she looked out over the garden where dozens of young men in Confederate uniforms wandered in groups, smoking cigars and drinking champagne, waiting to be summoned. Searching for Ben, her gaze swept past the glowing charcoal braziers which provided warmth, moving under the flickering clusters of strung lights to scan the garden which descended in terraced fields of rose bushes, where hundreds of frost-white blossoms had been forced into premature bloom. In the center, live swans floated in a marble pond. Nearby, she could see the two of them, Ben and Leopold; Ben pacing to and fro—Leopold with his arms stubbornly folded across his uniformed chest—Ben doing all the talking with an occasional violent gesture. She watched, her face clouding as the shadow of the war intruded, briefly, no more than a second. Then, at a curt nod from her, liveried Negroes, stationed and waiting, flung the doors open. She motioned for the violins to begin, softly; the music floated out, signaling the men to return.

Turning away, she glanced around the ballroom in a swift final surveillance. Stripped of excessive ornament and divested of color, the massive room gleamed with a glacierlike elegance. Pyramids of candles glittered in sculptured crystal like winter stars. The chandeliers blazed, a thousand hand-cut prisms glistening like icicles over velvet chairs which rose like snowbanks around the ballroom floor. Anna permitted herself a fleeting smile. The room was luxurious and insular, far from the battlefield; the room embodied a different kind of engagement and triumph.

How hazardous, Anna knew the women had whispered to each other, *to launch their charges upon Anna Calder's social sea. What risky auspices under which to steer their daughters into the haven of matrimony.*

Ben had sent hand-delivered letters, carefully worded. The whispers had ceased; the acceptances had poured in.

Moving regally across the floor, she halted just inside the entrance where she stood poised and waiting. On either side of the orchestra, huge mirrors reflected the image the women would confront. Her rich mass of hair had been caught and twisted to reveal a smooth arched neck, deliberately unadorned. Diamonds flashed at her earlobes like drops of frozen light. Emerald silk, boldly cut, plunged deeply to a shimmering bit of discreetly tucked lace; the color turned her eyes the translucent green of Venetian glass.

Ben touched her arm. She turned. Ben's eyes told her she looked magnificent. Then his eyes read her unspoken question.

"I've purchased a battalion for him—uniforms, supplies, monthly pay for the soldiers—everything."

"For Leopold?"

"I made the arrangements through Lambert. The battalion won't be sent beyond the boundaries of Texas."

Looking past Ben, her eyes sought Leopold among the young men, her heart leaping as it always did at the sight of his golden hair and slender grace. Sensing her gaze, Leopold turned and fixed her with a petulant look.

"He thinks he wants to be in the thick of it," Ben said gently. "He'll come around—"

Ben was gazing down at her; she could see the pulse in his throat rising and falling, beating like a drum. He looked suddenly young to her. The frost in his sideburns and the craggy contours of his jaw reminded her they had shared twenty years. She had no memory of those years. She felt them fall away, as if she were seeing him for the first time—as if she, too, were young and filled with expectancy and certain of her own desirability—like the girl who'd fallen in love with Eduard von Lanz at the ball in Berlin. Only this time it was Ben, she thought. How strange—how amazing—to feel those stirrings again.

She sent him an exultant smile. A vibrancy rushed through her, the dizzying power of years being shed—a new youth, this time, without innocence, she thought—feeling her cheeks flush and her spine straighten with pride. Ben's gaze was still fixed on her. She felt herself preen under it. In his eyes, she saw herself poised at the pinnacle of a life she had dared to live against the rules. The hardships had vanished. The war would soon be over; she felt protected from tragedy. She had beaten the forces that had set out to diminish her. She had flaunted fate, and now she was being given the peculiar miracle of falling in love again.

Again, Ben touched her arm lightly as the guests began to appear, passing in a parade that he had summoned from the most powerful families in Houston to bear witness to her triumph.

The women's eyes met hers, startled. She watched them deny their defeat. They patted their elaborate jewels and pressed the arms of their portly husbands a bit too tightly, and their voices echoed as they did on wintry streets and they moved cautiously like treading across an ice pond. She greeted them with the imperious generosity of the victor, feeling removed from them, encased in some glittering immunity. Ben's eyes never left her. She greeted them with the queen's grace of a woman loved.

Then the musicians struck out and—accompanied by a rolling *colonnade* of drums like the rattle of hail and whispered snatches of conversation—each girl was formally presented.

"Miss Florence Anderson . . . !"

—Her brother was killed at Gettysburg, remember? Poor girl—

—They say there've been fifty thousand Confederate deserters since Gettysburg—

"Miss Marybeth Buchanan . . . !"

—Lambert's niece, isn't she?—from Richmond? I hear there're bread riots in Richmond. Mobs of women looting the stores—

—Word's come through the copperheads that Lincoln's going to appoint Grant General-in-Chief. They say he has a plan to take Richmond—

—Grant's a drunkard—

—For a drunkard, he did damn well at Vicksburg—

"Miss Elizabeth Calder . . . !"

Anna caught her breath as Elizabeth floated out, shoulders rising from layers of crystalline organdy.

Around Anna, the whispers faded. The years rolled back—to the night Elizabeth had been conceived—to the night Ben had returned from the war with Mexico and their passions had exploded.

Elizabeth was like Ben, she thought. Elizabeth had Ben's chestnut hair and Ben's direct gaze. She had always walked with Ben's bold stride, and she rode like the wind, with a raw-boned grace, as good as any man on a cutting horse. Like Ben, Elizabeth had no fear of what was raw and untamed, only of what was civilized.

—I understand they asked Calder to help set up a textile mill in the penitentiary—

—He's refused—

The other girls were being presented. Anna paid no attention. Instead, she watched Leopold escort Elizabeth into the promenade on the ballroom floor. Leopold had been drinking again, Anna could see that: He strolled too casually and his mouth had a querulous look. Still, he was the most striking young man in the room, Anna thought. He looked like Eduard; he had the same moody eyes, the same aquiline profile. She had spoiled him. She had coddled him. The young and daring part of herself—the secret self she had cherished most—was preserved in Leopold.

—The Union's got command of the entire Mississippi River—

A slight shiver passed through her, like a warning.

Then "Donaulieder" began, and the strains of the waltz filled the ballroom with its special enchantment of hope and exuberance, of promises that would be kept or broken, of girls gliding across the threshold of new womanhood in the arms of young men in uniform.

Ben swept her into it. Taking her into his arms, he whirled her into the maze of the waltz, holding her lightly until she felt herself rising, airborne, like a gull skimming on wings across the dark pond of the ballroom floor. Mirrors reflected them at every turn: Anna saw only a dizzying glimmer of emerald green. She could feel the powerful thrust of Ben's shoulders under his evening coat and the beating of twin pulses, joined, indistinguishable. Tilting her head back, she sent him a radiant smile.

"Supper's not until eleven," she murmured.

His eyes skipped over her face in rapid inquiry.

Her own gleamed with sudden mischief. "No one will miss us."

His grin broke slowly.

She caught his eyes and held them. "I assume your intentions are dishonorable?"

"Have you no shame?"

"None at all."

His hand tightened around her waist. He spun her across the ballroom floor and through the doorway, keeping perfect time to violins that were drowned in bursts of shared laughter.

He was different.

Her heart was pounding.

She knew he had had other women. She wanted to ask: "Were they like me? Am I like them?" She wanted him to say: "You are my own true love."

She whispered endearments. She bruised his mouth. She drank in the sight of his rough muscular body, swaying over him in a play of violet shadow and milky moonlight.

His touch was the touch of a stranger, as if she had never been touched before.

From downstairs, she could hear the music and the dancers. Peals of laughter floated up. From the garden, she could hear voices, men speaking his name with anger and with awe. She saw who he was. She saw he had become everything the young Anna had ever wanted and more than the young Anna could have ever imagined.

The young Anna laughed until tears ran down her cheeks; the young Anna wept inconsolably.

Then a boundless joy welled up within her, spilling over, uncontained.

His mouth explored her, arousing every inch of flesh. She could feel his hunger; she met him freely. She could feel his need for conquest; she surrendered. She felt a wanting past flesh, a deepening of ecstasy, forbidden chambers opening in the depths of what had been herself. It was like moving through the heart of a fire, through a crucible of passion; at the center was something never touched before.

She was different. He had made her different. She heard herself whisper, *"You are my own true love . . ."*

He took possession of her again. In a slow grave rhythm of lovemaking, he uttered her name in a new way. She recognized love without innocence, love reborn from knowledge and experience and living. Her own need came in overpowering waves, without constraint, engulfing her. There were a dozen Bens, and a dozen Annas—she could feel them all—dozens of hands touching, trying to grasp a lifetime in motion, days that had passed and days to come, who they had been to each other and who they would be. Each breath he drew changed her, transformed her. She felt time race like the fleeting wind. Then she felt time halt and part for her, drawing her into a whirlwind through that knife edge between moments where she heard her own cry, like the cry of a wanderer being guided home.

It's too late, Leopold thought. He didn't know what it was too late for, but the phrase had locked in his mind and it kept repeating itself, over and over: It's too late.

He was carrying a beaker of champagne as he left the ballroom, striding with a rigid military air, like someone giving his body orders. He'd had enough to drink to have reached a dreamlike state, enough so that the ground felt unstable under his feet and he was relieved to hear his boots rapping clearly on the walk.

At his back, the strains of the orchestra swelled out through the french doors. The waves of music felt palpable; they tingled along his spine like the fingers of specters, prodding him. Around him figures blurred like shadows; he could hear crinolines rustling, the murmur of voices and an intermittent laugh. Someone called out to him, but he kept going, past the swans and the fountain and through a grove of oaks, leaving the garden behind.

When he reached the stables, he paused to drink directly from the beaker before he went inside. The red bay neighed when he entered, raising its long narrow head with protruding eyes and regarding him over the stile. Six of the eight stalls were occupied with horses used by the family and guests. The bay belonged to his father. An iron-gray horse, coarse and powerful and a bit vicious, was Elizabeth's. The mustang was his, taupe-colored with a black mane and tail. He went past the stalls without stopping. He'd never been a fearless horseman. He knew the animals sensed that; whenever he was alone with them, he felt they exhibited contempt for him.

At the rear of the stables, a rough stairway led to the groom's quarters, four rooms occupied by an old deaf-mute Negro named Worley and his sixteen-year-old daughter, Emily. He liked Worley. He sometimes played cards with Worley. Now, he called up the stairs and when nobody responded, he climbed to find Worley asleep in an old rocker.

Leopold shook him awake. "Where's Emily, old man?"

Rubbing his eyes, Worley peered at him through his knuckles.

"Do you want champagne?"

Worley shook his head.

"You know I'm going away to fight for you?"

Worley nodded.

"I'm going to go into the worst of it. I'll come back a hero—like Dick Dowling." He watched Worley warm his cracked palms in front of the cast-iron stove. The rocker creaked. "Don't you care?" Leopold asked. "Don't you care how the war comes out?" He was weaving slightly. "You don't care, do you?"

Worley was staring at the flames in the black hole of the stove's belly. His white bush of hair gleamed. Leopold took another swallow from the beaker. "It's too late, isn't it?" he said. He had no idea what he meant. Worley didn't look up. Setting the beaker on a newspaper-covered table, Leopold frowned, trying to remember why he had come. He couldn't remember, so he turned on his heel and left.

The night seemed colder than it had been before. A veil of clouds obscured the moon, and from faraway came the faint rumble of thunder. He was moving through the grove of oaks when he heard Elizabeth call his name. A white apparition appeared, floating toward him, and he wished he hadn't left the beaker of champagne upstairs.

"I can't find them anywhere," Elizabeth said, halting in front of him.

"Everybody's looking for them—and then you disappeared, too!" She scrutinized him. "You've had too much to drink, haven't you?"

He looked up at the sky. The moon mocked him through the clouds. "It's going to rain," he said. "You should be inside, dancing with all those eligible young men."

A furrow appeared between Elizabeth's brows. "You know about Joel Lewis. You know we made love before he left. You're the only one I confided in." She took his hand between hers and pressed it to the hollow in her throat. He could feel her pulse beating there. "I don't believe he was killed at Vicksburg. I dream about him—"

He took his hand away. He couldn't look into her face. She was wearing a small cameo pin on her breast. He focused on that.

"What is it?" Elizabeth asked softly. "What's the matter? You can tell *me*—"

He shook his head. "I'm not like you," he said. "I'm not like any of you—Alfred or Hannah or Elijah." Strange emotions stirred in him. He envied Elizabeth in some way he didn't comprehend. The alcohol released salacious thoughts that frightened him.

"You're being morbid," Elizabeth said.

"He bought me a battalion. Did you know that? He's a speculator. A traitor. I don't want a battalion bought with his money—" He broke off abruptly, feeling suddenly dizzy as though he might faint. He could hear Elizabeth trying to soothe him, talking gently as though to a small boy. He heard the thunder again, like an echo of something he couldn't fathom. "I owe gambling debts," he heard himself say. "More than I can pay." He wondered why he needed to say that. He wondered why it mattered.

"You can get the money from Mamma."

"Naturally." He spoke with disdain. "Whatever I want, she'll give me, won't she?" He straightened his shoulders. His mother would weep and make frenzied gestures and extract false promises from him. Then that peculiar disaffected look would cross her face and she'd throw her arms around him—he'd grown to despise displays of affection—and she'd bend, go back on her word, placate him.

"Let's go inside." Elizabeth was staring at him.

"Joel Lewis is dead."

"Don't be cruel." Tears sprang to Elizabeth's eyes.

"Do you know why he bought me that battalion? Because he doesn't expect anything of me. Did you know that? Did you ever notice the way he looks at me—like there's a flaw he can see and I can't."

"I won't listen—"

"It's true." It struck him he had never looked into his father's eyes and seen himself. It struck him he was going off to war without ever having been in bed with a girl. The two thoughts seemed connected, he didn't know how. "You're looking at me the same way," he said.

"No—I'm not."

"It's too late, isn't it?" He heard the thunder roll again. He wondered what he meant.

"Too late for *what?*" Elizabeth cried.

He grabbed her hand and started to run, pulling her after him through the garden. "Let's ask them to play a Virginia reel—" he shouted.

Anna's slippers barely grazed the ballroom floor. Eager hands caught her firmly about the waist and swung her around the edge of the circle, sending her soaring from one admirer to another. *"Radiant . . ."* a partner murmured. *"More beautiful than any of the girls . . ."* another exclaimed. *"Amazing . . ."* she heard from the sidelines, *"How does she do it?"* Anna threw her head back and burst into laughter each time she passed Ben and their eyes met.

Around her, faces gleamed. The mirrors blurred into rainbows of swirling color. Accelerated by the hearty tempo of the Virginia reel and heightened by the sudden burst of rain that spattered against the french doors, the gaiety climbed to its highest peak. Pale complexions flushed. Whispered compliments teetered on bold requests for assignations. Under the lights, shoulders glistened pearl-like and young breasts heaved, rising and falling, hearts palpitating visibly as the dancers merged and parted, caught up in the vibrant music and the thrill of shared secrets and the daring search for that special pair of arms, that certain pair of eyes.

Then the musicians started to play louder and faster and the dancers began to plunge in and out of each other's arms, spinning in dervishlike circles until they were dancing on the edge of frenzy—Anna could feel herself seized by it—whirling as though nothing beyond the dance had ever existed. The music rose, throbbing, and the dancers reeled even faster, like birds hurtling before the threat of the thunderstorm. Courting vertigo and filling the air with shrieks and cries, they defied the imminence of supper and the recognition that the evening was three-quarters gone, hurtling faster and faster as if the dance would never end.

Then something altered suddenly. A cold wind stirred and passed through the ballroom like a common shiver. As if a whip had cracked the air, the dancers halted. A whisper ran through the hall. A hush fell.

The musicians continued to play, slower and slower, like an animal crying.

Turning, Anna froze.

Like a ghost she had failed to exorcise, a wounded soldier occupied the ballroom entrance. He was no more than twenty, wearing a rain-soaked shirt of coarse cotton and mud-caked trousers which had once been Confederate gray. His left leg, amputated at the knee, was wrapped in a bloody bandage and, in lieu of crutches, he was holding his gaunt frame upright by two rifles placed under his armpits. From a face lined with despair, he stared out at them through eyes like burned holes. He stood silent and motionless. Then all at once, like a tree crashing, he fell.

The music ceased.

Somebody screamed.

Through the confusion, Anna rushed toward the fallen boy. She was bending over him when Samuel hurried over to her.

"There's more outside," he said. "There's hundreds."

A procession of doom filled the street.

The rain poured down on a ghost-train of wagons that snaked into the darkness as far as the eye could see.

The Negroes, their white livery instantly soaked, came out bearing their hurricane lamps aloft. Now the flickering lights illuminated a nightmare: bodies piled on bodies, with only the sounds of agony and the twitching of limbs to distinguish men from corpses.

"We've been traveling for weeks," the captain said. "The hospital's full." Rain pounded against his tattered epaulets. "We need a place to billet them—"

From under a cape held over her head like a tent, Anna's eyes moved down the street. A wave of protest surged within her. Then it crested and broke, like the sea crashing.

"At Chickamauga, fifteen hundred were wounded in one battle—"
The captain was addressing Ben; the rain streamed down his face like
tears. "They were sent to the railroad terminal on the river. The surgeons worked there, but there weren't enough—"

The captain's voice rang in Anna's breast. Lightning split the sky
and thunder rolled.

"At Vicksburg, Grant paroled thirty thousand. At least half were
casualties of some kind—" The captain's stare, fixed on Ben, was
strangely opaque. With a shock, Anna realized he was sightless.
"They're Texans, all," he said, "from around these parts—"

Ben whirled around. Striding through the rain, hands cupped around
his mouth, he called out over the wagons, "It's all right! Buck up,
there! You're going to get care! You're home!"

The ballroom was a sea of human carnage.

Bodies stretched out on makeshift pallets, filling the hall from end to
end.

And more arrived.

They were carried on improvised stretchers through the vestibule by
Negroes and men wearing velvet evening coats, past jeweled women
and girls in white dresses, weeping.

"There's no time for weeping—" Anna cried.

Orders poured from her.

"Bring straw from neighboring stables for more pallets . . . bring
blankets and linens from every house and brandy from every cellar
. . . get morphine and sulphur and iodine from the pharmacy . . ."

Young men in neat pressed uniforms, far from the war only minutes
ago, leaped to do her bidding.

"Rip up sheets for bandages . . . fill every kettle on the stove . . .
find Beatrice. Tell her to boil up supper's roasted partridges for
soup . . ."

The girls obeyed.

"Everybody out—except those who are willing to help!" Anna
shouted. She went looking for Dorsey who was a surgeon. "We'll need
instruments—"

And still more men came.

They came limping, or dragging themselves, staggering on bleeding feet across the ballroom floor, those who could walk supporting the others, faint from loss of blood or numb from pain, some wounded in two and three places. Blinking under the chandeliers, they came with shattered limbs and broken skulls, stinking from infection and rotting sores and unhealed wounds and blistered flesh, faces brilliant with fever and rasping with the hard labored breathing of pneumonia-ridden lungs.

They came with spirit seared as deep as flesh, with haunted eyes and mute pleas, voices immobilized from shock, some stunned into paralysis, some quaking and shuddering, others making gallant jokes or hoarse attempts at laughter, clutching at the remnants of rage or hope or patriotism, the tattered beliefs that had left them butchered, or grasping at the vestiges of remembered chivalry, a murmured *"Thank you, ma'am,"* or *"By your leave."*

A schoolmate of Leopold's went past . . . the son of friends in Galveston . . . a cowhand who had worked for Ben . . . a planter's boy from Beaumont . . . an Anderson cousin falsely reported as a deserter.

In the dining room, cleared of silver and china, Dorsey set up a medical station, instruments and medicines laid out, silver chafing dishes brimming with hot water. Dorsey, well past sixty, looked frightened. "We can't do this by ourselves!"

"We'll have to," Anna retorted. She looked around for Ben, but Ben had vanished.

In the ballroom, she moved among the wounded, giving orders to Elizabeth and the other girls, instructing them—dispensing soup and blankets and brandy and morphine—cleaning festering wounds, changing blood-caked bandages, lancing sores, making splints from broom handles and searing wounds with pokers from the fireplace—in an endless hopeless task of mercy.

"Oliver Hunter, ma'am—don't you remember me?"

"Albert Carney—my pa works at the sawmill."

"Only one thing I'm sorry about ma'am—is that I was wounded in the back. It makes me look like a coward."

"I'll tell you the way it is, ma'am. The minié ball, it leaves a hole. The shell rents the body. And the shrapnel, it cuts a gash like being thrust with a spear."

"See this powder burn in my Bible? If I hadn't been carrying it by my heart, I'd be a dead corporal."

Someone touched her shoulder. She looked up to find Ben standing with three men. She recognized one as the veterinarian who sometimes tended their horses. The second was a dentist wearing his nightshirt tucked into his trousers. The third was a pharmacist on Main Street. "Doctors," Ben said.

"Roused me from bed," the dentist said irritably, "at gunpoint."

Anna rose. "There's coffee in the kitchen and medical supplies in the dining room." She watched them pick their way around and across the wounded. Then, smoothing her blood-stained skirt with hands so chafed they were raw, she sent Ben a stricken look. "They're not enough."

Ben took her in his arms.

"I thought we'd seen the worst of it in our lives," she whispered against his chest.

Instead of answering, he drew her closer. She could hear his heartbeat. Listening to it, she felt her youth ebb away. His heartbeat, pounding in her ears, seemed to mark something passing from her life. She felt an imperceptible acquiescence occur, an acceptance of some inexorable thing that had no name. Then deep within her, a dam cracked to admit mortality.

He released her to a sense of overwhelming loss.

Somebody was singing:

"Jeff Davis rides a white horse
Lincoln rides a mule
Jeff Davis is a gentleman
Lincoln is a fool."

A young boy, in the throes of delirium, was crying out, still caught in vivid dreams of battle. Another shuddered in the first spasms of lockjaw. Another begged for morphine; lying directly beside him, his friend was dead.

Moving back among the sea of bodies, she did what she could. Time moved her. Duty moved her. Compassion failed her. She worked in a daze, as though something had snapped in her.

Three times, Elizabeth called her name before she heard her.

Elizabeth was cradling a boy whose face was swathed in bandages. "It's Mamma," she said to him. Her cheeks were wet with tears.

"I know you can't recognize me, ma'am," the boy said. "I'm Joel Lewis . . ."

"I'm going to marry him, Mamma," Elizabeth said.

The rain quit.

Through the french doors of the ballroom, Anna saw the first rays of dawn break over the garden. Looking up from tending a feverish soldier, she stared at the light like someone waking from a dream. Then rising, she moved wearily across the room to open a door and step out.

She had the feeling someone had called her. She could hear strange sounds, as if a crowd had gathered somewhere nearby. A need stirred in her to see her children, to account for the living. Were Hannah and Elijah asleep? Where was Ben? Where was Leopold?

The morning was cold. Broken lights dangled sadly in a brisk wind; wet ash filled the warming braziers. White rose petals, beaten and crushed by the rain, littered the ground. One of the swans, circling within its marble prison, feathers matted and head bent, cried out mournfully.

A tremor of exhaustion passed through her. Voices floated on the air, like people on the streets. It was too early, she thought. Confused, she looked back through the glass, her eyes scanning the rows of ravaged bodies until she found Elizabeth. Elizabeth's back was propped against the wall. Elizabeth slept, cradling Joel Lewis' bandaged head.

Joel Lewis . . . Anna thought. He was Leopold's age. She had looked into his eyes. His eyes were a thousand years old. "I love him," Elizabeth had said. Joel Lewis would live. And he would leave. And he would take Elizabeth with him.

She turned and walked out into the garden, away from the sounds. She thought about those who had died during the night. At the moment of death, their faces had filled with light, as if something had been freed in them. Was it because they were no longer bound to earthly pursuits—no longer driven by desire, or imprisoned by suffering? Was death nothing? Or did it bind one forever to all men and to all living creatures?

Something had changed in her. What? For an instant last night, when Ben was holding her, she had known what it was. Now it escaped her.

The roses would have to be dug up and replaced, she thought.

Moving farther from the house, she passed through the grove of oaks. The wind whipped the leaves. Another shiver passed through her. Then she saw Ben's figure emerging from the stables. When he was close enough, she said, "If you touch me, I'll cry—and I'll never stop."

"I watched you last night. Nobody else could have done what you did last night."

"Where have you been?"

"There's a mob out front. They've been coming all night. We had to lock the gates. God knows how they got word. They've come from miles around hoping their husbands or their sons are inside." He managed a tired grin. "Never let it be said that Anna Calder gave a ball and nobody came."

"Let them in," she said.

"Leopold slept in the stables."

"I'll see to him." She reached up and held his face between her hands. "Hannah and Elijah—make sure they're all right."

"Are you?"

She nodded. "Yes."

Inside the stables, she found Leopold in one of the empty stalls. He wasn't asleep. He had made a pallet of straw, like the wounded soldiers inside and, hands clasped around his knees, he was puffing on one of Ben's cigars.

"That's dangerous," she said quietly.

"Did he tell you?" Leopold's eyes were frightened. They made her afraid.

"What?"

"About the battalion?"

"He loves you," she said. It sounded hollow, without meaning.

"Does he?"

"Yes."

"I'm going to be a damned fine captain."

"You'll do well, son." The charade pierced her heart.

"I owe gambling debts. They won't take Confederate money. Before I go, I want to clear the family name—"

She saw he was manipulating her. She saw she had exercised a patience without limits, the kind one exhibited with an aging relative from whom one hopes to gain an inheritance or absolution. She wanted to weep and cradle him in her arms. His eyes told her he didn't want that.

"You'll clear my debts, won't you?"

Fatigue rent the veil. She saw him as he was. She saw herself and what she had done. She had given him power over her and robbed him of power over himself.

She wanted to say: *"Your father was Eduard von Lanz."* What would she say about him? *"He was a fine soldier."*

Instead she nodded.

"There's something else I want you to do for me," he said in a queer tone. "When I'm gone—I want you to take care of Emily."

She wanted to say: *"You were conceived from my first passion and born from my courage."* She wanted to cry out: *"How did this happen? Why do you not have more bravery than the others?"*

"Worley's daughter," he said in the same queer tone. "You know what I'm talking about, don't you?" He laughed. She heard the falseness in it, and the pain. She heard the lie. "I'm a man," he said. "Like Pappa. A bit too bold, maybe."

She saw it wasn't his lie. It was her own lie, and Ben's—Ben had collaborated in it. She saw the lie had robbed him of the truth.

She wanted to tell him. She couldn't. Instead, she nodded again. It's too late, she thought.

29

Dear Nicolai,

I write this on a high bluff overlooking the river. There was once a hamlet here. It has been burned, like everything else, to rubble. We have done that. The fires have driven off even the birds. Tonight, God is silent except for the call of one surviving whippoorwill and the occasional cry of a wounded man in sleep.

In your last letter, you said the Tribune reports the Union is winning this war. I hope so. As for this Red River campaign, if there is to be an invasion of Texas, it will take far longer and cost more lives than anyone imagined. A soldier in this wilderness is far from cries of glory, and our Moses—Commanding-General Banks—is neither leader nor prophet. The 13th Corps was cut to pieces at Pleasant Hill, and all that remains of the 130th Illinois is a youth in a coonskin cap. The 153rd New York fared not much better. I was hit by a ball that went through my knapsack. Something preserves me, perhaps your prayer that God should cover my head in battle.

You seem very far away tonight. For days, a feeling has nagged me that there's something wrong at home. To bring you closer, I remind myself of what it must have been for you to raise a son who wasn't yours and to carry him to freedom. You are to me the good man by whom I judge myself, and tonight I think: Nicolai would weep at the devastation.

Our retreating column commits nothing but destruction. Between

*Pleasant Hill and Grand Encore, the flaming countryside lit our way at
night—we were ordered to set torch to everything at hand. Cows and
horses, hogs and mules, lay dead along the road. In front of us, burning ambulances and wagons obstructed the path of the wounded and
men asleep from exhaustion in their saddles rode over our unburied
dead. We destroyed houses as well as cotton gins. Even the Negroes'
cabins were burned. Those we came to free wept in despair by
blackened chimneys. Others clogged the road, women walking like Af-
ricans with bundles on their heads, and homeless families riding mule
carts piled with old clothes and iron pots and babies. Ours is a Godless
exodus. They are the Jews and we are the Egyptians.*

How far away I am!

*Your last letter came a month ago. I pray the mails are at fault.
Your health concerns me. A New York winter takes its tolls of those in
open stalls, and I keep remembering that persistent cough that always
grips you in the spring. Before the fires here, I saw white cranes and
herons in the swamp willows, and wild magnolias, and cypress trees
heavy with Spanish moss. It was strangely beautiful. Sometimes I think
how much better when the war is over, this climate would be for you.*

*Be assured I still love Lincoln and our cause. The men here are my
boon companions and we fight fiercely. Yet, the South has touched my
heart. All these things are true.*

Your son,
Jacob Lubeck

30

The wagons were rumbling across the ranch again, too far from the house to be seen, but Anna recognized the sound; she had heard it since March, an echo in the earth before Ben disappeared for days at a time.

She was seated at her dressing table, brushing her hair. "In June," she said. Saying it aloud made her suddenly afraid.

Ben came up behind her. A slow grin broke his jaw. He met her eyes in the glass. "Are you sure?"

"I thought we might call him James—"

"You thought Elizabeth was going to be Alfred—remember?" He raised her to her feet and wrapped his arms around her. His arms felt powerful. They told her nothing could happen to her.

"Maybe the war will be over by then," she whispered.

It was a cold bitter December. The wind blew fiercely from the north and the sky was as gray as the schoolroom slate where the young tutor, Charles Ramsey, chalked the alphabet for Daniel. They had brought Ramsey back from Houston in March—wounded at Chattanooga, he limped badly. He had prepared Alfred for enrollment in Houston Academy. Now, he was teaching five-year-old Daniel to read. He was teaching Hannah, French and Eli, geometry. Anna left the lessons to Ramsey; they tired her.

She was thirty-nine.

The pregnancy threatened to drain her vigor; she denied it. By December, she was already losing her suppleness, but refused to acknowledge it. She was too old for childbearing, a small voice whispered; she was in the wrong season. The heart knows no seasons, another voice said.

She immersed herself in the books and the ranch records and she wrote letters for Ben. Often, weariness overtook her. The night before Ben left, she fell asleep at the desk in the study and he found her there, her head cradled in her arms and when he woke her, tears were streaming down her face.

"I was dreaming about Sherman. Men marching and burning. It was terrible—"

"Leopold's in Texas," he said gently.

"Union soldiers are in the Davis Mountains."

"The Comanches won't let them come any farther than that."

Tenderly, he lifted her into his arms and carried her upstairs and put her to bed like a child.

"I can never go back to that house in Houston." The image of the wounded soldiers still haunted her.

"We'll build a new one."

"A house like this one," she said. "Adobe brick. With courtyards and galleries." She closed her eyes. She could see the stone house in Houston, being used now by the Confederacy as a temporary hospital. She blotted it out. "I want it built on a rise," she said, "with huge oaks all around and a view of the river."

"You'll have it by summer."

"What shall we call it?"

"James." He smiled.

"The house—"

He bent over and brushed her forehead with his lips. "River Oaks."

"How long will you be away?"

"Not long."

"Don't go—"

"I have to," he said.

She threw herself into preparing for Christmas.

Samuel filled the smokehouse with hams. She set a half-dozen Negro women to making clothes for the servants and their families. She ordered a tree for the drawing room and another for the servants' quarters and another to be set up in the bunkhouse for the cowhands and the *vaqueros*. With Beatrice, she shelled nuts and preserved citron for the Christmas cakes. She did these things in bursts, with effort, despite a recurring feeling of foreboding. She missed Elizabeth, she told herself. She missed Ben.

She kept up with the books. The last three shiploads of cotton had brought two dollars a pound paid in gold. The wagons had returned from the Rio Grande with salt and blankets and munitions. The blockade had tightened, Ben had said. Garras had made arrangements for the ships to Matamoros to fly the Mexican flag. Going over the bills of lading and making entries in the ledger, she saw they were growing richer than she had ever imagined.

Lambert's regular letter said six more Calder warehouses had been completed at the foot of Main Street; the warehouses already bulged with cotton. The dredging of the ship channel was continuing, Lambert reported, deep enough to accommodate ocean steamers. He was putting to use hundreds of the slaves sent in from all over the South for safekeeping. Except for the military outpost, Galveston was a ghost town. When the war ended, Houston would reign as the major port—for the first year alone, Lambert estimated a million dollars in fees. Reading Lambert's report, she saw they would grow richer still, rich beyond her powers of conception.

The light was almost gone. Rising, she massaged her sore shoulders and crossed to the window. Buzzards circled at dusk. She watched one of them sail overhead, wings spread wide as it dipped and soared, followed by a smaller buzzard that duplicated its pattern exactly. Watching, it suddenly occurred to her that predators bred predators and raised them and taught them by example. It was a strange thought. She realized her hands had strayed to her abdomen even as she dismissed it. From the children's quarters, she could hear the piano; Ramsey was playing Christmas carols.

"Señora?" Garras spoke from the doorway. Anna turned. Garras' hair was wet, plastered to his head, and he had tucked a clean unpressed shirt into his dusty trousers. She saw he was still wearing chaps and his holster. "Samuel said you wanted to see me—"

"Yes."

Garras waited.

"Is it quiet this evening?"

"It seems so." Garras' hands rested lightly on his holster. "I doubled the patrols. I always do when he's gone."

A sigh escaped Anna. "Do you know how difficult it will be for Ben without you?"

"I'm sorry." His words had a bitter edge.

"Don't you understand?" She searched Garras' face. "To ask Ben to give away a piece of land is like asking him to give away part of himself."

A shadow fell across Garras' eyes. "There's nothing to talk about, *Señora*."

"I'm fond of you—you know that, don't you?"

Garras made no response.

Anna went back to the desk and sat down. "I understand why you wanted the land. I understand why you wouldn't take the money. You want his acceptance. You want to be recognized. I've thought about it a great deal." She opened a drawer and took out a map and began to unfold it. "I have a parcel of land of my own," she said. "I acquired it under unusual circumstances—nearly twenty years ago—it belonged to a man named Mueller." She hesitated. An image of Mueller flashed—Mueller's figure shattering under her shotgun blast. "The land certificates were recorded," she said. "It's all legal." Again, she hesitated. She had the strange feeling Garras had already sensed it was blood land, tainted. "It's isolated land," she said, "but it's good land—here—near the Rio Grande." She looked up. "I'd like you to have it."

Garras remained silent. Not a muscle moved. She could see the stubbornness in his face and the fierce pride. Then he shook his head. "As soon as he returns, I leave for Matamoros."

"You're twenty-six. How can you want to become a priest? And never marry? Never have children?" She halted. She felt a sudden discomfort. "Ben loves you," she said quietly. "He needs you."

"No," Garras said. "He loves nothing. He needs no one."

"You don't understand him. This is a man who's experienced more poverty and more loss than you can ever imagine. This is a man who was always driven by one thing—land. But he's always followed his own conscience, and he loves in his own way—" Something in Garras' face stopped her.

"It's you who don't understand him," Garras answered. Anna saw fire flare in his eyes. "This is a man who's loyal to nothing. I know the greed that comes from poverty. That's not what drives him. His is a different kind of greed. It eats up everything and everyone it touches."

"That's a lie—" Anna cried.

Garras came across the room. The desk was between them. "This is a man who turns everything into figures," he said. He gestured at the ledger. "Like these numbers—" he spoke quietly now, with unmistakable conviction. Resting his palms on the desk, he leaned forward. "These aren't numbers," he said, "they're men. Like me. For every bale of cotton you record, somebody risks a charge of treason or death by cannonfire. Do you know how many men have been killed on those contraband ships? Do you know how many men have been captured and are rotting in jail?"

"It's not your place to tell me these things—" Anna's heart started to pound.

"I know my place," Garras said. "He paid seven dollars for me. He taught me to read and to speak English and to use a knife and fork. He taught me to walk in his shadow." Garras straightened. "He taught me to love him and to hate him," he said.

"I won't listen to that." Anna's voice broke. It was too late. She had listened. She had heard. Garras' voice rang in her ears.

Garras stared at her. The bitterness in his eyes made her remember the creature Ben had brought back from the Mexican War. *"A little savage,"* Ben had called him. Against her volition, she recognized what she saw. It was pain.

"I'm sorry," she whispered.

"I want to be free," Garras said softly. "But I don't know how to set myself free. The only way I can do it is to serve a power higher than he is." His eyes flashed with a final bolt of departing anger. "He's bigger than all of us, but he's not God."

When she awoke, it was close to midnight. The lamp on the desk had grown dim while she slept. Beatrice had left a tray; the food looked cold and unappetizing. She hadn't heard Beatrice come and go. The sleep had drugged her without salvaging her. She felt a weight in her chest like unshed tears, as if Garras had held up a harsh mirror and, looking into it, she had seen a strange and cruel aspect of Ben and an Anna she had been unwilling to recognize.

When had it changed? At what point had it happened? When had the
urges of the heart become the demands of ambition? When had the
courage of survival become the habit of exploitation? And who was she
addressing—herself or Ben?

Once more, she crossed to the window. The night was black. She
could hear the eerie creaking of the wind and the tumbleweeds
brushing against the house. Overhead, a lone star glinted. A shadow
passed across the pale winter moon like the buzzard she'd seen earlier,
like a shadow of mortality. Again, her hands strayed to her womb, and
she suddenly saw the rekindling of her passion had been meant to
deflect aging; the act of procreation had been meant to defy death. She
had asked a question and now the answer came. She saw that ambition
and greed—like the child gestating within her—broke through as an
omen or a warning. Behind it were other truths; she knew Garras had
left them.

She shut them out.

Carrying the lamp, she left the study and climbed the stairs, listening
to the night noises. She climbed slowly, dreading the empty bedroom,
dreading the lonely bed.

Pregnancy had made her vulnerable, she told herself.

The fire was going. Samuel had added mesquite. As she entered, she
was struck by the beauty of the firelight flickering over the polished
bedposts and the fragile lace borders on the pillowslips and the veined
marble washstand. Each object seemed new and indescribably clear as
though she were looking at it for the first time. The air tingled. In it
was the faint scent of something like camphor or sage. Halting, she was
beset by the strange feeling that she was experiencing the room, not
through her own senses, but through the perceptions of some invisible
presence that contemplated the false peace while waiting to disrupt it.
She told herself she was foolish. She made herself cross the room. She
set the lamp down with a sense of someone watching her. In order to
turn she had to instruct herself. Then she felt her blood freeze.

He materialized from the shadows. He was tall and bronzed, at least
six feet, wearing a fringed hide shirt and leggings and a medicine bag
on his belt. His thick black hair was sheared into a Comanche scalp-
lock and fastened into a long braid laced with rawhide and hammered
silver discs and the fine glimmer of hummingbirds' wings. He wasn't a
warrior. She could see there was no red paint on his face—he was

painted instead, with white clay, the mark of an Indian seeking a vision —and around his neck, the polished stones of a sacred necklace glinted.

Fear constricted her throat. No sound came from it. He nodded as if he had silenced her. She heard midnight strike. She heard herself whisper, "What do you want?"

He turned around slowly. She saw the smear of fresh blood on his shirt. The wound was high on his left shoulder, near the nape of his neck. When he faced her again, he was brandishing a knife.

Once more, she tried to call out. He shook his head. Reaching behind him, he slit the rawhide shirt. She heard it rip, like flesh tearing. Then he stooped and sharpened the blade against the stone hearth and held it in the fire until it was white-hot. Rising, he offered her the knife. Immobile, she stared at it. He took her hand and closed it around the handle. Then he turned his back and knelt in front of her. She stared at his back. She saw herself plunging the knife into his back. She felt he could see the image cross her mind. She felt his certainty; he had no fear she would act on it.

Her legs moved; she brought the lamp closer. Her hands washed the wound and probed for the bullet. No sound escaped him. Downstairs, the clock ticked on. She could see their shadows on the wall, eerily connected, silent. When she found the bullet and removed it, he took a coal from the fireplace and seared the wound himself.

He rose and reclaimed his knife. Tears were streaming down her cheeks. He raised two fingers and touched her forehead. For a long moment, he looked steadily into her eyes. With a shock, she saw he was young, no older than Leopold, and his eyes were a startling blue.

"Tell him she's dead," he said. It was the first time he'd spoken.

"Who? Who are you talking about?"

He opened the medicine bag on his belt. She watched him extract a small bundle of herbs. He closed his eyes and chewed them carefully. Then he stooped and smeared a bit of the juice on the sole of each foot. On one, she caught sight of a mark, two interlocking circles, tattooed.

"I buried her in the mountains," he said, rising. "A party of Union soldiers came upon me there." As he spoke, he backed slowly toward the door. "Tell him her grave is north of the crabapple orchard, past the mescal pit and the Indian burial grounds." He paused in the door-

way. "Tell him Black Wing buried her where he watched the coyotes
eat the heart of a deer."

"Who? Who is *she?*"

"Selinda," he said. "My mother."

"Bendejo—?"

"Black Wing," he said. Then he was gone.

Trembling, she fell across the bed and wept.

31

It was over.

Enemies, wielding bayonets and firing muskets—cousins and strangers divided into armies by lines drawn on a map and by ideology most of them failed to comprehend and by opposing economic systems under which few of them would profit—were ordered to cease and desist. Official notice had been given: It was over.

"Not in Texas," Ben said.

"Outlaws and diehards—" Foster replied.

Colonel Foster was perched on a blue velvet chair in the drawing room, spine held upright and knees stiff, a husky gray-bearded man with weary eyes, his Union uniform dusty and rumpled. Ben was lighting a Mexican cigar. Beatrice had brought tea. Ben had laced it with brandy. Listening, Anna continued to stare out the window.

Leopold will come home, she thought. *Any day now.*

Only a part of her registered what they were saying. Peace, Foster called it. But a month had passed since Lee had surrendered at Appomattox and still they were fighting.

"—deserters swarming up the Buffalo Bayou from Galveston," Foster was saying. "You know they sacked the Ordnance Depot at Houston? They're pillaging stores in San Antonio. They're threatening to rob the state treasury and distribute the money. And it's only the beginning. There's going to be a rash of lawlessness—jayhawkers, guerillas, highwaymen—thousands of Negroes wandering and starving, looking for the *glory road*. And the damned Indians—"

"The buffalo are gone," Ben said. "Every winter when their supplies run out, they sue for peace—and every spring they go raiding again." He shrugged. "I've always made my own treaties with them."

"We need somebody who knows how to restore order to this territory."

"I'm a rancher."

Anna rose. She moved awkwardly, eight months with child. Hands crossed on her swollen womb, she took a seat at the window and looked out toward the road. It was May. The oleanders were in bloom. Dust blew in swirls close to the ground and the sky was china blue. She could see Foster's aides, three of them, mounted on horseback. She knew there were other Federal soldiers out there, out of sight, victors turned shepherds of the collapse of the Confederacy which would perish like a dinosaur, bellowing and flailing long past the end. It occurred to her that Leopold might be nearby, waiting for the soldiers to leave.

The new house in Houston was nearly finished. *After the baby comes, I'll take Leopold to Houston,* she thought.

"My business is land. Cattle," Ben was saying.

"We both know cattle are running wild around here," Foster answered. "For the next couple of years, you're going to be giving beef away." Foster was pouring brandy into his teacup. "Your real business is running this part of Texas."

"Why should I do your job for you?"

"Texans won't submit to blue-coat rule. We both know that. It'll only be another kind of war." Foster drained his cup and set it down. "You've got one of the larger stakes in settling this state back to normal."

"I might take it on if Lincoln were alive. Lincoln was bigger than the split. But Johnson—"

"If you were guaranteed a free hand?"

"There was never any question of that."

"And—"

"I'd need other guarantees."

"No interference with the port in Houston." Foster had risen; he was pacing, now. "Hands off all Calder property, including the contraband arms and the illegal cotton in your warehouses. We close our eyes while you transfer that fleet of ships you were running under the Mexican flag." Foster paused. "Have I missed anything?"

"Lambert."

"—immunity."

"There's a piece of land," Ben said. "It's up in the mountains near the Union fort. It includes some Indian burial grounds and a crabapple orchard—"

"Godforsaken land."

"To some."

"I'll see you get title."

"My son's in the Confederacy. Captain Leopold Calder. Cavalry. His battalion's somewhere near Brownsville. Nobody knows if they've gotten word yet of Lee's surrender."

"I'll have him sent back with an escort."

Anna turned from the window. Foster was extending his hand. She watched Ben rise and take it.

"When?" Anna asked.

"As fast as a horse can travel," Foster said.

The day came.

Before dawn, her eyes flew open in tremulous recognition that the day had arrived. Summoned from sleep by the erratic thumping of her own heart, and by the child awake and active in her womb, thrashing about in its amniotic sea, she succumbed to a foreboding which had no name. *Leopold will come home today,* she thought—but the incantation inspired only alarm.

Ben was lying beside her, mysterious and impenetrable in sleep, as still as the earth's breathing which could be heard only at night. She reached out to touch him, then drew her hand back, impelled by another, more vital demand.

She left him asleep and descended the stairs, drawn toward the dawn as if to a prearranged meeting. Clad in a dressing gown—trailing almond-colored silk in the dust outside, bare feet crushing fallen masses of withered oleander blossoms—she moved away from the house until the road was in sight. Then she stopped and, standing in the open, she watched the day break, a wall of light pushing up from the east over the naked land. The dressing gown billowed around her in the wind.

She gathered it to her and lifted her face to the sky, a face grown gaunt as her womb had thickened, as though the child had drawn everything to itself, leaving her bereft.

She stood, waiting. As she watched, phosphorescent strands streaked the fading darkness, like rips in a mourning veil. Then, all at once, a flaming aurora burst like a fire on the horizon to ignite the sky. She could feel the heat. Her eyes burned and the wind stung her cheeks.

The sun rose like a red cavernous hole through which she might be hurled to be tempered and transformed for worlds beyond. Mesmerized, she watched until it frightened her. Then she pulled her eyes away and turned them westward where the road snaked toward the mountains. The sun's rays severed the haze and struck the granite range like knife blades splintering. Sparks whirled in the air before her eyes and settled like specks of dust on the horizon. Far off, the specks moved. Shading her eyes with both hands, she peered out toward the farthest point on the road where it narrowed to a spot of dazzling light. She saw the specks were men.

Were they? Were they moving? Was Leopold one of those tiny dots, vanishing and reappearing through pockets of glare that obscured the harsh and barren earth? How many times had she been here in her mind's eye?—looking down this road, hoping to claim Leopold from among the stragglers and the angry soldiers trudging bone-tired and bitter from defeat.

It appeared to be a small band, traveling on horseback at an interminable pace. Was it? Yes. Were there four or five? Larger than specks now, they could almost be counted.

Beside her shadow on the earth, another shadow fell. Gently, Ben wrapped a cloak around her. His hand rested lightly on her shoulder. She was afraid to look at him. Like looking into the sun again, her eyes were drawn to his and she was blinded for an instant. He said nothing, but something passed between them, as if he knew what she refused to know.

She fixed her gaze steadily on the road again. Her ears strained for the thud of hoofbeats. She imagined how Leopold would be. Different, she thought. War had matured him, she thought. He had left as a petulant boy. He'd return as a man in his own right. The thought set her trembling. In the sunlit silence, she heard the wail of the wind.

Then the first clopping sounds cleaved the air and the figures swelled forward, moving into focus through a blast of white dust. She saw four horsemen. Three were wearing tattered blue, the uniforms of Union soldiers—the fourth wore gray. Time stopped. Her heart ceased. Her breath came in gasps. Fair hair flashed in the sunlight. She reared forward suddenly, but Ben's hand restrained her.

The figures blurred. Then she saw what Ben saw.

He looked like a fallen bird hunched in the saddle. Twisted, he swung from side to side, legs dangling and arms slung over his drooping head, flapping against the horse's mane, his hands strapped together underneath to hold him astride. The horse moved slowly, jerkily, like a mule being switched, reluctantly carrying its spiritless burden.

A treacherous chill overtook her. A shadow fell, like a cloud crossing the sun. She stood frozen. Then breaking from Ben's grasp, she bolted down the road.

The horsemen stopped. She reached out and touched her son. His eyes were closed. His face was wooden. She stroked his head. She laid her hand on his heart. She felt herself become a vessel. She felt sorrow pour through her, liquid as blood, with nothing to halt its flow. It rendered her heart useless.

"He's in delirium." The boy who spoke was a stranger. How dare he violate her? "Septicemia," he said, dismounting. He spoke in a murmur, clutching his cap in his hand. He told her Leopold was dying.

For a moment, she grew blind and deaf. Then fury rose in her. How dare he tell her? There was no need. She *knew*. She had known since she opened her eyes. Her hand, still pressing against Leopold's chest, felt no life throbbing in him. Her hand told her Leopold was no longer dying. The knowledge pierced her. It seemed quick and harmless— nothing more than a cold quick thrust, like being pierced with an icicle. Only as it dissolved in the sunlight, did she feel it as a mortal wound.

It was three hundred yards to the house.

Ben swung Leopold into his arms and carried him.

The sun swam overhead, red and futile. The sky turned hard and flat, pressing down upon her. Her cloak rattled in the wind, rising and falling like the wings of a vulture about to take flight with its prey. Shafts of pain struck her womb like flashes of lightning. Then she heard someone singing, singing in German, singing the sweet sad strains of an old lullaby. The strange high voice cut the dusty air. Then it quit.

The soldiers waited outside.

Inside, a ceiling fan swished and whispered. It was a strange place to

her, an alien place she had never seen before. She watched Ben lay
Leopold down on a sofa, a rose-colored tufted sofa; she watched him
place a fringed pillow under Leopold's head. A yellow sulphur light
streamed through the window and struck Leopold's golden hair.
Leopold was only sleeping, she thought.

A cry escaped her. Her fist flew to her mouth. Fire stabbed her
womb again. She bit her knuckle until she drew blood. Then whirling
suddenly, she flew at Ben, clawing and tearing at him.

"*You never loved him!*"

Ben caught her hands. She tried to pull away, flailing at him vainly,
uttering wild despairing cries. He grasped her shoulders and held her
still.

"I loved him best—"

"*Liar—*" she cried. "Profiteer! Murderer! *Liar—*"

"I loved him best of all," Ben whispered. "He brought me you."

Sobbing, she fell into his arms. Then pain struck her at her knees
and sent her falling, falling through a twisting well that had no end.

The boy was an intrusion. Ben glared at him, his mind not on the
boy, his mind still fixed on Anna upstairs. For hours, pacing the hallway outside the bed chamber, he'd been telling himself that Beatrice
had delivered the others, all of them since Alfred—only one stillborn
—it wasn't the child he cared about. It was Anna. One shock on top of
the other, Beatrice had said, mournfully. One dead and another one
wild to be born the same day.

He had come down to the study for brandy.

Then he had turned around and found the boy standing there in his
faded blue coat, shabby and frayed, badly mended. The boy was holding his cap in his hand, hands clasped together like they were
manacled, like his sentence had been to wait around all day, and he
hadn't any more heart for what he had to say than Ben had to listen.

"Say it," Ben said, swallowing down the brandy.

"Colonel Foster sent me to Brownsville. When I got there, I discovered your son had taken his battalion with Colonel Ford to Palmito
Hill. The Union had attacked—Colonel Barrett in charge—sixty-
second infantry, thirty-fourth Indiana and a few Morton rifles. Most of
the Union soldiers were Negroes."

The boy stood in a patch of failing light and spoke quietly. Anger rose in Ben, an urge to strike a blow at this boy who represented those who robbed him.

"Captain Calder fought on the edge of the Palo Alto plain," the boy said. "Three hundred horsemen galloped into the Federal Infantry flank—they rode them down to the last man and pursued Barrett's retreat to Brazos de Santiago. It was a Confederate victory. Only Union soldiers were counted dead in the field and floating in the Rio Grande. Two hundred and twenty out of three hundred in the thirty-fourth Indiana slain—"

Ben glowered at the boy. Tall and straight, the boy was strangely articulate. Wheat-colored hair and cornflower blue eyes—Ben found himself noting that—substance behind his presence, a vigor. There was something about the boy he seemed to know, as if the antipathy had forged a perverse bond.

"Get on with it," he said sharply.

"Both sides had heard the war was done with. Barrett attacked anyway. On the Confederate side—if Barrett had come with white troops, they would have surrendered—but Ford wouldn't give in to Negroes."

Ben stared the boy down. The boy didn't flinch. Ben's eyes narrowed menacingly. "The war was over, Palmito Hill was a futile massacre—and the only Confederate casualty was my son. Is that what you're telling me?"

"It was a minor wound. Blood poisoning set in. High fever. Ravings." The boy frowned. "There was nothing that could be done."

Ben spun, poured another shot of brandy, crossed to the fireplace and turned his back. Gulping the brandy, he stared sightlessly into the cold ashes. "Dismissed—" he said. Behind him, the boy didn't move. "You did your duty," Ben said coldly. "You delivered a dead boy. Now get out of here while you're still in one piece."

Behind him, the boy still didn't move. Ben stiffened. Clutching the empty glass in both hands, he turned slowly. The boy had tucked his cap under his arm and he was holding out a small leather pouch, coming toward him without caution, strangely unshielded.

"This is Captain Calder's property, sir."

Ben's eyes moved unwillingly over the boy again. "How old are you?"

"Twenty-one, sir."

Ben held out the glass. "Pour yourself some brandy."

The boy obeyed him. Ben watched him cross to the sideboard. He watched him pour two fingers of brandy and drain the glass and set it down. The dwindling light struck the boy's profile. Ben felt his skin prickle with the odd sensation of having seen what he was seeing before, of having known it somewhere.

The boy had left the pouch in his hands. Opening it, Ben saw the glitter of coins. He scowled. Another bolt of anger shot through him. "What are these?"

The boy answered in a queer dignified tone. "General Slaughter sold the Confederate Artillery to the Mexicans for twenty thousand silver pesos. Colonel Ford arrested him and distributed the silver among the men."

Ben stared at him. "Thirty pieces of silver?"

"No, sir."

"Who was the Judas?"

"I don't know what you mean, sir."

"Are you saying it was Slaughter? Was it Ford? Are you saying it was *me?*"

"No, sir."

Striding across the room, Ben thrust the pouch at him. "Take it."

The boy shook his head. "No, sir."

"Get out," Ben said quietly. His voice dropped, nearly inaudible. "Get out before I kill you."

The boy nodded. He obeyed without trepidation and without malice. Noiselessly, with that same odd dignity, he donned his cap and moved toward the door. Then he halted and turned. "I'm sorry for your grief, sir."

"Damn you. What do you know of grief?"

"A fair amount, sir. My father died last spring." The light was almost gone. Violet shadows crept over the boy's face. "He died in New York. He wasn't my real father, but he brought me from Europe—he was the only family I had."

Ben heard the sorrow in the boy's voice. Against his will, he felt a fleeting bond, a shared knowledge that life was effort and risk and blunders, that life was loss. Turning away, he dropped into the chair at the desk and pressed his fingertips against his temples. Anna's ledgers were lying there. The sight of them stirred his fears for Anna again—it was eight hours now; he closed his eyes, torn between anger and prayer. When he looked up, the boy was facing him across the desk.

"I need your signature, sir." Reaching inside his coat, he extracted a folded document. "It's my last duty, sir. I can't be released until you sign it."

Ben lit the lamp. Light flooded the boy's face, striking sculptured cheekbones and golden glints in his lashes. For an instant, he looked like a figure from a dream or a forgotten memory. Ben scowled again. "Why aren't you afraid of me?"

"I don't know, sir."

The boy had laid the document on the desk. Ben pushed it under the lamp. "What will you do when you're released?"

"I'm not sure, sir. I used to think about being a rabbi, but you have to prove your mother was a Jew. She wasn't. She was a Catholic, I'm told. Polish. I never knew her."

Ben dipped a pen and scanned the document. It was a military document, standard. He had no eyes for it. "You have spiritual aspirations then?"

"No, sir. My father's dream was always that we'd open a store together," the boy said. "A store of quality he had in mind. He was a peasant before the German Revolution. He became a peddler in Poland. In New York, he never had more than a stall—"

The words on the document blurred in front of Ben. Here and there, a phrase came into focus, then vanished. "You want to be a merchant, then?"

"No, sir. It may seem strange to you, sir—but I've grown used to this part of the country. There's going to be a lot happening here. Sometimes it strikes me I might wander around and write down what happens—it's my bent to see different sides of things—somewhat like a journalist."

"A store's more solid," Ben said tersely. He scratched his signature. He folded the paper and handed it back. Something he'd seen in the document wavered at the edge of his consciousness, a name—the boy's name.

"Yes, sir," the boy said.

"What?"

"I'm sure you're right, sir." The boy was gazing at him, clear-eyed.

The name bobbed just out of reach. What had the document said? Was he imagining it? "There's a man named Lambert in Houston," Ben said. "I'll give you a letter to him. If you decide on a store, he'll make all the arrangements for you."

"Why would you do that, sir?"

Ben scrutinized him. *"She was a Catholic,"* the boy had said. *"He was a peasant before the German Revolution."* "What's your name?" "Lubeck, sir. Jacob Lubeck," the boy said.

The sun was gone.

He stood in the wind, blinded by the wind.

The boy was gone.

Life had given him opposing sons and set them one against the other. Lilli's he had sired; Anna's, he had not. To Jacob Lubeck, he had not said, "I am your father." To Leopold, he had never said, "I am not."

Now, the boy was gone. And Leopold was gone. And Bendejo was gone, and Garras, too—gone before the Christmas tree was raised, candles burning on the branches, a dozen candles for every child—for Alfred in Houston, for Elizabeth, for Hannah who was falling in love with Ramsey, for Eli and Daniel, and for the child now tearing at Anna's womb.

The wind howled. The moon rose.

Standing in the wind, he saw that life would not stand still, like a stick upended in the ground while the days moved past. He saw that he could not—by his will—cause the sun to rise or set or the wind to blow or the rain to fall. He saw that he had been made witness to the changing seasons, that he had recorded each day that passed, had recorded the fact that this was so, that life existed. He saw that he had been both an agent of destiny and a tool of fate—he saw that time was the thing that would break his will.

But not yet, he thought. Not yet.

Closing his eyes, he bargained with God: *Take the child and spare Anna.*

32

A half-million acres of gullies and crags and naked stone. Will you fence it? Never, you say. What a man fences contracts on him; it turns on itself. A man goes for more or becomes less. I have no more heart for it. I have measured the size of my own hungers.

Impulsiveness is good for the young. One pays for it. It becomes courage.

In my own way, I have been as tough as you, my husband, and as ruthless. It will take two generations of women to catch up with me. Perhaps three.

You were always at home here. Inside myself, I sheltered an expatriate. You had nothing to lose. I clung to Berlin. I stretched as far as I could stretch. You brought me to a land of scavengers, columns of dust and tawny earth, nights as black as lava where stars swarmed like bees.

I shall miss the common miracles.

I can hear your thoughts. They flutter over me like hands, drawing me back. A cold voice whispers: Nothing lives beyond its time or dies too soon. It lies. I will not sunder myself from you. I shall take you with me. I shall leave myself behind.

Did you know I fell in love with you on the Armenius?—when you cast my trunks overboard?

I shall miss the touch of flesh.

How did it happen that our life together began with Leopold's con-

ception and now threatens to cease with his death?—as if he held it in his hands and dropped it, and it shattered and the pieces lie beyond repair. Was it God's plan—or were we windblown in an accidental universe? Was our bond an idea in God's mind that became a forgotten thought? Did He grow bored with our greed? Perhaps God was Leopold. Is it possible we give birth to our own gods?

I would not have changed a moment of it.

I shall miss the shadows of the windmills in the sunset. I shall miss the smell of bread rising, and the awkwardness of colts and children, and the eager cries of Christmas morning, and the winter rains, and the house you built for me in Houston that I shall never see.

I have had it all. I have had everything.

Oh God!—Why am I not ready?

BOOK THREE

1908

33

_____

They had sewed the eyelids together in the old days. Wild devils—hell to rope and prone to stampede. Temporarily blinded, they had to travel by sound. That's how the cowboy came to sing. Damned if they hadn't sung the Longhorn straight into captivity.

Are You out there, God? Are You listening?

Was there Someone looking down to find him, Ben Calder, on the trail again? Four hundred head including the Brahmin—all branded on the trail with the Calder crown. *Past eighty—and I can still run steer better than any nickel-plated puncher in Texas!*

When had he started talking to God? Ben couldn't remember.

Tonight, the Hindus had thrown cactus into the campfire before they prayed. To *Atman,* they prayed: *The Universal Soul.* Damned Hindu cowhands. It was his brother George's grandson—Ernst Calder—who had made the trip from Hamburg to Bombay and wired him from the Taj Mahal Hotel. Five coolies—Ernst had said—regular herders from Miraji would arrive with the Brahmin cattle. The cost was a hundred thousand dollars—forty-two bulls, thirteen cows, five heifers and three calves—all examined for disease at a farm in Poona, Ernst had claimed. Damned fool! When they unloaded the Brahmin in the New York Harbor, thirty-three were found to be infected with surra. Damned Hindus had wailed and rolled on the ground when those cattle were destroyed.

He had bought cattle in Wyoming. And cattle in Abilene. The best he could find anywhere. Buying cattle like a madman, some had said.

To save the rest of the Brahmin, he'd gone to Washington. *"The Brahmin look like hell,"* he'd told Teddy Roosevelt. *"Ugliest beasts you ever saw. But their sweat glands repel ticks. Give me a chance to crossbreed them and I'll produce the best damned range cattle in the world."*

Teddy Roosevelt understood cattle—he had owned a ranch in the Dakota badlands. In his youth, Teddy Roosevelt's first wife had died in childbirth—

It had brought Anna to mind.

Her name was Anna . . .

He had only her name—and a veiled memory of a lost time that had passed like a dream. Even now, when he searched for her, he lost her. He grabbed her memory—it slipped through his fists. The wind had blown through every corner she had been and left only shadows behind.

There had been women afterward. They had no names. He had hated them for not being Anna—and then he had forgotten the reason he hated them, and he had hated them from habit—and he had taken them only in anger.

Are You listening? How do I know if You're there?—If You're anywhere?

His last cattle ride: *"Calder's Folly"*—that's what those Washington reporters had written.

In the White House garden with the damned moviola camera going, Teddy Roosevelt had given his decision to the press. *"Remember the hills of Judea,"* the President had told them. *"It was the herdsmen who were selected by God to be the first to hear the angels sing 'Peace on Earth, Good Will Towards Men.'"*

"I have no reverence," Ben had roared. *"Nor will I."*

He rode with Manuel.

Manuel rode beside him.

Two months ago, on the coldest day in February, Manuel had appeared straddling a mule and wearing a letter pinned to his pitiful chest:

"Diablo Tejano," Garras addressed him. *"I write this from a jail cell*

in Chihuahua without knowing if I will see the sun tomorrow . . . I was not a good priest. The Church supported Diaz when he took the communal lands from the poor—I left without regret. Since, I have become a known revolutionary—first, following a man called Madero and now another, Zapata . . . I married ten years ago. She was killed by Diaz's Cientificas. It is for Manuel's safety that I send you my only son. He is eight years old and can read and write English—I taught him myself. For me, you paid seven dollars. Manuel Garras is free. Raise him as a free man . . ."

Had God watched him read that letter?

What made him give a damn? He had no use for God's judgments or for any—even those of his children—James, least of all. They had raised derricks on his grazing land. They drove horseless carriages and talked of heavier-than-air flight. How could they—so separated from the earth—know the truth of a man who'd never had anything more between him and the earth than a fine piece of horseflesh?

Did You expect me to weep? Me? Ben Calder?—who shed no tears when You took Anna, but made a vow instead: If I ever see You, I will kill You.

If You have taken Garras, tell him his son, Manuel, met Teddy Roosevelt, the President of the United States!

The air bristled. The sky turned pale and dry as bleached bones, dense as the earth, as stark and invincible. Dragon lizards leaped from the cacti and scurried for cover. Then the hot wind rose and the cattle wailed, moving blind like ghosts through stinging veils of sand.

"Sing! Keep moving—"

The *vaqueros'* voices rose. The sun set like molten fire. All night, the stunted oaks roared and the wind whipped every loose thing and sent it hurtling, pieces of trees and tumbleweeds, and the sand rose in billows, erasing all prints from the land, enraged by every mark that man had made.

I know it's You.

All right! I know it's You!

He had worn the talisman from the German forester Ott around his neck for sixty years.

The Hindus stared at him with bead-black eyes.

"You must fast for twenty-four hours," Ott had warned. Through the sandstorm, they had not stopped to eat or drink.

The wind was gone. The air was washed clean over the littered earth. Iguanas frisked again in the cacti. The herd of four hundred moved steadily—the crown brand of the Calders plainly visible in the morning light. Overhead, a few clouds gathered, promising rain, but no rain would come, only faraway thunder, and every day until the Indians prayed in midsummer, the Rio Grande would shrivel.

The land is dry . . .

He remembered. He could hear old Magda's voice.

"The land is dry . . ." old Magda had prophesied. *"The trees grow knives instead of leaves, and there are dragons in them. Four hundred will wear your crown . . ."* It had come about. It was here. *"Then you will see the face of God . . ."*

Was it time?

The Hindus cackled.

Inside Ott's bag, the thing was putty-colored, no bigger than a coin, an ancient forest mushroom from the Siberian woods dried stiff as leather.

The Indians poured sugar-water on the mescal and heated it over copal. He had no sugar-water and no copal.

The thing could not be chewed. He tore off chunks and swallowed them whole.

The Hindus chattered like birds.

Now, God—it's time!

Jewel-encrusted cacti glisten in the sunlight. The Brahmins, strange white beasts with severed wings, tread on shards of diamonds. The mountains lie flat against the sky, and as the twilight falls, the desert shimmers like an opalescent sea, swaying and undulating, beckoning to me to enter and swim and be lost forever.

I have heard Your laughter in the mountains, but only in the silence of this desert do I know the infinite magnitude of Your bag of tricks. Lying still, my ear pressed against the planet's hide, I can hear the blood rushing through the earth's veins, and I can hear the beating of its heart.

How heavy my limbs are! How many centuries have passed. How long since I've seen Your face? How long before I see Your face?

The law of Karma—the Hindus whisper—holds every human being to account for every earthly deed. The law of Karma declares the soul will be reborn according to its former deeds.

Damned Hindu cowmen! Why do I believe them? Because they say I will not die. And I believe them.

A steady fire still burns in me. Strange. The flames no longer lick at my bowels. They leap higher now, whiter, radiating from my chest and flickering at my throat and sizzling to my brain.

Why have You not shown me Your face?

Who is that lying there? Spraddled out in his Texas tuxedo, black broadcloth and velvet lapels—the one he wore to see the President— the coat cut to accommodate a pair of six-guns, and the trousers cut to slide over a pair of Lone Star boots. "He's gone where the cowfolk go," they're saying, "to bulldog a celestial steer."

Fools! I roar with laughter.

They've put him in a box. They call it a coffin. Damned fools. They've put God in a box, too—they call it a church!

Was that You, God—roaring with laughter? Was it?

What is this sudden silence?

What's that? I can't make it out. Slower—You're moving too fast— I'm an old man.

Is that You? No—

Your face?—Is it?

How can that be?

Oh, my God—no! It can't be—

Through the open window of his bedroom, he could smell the perfume of the wild-rose hedge in bloom. Forty miles of roses—windbreak for the Brahmin.

No one told him he was dying.

Manuel told him James' wife, Victoria, had gone into labor.

Manuel told him the child was meant to be a girl. She was meant to be called Anna.

James told him nothing. James talked of salt domes and arched beds and oil-producing rock.

Through his telescope, he could see the evening star, hanging low above the barns and saddle houses, winking past the bunkhouse and the blacksmith shop, a lone star among the pattern of derricks.

In the desert, he had touched that star. In the desert he had seen—

"A grandson," James said. James was holding the child. "What shall we call him?"

"Leopold," he answered. "Call him Leopold. For Anna."

In the desert, he had seen—

James handed him the sleeping child.

"Leopold," he repeated softly.

He had seen God's face. It was his own.

He held the newborn child and whispered Magda's warning. *"Let those who would be gods first learn to be human."*

BOOK FOUR

1920–57

34

In front of the barbershop, a Negro was running a sled-ferry across the quagmire that passed for Main Street. The boy hailed him. The mud was gumbo, three feet deep in some places. Last week, a boll weevil—beginners were called boll weevils—a Chinaman, who had worked only three days on a derrick, had finished off too much raw whiskey at Blue Mary's dance hall and drowned in a mudhole.

The boy gave the Negro a quarter and rode the sled like a rickshaw —the Negro pulling it—to the other side. The wooden sidewalk was slimy, oil-slippery. Sure-footed as a mule-skinner, the boy affected a swagger that, like his fancy boots and wide-brimmed hat, was a replica of his father's. He was carrying a satchel. He was a month away from his thirteenth birthday and inside the satchel was a million dollars in cash.

He moved through groups of Negroes and Indian half-breeds passing whiskey back and forth in the fading spring sun. Like the Mexicans, the Negroes were team drivers and ditchdiggers; unlike the Mexicans, the Negroes weren't allowed inside the saloons. He saw a knife flash. He heard somebody growl. Accustomed to violence—in the streets of Bell, he had seen countless men shot or knifed or beaten to death—the boy kept going until he reached a three-story wooden building with a swinging sign that said JESSIE'S.

Inside, the saloon was purple with tobacco smoke and thick with the smell of whiskey and sweat. Too early, not yet sundown, for the bar to be stacked with drillers and roughnecks and roustabouts, but he saw they were already there—a bad sign—shouting in German or cursing in Czech, most of them already drunk, ready to fight, arguing about women and wild wells and rumors of pressure in the reservoir falling. Hanging onto the satchel, the boy strode the length of the bar and then past the tables where the cripples gathered: Jessie's drinks were half-price for the men who'd been blinded by gas or maimed in falls from derricks or burned nearly to cinder by gushers that burst into flames. He heard chairs topple behind him and the crack of a shot ring out as he was climbing the stairs to the second floor.

The double doors were closed. Standing in the hallway, he removed his hat and pulled the bell rope. Jessie peered through a slat in the door before she let him in, enveloping him in her corseted three hundred pounds. Jessie was old, nearly fifty, with frizzled yellow hair and cannonball breasts that heaved when she laughed. Jessie had come in a mule cart from Butte, Montana, with an instinct for what his father called gooseflesh; nuzzling his ear, Jessie offered him Alice, the youngest of those who worked in the third-floor cribs selling gooseflesh. Her laugh struck his ear like the bark of oil traveling through pipes. Behind it, he could hear the spin of roulette wheels, the rattle of dice and croupiers, and the clinking of poker chips. Behind it, he could hear his father roaring, "—the rumors are lies circulated by Standard Oil."

Jessie released him, sailing behind as he made his way to the poker table where the reporters were still clustered around, firing questions. Pausing, the boy made an attempt to size up the scene. He saw his father was less drunk than he appeared to be and was performing for the reporters. Leaning forward in his chair and stroking his outrageous moustache, his father was pouring whiskey for Bradshaw Tate. The game was over. The boy saw the chips were stacked in front of Bradshaw Tate. Again, the boy wondered—with so much trouble in the field—why had his father locked himself into eighteen hours of poker, the stakes climbing to madness? And why with Bradshaw Tate? *Damned secret agent,* his father had said a hundred times, *trying to infiltrate for the Rockefellers. I'll see him in hell!*

The boy moved through the reporters who were vying with each other, having got wind of trouble and, like reporters did, blowing it up. The boy wanted to tell them there wasn't any trouble his father couldn't handle, though he didn't like the look on Bradshaw Tate's face, jowls flushed with pleasure and a smugness about the way Bradshaw was slouched in his rumpled suit and chewing on the stub of a burned-out cigar.

"What about the refinery you're building?" The journalist who asked the question was from the New York daily that had first called James Calder "Big Jim" in print. "They're saying that refinery's never going to be finished."

"I know what they're saying," Big Jim said, with a disarming grin. Seeing the boy, he waved him over. The boy obeyed, like he'd obeyed by going back to the office and cleaning out his father's safe. A million dollars was everything there was. Still, Big Jim took the satchel from him and set it on the table like it was no more important than a bag full of dirty laundry.

"They're saying I'm overextended," Big Jim continued, still smiling at the reporter. "They're saying I get rigs on credit from Calder Drilling Supplies and I transport my oil on credit in Calder Railroad cars and I make my payroll on credit from the Calder Bank. And they're *right*. There's nothing a Calder needs that another Calder somewhere in Texas can't provide"—the boy saw Big Jim look Bradshaw Tate directly in the eye—"and that's why the Bell field is one piece of the oil pie the Rockefellers' Standard Oil can't swallow."

Another reporter quit scratching in a notebook to ask, "Isn't it true you can't get any more oil out of the ground without pressure in the reservoir?"

"The reservoir's being stabilized," Big Jim roared. The roar made the boy nervous. Big Jim only roared when he was bluffing or running, the boy couldn't tell which, maybe both.

"What's your current production schedule?"

Big Jim let out another bellow. "The Allies wouldn't have beaten the Krauts without the Bell field. Henry Ford wouldn't be packing the streets with Model-Ts without the Bell field. Ten thousand barrels a day, the biggest strike in west Texas—and when the good Lord sees fit to take me to the Great Beyond, Leopold here's gonna be oil king of Texas."

"Lep," the boy corrected.

The New York reporter smiled. "Big Lep?"

"Shit—" Jessie chortled, "Lep can hold his whiskey and he's a helluva poker player, but he ain't a man yet."

"Man enough," Lep retorted.

"Damned right," Big Jim roared. He was opening the satchel and removing the stacks of bills. "My boy was born with oil in his veins. Print that. He's as good as his old man. Print that, too. He's crazy about the risk, the danger, the hard work and—most of all—the *money*."

The reporters were staring at the money. The boy watched Big Jim push the stacks of bills across the table, not even looking at them, like they didn't matter.

"You all know I owe Bradshaw Tate a million dollars," Big Jim chuckled. "There's some who said I couldn't pay. Well, here it is. Print that. Tell 'em Big Jim Calder pays his debts and never walks away from a wildcat game."

The reporters had gone silent. They couldn't take their eyes off the money. In the silence, the boy could hear his heart hammering in his ears, like something was going to blow, like just before the discovery well blew three years ago and nobody knew if they had a dry hole or a gusher.

Then Big Jim leaned across the table again and let loose another roar at Bradshaw Tate. "Have you got the guts to go for another million in chips?"

Bradshaw Tate nodded.

"Two million?"

The boy saw Bradshaw Tate hesitate before he nodded again. Then Bradshaw took the cigar out of his mouth and pointed it at Big Jim. "I'll back it in cash, you back it in Bell shares."

"Sonofabitch—" Big Jim bellowed.

"Two million in Bell shares," Bradshaw Tate said, pressing. "A dollar a share."

"Two million shares against three million in cash," Big Jim countered.

"Two and a half," Bradshaw said.

"Double the stakes?"

Bradshaw took a beat. "Agreed."

Lep stared incredulously at his father, but Big Jim had turned away, suddenly busy putting on a show, teasing two of Jessie's girls who had appeared with new cartons of chips. It crossed the boy's mind that, with all the trouble, Big Jim had cracked. For three years, Big Jim had beaten back Bradshaw Tate no matter how hard Bradshaw had begged and connived and set traps to get shares in the Bell field. Now Big Jim was pouring fresh whiskey and roaring like a steam engine at the spectators who had abandoned the dice tables and roulette wheels to join the reporters, jostling for position and making side bets. The boy's instinct told him it was a setup. But what kind? And whose?—Big Jim's or the Rockefellers'?

Then all of a sudden, Big Jim got up from his chair and the boy realized he was holding it out to him. "You take over for me," Big Jim said.

The boy froze. He felt Jessie push him down into the chair. The room spun around a minute, then Jessie was handing him a glass of whiskey and Big Jim's hands were on his shoulders, grasping his shoulders, like telling him he could do it, telling him he had to do it because Big Jim had something more important to do. What? Something Big Jim didn't want the reporters or Bradshaw Tate to know? Something worth more than two million shares of Bell stock or three million dollars? What? The boy turned around to look up into Big Jim's face. Nothing in it told him the answer. All Big Jim's eyes told him was to sit tight and play cards.

The boy took a deep breath, spit on his hands and rubbed them together. Big Jim bent swiftly to whisper against his ear, *"Get everything you can."* Then Big Jim let go and started to walk. The room threatened to spin again. The boy turned, half-rising, everything in him wanting to get up and go with Big Jim. But Jessie's hands gripped his shoulders where his father's hands had been, pressing him down into the chair again and, in the same instant, Big Jim turned on his heel as he left to roar at Bradshaw Tate,

"My boy's gonna whip your ass!"

To the boy it sounded like thunder. It sounded like rain spattering on the tent.

The woman swung her body about and wrapped her thin legs around him and emitted a noise, a sound between a moan and a whistle. Palms supporting his weight, the boy rode her, making her buck under him, like what he was doing was something to be done with, some angry resolve to be vented on the creature beneath him; she was one of those cheap prostitutes who worked out of the tents, who rode on horseback through the fields servicing roughnecks and pipeliners on a bedroll laid out on the ground. It was his first sight of dark shaggy pubic hair, moist; his first encounter with glossy brown nipples. He hadn't even taken his boots off.

From outside, he heard the thunder grow louder, the crackle of lightning. Plunging into her, as if he were boring a well at three thousand feet past sand and shale, he had the same fear of the bit breaking. Then a shudder racked him, a release that was involuntary, like a dry hole erupting into a gusher, spewing out of control as the well blew in.

He gave her three dollars. She was already scurrying into her clothes. Outside, he heard the noise change, growing louder, not like rain at all. Then he heard the siren shriek and he understood he was listening to the roar and sizzle of flames.

The tent flap parted and Jessie bent over—a red glow behind her— shouting at him, "Get the hell out of here!"

Burning oil struck the ground, exploding. Flames leaped and fell. Jessie whipped the horses, maneuvering the oil wagon around the edge of the blaze, shouting at him over the roar of the flames,

"Why'd you run away? You got your paw's million back from Bradshaw Tate—"

"I lost all those shares."

"Christ almighty—didn't you know Big Jim wouldn't give Bradshaw Tate a crack at Bell stock unless it was worthless?"

"Worthless?" Behind Jessie, he could see towers of flame sending up corkscrew spirals of smoke. Hundreds of blackened figures were running and screaming orders, trying vainly to fight the fire with steam. Streaks of sparks shot up through the low strata of clouds and rained down again like comets.

"The field's a bust," Jessie cried. "It's all over—"

"You're a liar—" He looked back. The shifting wind was moving the fire like a tidal wave. A great cloud of flame burst, illuminating the smoke-darkened night.

"Big Jim tried to acidize. It didn't work. He ordered them to explode a couple of wells to get them started again. The wells blew. They tore the derricks to splinters and"—Jessie crossed herself—"the men to eternity."

A blast shook the earth as the storage tanks exploded. The fire roared like an inferno. The horses reared under the impact, screeching. Jessie cracked the whip, heading farther away from it.

"Big Jim?—was he—?"

"Not a scratch—"

"Take me back," he ordered.

Jessie kept going, rocketing down Main Street through the mayhem of men running and horses squealing, mule wagons paralyzed in the street, and shrieking dance-hall girls scurrying and weeping and wringing their hands. All the buildings were red, lit by the fire. The faces had the look of sinners fleeing from Hell.

"*Take me back*—" he shouted again. Jessie ignored him. Jessie kept whipping the horses, the wagon veering and careening right through the chaos past the edge of town. He turned to look back. The town was a tinderbox under a fiery sky. Behind it, the flames were spreading in leaps and bursts. Hurling himself in front of Jessie, he grabbed for the reins. She fought him for them, twice his weight and strong as an ox. He reared back and punched her in the jaw. She went reeling sideways. It took all his strength to bring the horses to a halt.

"Why'd you go with that two-bit whore?" Jessie shouted at him. "I was saving Alice for you."

He was already climbing down. Jessie seized his arm. Her grip was like iron. He tried to pull loose. She held on. Then she let go, suddenly, sending him tumbling into the mud. Leaning over the wagon, she hollered, "It's Big Jim's orders—"

Stumbling in the gumbo, he reached up and grabbed her. Caught by surprise, she yelled as he pulled her over. She fell like a heifer, rolling in the mud. Bills sprayed from her bodice. She scrambled for the money, stuffing it back and cursing him.

"I've got a million dollars stashed in my corset, you bastard!" She lunged at his leg and sent him toppling again. "Bradshaw Tate's hollering fraud and looking for his money. Big Jim wants you and that money at the *ranch*—"

She was grappling with him, trying to pin him against the wagon wheel. He thrashed under her grip. She clamped her hands on his shoulders and pushed him down until he was half-submerged in mud, still yelling at him.

"The creditors are gonna descend on the ranch like vultures, Calders all of 'em—"

"Let me go!"

"—just itching to divide that land between 'em."

"They can't. My grandpaw left the ranch to me. It's mine."

"Not any more, it ain't. Not with it mortgaged up to your ears and twenty million in debt on top of it."

"You're *crazy*. I don't believe you—"

"Big Jim says you're to dangle a piece of the million in front of each of 'em. Under the table. What you're gonna buy is the right to pay 'em back in twenty years." She loosened her hold. "If they won't give you twenty years, take fifteen."

He wanted to strangle her. He wanted to pummel her with his fists. He wanted to bury his face in her massive breasts.

Jessie let him go. Dripping mud, she rose to her feet and stood with her hands on her whopping hips, looking down at him. "There's a Model-T down the road all gassed up and waiting."

He pulled himself out and stood up, covered with gumbo, glaring at her.

"You're a sorry sight," Jessie said.

"So are you."

"You look like an *ape*." Jessie grinned.

"You look like a *whale*." A snicker escaped him.

Jessie started to laugh. Her bulk quivered and churned. Mud rolled and spattered. She stretched out her arms and he fell into them, wrapping himself in her mountainous flesh, both of them slipping and sliding and hanging onto each' other, shaking with laughter. "You're a Calder bastard, all right," Jessie chortled, "but you can't learn about women from a two-bit whore."

Behind Jessie, the boy could see the red glow of the Bell field burning.

"Somebody's gotta teach you about women," Jessie said, taking his hands and pressing them against her mammoth breasts.

The sound that came out of him was Big Jim's roar.

They brought his father's body back wrapped in burlap.

Big Jim's heart gave out, he was told. Big Jim's heart broke.

Twenty million dollars in debts, the lawyers said.

His mother wouldn't stop weeping. His mother floated through the house, clutching a lace-edged handkerchief to her nose and reminding him through her tears he was her only child.

He found himself shouting at her, "Leave me alone. I'm a man now."

He couldn't cry. Even when they set up the coffin in the parlor, he didn't cry. They set the coffin at the end of the parlor under Ben Calder's portrait, painted the day Ben Calder died—the painter had worked from Ben Calder's corpse—the old man on horseback. Big Jim's coffin was closed. In the middle of the night, before the day of the funeral service, he went downstairs and opened the coffin. The mortician had brushed Big Jim's sideburns and waxed Big Jim's moustache. Big Jim was asleep, he told himself. He stared at his father's rigid figure, trying to make himself believe death might be one of Big Jim's pranks, imagining Big Jim climbing out of the coffin and roaring with laughter about how he'd fooled Bradshaw Tate into thinking he'd gone to the Great Beyond and how, in the bottom of the coffin, Big Jim had a bottle of whiskey and twenty million stashed. But a long time went by, the clock striking in the parlor and every minute telling him that life was not to be counted on or trusted, and there was nothing more than Big Jim's last words to him, *"Get everything you can."*

Still, he didn't cry.

In the morning, Manuel came in from spring roundup.

Stocky and weather-burned, Manuel stood in the sun with his hat in his hand and paid his respects.

"The Bell field's gone bust," Lep told him.

"I heard," Manuel said, no regret in his voice. Lep heard something else. Manuel, like Ben Calder, had hated oil.

"I'm in charge now," Lep said. "I'm the *patrón.*" He watched Manuel nod, no servitude in the nod. Lep sensed something else. He knew Manuel had remained Ben Calder's "boy," sent on a mule from Mexico to Ben Calder who'd made him a *vaquero* before he was eight. Now, at twenty, Manuel was corral boss and foreman; Big Jim had left the cattle operation to Manuel while Big Jim chased oil. "I'll need cash to keep the ranch going," Lep said. "How much can we get for the cattle?"

"The new strain looks good." Manuel answered in the same strange tone. Lep remembered it was Manuel who had fought to crossbreed the Brahmins Ben Calder had brought back before his death.

"How good?"

"Maybe two hundred thousand," Manuel said. Lep saw something in Manuel's eyes he didn't want to read.

"Get everything you can," Lep said.

The funeral service took place at three o'clock in the afternoon. His father's lawyers were there. All the Calders were there. The Mexicans and the cowhands came in from the range. Bradshaw Tate's wife came with a four-year-old child she called Sugar. Bradshaw Tate didn't come. Neither did Jessie. The parlor was filled with the smell of roses. Tons of roses. The Negro house servants lit tiers of candles. His mother cried through the eulogy. Failing to reconcile the elements of Big Jim's nature or the events of his life, the minister consigned Big Jim's soul to Heaven anyway, concluding, "—the hounds of Heaven are stronger and faster than the hounds of Hell." Then each of the Calders placed a rose on his father's coffin and Lep watched each of them, afterward, corner the lawyers to schedule appointments for the following week. Afterward—he was standing with his mother under Ben Calder's portrait as the mourners filed past—he bolted. He was fleeing through the crowd when he heard his mother cry out,

"Leopold's heart has turned to stone!"

He rode into the sunset. He rode as hard as he could and as fast as he could, still wearing his mourning suit, digging his heels into the mustang's flank, riding in a cold sweat as though devils were chasing him. He rode until he was beyond the smell of wild-rose hedges and beyond the cattle pens and the grazing land. He rode into the hard stony hills and into the flatland littered with rocks and stunted oaks, land that was good for nothing, except to own, except to know that you owned it. Like being torn from a dream, he found himself crying, tears rolling down his cheeks, tears of grief and rage. Then he felt the fear. He was seized by a terror of being nobody, a fear of dissolving into nothing—unprotected by land or money—a disappearance of self into the quicksand of pain and struggle. The sound of Manuel's voice came back to him, the look in Manuel's eyes. In Manuel's pride, he had glimpsed his own terror—that he, Lep Calder, cast into an ordinary world, would be less, far less than Manuel.

His tears were spent when he got back. It was long after dark. It was late. He couldn't tell how late. He didn't care.

Light was coming from under the closed doors of the second parlor. He knew the lawyers were still there, closeted with his mother, trying to explain what they called the "unfortunate circumstances" to his mother.

He went upstairs to his room. The money was packed in a saddlebag under his bed. He retrieved the bag. Then he went downstairs to Big Jim's study where he took a rifle off the gun rack and loaded it. The saddlebag slung over his shoulder, he picked up the rifle and went down the wide hall to the second parlor and pushed the doors open. The four lawyers were gathered around his mother who was clutching her handkerchief, still weeping. He leveled the rifle and waited. He didn't have to say a word. One by one, the lawyers felt his presence and turned, staring or sputtering. "I'm in charge now," he said, "not my mother."

He crossed the room and let the saddlebag drop onto a rosewood table. With his right hand, he kept the rifle leveled at them. With his left, he unbuckled the bag and tipped it so that the money spilled out. "A million dollars," he said. He spoke quietly, telling them what he wanted them to do and what he wanted from the Calders. When he was finished, he crossed the room again and stood at the door and said, "You can go home now." He stood there as they went past. He kept the rifle on them, following them until they reached the front door. "If you can't get twenty years," he said, "get fifteen." He opened the front door for them. "Get everything you can."

He shut the door. He turned around. His mother was standing at the foot of the stairs, holding onto the balustrade, weeping. "Go upstairs," he said. She obeyed him. He went into the parlor. The candles were still burning. He crossed the room. Then he stopped and aimed at his father's coffin. Peering through the gunsight, he cocked the rifle. Candlelight flickered on the coffin. A long time went by. Slowly then, he raised the rifle until the barrel was in a direct line with Ben Calder's portrait. Astride an Arabian stallion, the old man looked back at him. He laid his finger on the trigger. He could hear the clock ticking. The clock struck the half hour. He lowered the rifle. Then he turned his back and walked out.

35

In 1935 he was twenty-seven, conspicuous in Berlin in his Stetson and high-heeled boots; heads turned at the Kaiserhof. Herr Calder, they called him in the lobby. He spoke a reasonable German. The girl in his bed spoke none. Nobody in Texas addressed him as Leopold, he told her, pulling off his boots. In Texas, he was Lep.

"Are you always so fierce?"

"Why?"

"That's what I mean. Why?"

He laughed. Texans were fierce, he said. Calders were fierce. He didn't say that. There were other things he didn't say. Like why he had come to Berlin. She turned in bed and giggled. Was he a cowboy? A Texas oil millionaire? She could feel a power humming in him, a beast in him, she said, kissing his eyelids closed, stroking his hair. She hoped it was a lion, running her hands over his spare rangy body which— more like the Texas rattler, he told her—was surprisingly dry to the touch.

She was American, no more than nineteen. In the lobby, registering, he had first seen her from the back, attracted by her waist-length copper hair which she wore straight and sleek as a sheet of copper. A dancer, she told him. Under her woolen cloak, she'd been wearing a spangled bra and tights and silver stockings; fastened to her forehead had been a pair of rhinestone horns. She was working at the Rio Rita with the young Persian boy with thick black eyebrows. Not her lover, she said—only the toreador—in black satin trousers, a tri-cornered hat, a jacket adorned with rosettes of mango-colored braid. She was the bull. The Persian's cape was fashioned of tiny mirrors. She complained it blinded her.

She was a diversion. Lep found her as oblivious to the forces gathering in Berlin as the sparrows that chirped in the middle of traffic. Earlier, as the bitter March twilight fell—patches of fog on the Spree, a cold setting sun on the linden trees and startling moments of crystalline light—he had stalked the crowded boulevards, feeling Hitler's presence in the exuberance that had risen from the passing of starvation and the depression and post-war disorder. In place of chaos were bursts of new building, housing and parks, austere forms of architecture, a heady promise of affluence.

"The accounts of barbarism in Germany which have reached the foreign press have been greatly exaggerated," Ernst had written.

Later, waiting for the girl in his room, he had gone over the letter again. It had been sent to his offices in Houston and forwarded. In the wildcat oil field, on horseback, he had first read the letter from his cousin Ernst—a man in his fifties whom he'd never met—empowered by the authority of one of the great industrial autocracies of Germany. The content had reeked of Prussian formality: Ernst's father and Ben Calder had been brothers; the references had been to family connections, the ties of blood. Even so, it had been less a request than a summons, a promise of a profitable alliance, the overture of a business titan who had done enough Texas research to know Lep's fifteen years were nearly up and he was four and a half million short.

He had come because of that. Yet, something more had impelled him, something unnamed, whirring in the sound of the propellers of the two-motor Douglas that had brought him from Zurich, coming in from the south, the immense maze of the newly revitalized Berlin sprawling below. Then, descending at the Templehof onto the landing field that had once been the goose-stepping parade grounds of Frederick the Great.

What he had felt was the ferment, money and power bubbling. Everywhere, ruddy-cheeked young men in the gray-green uniform of the new Wehrmacht were wearing the glazed expression of zealots, and he had wondered what position Ernst held in the ranks of a Hitler who had staked out a claim to divinity.

"—good angel," she said.

"What?"

"Acacia—" She was telling him her professional name. It meant: good angel. Her real name was Eva. Somewhere in the Midwest, there was a widowed mother and a two-year-old child, hers. She turned on the light and showed him a photograph: a dumpling daughter with blank dazzling eyes, like her mother's, like pieces of broken glass. She showed him the picture shyly, as if she were offering him a gift, wanting him to understand that her real treasure was not her body but what had come from it. She had that buttermilk skin that redheads sometimes had, rich and curdled. Making love to her, he felt like a cat lapping up cream.

He sent her away afterward. Her perfume remained, the faint smell of vanilla. In retrospect, he felt there had been something dull about her, like sun striking a dingy window. He was lying in bed. He turned on the radio and listened to the sounds of Berlin. He fell asleep with the radio on: somebody, somewhere singing *"Deutschland Uber Alles."*

By day, even the garbage wagons shone. Sitting in the back seat of a chauffeured open car, Lep listened to Ernst dismiss the news reports in the States—the rumors of terrorism, tales of raids and arrests, truckloads of Jews and Socialists vanishing into nowhere—all exaggerated accounts.

"It's true the trade unions have been broken, but the average worker is better off—" Ernst's gesture encompassed chimney sweeps on bicycles, students darting through traffic, workmen carrying blue-enameled lunch boxes and whistling.

"What about Dachau?—and Orienburg?"

Ernst smiled. "Guards with machine guns? High-voltage fences? Labor camps filled with intellectuals and artists whom we starve and beat? Is that what you've heard?" Ernst shook his head. "Falsehoods. Emil Jannings is still with the theater. Furtwanger is still with the Berlin Philharmonic—"

Ernst pointed out Goering's forty-room house in the Leipzigerasse.

"Before Hitler, there were strikes, riots, unemployment, bankruptcy. Hundreds slept in the Tiergarten every night. Cripples and beggars filled the streets—"

The car had halted, waiting for traffic. The street was crowded, filled

with shops and flower vendors and sidewalk cafes. Up ahead, Lep saw
a military truck had blocked traffic. As he watched, a half-dozen
storm troopers leaped out and started dragging a woman away from an
outdoor table.

"Make a U-turn," Ernst told the driver.

The woman was screaming. Sunlight struck her frizzed blond hair.
Huge, more than two hundred pounds, the woman was fighting like a
tiger. Lep realized the woman looked like Jessie.

The driver was wheeling the car around. Lep looked back. The
woman was being beaten unmercifully and hauled into the truck. Lep
reached for the door. Ernst caught his arm. Lep whirled. Ernst's jaw
had squared, the Calder jaw. Ernst's eyes were cobalt, the Calder eyes,
glinting. The word that came to Lep's mind was *gewalt:* divine violence.

The car turned a corner back into the boulevard.

"Morality is the refuge of the impotent," Ernst said, "the weak man's
compensation for having failed to gain power." Ernst smiled. "However, I'm sure you understand—you have that choice. What better
place than Berlin to be tested?"

"I came to do business," Lep snapped.

"Yes. Business. Of course. But that's not all that drew you, is it?
There's more. You're a Calder. You're a German and an Aryan. Don't
you feel it?"

Lep stared at Ernst. "What?"

"Blood knowledge," Ernst said.

At two o'clock in the morning, the telephone startled him. "It's
Acacia," she said. "Eva—" She had just returned from a late performance at the Rio Rita. She was ringing to see if he wanted her.

He was awake, the blueprints laid out in front of him along with the
details of Ernst's proposal.

"In fifteen minutes," he told her.

He poured another shot of whiskey and went back to the documents.

"In 1917, your father wildcatted the Bell oil field," Ernst had said.
"As far as we can tell, nearly all those leases are still in your name."

Ernst's estimate was 80 percent of the oil was still in the ground.

Ernst's proposal was simple. Water pumped underground might
force the oil from the rock except that water was less viscous than oil.

The addition of a German miracle chemical—a colloid used in nylon and plastic—mixed with the water would produce a gel heavy enough to prod the thick stubborn oil upward.

It was risky, expensive—for every oil well drilled, a second well had to be drilled to pump in the gel—and there were no guarantees.

Ernst had offered him a four-and-a-half-million-dollar advance against a partnership: German technique, German chemicals, German financing. Any loss would be in German marks. The gain, if it worked, would be payment to Lep in cash—top dollar for his half of the oil— all of it to be shipped to Germany.

Ernst's estimate was twenty million barrels.

Lep finished off the whiskey. He thought about Jessie, and the woman he'd seen assaulted by storm troopers. He thought about Bradshaw Tate, how to get Bradshaw Tate to give him back more than a million shares of Bell stock. He thought about Big Jim and the legacy of debt that had driven him for fifteen years. When he added it up, it was ten million barrels of oil at four dollars a barrel. It was forty million dollars.

He knew there was more. Ernst had said there was more. *"Business. Of course,"* Ernst had said. *"But that's not what drew you, is it?"* Lep had asked to go over the figures, knowing he'd accept them.

She knocked on the door. He opened it and watched her take a look at his face and see something she couldn't interpret that made her say, softly, "I'll make love to you."

He let her stay afterward.

Just before dawn, the screeching of peacocks woke him. Crossing to the window, he saw that the birds, usually confined to the courtyard garden, had somehow escaped and were fleeing like outlaws in the Wilhelmplatz below. From the window, he could see the Reichschancellery where lights always burned. Then he turned and he saw she was sitting up in bed wearing his Stetson which covered all but the lower third of her face.

"How much does a ten-gallon hat hold?"

"A gallon."

"Why call it a ten-gallon hat, then?"

"Because Texans have a ten-gallon head. For whiskey." He poured himself another shot and offered her one.

She shook her head, taking off the hat with a sigh. "When I was a little girl, I always wanted a horse—"

"Where do I send it?"

"Muncie, Indiana." A bubbling laugh escaped her. "Do you think it's true that Goebbels really has a pet lion?"

"Goering."

"I always get them mixed up," she said.

During the day, he forgot her.

It was easy to forget her. She slept all day and most of the time when he returned from his meetings with Ernst, she had left for the Rio Rita, and his mind was on other things. There was more: the right to the German colloid processes in the States. Ernst congratulated him on his acuity. But Hitler was concerned about petroleum reserves. Negotiations would be considered only in oil.

"Texas was settled by Germans," Ernst said. "By men like Ben Calder who wanted to own as far as they could see—"

They were having supper at Horcher's. Ernst had ordered a bottle of Clos Bougeot and the waiter had delivered two platters of oysters. The more civilized the surroundings, the more treacherous the game—Lep understood that. A bond with Ernst had been established. In going for more, there was no going back—he understood that, too.

"Of course, the airplane changed our perspective," Ernst was saying. Ernst's voice chilled him. "Think about the first American going up. When the American looked down, everything he could see already belonged to him—all the land and the resources between the Atlantic and the Pacific to be conquered and exploited. And the first Russian— what he saw was his own vast hinterlands. But the German—when the German went up, he saw Austria and Poland and Czechoslovakia." Ernst shrugged. "What are we Germans to do with our aggressive vitality?"

Lep looked up from his oysters. "What the Japanese did in Manchuria?"

"In that case, American oil companies might grow uneasy about selling to Germany."

"Or jack prices?"

"Exactly. Unless"—Ernst paused to fork an oyster. Then he met Lep's gaze. Ernst's eyes were ice-blue, waiting.

"Unless somebody provides you with a legitimate front to buy up American oil and ship it to Germany?"

"At an agreed price, of course."

"Market price—"

"To be paid out of a percentage of profits from the colloid process in America."

"How much of a percentage?"

Ernst smiled. "Calders have a talent for projecting the future and profiting from it. For men like us, it's less a matter of figures than a matter of possibilities. Vision. Don't you agree?"

Lep hesitated. He felt Ernst assessing him. He felt another question, unspoken, under the question Ernst had asked, another offer of more. "I agree," he said.

"I've arranged for you to meet Wernher von Braun. Do you know who he is?"

"No."

"He's a rocket designer. A genius. Not very many people can grasp what he's doing. He believes rockets are the key to space travel—" Again, Ernst paused to make an assessment. "In case it hasn't struck you, if you can ever send a manned rocket into interplanetary space, the view from there is of the planet."

The Berlin post office was the most efficient in Europe. There were four mail deliveries a day. A letter, posted in the morning, arrived at its local destination four hours later. Eva gave him a letter. To her mother, she said, in Indiana. He agreed to post it after she left. It was seven o'clock in the evening and she was standing in the crowded lobby waiting for the Persian boy. The elegant decor of the lobby seemed all wrong for her. She was dressed in the foolish costume, her eyes smudged with kohl and glitter on the lids, wearing the rhinestone horns, looking particularly inept and touching.

"What if I said I'd fallen in love with you?" she asked.

"I'm getting married when I go back." He was surprised at how easily the words came.

"I didn't know—"

"Her name is Sugar," he said. He had calculated how old Bradshaw Tate's daughter would be. Eighteen. Probably not married yet. It didn't matter. "Sugar Tate," he said.

Eva reached up and touched his cheek as if she were practicing a gesture of farewell. There was a stoicism in the brush of her fingers, some decision she had made to neither yearn nor mourn. It made him feel strangely sad.

"They say Hitler's going to be at the Rio Rita, tonight," she said.

The rocket exhibition was being filmed, Ernst explained. Still, Lep was an American. Lep's presence had required special permission. Von Braun, who was designing rockets for the army, had been given leave to supervise. What Lep would see would be a demonstration firing— an updated version of a German rocket that the Americans had tried to copy and test a year ago on Staten Island.

The night was clear, filled with stars. Lep felt an odd excitement as Ernst's car approached the northern suburb of Reinickendorf. The firing would take place on a three-hundred-acre field, Ernst explained. Originally an abandoned ammunitions dump, the acreage had been the rocket airfield for the German Society for Space Travel. The Society was no longer in operation, Ernst told him. Financial difficulties. There was no more private rocketry in Berlin.

Gestapo guards were ringed around the field. Ernst explained to Lep he wasn't allowed beyond the edge of the field where a shelter of earth-works had been constructed. Von Braun appeared and spoke privately to Ernst. Lep heard the words *"Kummersdorf"* and *"A-1."* Before leaving with Von Braun, Ernst introduced them briefly. Von Braun explained that a mixture of propellants—part liquid oxygen and part ethyl-alcohol—would burn at the rate of a hundred pounds per second. The propellants would produce a one-minute thrust. The rocket weighed ninety pounds. It would reach an altitude of sixty-five hundred feet. A parachute would bring it back to earth. Von Braun shook Lep's hand. "Perhaps we shall all live to see the rocket open the universe to human exploration."

Lep was left alone. There were lights on the field, and cameras. The mechanics wore white. Voices floated across, like Von Braun's, clipped and brusque.

Lep studied the rocket. Mounted within a steel tower that looked like an oil derrick, it was about five feet long, with a cone-shaped nose and fins. He was offered ear-plugs and a pair of infra-red glasses. He refused both. He was told to kneel behind the earthworks. He did.

All but a few lights on the field were extinguished. A silence fell. Kneeling, Lep waited. In the quiet, he could hear the thud of his pulse-beat. Suddenly, he saw a blast of flame. The tower started to shake. He stared, hypnotized as a cascade of fire poured downward and the bullet-shaped structure erupted skyward with a deafening roar.

Lep's ears rumbled. He felt his spine tremble. He soared with the rocket. Kneeling, as the fires of hell burned up the German sky, he knew this was why he had come to Berlin. Following the path of the rocket, speeding with it, he understood there was more, and the more was the future.

He heard the echo of Von Braun's voice and he saw a future where men would be given powers designated only to gods.

Eva didn't call.

At half-past three, still wide-awake, he called her room. No one answered.

He poured a double shot of whiskey and, stretching out on the bed, he tried to decipher the books Ernst had given him, written in German, describing the technical aspects of rockets and space travel. He found them hard going. At five o'clock, he put them aside to be translated into English when he returned to Texas.

He called Eva's room again and listened to the phone ring. Seeping through his own excitement was a conviction that something had happened to her. He told himself he was being absurd. The absurdity passed. He fell asleep, finally, to dream of rockets as the sun began to rise over his last day in Berlin.

It was late afternoon when he woke. He called Eva's room again. A strange woman answered. She identified herself as Frau Weingarten. He argued with her. Herr Weingarten came to the phone—they had arrived from Stuttgart this morning and had been given the room.

He dressed and went down to the desk in the lobby and inquired about her. He was told no such person had ever been registered. He was told no such person existed.

He had forgotten to post her letter. There was no letter inside, only a money order for ten thousand dollars. He made a note of her mother's name and address, then resealed the envelope and posted it.

He took a taxi to the Rio Rita. The place was locked tight. He banged on the door until a porter appeared. Pushing his way inside, he thrust the porter against the wall and threatened him.

Three storm troopers pulled him off. They pinned his arms behind him and hustled him off to the curb. Two more guards wearing machine guns were reaching down to haul him into the rear of a truck when Ernst's car pulled up alongside. Ernst leaped out and ordered the guards to turn him over. A hasty discussion took place out of earshot while a pistol was held to his head. Finally, the guards gave in. Ernst hurried him into the car. The driver sped off.

"Their orders were to arrest you for conspiring with Hitler's enemies," Ernst said.

He stood with Ernst on the north end of the bridge facing the curve of the Spree. Behind the Reichstag, the sunset cast a red glow on the ornate dome and the gilded horsemen. Above, a cloud of gulls gathered, crying in the twilight, as if they were crying for Eva.

Ernst's voice was clipped, quiet. "Hitler appeared last night at the Rio Rita," Ernst continued. "At a ringside table. He was accompanied by his retinue of bodyguards and the surgeon who goes everywhere with him in case of an accident or an attempt at assassination." Ernst paused. "Midway through her performance, Eva raised her hand and—as though surprised to find a pistol in it—she froze and stared at it until they took her away."

"Where did they take her?"

"The pistol was a thirty-eight. On her, they found two cyanide tablets meant to be placed under her tongue directly after firing."

"What will happen to her?"

"They arrested the Persian boy, too."

Lep turned away. A bent old man had stopped at the bridge rail and, digging into a paper sack, was flinging lumps of dried bread at the gulls. "Did they kill her?"

Ernst didn't respond.

Past the bridge, Lep could see the old architectural forms being razed for subways and elevated trains and tall buildings the Germans called cloud-scratchers—in that instant, he saw them not as progress but as a perversion of a lost dream he had meant to fulfill and now couldn't name. Marching, a troop of twelve-year-old boys came across the bridge, wearing the uniform of the Hitler youth and singing *Horst Wessel*— ". . . *when Jewish blood flows from the knife, things will go better*—"

He looked down into the river. The water glittered like Eva's spangled tights. He reminded himself it hadn't occurred to him to love her in life—to love her in death would be sentiment.

Ernst's hand on his shoulder snapped him around. "I understand your distress."

He read the rest in Ernst's eyes. From the beginning, he'd been followed. "She was a plant, wasn't she? She was a setup?" Nothing in Ernst's eyes confirmed it. "If I'd said no any step of the way, my arrest would have taken place?"

"You invest too much meaning in the death of a stranger," Ernst said quietly.

"Blood-knowledge," Lep said.

"Your plane's waiting," Ernst answered.

36

Lep followed Bradshaw Tate into the library. Bradshaw locked the door. The room was imposing, mahogany walls lined with Texas oil maps—a boll of cotton preserved under glass—Bradshaw had been a cotton broker before he'd become an oil promoter. Now, dressed in a cutaway that matched Lep's, Bradshaw started to pace. Lep helped himself to a shot of whiskey and waited, noting that Bradshaw looked paunchy, a bit stiff in the joints, all deceiving aspects; Lep knew Bradshaw was after a final reckoning.

The strains of an organ, warming up, drifted in from the garden. Lep could feel Bradshaw listening. He could feel Bradshaw remembering the Beaumont Cotillion—Sugar floating on her father's arm, as fragile and shimmering as a blown-glass figure, appealing in the way virgins were appealing, naïve and untouchable and longing to be broken.

"I can still put a stop to this wedding—" Bradshaw began.

Lep crossed to the window. Through leaded glass, he could see the chairs lined up, guests already arriving. Upstairs, Sugar was getting into the dress that young Sol Lubeck had brought back from Paris, seven tiers of lace and a train that required four page boys to carry. The bridesmaids would wear mauve, eight bridesmaids surrounding Sugar like a bouquet of peonies. "We made an agreement," Lep said. Turning, he saw Bradshaw had quit pacing. Lep smiled. "We agreed the best husband for a Texas girl is a Texas bastard."

Bradshaw had abandoned his cigar. He was unlocking a drawer in an inlaid Chinese desk. Reaching inside, Bradshaw pulled out some papers. "One of these documents transfers the Bell stock back to you. All I have to do is sign it."

"Sign it," Lep said.

"You know what these leases cost me. Worthless, then. The Rockefellers wouldn't pay. I got stuck with the million that nobody ever found."

"It's all in the family."

Bradshaw looked up. "Not yet."

Outside, the organ chords quit. Lep saw Bradshaw's bulldog jowls quiver. He saw a man resisting the image of his daughter's seduction: Sugar's frail, delicate body—Lep had gone about arousing it like a Catholic counting off rosary beads, with the same devout attention to ritual. Sugar knew nothing about sex. She had trembled in ecstasy at his slightest touch, giving herself over like a child, unpremeditated, eyes glistening with tears, emitting small gasps of surprise. No one had ever touched her before, and because she believed her rapture lay not in her body but in his—because she disowned it—he now owned her. That was his leverage. "It would break Sugar's heart to be left at the altar," Lep said quietly.

"Better now than later," Bradshaw answered.

Lep came across the room. Setting his whiskey glass down, he extracted one of Bradshaw's cigars from a humidor and lit it. Lep thought about now, and later. He thought about Sugar's rose-petal breasts, Sugar's narrow pelvis without experience or intuition. He knew, later, Sugar's innocence would turn to grief, like a tree in winter that had never flowered. He wondered if Bradshaw knew that, too.

"Four and a half million," Bradshaw said. "That's your deal for the Bell field. You'll pay off the Calder ranch and the house in Houston—"

"That's right."

"A gamble against forty million in oil and a crack at the chemical industry—"

"Those are futures."

"Exactly. Futures. Right now, Sugar thinks she's in love with you. Right now, Sugar's got stars in her eyes." Bradshaw was holding out a document. "Maybe you'd better look at this."

It took Lep only a moment to read it all the way through. It was a property settlement. The date was blank. The figure was blank. There was a place for his signature.

"If you ever divorce her, my lawyers will fill in the date and the sum. It'll cost you everything you've got," Bradshaw said.

Lep ground the cigar out in an ashtray. He picked up his whiskey and drained it. "What if she's pregnant?"

Bradshaw held out a pen. "She's not."

In the garden, the organ began to play *"Lohengrin."*

37

The wild horse was a devil. A pure albino, treacherous as a streak of white lightning, it was called ghost of the mountains by the *vaqueros* who believed it to be possessed by demons. Manuel had captured it anyway and brought it back to the ranch, penning it up alone where it snorted and reared like an angry wraith. The *vaqueros* wouldn't go near it. Lep ordered Tate not to go near it.

Lep meant to break the horse himself—at forty-six, he could still break any horse alive—he meant to give the *bulto* to his son for his tenth birthday. But the next morning at sunrise, crossing to the bedroom window, he saw the boy climbing onto the roof of the stable where, crouching, Tate sprang suddenly onto the horse's back to be instantly and mercilessly thrown.

Through July, Tate wore a cast on his right arm and tape on his ribs, becoming more and more withdrawn as though he saw it had pleased Lep to be disobeyed. And sometimes Lep saw anger blaze in the boy's eyes, as though Tate knew mounting the albino had been an obliging— a son showing his father there was that kind of wildness in him—and he hated Lep for wanting that from him.

"The boy's too sensitive," Lep told Sugar. The boy had daring in him, but not fierceness—no fear but too much pity. "You leave him to me," he told Sugar. Sugar was drinking too much. She was thinner than ever, pliable as a reed. Over the years, she had suffered four miscar-

riages before giving birth to Tate. It had taken nine years and then she
had borne twins—only Tate had survived—and sometimes Lep
thought Tate had gotten the crazy idea from Sugar that a part of himself was missing and the boy was always searching for it. Lep's tone
was impatient. Nineteen years of marriage had come down to watering
Sugar's gin. There would always be other women, but there would be
no more sons. He had begun to see that as Sugar's revenge. "You leave
Tate to me," he repeated.

The cast came off in August. Tate's ribs had mended, so had the
arm.

In the kitchen, Lep found Sugar hovering over the boy at breakfast,
like a tailor who was always measuring him for a suit nobody had ordered but which, if left to Sugar, Tate might have to wear for the rest
of his life. "Let's go," Lep said to him.

The albino was penned, still unbroken. Lep saw the boy looking at
the stallion from that secret corner of himself Lep had never been able
to probe.

"You set out to subdue a wild thing," Lep said harshly. "There's a
law in that." A rope hung across the fence. "The law is—it's either you
or it." With one hand, he offered Tate the rope. In the other, he held
out a 44-caliber Walker Colt. "Either you tame the bastard or you
shoot him."

Tate took the rope. Lep watched him vault the fence. The stallion
fastened its ghostlike gaze on Tate, snorting. Tate moved in obliquely,
casting the rope, catching the albino on the first try. The animal reared
and soared, teeth bared, roaring. Tate caught hold of the rope and
leaped onto the animal's back. Crouching between its shoulders, he
brought the rope in enough for the stallion to roll beneath him, sliding
and lunging but unable to shake him. He stayed on for a full minute
before he released his hold, slipping off in a ball and rolling in the dirt
under the rails of the fence to get out of the way of the crashing
hooves. Then Tate scrambled to his feet and unlatched the gate and set
the albino hurtling free.

Lep gave Tate two hunting rifles for his thirteenth birthday.

One was to be kept at the ranch. The other rifle would take its place
in Houston among Lep's personal gun collection, three glass cases in
the library filled with Walker Colts and Diamond Backs, every kind of

rifle, automatic and single shot pistols—Magnum revolvers and Browning automatic lugers—none of them purchased at those gun shows which also offered Nazi memorabilia, iron crosses and Wehrmacht helmets. Lep had brought the luger back himself from Germany in the spring of 1945 when the Third Reich was being obliterated by American and Soviet armies, and he had been instrumental in convincing Wernher von Braun to transfer the German V-2 rocket operation—fifteen hundred people and fourteen tons of paper filled with mathematical equations—to the American theater of operations.

All summer, he'd had no time for Tate. The rifles were to make up for that, and the hunting trip. Lep ordered a Jeepster outfitted with airplane landing lights and had Manuel teach Tate to drive it. The first weekend in September, Tate and the Jeepster were delivered to Brownsville for a whitewing dove hunt along the Rio Grande.

Lep came in from Washington, from meetings on the Libyan oil strike and the ensuing glut—oil imports rising so sharply they threatened to put Texas producers out of business. He had spent an hour with Eisenhower arguing for import quotas. Then he'd raised the issue of space. According to Wernher von Braun, the Russians were about to launch an artificial satellite capable of remaining in orbit a thousand kilometers from earth. To catch up, Von Braun needed funds, government support, the firing up of national spirit. Eisenhower was a military man. Wasn't it clear that Hitler could have won the war? Hitler had Von Braun, advanced rocketry—Hitler hadn't used it because Hitler's idea of a General was Napoleon. The psyche lagged a hundred years behind the times. Nobody wanted to get caught a hundred years behind the times.

It rained for five days. The hunting was rotten, not like the old days before the freeze of '51 when the air had been so thick with doves a man could bag a hundred birds a day without taking aim. Lep tried going out at night, crashing through the rain-soaked marshes in the Jeepster, the airplane lights turning midnight to day. Snakes scurried from hiding. An owl hooted. The rain broke, suddenly, briefly. A covey of birds took flight. The boy didn't raise his rifle. Withdrawn under a duck-billed cap and huddled in a soggy mackintosh, Tate never fired a shot.

"Do you want to drive?"

Tate shook his head. "No."

Lep studied the boy through narrowed eyes. Tate's expression was grave, no eagerness in it—reckless and stubborn in his own way, it wasn't Lep's way. Lep had a need to provoke the male violence in him. "Don't you like hunting?"

"I don't like killing."

Lep swerved the jeep around and headed back. Over the river, the moon showed its face through a rift in the clouds. "What do you like? Church? All those prayer meetings with Sugar? Billy Graham? Do you believe Texans are going to spend eternity in Hell?"

"No."

"School, then? You like school?"

"Sometimes."

"When I was your age, I learned from a three-hundred-pound whore and from men who'd knife you as quick as cutting butter." Lep frowned. "Life's a cold-blooded business. I'm trying to get you ready for it. Do you understand that?"

"No."

"Do you see that moon up there? It's no bigger than Africa. Did you know that?"

"No."

"One day we're going to send a man to the moon. We're going to do that from Texas. One day there'll be Calders in space. Do you know why?"

"No."

"Is that all you can say? No?"

"I'm sorry."

"A Calder's never sorry. You can't be sorry and get there ahead of everybody else. How do you think your great-grandfather tamed Texas? How do you think your grandfather made and lost twenty million dollars in wildcat wells? How do you think the Calder Refineries came about?—and Calder Chemicals? There's been a Calder on every frontier, and the next one is space, and thirteen's not too young to start thinking about it."

"I'd rather be a doctor," Tate said.

Lep scowled. Then he laughed, suddenly. "You been laid yet?" The boy didn't respond. "You'll change your mind," Lep said.

The boy slept. Lying beside him, wrapped in a bedroll in the sanctuary of the tent, Lep smoked quietly, two pairs of scarred boots, nearly the same size now, were drying beside the embers of the fire pit. Rain was beating on the canvas again. He saw Tate shiver in his sleep, fending off nightmares. Then the boy's face changed, taking on a strange and luminous quality, as if he had traveled beyond sleep into some stream of savage light. For a moment, the boy turned rigid. His hands clenched the bedroll and a slight film of sweat formed on his forehead. Then Lep saw the boy yield, and Tate's face took on an awesome beauty not unlike the strange purity of the albino stallion he had freed —Lep had ordered the animal run down and shot, but no one had ever seen it again. Now, watching Tate, unguarded in sleep, Lep felt the same kind of impulse stir in him again—a hatred for the part of the boy that eluded him, a fear of what he sensed might be a spiritual mystery, some quality of freedom that existed beyond him. Uncertain of what he saw, he felt only a powerful need to destroy it.

The next evening, he drove the boy across the border. Rain-saturated hunters trudged through the streets of the *zona roja,* still shouldering rifles and drunk on tequila, spilling in and out of the cantinas of the red light district. Five days of straight rain had turned the Mexican streets into swamps, but the mud hadn't deterred the urchins begging for coins or the whores who'd come all the way from Mexico City for hunting season.

The old woman had come from Torreon. She had brought her granddaughter, a rouged twelve-year-old—guaranteed to be a virgin—onyx eyes blinking in a full round face and a great mass of black hair, the body so stalk-thin she looked like a sunflower. Lep put Tate next to her at the table in the crowded cantina. The old woman, peering at both of them from under withered lids, was eating enchiladas dripping with pork fat and covered with raw onions. Lep kept filling Tate's glass from a pony of Mexican beer. Finally, he asked the old woman, "How much?"

"A hundred and fifty pesos," she answered.

"Too much."

They bargained. The old woman settled for half. Lep paid in dollars.

"I don't want her," Tate said.

Rising, Lep took the girl away.

When he came back, the cantina had emptied, the woman was still eating. The boy was asleep, slouched over the bowlegged table. Perched on the back of an abandoned chair, a rooster crowed and flapped its wings. Tate woke at the sound. Lep looked at the girl through Tate's eyes. The girl had smeared her mouth with fresh lipstick; it looked like she was bleeding. *"Diablo,"* the girl was saying to the old woman. The girl started to weep. Coming from her was a smell that made Tate's nostrils quiver. The boy couldn't quit staring at her.

Lep laughed. "Do you want her now?"

Stumbling to his feet, Tate grabbed for his rifle. The blast missed Lep by a fraction of an inch. The rooster shrieked, struck by the blast, and dropped to the floor. The old woman twisted the bird's neck and began to pluck it. Tate started to shake. Lep didn't move. Tate's teeth chattered and a violent trembling assaulted him, sending him to his knees where he vomited on the floor of the cantina.

Lep was asleep.

Sliding out of the bedroll, Tate got into his boots and his mackintosh and left the tent.

Outside, dawn was trying to pierce the cold steady rain and he could hear the rush of the Rio Grande lost in the mist. He walked a few yards and stopped, watching the rain form strange images and listening for the echo that he sometimes heard when the *vaqueros* sang around the campfire, the sorrow and the rage that he'd always heard as Ben Calder's voice.

He knew it would come.

Waiting, he thought about not going back to the ranch. He thought about not going back to Houston, not going back to school. The boy in him harbored these thoughts. At the same time, another part of him— he felt it split off from the rest—went searching through the mist for a glimpse of the old man mounted on the back of a smoke-colored stallion and galloping through time.

He carried Ben Calder inside of him—he'd never told anybody that —never sure what it meant, only that it was so and, sometimes, like now, he could make out the figure of the old man and he could hear the stallion's hoofbeats, as clear as in a dream.

He heard something. The echo came, less an echo than an imprint on his mind.

So remember this . . .

A hidden mystery stirred within him, uncomfortable, bewildering, like something lost demanding to be reclaimed.

Let those who would be gods—

He waited.

—first learn to be human.

BOOK FIVE

38

The cafe was an old storefront on the fringe of Houston's fifth ward. A dingy pink curtain covered the window where somebody had painted two garish fighting cocks above worn green lettering that read: ROSA'S. Inside, there was no sign of Rosa. The place was run by her husband, Antonio, a pie-faced *Chicano* with slitted eyes and a laugh like a rusty cowbell. Rosa had run off four years ago with an oil rigger. Rosa had been a shrew. The first tequila was always in honor of Antonio's good luck.

Now, Antonio's luck had run out.

Fifteen years in surgery, Tate thought. Surgery had trained him for everything except how to tell a man his luck had run out.

Carrying his glass, he made his way through the crowded tables, ducked through a low doorway, dropped a coin in the scarred pay phone at the rear and dialed his answering service. Lola was on the board. "Call home for me, will you?" The kitchen door was open; he could see Antonio's ancient *tia* stuffing tamales. "Tell Joanna I won't be in until"—he looked at his watch. It was almost midnight—"late," he said.

"Which is it tonight—an aortic valve or an emergency bypass?"

"Use your *Merck's Manual*."

"Maggie Wilson's called three times."

Maggie Wilson was a scrub nurse. "You're a woman, make up something."

"You're a bastard."

"You're the only one who understands me," he said.

A neon-lit jukebox was playing Mexican cantina music. Tate settled onto a stool under a life-size blowup of Lola Montez which hung over the bar. Below it was a sign in Spanish which translated: ACCEPT LIFE AS IT IS AND LEAVE ROOM FOR MIRACLES. The sign had gone up two and a half years ago. *El toro,* Antonio had said: cancer was a peevish black bull. Six weeks after surgery, Antonio had been behind the bar exuding triumph, a belief in miracles which had taken the form of a dozen candles to the Madonna, and a lusty appreciation for a new life which he intended to spend exactly as he had spent his old one.

Now, Antonio needed another miracle.

The *guacamole* was loaded with enough garlic and chiles to spice a whole suckling pig. The *tostadas* were hot, newly fried. At a nearby table, two men had started to arm wrestle, sweating, and Antonio was moving around, taking bets. Tate laid two dollars on the older one, betting on experience over youth; he was nearly forty, it was time for that. Around the curve of the bar, a woman was watching half-heartedly, heavy rouge and mascara applied in a defiance of mortality that went all the way back to the ritual of dancing with skeletons on All Saint's Day. She fastened her eyes on him and he read them: *Do you want me and how much will you pay?*

In the cloudy mirror, he could see himself: over six feet, chestnut-haired, blue-eyed, a *gringo. Gringos* showed up to buy what shouldn't be sold and take what couldn't be bought. It was an old Texas tradition. You took a land that essentially belonged to another people and then created a supernationalism devoted to blotting out those people. Then you went looking for grit and earthiness among the people who no longer existed but who somehow embodied the qualities you had lost.

He knew his father would have argued with that. From the tower of Calder Enterprises, Lep looked out over Houston and saw nothing but progress.

He reminded himself he had sworn not to think about Lep.

He moved to a table and ordered a second tequila. He had a need to get drunk, a need to obliterate the last few days: the hairless twelve-year-old in the cancer ward at Sam Houston Memorial Hospital who slept with her tap-shoes under her pillow; Donna Luigi. He had lied in Italian to Donna Luigi: no metastases. The old couple at Calvary Hospital who'd been admitted with matching coronaries—the old man had died on the operating table and the woman had survived to keep asking over and over "Why do I keep seeing stars?"—Joanna's profile; Antonio's X rays.

The tequilla went down like lye. He seldom drank heavily, only at *Rosa's*—something in it deliberate and perverse. Liquor unleashed other presences. He could feel them breathing, waiting for the crack that would signal their release.

Cheers punctuated the end of the arm wrestling. The younger man won; Tate lost the two dollars. The winner, a beefy *Chicano* with thick black hair cut Indian-style, rose and came lumbering over to the table.

"Your name Calder?"

"Yes."

"Doctor Benjamin Tate Calder?"

"That's right."

"You tell your old man if he doesn't watch his step, he's gonna start another Mexican-American War."

Tate rose slowly. He wanted to say: The Mexican-American War was like Vietnam—nobody human wanted it. But the arm wrestler's eyes reminded him that his great-grandfather, Ben Calder, had fought in one and he had fought in the other—and, only a month ago, a chemical worker named Rodriguez had been beaten to death and dumped in the Ship Channel not a half-mile from the Calder Refinery.

"Tell him yourself." Tate heard his own anger. He knew what was underneath. He had spent a lot of time not looking at what was underneath.

He felt the arm wrestler's hand on his shoulder, powerful, like a vise. He watched the arm wrestler's face redden, threatening. *"Quiere repetir eso?"*

Lubeck's Emporium was closed. The escalator was static, reduced to a set of metal stairs. Over it, an eighteenth-century French clock encrusted with gold buhlwork struck midnight in clear precise tones.

Below, moving beneath the blazing crystal chandeliers, Joanna crossed the ground-floor followed by an entourage of *Lubeck's* employees and a pair of Brink's armed guards. Heels clicking on marble, she crossed to the southeast corner of the store where she paused—a slim study in shades of brown—linen trousers and pima shirt, a raw-silk jacket, sleeves pushed up to her elbows. Then she nodded, waiting as the guards moved forward and unlocked the scrolled iron gates that protected a discreet sanctuary tucked away from public view. She pressed a switch. Inside, in a dozen velvet-lined cases, recessed lights flared. Rubies sparkled. Emeralds and diamonds gleamed.

At night, the room looked a bit like a coffin, maroon-velvet walls and matching rug. Entering—accompanied by a pudgy prematurely balding man wearing a painter's smock and carpet slippers—she moved quickly behind the main case and stooped to spin the combination lock. The lights sculpted her cheekbones and cast golden highlights through her mass of hair. For a moment, the lights blanched her face, giving her an odd tremulous look. Then the doors slid apart and she rose, as if gathering her authority, and stepped around in front. One by one, she pointed out the most expensive necklaces. One by one, the pudgy balding man—rosy-cheeked and prone to extravagant gestures—removed the neckpieces and, beckoning to four girls who were carrying wire cages filled with white rabbits, he fastened each jeweled clasp around a rabbit's neck. "Another triumph!" Quinn chortled.

Joanna smiled affectionately. Quinn's real name was Cohen. He came from Sweetwater, Texas. Seven years ago, her father had hired him as Art Director because he had presented no credentials except a promise "to make Nieman-Marcus look like the five and dime." It had been Quinn's brainstorm to "bejewel the furry beasts" for the Easter windows which, he predicted, would be unveiled tomorrow "with more local press coverage than the discovery of the Dead Sea Scrolls."

Before his illness—she always called it his illness and never its name —her father had supervised Quinn. Her brother lacked imagination, her father had said, and Quinn needed boundaries. She had freed as much time as she could, coming in between the children's schedules and the Symphony Board and the Houston Ballet and the *Casa de Vida,* her own project for Hispanic women; she had cut out the dance classes and canceled her regular tennis game and extracted herself from what had been the possibility of an empty love affair. Remembering— he had been third-generation Natural Gas with a reputation for inter-mittent rages—she felt a swift pang of need and a flutter of fear. She wondered where Tate was tonight. With a woman, she thought. Maybe not, she thought.

It didn't matter, she told herself. *Liar,* she thought.

She locked the case. The guards secured the gates and provided an escort across the main floor to the windows which had been dressed to give spectators the illusion of peering through a series of cloisonné Easter eggs. Her father liked opulence and historical allusion. Quinn had discovered the Easter rabbit had been born on Texas soil; he had ordered hand-lettered parchment for every window:

> *In 1845, in a small German settlement in West Texas, immigrant farmers engaged in the traditional peasant ceremony of lighting Easter fires to ensure fertile crops. Roused by the flames, hundreds of jackrabbits went fleeing across the Texas prairie casting ominous shadows. To soothe her frightened children, a pioneer mother invented the tale of the Easter bunny.*

"Dazzling, no?" Quinn was spraying the rabbits with perfume, a mixture of musk and tea roses.

"Spectacular."

"Incredible."

Joanna glanced at the clock, murmured another superlative, and headed for the escalator, climbing quickly. She was almost at the top when she heard one of the girls moan, "Shit!"

She stopped and looked down: One of the rabbits had escaped and was scurrying across the marble floor wearing thirty thousand dollars worth of diamonds and freshwater pearls. As she watched, a guard gave chase, knocking against a cage and freeing two more. She suppressed a smile. Distraught, Quinn was plunging after the animals but they evaded his grasp and disappeared under the handbag case, one of them wearing a fourteen-carat emerald pendant and the other a hundred-thousand-dollar replica of a bauble given by Napoleon to Josephine.

Joanna turned and kept going.

Upstairs, it was quiet. At night, the store's silence held the same promise as an empty theater; it said: Here, soon, magic will take place. Lights burned in the Designer's Salon. She stopped to pick up a scarf that pleased her—then an apricot silk robe and a boucle sweater the shade of Texas spring bluebonnets—aware that all of it was superfluous and none of it would provide balm for the recurring bouts of disquiet that had lately beset her.

Inner tremors, she thought. The rift in the marriage was beginning to create a rift in herself.

The Salon was circular, walls of eggshell brocade set off by thick white carpet. Surrounded by piles of clothing strewn over gilded chairs, Allison was turning in front of a three-way mirror.

The suit was panne velvet; the blouse was antique lace, a web of old antimacassars and shimmering chiffon. Catching sight of her daughter, it struck Joanna that Allison was exactly the age she had been when Allison was born. Child of her first passion—a brief intense marriage that had consumed her innocence—Allison had always been special, different from Cissy and Benjy, her children by Tate; Joanna carried that tucked away.

"Dazzling," she said, giving the word Quinn's emphasis, and moving close enough to see their two reflections in the mirror—alike and not alike—her own image more fluid and vulnerable than she imagined herself to be.

"I wish I looked exactly like you," Allison said. "I'm all over the place—and you're sexy and glamorous. I mean, you're already there."

Joanna smiled at Allison in reflection—leggy and golden hair foaming around her shoulders like spilled beer. "You're beautiful."

"Then you're not angry with me?"

"Only a little."

"I know you don't like my leaving the store to work for Lep—"

"Turn one more time. Let me take a look." Joanna watched Allison slowly pirouette. "How is it at Calder Enterprises?"

"Exciting. Merritt Lockwood's training me." A slight uneasiness crossed her face. "I'm not supposed to talk about it." She caressed the sleeves of the velvet jacket. "Do you like it?"

"Staggering."

Allison removed the jacket and dropped it on an already overflowing chair. "Is it true Merritt Lockwood's been Lep's mistress for twenty-five years?"

"Thirty."

"What about this?" Allison held up a sleeveless lemon-colored silk.

"Smashing."

"Why did Lep stay married to Sugar?"

"Why don't you ask him?"

"Do you think I'm afraid of him? I'm not—" Allison dropped the lemon-colored silk on top of the jacket. Then she stepped out of the skirt and unfastened the blouse. Underneath, she was bra-less. Peering into the mirror at her breasts, she made a gesture of dismissal. "Too small—"

"Perfect," Joanna said.

The same trace of uneasiness flickered a moment in Allison's eyes. "Guero led the march against Lep last night."

"Somebody had to," Joanna said quietly.

"Merritt Lockwood says they're making up lies. Maybe there are chemical hazards—maybe that's true. Maybe Rodriguez had medical reports and maybe Rodriguez was going to sue—but Lep wouldn't order the police to kill *anybody*." Tears sprang to Allison's eyes. "Sometimes I think Guero hates the Calder family—all of us."

"He doesn't hate you."

"Because I don't have to deal with things like money or where I belong in the world—because I'm not part *Chicana,* he thinks I'm *free.* But I'm not, am I? I don't feel free."

Joanna shook her head. "Freedom's different for everybody. It's like love—"

Allison got into a faded western shirt and tucked it into an old pair of jeans. "When you fell in love with my father, how did it feel?"

"I was your age—"

"I know. And Malone was ten years older—and his grandfather was a Comanche *shaman*—and he was a crazy test-pilot genius—"

"I was like you. I'd always had everything I wanted." Joanna bit her lip. "Malone didn't care about *things* or what people thought. He was like—a shooting star. I knew it wouldn't last. I wanted him anyway." She brushed a tear from Allison's cheek. "You're like him. Enough. Not too much. Just enough."

"And Tate? How did you *know?*"

"When you fall in love, you know."

Allison turned away, picked up a striped linen chemise and held it out. "I think this would look better on you."

"I'll take it home and try it."

"Can I ask you something else?"

"About Guero?"

Allison flushed. "No. About you." She hesitated. "I know there's something wrong. Not between us. But there's *something.*"

Joanna took refuge in the motions of folding the velvet suit. "It's nothing."

"You seem a bit—shaky. Maybe that's not the right word. Like you feel something the rest of us don't—and you keep trying to bury it."

Joanna turned. "Listen to that—" From downstairs, came the faint echo of mayhem. She flashed a bright smile. "Do you believe Quinn's down there chasing rabbits wearing a king's ransom in diamonds?"

Allison giggled.

"Quinn—the security guards—they're all down there on their hands and knees," Joanna said, giggling with her.

Allison threw her arms around her. In the mirror, Joanna caught a glimpse of the two of them, like the last two women on earth, hanging onto each other and laughing.

"Por Dios—no!" Antonio was shouting. He had moved between the arm wrestler and Tate and he was gesturing and shouting in Spanish so rapidly that Tate could only catch phrases. *"Manos de oro—* golden hands!" he was yelling. "The Virgin Mary will rain curses on your head! Your mother will lie down with the Devil!"

The arm wrestler shrugged and lumbered to his table.

Tate eased back into his chair. "I could have taken him."

*"Por Dios—*I need you in one piece." Antonio produced two glasses and a bottle. Turning a chair around, he straddled it and poured tequilla for both of them. "Did you look at my pictures?"

"In black and white, you're a ringer for Ricardo Montalban."

"El toro?"

"El diablo," Tate answered.

"I had a dream. In my dream, I was in church. I kept trying to light a candle, but every time I lit it, it went out. Then I ran out of matches."

"We'll have to go in again." Tate drained his glass.

"You mean cut?"

"Yes."

"This time, you'll get all of it?"

"I don't know."

"No more cutting," Antonio refilled Tate's glass.

Tate stared into the tequilla. "We're dealing with crazy cells," he said. "They keep doubling. They go from two to four, then from four to eight, then from eight to sixteen. They go from five hundred to a thousand. Even if I can't get it all, I can set back the progression—

you'll be back to two again, or four. You'll have time. During that
time, a cure might be found—" He heard his own voice. It sounded
ragged and angry.

Antonio sloshed the tequilla around in his glass. "When Rosa ran off
with everything, remember?—you gave me twelve hundred dollars to
pay the bills and keep the place going." He reached across the table,
gesturing in front of Tate's face. "I gave you a paper, ten percent of the
profits of a business that's never had a profit. So you come here three
times a year and you get drunk and you tear the place up—"

"—only ten percent of it." Tate slugged the tequilla.

"I'll give you fifty percent," Antonio said, "seventy-five percent.
More. Anything you want." His hands swept the cafe.

"No charge for the surgery," Tate said.

"No," Antonio said, "I'm not talking about cutting. I'm talking
about what you do in Mexico City." He leaned forward and whispered,
"They say you take out the blood and you boil it."

Tate laughed. The sound spilled out of him like the tequilla which
Antonio was pouring, spilling over the rim of his glass. There was a
jagged edge to the laughter, something dangerous underneath. "Who
told you that? They're *loco*." From the corner of his eye he could see
the arm wrestler was watching him.

"My cousin Pepe told me," Antonio said. "His mother told him. Her
sister's mother-in-law has a nephew who worked in that hospital in
Mexico City. You've been going down in your papa's plane." A pleading look crossed Antonio's face. The neon from the jukebox cast an erratic rainbow of colors over the bridge of his nose. "Next time—I want
to go with you."

Tate shook his head.

"No cutting." The whites of Antonio's eyes turned yellow. "You boil
my blood instead of cutting. Do it here. Do it tonight."

"It's not legal here. That's why I go down there."

"Legal? What does that mean to me—legal?" The jukebox turned
Antonio's eyeballs green.

"The patients are Mexican—"

"What am *I*?"

"You *sonofabitch*," Tate said.

Antonio stood up. He wavered a bit. His eyes misted over. The
woman at the bar slid off the stool and came over to the table. "Go

away," Tate told her. *"Vamos!"* She leaned over, flashing a breast at him. He could see the edges of a brown nipple. He had a fleeting urge to bury his face in her breasts. The urge infuriated him. *"Vamos!"* Tate repeated.

Somebody laughed. The woman was making extravagant gestures and accusing him of something. The arm wrestler reappeared, and grabbed him, menacingly. Tate hurled himself up, diving with enough force to overturn the table. Antonio backed off like a man resigned to watching Tate take his own prescription. The first blow struck Tate in the abdomen. He doubled up, breathing heavily. Then he sprang forward again, battering at the arm wrestler's face as if it were no more flesh than a punching bag. Snorting blood from one nostril, the arm wrestler lunged, landing a blow like a thunderclap against the side of Tate's head. A second blow followed. The third blow, Tate ducked. Circling, they eyed each other. The arm wrestler moved first. The blow whistled over Tate's head. He crouched, catapulted forward, grabbed his opponent around the waist and, with enormous force, sent him sailing across the bar. Bottles toppled. Glass flew. Slumped over the bar, face down, the arm wrestler's hands twitched for a moment in a reflex action. A bleat escaped him. Then he slid slowly and silently to the floor.

The washroom was next to the telephone. Inside, he checked his hands. Nothing was sprained. There were, miraculously, no bruises. In the mirror, he saw there was a cut below his left cheekbone, three inches long, crescent-shaped.

When he emerged, the jukebox was playing "Mexicalli Rose." The customers were back at their tables; nobody looked at him. The woman was gone. So was the arm wrestler. Antonio was sweeping glass into a long-handled dustpan.

"In three weeks—" Tate said. "The twenty-eighth of April. Sunrise. Meet me at the airport outside the Calder hangar."

Antonio looked up and grinned. His eyes disappeared into the pouches underneath.

Tate touched his shoulder. *"Mi amigo,"* he said. "It's experimental. You have to understand the risk."

Antonio nodded. The pouches jiggled.

Tate went behind the bar and poured himself a shot of tequila. "We'll need a new sign," he said. What came to his mind was the one line from Martin Luther that had come down through Lep from Ben Calder. "Love God and sin boldly," he said.

He stopped at the hospital. An intern sutured his cheek, seven stitches. He didn't wait for a bandage.

Joanna wasn't asleep. He found her propped against pillows in the four-poster bed, making notes on a clipboard. When he came in, she looked up and took note of the half-moon cut on his cheek and asked, *"Rosa's?"*

His response was a curt nod.

"Who were you fighting this time?"

"Does it matter?"

"Ben Calder? Lep? Yourself? Who won?"

He spun on his heel and headed toward the bathroom.

"I'm sorry—"

He turned around. "Why don't you just say you're glad it was a brawl and not a woman?"

"I'm not glad. I know whenever you end up at Rosa's it's because you're wrestling with demons. Calder demons. Sometimes I feel them, too. Sometimes I feel Anna Calder lying in this bed—" She halted, uncertain. "Do you think they're trying to tell us something?"

He knew what she was asking. When did we start sleepwalking? How did we get to be one of those couples who've inherited everything and are certain of nothing? "I don't know," he said. "Somehow—I don't know how—the connections were cut. To the past. To each other. To ourselves—"

She laid the clipboard down. "You look tired."

He took a step toward her. "I'm going back to Mexico City. In three weeks." He felt her stiffen.

"What was her name?"

"Who?"

"The woman in Mexico City."

"I don't remember."

"Annabel? Jezebel?"

"Isabel."

"It's not jealousy," she said. "I'm not jealous."

"Can you clear your schedule?"

"For Mexico City?"
"Come with me."
"Why?"
"Forget it," he said.

39

The garage door was open. Tate's Porsche was parked next to Joanna's Mercedes. Directly behind it, Manuel's battered pickup blocked his exit. The pickup was filled with rosebushes, the keys weren't in the ignition and Manuel wasn't around. Tate reached inside the pickup and blasted the horn.

He heard Manuel whoop. Then Manuel came reeling around the house, carrying a squat iron shovel that weighed as much as he did. Somewhere near eighty, only the pull of gravity held Manuel upright, slightly askew, at a tilting angle to the earth so he walked with the rolling gait of an acrobat in a high wind. *"Que pasa?"* Manuel's face creased at the sight of him. *"Que pasa, que pasa?"*

"You think my Porsche has wings?"

Manuel grinned, showing a treasure chest of gold and silver. His head bobbed on a crone's neck, a rooster's gullet which he wore proudly as a mark of virility—*cahones* in the throat he called them; testicles. Manuel was patriarch to eleven grandchildren, all named *Garras*—a name that went as far back in Texas as Calder and had traveled the same places.

"The old man came to see me last night," Manuel said. "He left a message for you. He said, *'Go and tell him it's going to all come around again.'"*

"I'm due in surgery—"

Manuel struck his forehead. "Ben Calder comes to me because *you* won't let him in. I'm an old man. I have work to do. How can I do my work if he keeps me up all night?"

"The keys to the pickup." Tate stuck out his hand.

Manuel set the shovel down and pawed through his pockets. "I told him—all right—so you bought my father for seven dollars and raised him as your own son. You had your own reasons." Manuel rolled his eyes. "Then I asked him—if we were all the same family, how come Lep Calder's the biggest coyote in Houston and my old man died in a Mexican jail? You know what he said? He said, '*Okay—money is thicker than blood.*' Then he rode off on his horse." Manuel climbed into the truck and took his time fumbling with the ignition. "Sometimes it doesn't start."

"Okay—what do you want?"

"Not me. *Him.* One of those machines. You push a button and talk to it. Then it talks back."

"A tape recorder?"

"He wants me to write it all down. The *truth,* he told me. I'm an old man. I can't write that much truth." Manuel poked his head through the window. "I figure—I can sleep and he can talk to the machine. One day, somebody'll listen." Manuel turned on the motor but the truck didn't move.

"Okay," Tate said impatiently. "A tape recorder for ghosts. You've got it."

Manuel reached through the window and laid a calloused hand on Tate's shoulder. "You look more like old Ben Calder every day."

Tate grinned. "You mean he was a *sonofabitch?*"

"He was the *worst,*" Manuel said, throwing the truck into gear. He rattled off a string of Mexican oaths. *"Un diablo,"* he shouted over the roar of the motor. The pickup backed down the driveway in a cloud of exhaust. The brakes squealed. Then Manuel's head appeared once more as he uttered the final epithet. "He was *un diablo Tejano!*"

40

The limousine slid to the curb and nestled there, sleek as a wet otter stretched out in the noonday sun.

A black porter quit slinging bags, mopped his brow and hurried over to rap at the window. "Check your luggage, sir?"

Inside, where the air conditioning hummed softly, the driver shook his head. He wore a white jacket, polyester sharkskin, a black nylon shirt, a gold tie. Above the patent visor on his cap and embroidered on his left lapel was the same black-and-gold insignia that adorned four thousand gasoline stations west of the Mississippi: a five-pointed crown struck through with a bold "C." Tilting the rearview mirror, Pavlik looked at the girl in the back seat. "Do you want me to check the plane's arrival?"

"In a minute," she answered. She watched Pavlik studying her in the mirror, looking at her the way one watched shifting sunlight, as if she hurt his eyes—as if he found it hard to tell where flesh started and wheat-colored silk left off. She frowned. Pavlik irritated her; his obsequience irritated her. She wondered if what happened after years around Lep—after being constantly in the magnetic field of someone like Lep—was that you either became supercharged yourself or, like Jan Pavlik, you collapsed.

The thought set her wondering again about Lep. When she was a child, Lep had frightened her. Tall and striking, silver-haired even then, he had seemed bigger than anyone else. Lep glittered, she thought. He made you look at him. He pulled you in. Now, at eighteen, she was learning what it was: power.

She leaned forward and parted the glass. "Would you go over the schedule again?"

Pavlik pulled a list from the glove compartment. "We've already picked up Japan, Israel and Australia. That leaves England and Saudi Arabia."

"What about Red China?"

"This afternoon."

"This is the Russian journalist, isn't it?"

"Mikhail Kostov."

Pavlik had left the glass open. She watched him adjust the rearview mirror, pretending he wasn't still looking at her. She was still a virgin. She wondered if he could see that. She could hear Pavlik thinking: *It'll have to be a special one to tame her.*

"You'd better check the flight now," she said.

Pavlik nodded. She watched him disappear into the terminal.

Maybe the Australian, she thought.

Unless the Russian turned out to be more attractive.

She was aware of her effect on men; she was aware that every man she met wanted to make love to her. It seemed strange to her, as if what they wanted had nothing to do with her.

She thought about Guero. Whenever she thought about sex, she thought about Guero. To Guero, she was a child. To Guero, she was a Calder. She wondered if she might go about sex the way she went through the Designer's Salon at *Lubeck's,* with the idea of taking what she wanted, wondering if the bill would be paid elsewhere, by somebody else—wondering if what she selected, she would wear only briefly, a temporary deferring to fashion that would be discarded after a season.

She had read somewhere that the Japanese had no pubic hair.

Maybe the Israeli, she thought.

She had the idea that all Russians looked like bears.

This one didn't.

The man following Jan Pavlik through the door of the terminal had an easy stride, more like an antelope—somewhere between thirty and forty—a copper beard hid his face.

Pavlik opened the door for him. She watched Mikhail Kostov's face crease with pleasure at the sight of her.

"Dobroposhalovatj v Houston," she said.

Kostov smiled. "A beautiful greeting," he answered, in perfect English.

Pavlik opened the recessed bar, popped the cork on a bottle of iced champagne and filled two long-stemmed glasses.

She lifted her glass and sent Kostov a brilliant smile. "I'm Allison Calder," she said. "Welcome to Houston."

41

Tate watched the heart tremble like a frightened animal perched on the brink of an abyss, uncertain. Then the organ leaped into life, beating on its own.

Next to him, an assistant was waiting with fibrillator paddles in case the heart needed an electrical jolt when it came off the artificial pump. Tate nodded for him to put them away. The radio was still playing, but nobody was cracking jokes anymore—the tension was over, the patient would live.

Tate started sewing.

The sewing was mechanical, automatic; it was nearly twenty years since he had opened and closed his first cadaver—the victim of a prison fight; nobody had claimed the body. He and his partner—they had worked in twos—had been digging around in the intestines the way a child explores a can of fishing worms, and he had suddenly fainted, standing on his feet. He hadn't keeled over, but his eyes had rolled up in his head and his mouth had dropped open and he had started to slaver. Before the lab was over, word had gotten back to Lep. The first fifty million that had built the Texas Medical Center was oil money— the pipeline had always been direct—Lep had sent a chauffeur with the limousine and a bottle of Dom Pérignon, an offer of a one-way ride back to Calder Enterprises, and he had stood on the curb shouting,

WILD SEED   299

"Go back and tell him I'm going to be the best goddamned surgeon in Texas!"

He checked the monitors. The vital signs were stable—no plunge in blood pressure, no abnormal rhythm of heartbeat. The weakened blood vessel had been excised and replaced with a Dacron graft. It was routine now. The patient became a man again, an identity beyond an aneurysm; the patient became Joe Sherwood again, ex-sprinter at the University of Texas where he had once run the hundred-yard dash in 9.8 seconds. Sherwood looked good: pulse rate steady; the heart beating away, as good as new; better than new, repaired.

"Wrap it up," he said.

"Who's being sued?"

"Jaeger Laboratories. A defective valve. Three million dollars." Ellie was ginger-haired, slightly built, a dynamo receptionist. "Foley's been called as an expert witness." Ellie's fingers never left the typewriter. "The trial's in Scarsdale."

Tate nodded, let himself into Foley's office silently and lowered himself onto the sofa out of the range of the camera. Foley was seated at his round table facing a closed-circuit television set which was transmitting the courtroom proceedings.

"Were you aware, Dr. Foley," the prosecutor was asking, *"that the valve was defective when you implanted it in Mr. Vallone?"*

"The defect wasn't visible," Foley answered. Tate saw what the jury in Scarsdale would see. Past sixty, Foley was still fit, still imposing, no sign of the problematic eyesight—a slowly detaching retina—only the demeanor of a veteran surgeon, head of a five-man team that averaged thirty heart operations a day.

The heart was a pump. In an average lifetime, the heart beat more than twenty-five million times and pumped thirty-four million gallons of blood through its two ventricles. Hippocrates had said: *"A wound to the heart is mortal."* Foley had said: *"A pump can be fixed."*

"If Mr. Vallone had not been implanted with the defective valve," the prosecutor was asking, *"if he'd been given one in proper working order—would he be alive today?"*

Foley took his time. "It's always puzzled me," he said quietly, "this tendency to address doctors as if they were God." Foley smiled, a brief smile, like the pop of a flashbulb. "I'm afraid I'm not qualified to answer that question."

The screen went blank. Tate got up and poured coffee while a burly technician wrapped up the cable, removed the set and rolled the camera out. Foley swiveled in his chair, switched on his own closed-circuit television monitor and scanned the surgery that was taking place in six of the eight operating rooms. "Medicine's a power game," Foley said. "Not healing. Medicine. Few doctors understand that."

Tate carried two coffee mugs over to the table. "What's your point?"

"Your hyperthermia experiments on cancer patients in Mexico City—"

Tate scowled. Three days a week, at Calvary, he performed cardiac surgery. Twice a week, at Sam Houston, he performed cancer surgery. Foley had never been crazy about the way he divided his time, and Foley was even less enamored of his current experiments with heat therapy. "What about them?"

"You're working outside of the country. You haven't made progress reports—"

"It's tricky. We've got to change their blood entirely—run it through tubes into the pump and alter the temperature. When the blood's heated to forty-two degrees centigrade, the cancer cells seem to be deprived of enough oxygen to self-destruct and the normal cells aren't affected. The real problem is how to keep the rate of dead cells down to a point where the body can slough them off. A few more trips down there—"

"No more trips to Mexico City," Foley interrupted. "HEW. New regulations. I don't like them any better than you do."

"The regulations only apply inside the United States."

"The Board disagrees."

"The Board's filled with laymen. Experiment's a dirty word. All they're concerned with is the complications of the treatment. They forget the complication of the disease is death." Tate's voice rose, angrily. "They've got no jurisdiction over experiments in Mexico—"

"Not legally." Foley leaned forward. "Houston used to be an open town—back when Lep was wildcatting for oil and I was doing wildcat bypass operations—nobody was watching Houston back then. Now everybody's watching Houston."

"What the devil does that mean?"

"I've got a patient for you. Lyle Morrison. The Vice-President of the United States."

"What's his problem?"

"Sonofabitch has got a heart that should have killed him five years ago. The Washington medical reports will be here today. He'll be brought in by private plane tomorrow. They want him registered as Carlson. Top security. No leaks. What they don't want is a three-ring circus for the press."

"I'll make the arrangements."

Foley rose, switched on the monitor, glanced briefly at the surgery and started across the room. Tate spoke as he reached the door. "About Mexico City. You know I'm going back."

Foley turned. A frown puckered his forehead. "I'd rather you wouldn't."

"It's the same decision you'd make."

Foley shrugged. "I'm not always right. I figured that prosecutor in Scarsdale for a hatchet, and he turned out to be carrying a scalpel."

"From what I saw, it was your operation."

"Hell—" Foley smiled. "I don't even remember Mr. Vallone."

42

"I've decided to make this record public because I'm aware there will be questions—"

Pacing, Lep spoke into the microphone.

"I'm aware that the dimensions of my current project and its effect on the nature and quality of life on this planet may appear to some to be exploitive and to others to be immoral. I'm aware also that there are men and women who are capable of grasping the impact of a daring and creative vision. It is to them that I address myself—"

He paused. Returning to his desk, he replaced the microphone in the panel that housed a sophisticated electronic dictating system. No machines were visible. Cassettes were inserted and injected by the slight press of a finger. By means of the same touch system, he could dictate one tape as he listened to another. Leaning back in his chair, he activated the tape he had dictated earlier.

He heard himself say: *"I never saw Hitler personally."*

It was not how he had intended to begin the evening's dictation. It had happened anyway. He heard his own voice capture the memory:

"I arrived in Berlin in March 1935, a month before Hitler's birthday. I stayed at the Kaiserhof . . ."

His own voice filled the silence. It was Sunday. The building had emptied out on Friday evening. Now, at seven o'clock in the massive tower of Calder Enterprises, his desk thrust boldly into the sunset, soaring like a solitary bird over Houston's skyline. Octagonal-shaped, thirty feet high and forty feet across, the penthouse office was constructed entirely of glass. Even the transparent dome of the elevator and the outlines of the plexiglass furnishings disappeared into an expanse of snow-white carpeting. Seated at his desk, Lep had deliberately created the illusion of a man suspended in space.

Lep smiled, the smile of a man who had, in fact, transcended not gravity, but time—the satisfied smile of a man who was aware he was still strangely attractive, still lean as a cowboy, still a man who burned and hungered, not yet finished with sexual restlessness and a need to conquer.

Around him, the shadows of twilight competed with the fiery sunset, casting a nimbus of ocher and violet; the colors of a bruise. Then a fistful of stars appeared in the red sky as if sprayed there by the telescope which was the one object of substance in the room.

He shut off the tape and left his desk again. Carrying the microphone, he crossed to the telescope, adjusted the lens and swung it around to survey the skyline.

Twilight wrestled with the sun to claim the sky. Hovering on the brink of oblivion, the sun resisted its own descent and, in a last act of revenge, set the city ablaze.

Connected by a web of freeways, pockets of skyscrapers dotted the city with willful imperiousness in a mixture of architecture that charted Houston's progress. The early modern buildings, made of granite and stone or of steel and concrete, massive thrusts of power and engineering, stripped of all ornament, earthbound, rose, gray and dense in the incendiary light. Afterward had come the buildings as transparent as crystal, vitreous, looking like columns of trapped fire in the sunset's finale, design pure enough to fly. The Calder building had been the first of those. Now, the newest were mirrored—an architecture of reflective glass, black and silver and bronze—each building mirroring another, mirroring the streets and the people on the streets, endlessly multiplying like the city itself, creating both a maze of illusion and the reassurance of a real existence.

An eastern journalist had called the latest architecture Houston's narcissism. It wasn't. Lep could pinpoint the moment in time when the buildings began to go up: It was right after Campbell Malone had walked on the moon, and every man, somewhere in his unconscious, had registered the fact that he was living and propagating and searching for immortality on a planet that was too small for the human race.

He switched on the microphone. "The official name of this project is META," he said. "M-E-T-A. The initials stand for *Mobile Extraterrestrial Agency*. Its official purpose will soon be announced. Unofficially, however, I am engaged in a more immediate purpose of far-reaching consequences—"

Looking west toward River Oaks he watched the boulevards curve with studied grace, turning black and sluggish in the streaked light, like rivers, like the Nile and the Amazon and the Rio Grande, emanating immunity. The old oaks rose, their trunks as big around as oil drums, protecting the cloistered River Oaks estates which had been copied from Tara or Versailles or transported intact from the English countryside. In the center the Calder estate, red tile and adobe—Ben Calder had built it for his wife, Anna—a rambling hacienda, built the way the Mexicans used to build them, around a U-shaped court, adding rooms as they were needed. Lep had moved in there when he married Sugar. Now, it was Tate's.

That same eastern journalist had said, "Houston is the capital of Arabia." It was. And, "River Oaks is the Camp David of international finance." It was.

Shifting the telescope again, he pointed it downward, toward the streets, seventy stories below, where he could see a group gathering in front of St. Joseph's Church at Houston and Kane. Close to a hundred people, mostly *Chicanos,* filled the sidewalks and the steps of the church, carrying signs: *MARCHA ENCONTRA BRUTALIDAD CHEMICAL.* ABOLISH CHEMICAL HAZARDS. They stood quietly as a priest addressed them. Then a young man, hoisting a bullhorn began to dart about, shouting orders. Lep frowned as he recognized Manuel's grandson, Guero. The crowd fell into line. Guero was leading the procession as he had led the protest against dangerous working conditions in the chemical plant; it was Guero who had made the accusation that uninformed handling of a new substance called DOM had caused the death of a young *Chicano* named Rodriguez. It was Guero who had led the demand for a federal inquiry. An old-time cop had said, "Every Texan's raised to vote Democrat, love whiskey and hate Mexicans." The eastern journalist hadn't printed that as truth; it wasn't.

He turned the telescope east, scanning the tenements, the Barrio, the borderline blue-collar neighborhoods, the fifth ward which was black and poor, the lowest per capita income in Texas. There were no zoning laws in Houston. It was money—or the absence of it—that produced bedfellows, and in the absence of money, bedfellows produced children, and the planet Earth, which was only a small satellite of the setting sun, offered no more frontiers to the oppressed and the outlaw.

Not yet.

When Tate was four, he had looked through the telescope and asked him, *"Who owns the stars?"*—and he had answered, *"The Calders."*

Below, twilight fell on the marchers. He saw they had halted at the edge of Buffalo Bayou and somebody, a woman, was tossing a wreath of flowers into the water—presumably, the current would carry it out to the Ship Channel where Rodriguez' body had been found. An autopsy had shown irremediable damage from DOM. On the opposite bank, a group of armed policemen watched silently. Then Guero began to herd the crowd into line again, touching base everywhere at once synthesizing the diverse elements into a compatible mass that moved as one.

Lep crossed back to his desk, picked up the phone and dialed the Police Chief directly, a private number. "Are they going to follow that funeral wreath down to the Ship Channel?"

"They didn't get a parade permit, so we don't know what the hell they're doing." Dixon Amory's voice was aggrieved. "City Hall said to leave 'em alone as long as they're orderly."

"I don't want anybody frying themselves on a Calder Refinery fence out there."

"What do you want me to do?"

"Pick up Garras. They call him *Guero*. No formal charges. Just lock him up until you hear from me."

"That's *your boy*, isn't it?" Dixon made a gutteral sound that passed for a laugh. "Manuel's grandson, isn't it?"

"I don't want him roughed up, just locked up."

"Hell," Amory said, "my cops are knitting bun-warmers for flies these days."

Lep hung up. Addressing himself to the microphone again, he said, "The future of man depends upon the conquest of a new source of energy . . ." At the same time, he applied his left foot to a panel beneath his desk. A series of clicking sounds occurred, then a portion of the floor in front of him lifted back like a massive trapdoor, revealing a deep well. From it, a huge acrylic bubble slowly emerged.

Carrying the microphone, Lep rose and entered it.

Once inside, he paused. Inside was a replica of the galaxy. He appraised a cloud-obscured Venus, a ringed Saturn, a flaming Jupiter, which was a hundred and twenty times larger than Earth and was rotating twenty-eight times faster, the gold and orange and blue-gray of a Mars, which was half Earth's size, a sea-green Mercury and the twins, Uranus and Neptune, and a cold pale Pluto four billion miles from the sun.

Emperor of this universe, Lep manipulated the dials of a control panel. A replica of the space shuttle hurtled over Earth, looking like a mutation, a bird swimming in the sea of space, the nose and rudder of a shark and the wings of a hawk. From the metal womb of its cargo bay a pair of mechanical arms emerged to toss out a satellite. A beam extruder began to emit structural components with the speed of a machine gun. An antenna farm took shape, looking like a series of Japanese parasols, and robot craft crawled like space spiders, weaving airy webs of solar-cells. Then music filled the bubble, the throbbing boldness and the sharp melancholy of Mahler's *"Resurrection,"* the sound of utter solitude which accompanied only those isolated travelers on the path to death or to progress. He waited for that portion of swelling music which proclaimed the power of man's vision. Then he spoke once more into the microphone.

"META is a logical step in man's ongoing search for energy. *META* is a leap in the evolution of man's personal power to control and create his own environment. *META* will ensure the future of man."

He set a series of dials and stepped out again to cross to the window and look out once more at the darkening skyline. Forty-five years ago in Berlin, he had told Ernst: *"As an American, I have inherited the same love the Greeks had for freedom and inventiveness."* He had seen Texas then as the promised land.

He had told Ernst: *"And from my German ancestors, I have inherited a talent for the principles of energy and the control of matter."* He had seen Texas, even then, as a center of power.

Now he saw beyond that.

META was also a Greek word that meant *"beyond."*

He turned. Inside the planetarium, two mechanical astronauts piloted flying robots with mechanical arms. The robots were arranging a network of beams into a floating platform. Watching, Lep went back to his desk and reactivated the Berlin tape to make a final entry. Then he listened as he played it back.

"When I concluded my final arrangements with Ernst Calder in Berlin, I returned to the ranch where I instructed that a horse be sent to Muncie, Indiana. It was a blaze-faced sorrel mare, gentle enough for Eva's two-year-old daughter. I also sent a saddle and a split-fringed buckskin riding skirt, size two. Everything was accomplished in a manner that preserved my anonymity."

He ejected both tapes, marked them and locked them both in the safe.

Then he entered the planetary bubble again, adjusted the dials, scrutinized the formation of beams and took some measurements. Mahler's *"Resurrection"* rose to its final crescendo. Night fell outside. The clouds parted and the moon looked down on a man playing with the stars.

43

Joanna's dream shattered. Like a badly cut diamond, the dream broke into shards.

She had heard Tate leave, refusing to wake fully, only enough to become aware of a tremor invading her body, a slight electrical shock, like two wires being spliced together. Then Malone's image had hovered, Malone circling the Galveston beach like a raven until he had stopped and, with his hands, dug a place in the sand where, protected from the wind, they had made love. Malone, saying: *"Sexuality is a need to transcend the container of flesh—the urge to touch, if only briefly, all the ancient and insoluble mysteries."*

Malone had said: *"Black Wing was his name. My Comanche grandfather was a ceremonial runner. He could turn into a hummingbird. His spirit could fly. He could communicate with rocks and rivers and trees. He knew everything was alive."*

Malone had said: *"Some people are more alive than rocks, and some aren't."*

She got up and wrapped herself in an apricot robe, silk, light as moth's wings. She heard Tate's Porsche start up outside.

Tate had been in Vietnam—Tate had been in Nha Trang when Benjy was born: July 20, 1969. She'd come back from labor and one of the nurses had turned on the television and the first thing she'd seen were Campbell Malone's footprints on the moon.

Lep had turned up with the deed to the Calder estate.

Her father had arrived bearing a dozen potted orchids and an exact replica of the layette *Lubeck's* had provided for the latest heir to an Arabian emirate. Children were a woman's inventory, her father had said.

Last Sunday, from his hospital bed, her father had said: *"At Lubeck's, you can buy a full-length Russian lynx or a pear-shaped diamond as big as your thumb—but, even in Houston, you can't buy time. Even if you're Sol Lubeck."*

She crossed the bedroom and opened the shutters and looked down. She watched Tate's Porsche slide out of the garage. She tried to remember when Tate had begun to use phrases like "aggressive surgery" and "war on cancer." She closed her eyes briefly, trying not to think about her father—trying to pinpoint, instead, at what moment Tate's rebellion and idealism had compressed itself into the closed world of the operating room. When had her own been siphoned off into the *Casa de Vida?*—a rescue-center of Mexican women?

We're doing Lep's laundry, she thought. It was somewhere in there —reparation for the sins of the fathers—a sign of time catching up, the fact that she was thirty-seven, prey to the fears and the yearnings that gobbled up the shadows of women who'd reached an age they'd never planned to be.

She watched Tate's Porche head down the drive through the delicate patterns of light and shade that trailed imperiously like smoke colored from the arthritic limbs of the grande-dame oaks. The sun shifted. Needles of light pierced the branches and offered to blind her.

She turned away. She crossed the bedroom and picked up the phone. It took a few moments for the line to connect, a long-distance number, public, available to anyone.

She reached a machine, a recording of a male voice that began:

"Astrosight, the second of two Interplanetary Navigation Spacecraft, is continuing to send information and transmit images back to Earth as it prepares to approach the planet Saturn. The boost in speed acquired from Jupiter's gravity has assisted Astrosight in covering the five hundred million miles between Jupiter and Saturn. The spacecraft has been programmed to take an orbital position two hundred thousand miles from Saturn's surface where it is expected to confirm many of the startling revelations transmitted by its earlier twin, Explorer One . . ."

She didn't listen to the words. She immersed herself in the voice, listening for echoes—like holding a seashell to her ear in order to calculate the ocean's depth.

"*. . . Reporting through the Deep Space Network from a position approximately nine hundred million miles from Earth, Astrosight is now being navigated by quasars at the outpost of the cosmos. The light from these quasars has been traveling through space since before Earth was formed . . .*"

She imagined the vehicle spinning in outer space, probing the secrets of Saturn. She knew the image represented her own longing for risk.

She opened a drawer and dug around until she found what she was looking for—a photograph. The image was blurred, more light than form; the substance had been fractured by the camera into a shimmering ball of fire.

"*. . . Astrosight will provide another exploration of Titan, the largest moon of Saturn. The probe of Saturn, which is surrounded by a huge ring of rock fragments, will begin next week. Astrosight will eject the probe which will radio back information as it descends through the atmosphere, measuring atoms and molecules by means of a mass spectrometer which has the capacity to prove or disprove the existence of large molecules that could be the building blocks of living matter . . .*"

The line fell silent. In a crystal sphere beside her bed, the clock didn't tick; its numbers captured time silently, refusing to break the continuum of time and space.

She turned the photograph over. On the back, she had written: *The fourth dimension.*

The recording said:

"*. . . This has been a status report on the Astrosight Interplanetary Mission from the Jet Propulsion Laboratory in Pasadena, California.*" Then the voice signed off, "*Campbell Malone, speaking . . .*"

44

Tate's gesture dismissed the Band-Aid on his cheek. "Shaving—" he lied. Loretta Tibbs was on the desk. Chief nurse and earth-mother, Loretta's expression told him whatever was boiling away underneath his stethoscope was threatening to rupture the surface. "What's the gospel?" he asked. The gospel was the list of the dead, those he'd lost during the night.

He watched Loretta pull the charts. Patients responded to everything else as a disease, they responded to cancer as a curse—it was Loretta who'd told him that. Over at Calvary, Loretta had said, being a surgeon was enough. Here, at Sam Houston Memorial, he'd have to be doctor, witch doctor and priest. Loretta had turned out to be right. Loretta was usually right. "Everybody got through," she said. "Even Donna Luigi's asking for pasta for breakfast."

"See that she gets it."

"Sure—one more ounce of cholesterol and we'll deliver her to you at Calvary for heart surgery."

He started to say, *"Donna Luigi's terminal."* He stopped himself. The one time he'd used that phrase with Loretta, she'd snapped, *"So are you, so am I."* Instead, he asked, "How's my father-in-law?"

"He looks better than you do."

"Don't be a dragon."

"How could you see yourself as St. George without a dragon?"

He took the charts from her. "Call the lab while I'm making the rounds, will you? Tell Stillwell I want the black-and-white mongrel put on the heat exchanger—the one in cage D."

"Listen, it's none of my business"—Loretta reached for the phone—"but I've seen a lot of burn out in doctors. Those who don't implode—explode." Her eyes met his. "There's always a look they get—"

"You're dead wrong," he said.

The Aero-Jet Commander dropped through a blanket of clouds and soared down toward the runway. From inside, Isabel saw sunlight touch the naked wings—no White House emblem; the plane was unmarked.

She rose before the plane halted, waiting at the door as it slid open. The metal stairs unfolded. She saw two Secret Service men emerge from a sedan and approach her as she came down. One was wearing sunglasses—she could see her own reflection: mahogany hair grazing her shoulders, an elegance in her stride, an athletic fitness still like the girl at summer camp who'd been taller than anybody else.

"Mrs. Howard?"

She nodded. She watched two paramedics pull a stretcher out of the rear of the parked ambulance. They came past her, carrying it onto the plane. "Is the route taken care of?"

"There's another car outside. There'll be one in front and one in back. Do you need a lift?"

"I'm being met, thank you."

Frances Morrison was coming down the stairs, unobtrusive, genteel, a rounded figure like goosedown plumped up under a wrinkled navy linen suit. Lavender shadows around her eyes betrayed the fact she hadn't slept. Then the paramedics came out behind her carrying the Vice-President.

Lyle Morrison was covered to the neck, but there was color in his cheeks and he looked strangely robust, smiling, as if he expected reporters.

The nurse came last, a tall bony woman with drooping shoulders, blinking in the sunlight, rubber-soled shoes squeaking on the metal stairway.

The Secret Service men returned to the sedan. The paramedics settled the stretcher in the rear of the ambulance. Isabel watched Frances Morrison climb in, followed by the nurse. The ambulance pulled off. The sedan followed. Isabel felt a moment of tender concern—slightly inappropriate—not official.

The airport cart arrived to carry her to the terminal. Inside, she bought a copy of the *Houston Post*. On the third page, a UP squib from Washington reported the Vice-President and his wife were vacationing in a secluded cabin in the Rockies; the Press Secretary was doing his job. Walking as she read, her thoughts moved back to Washington and the White House, to the daily onslaught of political demands and personal assaults that faced the President. She was the one he kept around who perceived him as human, as one of God's struggling creatures who had coveted America's number-one driver's seat. He trusted her. He had sent her to Houston because he trusted her. More than Texas was being run by Lep Calder he had said. There was that in this Houston trip. And Lyle Morrison. Patients died on the operating table, or recovered slowly, or not at all. Walter Talbot, the Speaker of the House, was a wicked gnome in his late seventies. Talbot would move up—which meant in the '84 election, the vice-presidency could be up for grabs. There was that specter too, in this Houston trip.

The terminal door opened. A limousine was parked at the curb. A chauffeur stood beside it, waiting, a burly man with a pugilistic neck, wearing a white suit, a black shirt, a gold tie; when he tipped a visored cap to her, he revealed a stand of quill-like hair.

Inside, the air conditioning was running. It was fifteen degrees colder inside. Isabel shivered. The chauffeur climbed into the driver's seat. A push button opened the glass panel.

"Calvary Hospital," Isabel said.

"Mr. Calder has registered you at the Houston Oaks." The driver was scrutinizing her in the rearview mirror.

She leaned forward. "Calvary," she repeated.

The glass panel closed. The chauffeur put on a pair of silvered sunglasses and adjusted the rearview mirror. The limousine pulled off, purring.

Isabel turned away and looked out of the window. A freeway sign said: KENNEDY DRIVE. They went past it. Pressing her forehead against the window, she closed her eyes. The stereo went on, soft plaintive music with a Latin beat that took her back to November.

In November, Mexico City had been cool and dry. In November, there were tremors in the earth—echoes of an earthquake past or one to come.

The Texan had been registered at *the Hilton.*

Crowds had filled the *Avenida Juarez,* carrying torches and candles, weaving to the sound of flute and drum. On the *Paseo de la Reforma,* she had joined the throng, three miles to *Chapultepec Park,* surrounded by masks—the Devil, Death and Time—painted blood and gilded Christs. The *Feast of the Day of the Dead* took place every November —to cleanse the souls of the departed, to pray them out of purgatory, to intercede for the dead. She had chosen to go back in November.

The Texan had found her. A surgeon, he had said.

She had expected only minor tremors, less than that. But the drums had continued to beat all night long outside the hotel window.

Isabel opened her eyes. The limousine had left the freeway. The first billboard she saw on the side of the road said: HOUSTON: THE AFFORDABLE DREAM.

A surgeon, he had said. From Houston.

Calder, he had said. Dr. Benjamin Tate Calder.

The mongrel was dead.

Stillwell was claiming he'd done everything right.

Tate checked the shunt he'd implanted in the dog's anterior thigh a week ago—Stillwell had annulated it correctly and connected the tubing to the heat-exchanger. "Did you forget to anticoagulate the blood?"

"I used Heparin." Stillwell was nervous, defensive, another baby-faced intern who hadn't yet learned what medicine was—no demon raging inside of him, shaking invisible fists at invisible deities, no urgency making impossible demands.

Tate's voice rose, anger spilling over. "What about the peristaltic pump? Was it working properly?"

"I had perfect control of the blood flow—"

The dogs in their cages started to howl. The lab boy, Leroy, was slapping a dirty mop around the terrazzo floor. The place smelled like a latrine. "Did you monitor the temperature?"

"Of course."

"Goddamnit man, the animal's *dead.* Overheated—"

"The temperature never rose over 42.5."

"How'd you keep track of it?"

"Rectal temperature."

"The rectal temp registers two degrees lower than esophageal temp. I left explicit instructions to monitor by esophageal temp."

"You didn't—"

Tate grabbed him by the lapels of his lab coat. "Are you calling me a liar?"

"No, sir." Stillwell paled. In Stillwell's eyes, Tate caught a glimpse of his own fury. Tate let go. Stillwell went flying backward, striking the counter. Flasks spilled from the counter, crashing to pieces against the floor.

Tate whirled, shouting at Leroy. "Get that dead mongrel out of here and get this place cleaned up!"

There was grass under his feet. His feet were moving but his legs felt wobbly and there was a buzzing in his ears.

He'd been working too hard, he told himself—sixteen, eighteen hours a day. He'd been in pursuit of something important, a possible cancer cure, a man chasing a beacon of light that had hypnotized him —afraid to stop, afraid it might blind him.

Liar, he thought. Somehow, somewhere, he'd quit chasing medicine and started to run. From what?

Stillwell hadn't betrayed him. Medicine had betrayed him. Medicine had promised to take care of his doubts and fears; it hadn't. Medicine had promised to resolve the struggle with Lep; it hadn't. Medicine had promised to ennoble him, to endow him with integrity. Medicine had promised to reconnect him to the original humanity which had flowed in Ben Calder's blood.

What was there in it that had provoked his own seething anger, a rumbling within—a sense of impending catastrophe?

He spun around and headed in the direction of his car. *"Maybe they're trying to tell us something,"* Joanna had said. When had he abandoned his place in time? When had he severed his connection with the ghosts of Ben and Anna Calder? How had their immigrant's daring become, in Lep, an armchair tyranny? How had their original assertion that had tamed the outer wilderness become, in Lep, an inner savagery? And how had he, Tate, lost touch with the heart and the courage that he'd vowed to restore as the Calder legacy?

He got into the Porsche and gunned the motor. He threw the gear into reverse backing out into the sunlight when the beeper in his pocket started to blare.

He cursed it. He reversed gears and pulled the car in. Then he got out and started to run. From the nearest phone, he called in. The service connected him to Ellie. "You're needed at Calvary," Ellie said. "Now. Right away."

45

The bedroom was streaked with sunlight, pale muted tiger stripes that undulated across the floor. Allison saw the mirror glisten where last night's image was still superimposed: the upper half of her own torso welded by lovemaking to Zev Malachi's powerful legs.

The phone had been ringing last night when she came in. Zev Malachi, he had said. The Israeli correspondent. Did she remember him? He'd been ringing all night, he said.

Now, he lay sleeping next to her, breathing softly.

It hadn't been what she had expected.

She had expected to take shape under his hands. She had wanted a map to herself, a guide through the labyrinth of her inner being, through a maze of undiscovered rooms and hallways, secret passages, hidden catacombs.

It hadn't happened like that.

Under the need to rid herself of the burden of innocence had been an image of Guero, the unlived love affair with Guero.

Rising, she wrapped herself Indian-style in the batiste coverlet and padded silently into the living room and pulled the drapes. Her apartment was on the tenth floor. The terrace faced downtown Houston, morning breaking over the skyline, which changed every day, expanding, exploding. The sun sparkled on the glass tower of Calder Enterprises, dominating everything. Last night, for a moment, she had teetered on the verge of a precipice much like the tower, Zev urging her, pushing her toward the edge. She had resisted. She had wrapped herself, instead, in the glass enclosure, safe and impervious as Zev flung himself into darkness.

She heard him stir in the other room. Then he called her.

She went back into the bedroom and stood at the foot of the bed, studying him. He was dark, the kind of tan that came from the Negev where the sun penetrated to the bone. Black springy curls framed a pock-marked face. He was the youngest of the journalists Lep had summoned, only twenty-seven. She had met him at the airport. There had been a rawness about him that had attracted her. Now he looked alien, out of place against the straw rug, the wicker chaise, the iron bed that was painted white and filled with ruffled pillows. He was smiling. A sunburst of crinkles fanned out from his eyes. "Come back to bed."

"I saw Tel Aviv," she said. "I was fourteen. My grandmother took me to a cafe on the Diesengorf. It was filled with soldiers and drug pushers."

Zev's smile receded. A puzzled look crossed his face.

"There were rows and rows of box-shaped apartment houses," she said. "All exactly alike, built with American money—everything in the same state of disrepair. And there were no flowers. No flowers anywhere."

Zev rolled out of bed and stood facing her. She saw he had an erection; he wanted her. She turned away. "I didn't feel anything," she said.

"What are you telling me? Was I the first?"

She didn't answer him.

"Weren't you ever in love?"

"Yes."

"But you didn't make love to him?"

"No."

"Why not?"

"He's never asked me," she said.

Zev came toward her. He reached out and loosened the coverlet she had wrapped around herself. It whispered to the floor, leaving her naked.

She slapped him. It was unpremeditated. The burning in her palm surprised her.

He didn't acknowledge the blow. Instead, he reached out and put his hands on her shoulders and applied pressure until her knees buckled. She dropped to the floor. He knelt beside her, pressing her backward until she could feel the bristles of the straw rug against her back, like small knives.

"At night, the Mediterranean turns silver," he said, "and the jeeps patrol the sand—starting, stopping, turning their spotlights. You make love to that light coming in your window. Then afterward, you go out and you look up and you see the same stars that Abraham saw, and Isaac and Saul. Only up there, planes are crisscrossing—there are sentries in Abraham's sky."

She turned her head away.

"When you live with war," he said, "everything becomes precious. Every time you make love may be the last time you make love. You don't throw it away."

He cupped her chin and turned her head back until she faced him again. His eyes were black, no light in them.

"What's his name?"

"Guero," she said.

He let go of her. He stood up, slowly. The phone started to ring. He picked up the coverlet and held it out, wrapping it gently around her as she rose. The phone was still ringing. He pulled on his trousers. "Answer it," he said. "I'll make coffee."

Joanna went through her closet. There were seventeen furs. Wearing any of them, she looked a bit arrogant; she had a need to look arrogant. She settled on a gray caracul vest and western-style pants, tight as a second skin. Too young, she thought. She had a need to look young. She pulled on ostrich boots, making a choice from a hundred and twelve pairs of shoes. She kept an inventory on her dressing-room door. Every three months, a buyer from *Lubeck's* came out and brought the inventory up to date and distributed the castoffs among the thrift shops dedicated to charity.

Pausing in front of a full-length mirror, she brushed carelessly at her hair, fastened ivory hoops in her ears and appraised her image. What she saw pleased her. Like shifting gears, she had reaffirmed a sense of her own power; a sleek superiority had settled over her, impervious and reassuring.

Lupe was in Cissy's bedroom, changing linens.

She stopped long enough to give Lupe a grocery list to order from *Jamail's Market*. Lupe seemed preoccupied, withdrawn. Only four years older than she, Lupe had traveled the path of most Mexican women—having crossed, in the blink of an eyelid, that invisible line which transformed the passion of youth into pride and stoicism and a fierce sense of privacy.

"What is it?" Joanna asked.

The sheets whipped in Lupe's hands. Lupe's face took on that strange combination of suspicion and tolerance for the Anglo's ways— the need for power and the love of acquisition and the curious deterioration of all human feeling into formality and habit. "Nothing," Lupe said.

"Is it Guero?"

"Lo que Dios quiere," Lupe answered. Whatever God wills.

Allison took the North Central exit. "Across the bayou," it had been called for as long as she could remember. It had once been separated from the rest of Houston only by Buffalo and White Oaks Bayous. Now the division had been further widened by the largest expanse of freeway in the city—a rift of traffic lanes that separated the minority groups from the booming expanding city.

Guero had made her aware of that.

Driving past Holy Cross Cemetery, she remembered Guero once taking her there, pointing out the photographs and portraits of the early Italian immigrants who were buried there, their likenesses still attached to the headstones, still testifying to an earlier time when the North Central area had been a stopping-off place for those on their way into the mainstream. Then the bridges had been cut and the mainstream had dammed up.

Guero had made her aware of that, too.

Overhead, the clouds thinned, leaving a bright pitiless morning, glare without sun, not kind to the damaged streets. Skeletons of razed buildings rose, boarded-over gaunt and bleak, like specter guardians of an old and tired war zone.

She pulled into a narrow alley, guiding the red Fiat past broken bottles and treacherous potholes and parked in front of a stucco apartment house. A blotched coat of salmon-colored paint peeled from it, in layers, like a bad sunburn. A scrawny tomcat arched its back and snarled at her from a nest of overflowing garbage cans. On one of them, somebody had scrawled: EXXON SUCKS.

The apartment was up four flights of rickety stairs. The hallway smelled rancid. There was a newspaper photograph of Rodriguez's funeral pasted on the door and scratchy Latin music coming from inside. When she knocked, a young *Chicano* answered. Tall and lean, he wore sneakers, a khaki T-shirt, frayed dungarees. His jaw was scraggly with the beginnings of a beard.

"Are you Carlos?"

She watched him scrutinize her, scowling at the silk and cashmere, the single topaz on a chain, the lizard purse and matching belt wrapped low on her hips. She could feel his contempt. "You said it was important. You didn't want to talk on the telephone—"

He looked past her, down the hallway, as though he were checking to see if she'd come alone.

"Please—" she said. "You told me it was about Guero—"

"The cops picked him up again. No lawyer. No phone calls. Not even a record of the arrest. You're a Calder," Carlos' lip curled. "You're the only one who can get him out."

Joanna sped through the Rice University campus. She had stopped at the printer's and ordered the invitations for the Houston Ballet Ball which was three months away. She had picked up the new little league uniforms for Benjy's team—the second stop had made her late for her weekly lecture.

She parked in a red zone and hurried up the stairs. Inside, the class was crowded. Out of the five thousand newcomers who moved to Houston each month, more than a hundred had signed up at Rice to learn how to be Texans.

She set her notes on a lectern and started with slides: jalapeño lollipops and O'Neil Ford's architecture. She played a portion of a record: the Austin sound in music. She read them excerpts from frontier poetry and cowboy lore and the legends that claimed Texas had been populated by Germans and Czechs, by renegades and mavericks, by those who couldn't read the signs at the Oklahoma border and those who got lost on the way to California.

The class was two hours. There was a ticket on her car. At half-past twelve she pulled up in front of *Tony's,* gave the attendant her car and tore up the ticket.

The restaurant sparkled. Refracted light splayed over oriental gold foil murals and red velour. Waiters rushed to hover around her. Heads turned. The captain snapped orders, murmured a compliment and ushered her to the Calder table.

Sugar was already there, wearing something long-sleeved and filmy, peach-colored, wisps of white hair curling around her face and pinned by a tortoise-shell comb into a Victorian twist. Sugar was sipping gin over cracked ice. When Sugar drank, the remnants of Beaumont became visible, and Joanna caught a glimpse of the girl called Sugar Tate who had grown up on the eastern side of the Balcones fault line which split Texas, distinctly dividing Old South from Wild West. Sugar still used words like *"nigra"* and penned weekly letters in an exquisite script to girlhood friends.

"You look stunning—" Sugar's voice was shrill and breathless. "Stunning," she repeated before plunging, as always, into the middle of a sentence nobody had started. "—divine idea for Easter Sunday," she said. "Two dozen Tahitian girls—floating on rafts in the swimming pool. They can dive for the lobsters—"

"A split of Pinot Chardonnay," Joanna told the waiter, "and lobster salad."

"I mean, for two hundred and fifty dollars a head, the caterer should come up with *something,* shouldn't he?"

"Absolutely," Joanna agreed. Listening to Sugar was like putting together a jigsaw puzzle; eventually, all the pieces would fit.

"I'm sick of Texas *barbecues.* It should be *elegant.* No more than a thousand. We'll only have people who are under thirty or very rich." Sugar turned to the waiter. "Cold salmon," she said. "and *another*—" Sugar tapped her glass and sent Joanna a guileless look. "You look stunning," she repeated.

"Thanks."

"A bit bold."

Joanna smiled.

"It seems to me we might as well make it a *celebration*—"

"What are we celebrating?"

"Suppose the children were killed in an automobile accident? They'd go straight to Hell, wouldn't they? I mean, so what if they're already ten and twelve? When I was a child in Beaumont, I attended the baptism of an *eighty-seven*-year-old woman. Of course, they only *sprinkled* her. They were afraid of pneumonia, you see? The creek at the ranch is lovely, don't you think? Or maybe we should build a baptismal font? Something out of *marble*—"

"For Benjy and Cissy?"

"They're my grandchildren, aren't they? My only son's children. It's not as if they don't have a *birthright*. You're an open-minded woman. You've always been open-minded. I mean, it's not my style, but I *admire* it—"

"You know I'm Jewish," Joanna said.

"Of *course*—" Sugar said. "You're Jewish and Tate's Methodist and they're *Texans*. They'll inherit *everything*, won't they? I'm only trying to protect their *spiritual* birthright—"

The waiter appeared with Sugar's gin and a silver bucket of iced wine which he uncorked and poured for Joanna. "Fine," she said.

"My stock goes all the way back to Justin Tate of Virginia who was Jefferson Davis' spiritual advisor," Sugar said. "After the Civil War, he tried to reunite the Southern and Northern Methodists. Of course, he *failed*—" Sugar sipped at the gin between sentences. Then she leaned toward Joanna and lowered her eyes. "Of course, you know why I never paid any attention to Lep and the Lockwood woman?"

Averting her eyes, Joanna sipped her wine.

"Of course, you know what I mean," Sugar continued. *"Everybody* knows what I mean. What they don't know is—Lep can't love *anybody*. Lep doesn't know how. At first, she probably didn't know that. But now—after all these years—she must know it *now*." Sugar paused to finish the gin. "If you're *married* to a man who doesn't know how to love, at least you're his *wife*. You have the power of that—social power, economic power. Those things don't help the loneliness, but they compensate for the *loss*. Do you see what I mean?"

Joanna kept her expression noncommittal.

Sugar wiggled a forefinger at the waiter. He brought another gin. "Lep's like a man who was born without a *heart*," Sugar said. "I don't know *why*. What I mean is—this baptism is for *me*. It has to be done in the right style because of our position—you understand that? But if you can't have a man's love, you have to have God's love." Sugar's voice broke. "You have to have *something*, don't you?"

"I don't know," Joanna said quietly.

"You're an open-minded woman," Sugar said. "You've always been an open-minded woman."

"No," Joanna said.

"Think of it as *secular*—" Sugar cradled the gin and sipped it. "Think of it as Sugar's *madness*. It is, you know. But it doesn't *matter*, does it? I mean, I couldn't *sleep* with Jesus, could I?"

"I'll have to ask the children."

Sugar smiled. "I'm worried about the chlorine. Do you know if lobsters can stay alive in chlorine? Maybe I should drain the pool?"

"The chlorine'll kill the lobsters," Joanna said.

46

"Dr. Calder," Tate said. "Staff surgeon." He raised the bed to a 45°
angle. Somebody had recently shaved and shined the Vice-President,
leaving him smooth and pale as a porpoise, a cloud of white hair at
odds with turquoise silk pajamas—Tate's guess was the pajamas had
been purchased by someone other than Morrison's wife.

"Related to Lep?"

"Sonofabastard."

"We'll get along." Morrison's voice was hoarse, a two-pack-a-day
voice.

Pulling up a chair, he applied a stethoscope to Morrison's chest and
listened, mentally filing the irregularities, the labored breathing. He felt
a brief rush of feeling for Morrison, that odd affection inspired by public
figures who were known strangers, flag-bearers for those like himself
who'd lost touch with their roots. "I admired you through the sixties."

"And the seventies?"

"They went by me."

"You mean you defaulted. When the rebellion burned out, your generation left it to my generation, and now you're not even sure how we
made such a rotten mess of it." Morrison cranked up a grin. "You're
listening to the problem," he said. "A failure of heart."

Morrison's voice rang in his chest cavity, off-key, like a neglected
piano. Morrison's heart was ravaged. What Morrison had said was he

knew his heart had been beating too hard and too fast for too many years—his heart had failed to synchronize what he saw as false hopes and failed dreams. Morrison's drummer was tired.

"What do you hear?"

Tate looked up. "It's not perfect."

"I had rheumatic fever when I was a kid."

"We'll run a few tests."

"Political stress," Morrison said, "occupational fatigue, cheap gin—I like cheap gin—too many Galois cigarettes, issues nobody else wants to deal with, southern fried anything, sex in a limousine—and I don't want to give any of it up." Morrison met Tate's eyes. "What kind of tests?"

"Cardiac catheterization. We inject a dye into your arteries and take pictures as it travels to your heart."

"When I was your age," Morrison said, "I saw myself as a mountain climber. Trackless ground, that kind of thing. Now I know better." His eyes traveled over Tate's face. "I've only got one fear," he said. "An aimless life. I don't want to turn into an old man shuffling along to nowhere."

Tate sent Morrison a swift reassuring smile. "We'll work on it."

Morrison's eyes had trapped his. Tate heard a faint erratic buzzing, like a gnat trapped in his inner ear. A sharp pain pierced his chest, as quick and unexpected as the materialization of a hairline crack in bone. He was still smiling at Morrison when he felt the thrust of an embryonic force against his own thoracic cavity which seemed suddenly as fragile as an eggshell.

The hospital room was filled with plants and flowers. The color television was going. Her father never looked at television. It was a bad sign, her mother had said: Sol spent too much time staring at it, not looking at it, just staring at the pictures.

He turned it off when Joanna came in. His eyes seemed too bright. His hair had grown thin at the top and his sideburns were white, but his moustache was still black, like a charcoal smear on his upper lip and there was something peculiar about his hands. Then she realized her father was a man who gestured constantly; in all her life, she'd never seen his hands at rest.

She had brought the photographs of *Lubeck's* Easter windows. He went through them slowly, looking at them the way he'd been looking at television, not seeing them.

"Good job." His face had changed. It was an open wound. The pain was blatant, the battle between suffering and healing going on in the open. It embarrassed her to look at it. It shamed her to look at it.

"Can I get something?"

"Don't address my illness," he said. "That's what everybody does, you know—they address the illness, as if I don't exist anymore."

"I'm sorry—" Next to the sofa was a formica table. He reached into the top drawer and pulled out a brown envelope. "There's a passbook in here—a hundred thousand dollars in a savings account. It's in Allison's name. There's also a packet of oil stocks and some municipal bonds—"

"No," Joanna said. "I don't want you to do that."

"When I was Allison's age, your grandfather told me money was to be *used*." He dropped the envelope in his lap. "'If you save a dollar a day, every day of your life,' he told me, 'and if you live to be seventy, all you'll have is twenty-five thousand dollars.'" A smile appeared briefly. "I always understood that part. It's the other part," he said, "—that even a long lifetime is only twenty-five thousand days."

"Don't—"

"Cissy and Benjy are Calders. Allison's not. Tate adopted her, but we both know she's *your* child. Allison's a *Lubeck*."

"She's Malone's daughter."

"It's not an act of forgiveness," he said.

She knew he was remembering how she had been at Allison's age—a neophyte, she thought—taking the generational oath of the children of Croesus: the watchword had been *no*. In the sixties, personal revolt had seemed a political act—chaos had been anarchy and defiance had been insurrection—from those beliefs had come her marriage to Malone—and from those beliefs had come Allison. From those beliefs had come the split with her father. "I was hoping it might be."

"When you were a child, I always had the feeling that you found me absurd. You had old eyes," he said. "Sometimes I believed you weren't a child at all—that you understood things I'd forgotten. Maybe that's why I was so hard on you. When you married that fellow—"

"Campbell Malone," she said.

"Nobody remembers his name anymore."

"He walked on the moon."

"Who cares?"

She stooped and embraced him. He patted her clumsily. Then she rose and he held out the envelope and she took it.

"There's one more thing," he said. "Benjy's going to be thirteen in July. I expect to hang around at least until then." He managed a rueful grin. "I'd like to see him bar-mitzvahed," he said.

"Isabel Howard," she said. She was waiting in his office.

She made him catch his breath. She made him remember a man lived two lives.

There was the life he inhabited which was made up of others, the sometimes orchestrated, sometimes chaotic demands of time and place and blood where commitments were institutionalized and impulses were enshrined: Church and State and Marriage, even Medicine; holier than Thou.

"Dr. Calder," he said.

"I remember."

The second life was an underlife.

She smiled.

Looking at her, he understood Joanna belonged to the first life; Isabel Howard belonged to the second.

"I came in with the Vice-President from Washington." She produced a set of credentials. He found himself looking at a card with her photograph and a White House Seal.

He took momentary refuge in amenities, professional courtesy. He offered her coffee.

She shook her head. "No thanks."

His office was a cubbyhole, nearly filled by a desk, a chair, and two overhead shelves which held medical books, a few volumes of poetry and a framed collage of snapshots, most of them of Joanna with Cissy and Benjy. He had a sense that before he entered, she'd been studying the snapshots.

"How serious is the Vice-President's condition?" The question surfaced through the scent of crushed tea roses.

"I don't know yet."

"There's a great deal involved," she said. "There's the office—all the contenders, the political ramifications."

"That's not my area."

She sent him a cool languid gaze, like sea water. "I never expected to see you again."

She was direct, he remembered that. He wondered if she had arranged to be sent here. He wondered if some part of her had been holding onto that night in Mexico City and if so—why? He thought about Lep again; Lep handing over the Vice-President. He felt another rush of anger. The anger was at himself.

She was talking quietly, in that direct way. She was saying: somewhere, about the time she hit thirty, she had grown bored with seduction. Something had happened to her sexual instinct, she said, a change in quality, a shift in tone. The criteria by which she had chosen men began to change. Men had been to her—as women were to men—objects of sexual need, rarely to be investigated beyond that; so few of them had instilled in her a desire to investigate beyond that. He was one of those.

He remembered her in bed. He had been crazy about her in bed.

She was running her fingers lightly over the volumes of poetry—over Plath and Sexton and Berryman. "Did you ever wonder why they all committed suicide?"

"After they diagnosed the human condition, they had to face the fact that it was inoperable," he said.

"Is that an oblique answer to my question about Morrison?"

"No."

Her voice dropped, almost to a whisper. "Why do we divide the world into those we can touch and not know—and those we can know and not touch?"

"That's an oblique question."

"I'm at the Houston Oaks," she said. "Suite ten thirty-six."

47

She could hear Malone's voice.

Everything Malone had ever said to her was stored on a tape inside her head.

"Yuri Gagarin wrote poetry in space . . ."

Malone never met Gagarin. Malone had wanted to meet Gagarin.

"The Americans' Redstone Rocket was a Model-T." Then, in April 1961 the Russians sent up Vostok I and Gagarin became the first man in history to orbit the earth. A month later Kennedy had announced that before the decade was out, America would land a man on the moon. The next day, Malone had applied for a place in the Mercury program.

He'd been an aeronautical research pilot at Edwards Air Force Base in California—living in a primitive log cabin, no plumbing or electricity, five thousand feet up in the San Gabriel Mountains—testing the X-1 rocket airplane and the X-15 which he'd flown to a height of two hundred thousand feet at a speed of four thousand miles an hour. Nine months later, in February 1962, while John Glenn was orbiting the earth three times in less than five hours, Malone was accepted as a candidate for the deep space program and summoned to Houston.

Joanna switched on the car radio, then switched it off again.

"Yuri Gagarin heard music in space . . ."

The traffic quit moving, snarled up ahead.

Malone's image took shape against the sun-streaked windshield: tall and lean, taut as a harpstring—dark expressive eyes, a bit askew—he'd had the off-kilter face of an icon chiseled by a Mexican thief.

How often had she returned there in her mind—and why now?—to that eighteen-year-old girl who'd lived, for a time, on the border of two worlds—a time like dawn or twilight when mysteries promised to emerge—a series of shimmering instants, uncaptured? Remembering, she shivered, plunging back into it like diving soundlessly into the ocean's depths, feeling the fierce passion he had stirred in her, blind and instinctual, a flounder darting radiant and sightless on the ocean floor. Malone took from her. Nobody had ever taken from her before. For eighteen years, people had given her things. Her life had been a getting. Taking, he had lightened her, made her weightless enough to float, insubstantial enough to be uncertain of her own existence. He had affected her like a drug. She had felt brilliantly alive.

Traffic was stalled. There was an accident somewhere up ahead, a car burning; Joanna could see clouds of gasoline smoke. The Loop was packed, horns honking, cars with their windows closed, air conditioning going.

"Yuri Gagarin saw visions in space . . ."

Malone had been complete, contained within himself, a dream animal, dreaming his own world—being complete, he could love completely and not at all. She'd known there was a part of Malone that could never love anybody. She made up for that by taking vows to love him completely.

She was three months pregnant when they drove to Laredo and across the border for a Mexican wedding. They moved into the old Victorian house in the Montrose area. It was too big for them. She painted it robin's-egg blue. She cropped her hair and dyed it an improbable shade of red, she wore feathered earrings and long flowered skirts, chains and beads clanking like castanets, the curve of her swelling breasts visible under a series of gauze blouses; she smiled at strangers. Malone wasn't a husband, never became a husband, and became a father only in the sense that his genes were perpetuated—his Comanche heritage had endowed him with different dreams of perpetuation. It was a kind of madness.

The cars had backed up. She was wedged in. There was a camper in back and a chocolate-brown Jensen ahead of her. The driver of the Jensen was studying her in his rearview mirror. His eyes caught hers, brazenly; she saw an appreciative smile break his jaw. Then he got out of the Jensen and rapped on the window. He was wearing an expensive suit, custom-tailored, a Sulka tie. "Real estate and oil leases," he said as she rolled down the window. His face was lightly freckled and his eyes were grainy. He rested his hands on the glass. There were tufts of reddish hair on his fingers, crisp, electrified; she imagined the fingers stroking her. "Do you have the time?"

"Yes," she said.

48

Inside the space capsule, the Calder logo was stamped on the silver ice bucket and the gold-bordered napkins and the champagne goblets. The tableware gleamed against the starkness of technological miracles and the massive panels of controls and dials which promised to carry the wonders of civilization into space.

"The orbiter's a *mock-up*," Lep said, "—a scale model of the first free-flyer to go into space. It'll have autonomy. It'll be completely self-contained."

A Mexican couple was serving. Wearing black-and-white livery, wearing white gloves, they passed silver platters of hors d'oeuvres. Isabel said no to the champagne, yes to Perrier and sturgeon. Sipping whiskey, Lep watched her.

"This represents only the first phase of META," he continued. "The space shuttle will launch it. The components will be carried by the shuttle in the cargo bay, and it'll be assembled in space."

He went through a brief technical description supplemented with figures and statistics. He knew she was familiar with most of it: congressional cutbacks had devitalized the space program; NASA's solution had been to extend an invitation to private industry, beginning with rental of space on the shuttle. Those with foresight predicted a third industrial revolution in space—NASA providing the technology; big business providing the funds.

"The President feels a moral responsibility to be certain how
META's going to be used," Isabel said. "I assume you're aware the reports you sent to Washington are less than adequate."

"I'm not accustomed to being accountable—"

"I know." She didn't smile. "Calder Enterprises is privately held. It
has a reputation for secrecy—nobody really knows how many sub-
sidiaries you have or what they produce. You're not subject to SEC
regulations and you're even immune to federal investigation."

"It's called free enterprise."

"That's not quite the same as a free hand—"

"Let me go over it once more," he said. "Once we launch the free-
flyer, we'll have a virtually self-supporting vehicle. From there, a crew
will build a platform in space. We'll build antennas, dishes, energy
collectors—it'll be available for lease—"

"To whom?"

"The electronics industry, for one. Zero gravity makes it possible to
grow large structurally perfect crystals."

She was listening. He knew she heard the sterility of technology, the
maleness of it, the calculating vision that had brought it into being. He
could feel it stirring the opposite in her—a commitment to passion, a
rebellion against the cold forces that promised to redefine man. The
Vice-President had gone on record, saying: *"Sometimes we must refuse
to go in the direction of history when history is no longer going in the
direction of man."*

"The aircraft industry, for another," Lep said. "Turbine blades. If
you encase an ordinary turbine blade in ceramic, then melt it in space
and let it rigidify without surface tension forces, there'll be no flaws in
the blade . . ."

Lep kept his eyes on her. He could feel her response to the space vehicle, something like being in church, the awesome silence, the same
promise of contacting worlds beyond this one. He could imagine the
young Catholic girl she had been, watching light pour through a
stained-glass window, probably experiencing a feeling of spinning while
reciting prayers to St. Jude who was the saint of the impossible.

"Also, pharmaceuticals," Lep said, "like urokinase. It prevents
blood-clotting. It's extracted from human urine and takes four hundred
gallons to produce one dose—at a cost of a thousand dollars. In space,
the specialized kidney cells that produce urokinase grow at a faster rate

than they do on earth and they're easier to purify. Space production would cut the cost to less than a hundred dollars a dose, including transportation."

She was silent. He knew some instinct told her the content was irrelevant, a complicated overture to something up ahead, or a cover for something underneath—he saw she couldn't tell which, only that she suspected he was lying.

"I see myself as a broker," he said, "offering a commodity to subcontractors who want to make use of what I provide—volume, power, heating, cooling, all the consummables—a fully equipped place in space."

He leaned back suddenly. The silence rang. The Mexican couple had vanished. In the vacuum, he imagined her in Washington, meeting at places like the *Sans Souci* where the men gathered, tense and honed, energized by power, the proximity to power, the quest for power; for the women, he knew the idea of power was an aphrodisiac. "*I see myself as a broker,*" he had told her. She'd know that was a lie. He knew she understood that power created or destroyed; power didn't serve, it ruled.

"Piracy," he said. "That's the truth of it. It's in the Calder genes. The biggest acreage in west Texas. The first cattle run to Kansas. The first independent oil company to beat the Rockefellers." He picked up the silver coffeepot and refilled her cup. "Now there's all that territory out there in space. I want the government to cooperate. I want the military to protect me. Why not? That's the way Texas was settled. It's the way the railroads were built and the oil companies were founded." He flashed a seductive smile. "Go back and tell the President I want to rearrange the stars in the Milky Way to form the Calder brand."

"I'll add that to my report."

"You're an extraordinary-looking woman. I suppose you know that?"

"I don't think about it."

"Only very beautiful women can afford not to think about it. The way the rich never carry money."

"And a man who's sure of his power is the most disarming?"

"I can see why the President's attached to you." Lep flipped open a slim gold cigarette case. "Do you smoke?"

Isabel shook her head. "Rarely."

"But then it's traditional, isn't it? Roosevelt had Lucy. Eisenhower had that Wac—"

"I'm not the President's mistress."

"Don't be linear."

"Vertical," Isabel said.

Lep selected one of the brown cigarettes and lit it. "What's your personal estimate of META?"

"There's the criteria of the Harvard School of Business. After the pioneers have taken the risks, it's time for the businessman to move in and take the profits."

"Class of sixty-seven, wasn't it—the year your ex-husband graduated from Harvard?"

"Class of sixty-eight."

"Mexican, wasn't he?"

"French-Mexican."

"Of course. His mother was from New Orleans. That was your home, wasn't it? Lace-curtain Irish, I believe. St. Ursuline's convent, Dominican College—then a Cinderella marriage to André Mendoza. A Catholic ceremony in Mexico City—in the Basilica, wasn't it?—to the Virgin of Guadalupe. Do the peasants still cross the plaza on their knees?"

"Yes."

"You do go back regularly, don't you? The last time was November, wasn't it?" Lep paused. "To see your daughter—Francesca. Under Mexican law, your ex-husband has legal custody. That must be difficult for you."

"I wouldn't have imagined any of that would interest you."

"On the contrary, I have a wide range of interests. Take *Mendoza Construction* for instance. The company's very shaky at the moment. However, with the proper capital behind it and a discreet word to *El Presidente*—"

"I'm not concerned with my ex-husband's business."

"Even if the business arrangements were not to be concluded until the necessary papers were drawn up giving you legal custody of Francesca?"

"I'm not sure what you're saying—"

"I'm offering you the right to take your daughter out of Mexico. The right to live with her anywhere you choose."

"Why?"

"Any friend of the President of the United States is a friend of mine."

"I think I'll take that cigarette now."

Lep took his time opening the gold case and lighting the cigarette for her. "No state secrets," he said. "Nothing classified. All I want is advance knowledge—up-to-date reports on anything that's on the drawing board that may affect my business."

"That's everything, isn't it?"

"Not quite."

She leaned back. He watched her raise her eyes to stare at the maze of cables that crisscrossed the ceiling. In silence, her eyes fixed there, she smoked the cigarette down until it burned her fingers. Lep held out a silver ashtray. Slowly, she ground the cigarette out in the Calder logo.

"I won't be your woman," she said. She rose and crossed to the entrance and stood on the threshold, looking out. After a moment, he came up behind her. "I'm not the President's woman," she said. "I'm not anybody's woman. I've never been on two payrolls. I've never sold my allegiance."

She walked outside, moving in an easy stride, hesitating only a moment before veering away from the place where the driver waited in the Calder limousine. Lep accompanied her, without responding, letting her take the lead.

"It's wired in there, isn't it?" She was making a statement.

Lep smiled. "Of course."

"And the limousine?"

"You know that's standard."

Isabel stopped. They were standing in the open. Lep watched her assess the prairielike land with nothing to break it, the fact that the limousine and driver were out of earshot, and the nearest cluster of utilitarian buildings were perched far away on the horizon. "I assume you're aware of the importance of the President's Energy Fair?"

"I made the arrangements for the use of the Astrodome."

"Of course."

"A massive display of alternative energy sources—to prove to the public that solutions are going to come from the American imagination."

"It's going to be more than that," she said quietly.

"How much more than that?"

"I want my daughter," she said. "I'm willing to pay for that. Not every day. Not every time I enter the President's office or attend a meeting or witness a decision. I'll pay for it only once. Right now."

"Go on."

"I'm not sure what you're after," she said. "It's hiding between all the words, all the technical explanations. I know it's not what you say. I'm also aware it's beyond my powers of speculation. But I can sense what the area is because I know what's coming in. You want to be the man who brings it in—like a gusher." She paused. He knew she was leaving room for a disclaimer. He didn't bother. "Solar energy," she said. "If I'm right and that's the area—I'll offer you a one-time trade. One piece of information in exchange for my child."

"It better be one hell of a piece of information."

"You'll have to gamble on that."

"Done," he said.

49

"Bourbon," Malone said.

The stewardess smiled, impersonal, not even one of those smiles that said: "*I know you're somebody, but I don't know who.*" She was young. Fresh out of high school, Malone thought, probably no more than five-years-old when his face had peered through the window of his space suit from the cover of every magazine in the country. He still gauged people that way, by figuring out where they had been in nineteen sixty-nine.

Lep understood that, he thought. Lep was smart enough to know that.

He nursed the bourbon, making it last. Next to him, a ruddy-cheeked executive wearing bifocals was engrossed in the contents of a briefcase, running a small hand computer and making notes in the margin of a complicated set of figures. Malone could multiply faster in his head. Bored, he turned away to look out of the plane window.

Take a man in exile—he thought—a man in exile from his natural habitat which was the air. Take a man deprived of the technological extensions that gave him access to his own destiny, and offer him wings.

He could hear Lep thinking like that. He had heard the offer under the offer: "*It's a chance to be hauled back from obscurity.*" "No drinking," Lep had said. "*Your image will legitimatize my project; my proj-*

ect will reinstate your image." "No press interviews," Lep had said. *"My terms or not at all."*

He had asked for twenty-four hours to think it over.

He had listened to Lep describe META, and he had known Lep was lying and he had agreed anyway.

Now, looking down, he could see the Grand Canyon; halfway to Houston.

He thought about Joanna. And Allison. Allison had been an infant when he'd left the first time. He'd been transferred to Huntsville, Alabama, to train. He remembered trying to explain to Joanna—simple terms—that in the third dimension reality was divided into opposites: into light and dark, into life and death, into love and freedom. In the third dimension people married, had children, lived linear lives, encapsulated by geometric space. He had to go beyond that, he'd said. Into the fourth dimension, he'd said.

"Bastard," she'd shouted at him.

He went to Huntsville alone. He spent two years steeped in physics and aerodynamics, saturated with psychiatric interviews and stints in the isolation chamber and months of practice in the weightlessness tanks. He was told to concentrate on the technology. He was told not to think about the larger meaning, not to ponder the implications of a species that had started with Adam presuming to go to the moon.

He didn't write. He didn't call. She sent a few snapshots of Allison. After that, he didn't hear from her.

At the end of two years, he was sent to Cape Kennedy to work in the simulators.

He was transferred back to Houston in '67: Allison was nearly four. There had been no divorce. Tate had moved into the Montrose house; Joanna and Tate were living together. He remembered the first time he'd laid eyes on Tate. He'd expected to feel malice. Instead, he'd experienced a shocking recognition—like catching sight of a brother—they loved the same woman, there was that. And something else, more profound—he'd never been able to articulate it beyond a crazy image of an ancient Vedic figure that melded the two of them: the lame man with good vision riding on the shoulders of the blind man with good legs.

Tate had been in residency under Foley. Lep had appealed to Foley for NASA. The moonshot involved millions. NASA wanted to avoid any possibility of an aborted mission because of a medical emergency. NASA wanted a half-dozen potential space jockeys taught the rudiments of surgery.

Foley had assigned Tate. Tate had started them out in the dog hospitals, teaching them to cut and sew, to close simple wounds, tie off an artery, clamp and tie bleeders. Then Tate had bootlegged them into the operating rooms at Calvary. McKay had fainted. McKay had been working his way through the Texas Rangerettes. The word on McKay had been: If that sky-can's not shaped like a cunt, they'll never get him in it.

McKay had died in a flash fire that asphyxiated him inside the spacecraft during a simulated launch at Cape Kennedy.

Malone frowned at the memory. Looking down, clouds obscured the geometric patterns of the earth, snow-tufted mountains and silver streams, patches of woods and furrowed farmland—still, the view seemed earthbound, too close to gravity, too far from the mystery he'd set out to explore.

He asked for another bourbon. Fifty-three minutes to Houston, the stewardess said.

He found himself wondering if Allison looked like Joanna now.

It was fourteen years since he'd been back.

Fourteen years ago, Joanna had boiled crayfish in beer with garlic and the three of them had sat around the kitchen table at midnight, eating the crawfish directly out of the pot, sucking the meat out and licking their fingers—they'd gone through too much red wine and laughed too loud and he'd heard himself ask, *"How do we know there were only two people in the Garden of Eden? What about the snake? Who the Hell was he?"* And Joanna had answered, *"He was a Bible salesman,"* and they had broken up, laughing; only Tate hadn't laughed.

It was fourteen years . . .

He had wakened to a throbbing head in the third-floor bedroom of the Montrose house and the sight of four-year-old Allison perched on a windowsill watching him. *"What's that?"* she had asked, pointing to the sole of his left foot where two intersecting circles had been tattooed by his mother three days after his birth. *"It's a Comanche mark,"* he had answered. *"It's magic. It means I can fly."*

He had expected her to giggle. Instead, she had nodded solemnly as if she'd understood exactly what he was talking about. *"I know,"* she had said.

"How do you know?"

"My mother told me."

"What else did she tell you?"

"That you're my father."

It was a Holiday Inn. The Jensen had pulled in next to her. He was carrying a key.

The room was on the second floor. Neat. Anonymous.

He didn't look like Malone. Joanna turned her back to undress, wondering why—now—she was thinking about Malone.

Because he had been her first? Lover. Husband. She had released herself from the power of a first commitment and from the pain of a first loss. Then Malone had come back—and, for all of them, it had been like touching a match to a parched field of Mexican poverty-weed; like finding themselves caught in the path of a Texas twister.

"Life's a laboratory," Malone had said.

"Two is always a dichotomy," Malone said. *"Two people polarize, become adversaries, freeze in opposition. Three is dynamic, fluid, always in motion."*

At night, watching television in the second-floor sun parlor—watching clips of Vietnam, Civil Rights, Indian Grievances, Brown Power and Black Equality—she and Tate and Malone had agreed that the world had been civilized without being humanized; they had agreed that the times were apocalyptic, human pioneering was vital and marriage certificates were obsolete.

They had agreed to experiment. They had agreed to lend themselves *"to the forces of fate,"* Malone said.

Now, she was in a Holiday Inn. The drapes were closed. The stranger was climbing into bed.

He had a bearlike warmth.

He had copper hairs on his chest, bristly, metallic, like wire threads.

He didn't feel like Malone.

"To choose one man," Malone had said, *"is to deprive yourself of another."*

She could feel the old humming in her blood; she could hear the sound of wheels spinning, a night train carrying her far from herself.

Malone had released her sense of magic. He had returned her to mystery. He had restored her sense of wonder.

Tate's passions had rushed out like primitive demons, crude and unbridled, defiant and earthbound.

And once the three of them, she and Tate and Malone, had made love together like pagan creatures dedicated to the pleasures of flesh, and afterward she had felt the same brief rush of mourning pass simultaneously through all of them, like a shadow, to remind them it was a strange and mysterious time that was destined to pass.

She had a sense of the three of them connected to one heart, beating; the heart was a ticking clock.

"Malone's crazy," Tate had said.

"Maybe he's not," she had answered. *"Maybe the rest of the world is."*

That had been in May.

June, Tate had spent in the Intensive Care Ward of Calvary Hospital.

"Come to bed," she had said quietly, the night before he left.

Tate had stared at her. *"What are we doing?"*

"We're living by our own rules."

"No, we're not. We're playing a game. We're playing it and we're watching ourselves play it and we're applauding—" he had stopped abruptly. *"I hate the sonofabitch."*

In the morning, he had dressed to go to Calvary. He'd be there for thirty days. He'd start with patient number one, work his way through fifty-four beds, then start over again.

His car hadn't started. Malone had gone out and hooked up jump cables. She'd heard the engine turn over. Then she'd heard Tate ask Malone, *"Are you in love with her?"*

"Are you?"

"Are you going to divorce her?"

"I don't know."

"When I come back, I want you out."

Now she was in bed in a Holiday Inn. She could hear the traffic outside.

He was smiling. His teeth were white and even. His hand was scuttling tentatively, crablike, circling her left breast.

He built shopping centers and apartment complexes. He was in from Los Angeles to bid on the Galveston project. Years ago, Houston had stolen the port and turned Galveston into a ghost town; now Galveston had talked the federal government out of enough money to restore the pirated city to its former glory.

Did she know Galveston?

Yes, Joanna said.

Her eyes were closed. She could see the rented house in Galveston, the gables and porticoes and widow's walk; it had been one of the earliest houses rebuilt after the turn of the century when cyclone winds had whipped up a tidal wave that demolished the mainland.

It was June.

She could feel the humidity.

Malone had been drinking . . .

In the afternoon, he had carried Allison on his shoulders, striding knee-deep in the waves.

Allison was asleep on the sofa . . .

The evening before, Malone had cooked pompano over an open fire and told Allison stories of Jean Laffite and buried treasure in the Galveston coves.

"*In 1937,*" Malone was saying, "*the bridge fare across the Rio Grande had been fifteen cents. When my mother went into labor, my father drove her across the bridge from Villa Acuña, Mexico to Del Rio, Texas, so that Campbell Malone might be born on American soil.*"

It had started to rain. Outside, the rain was making rusty rivulets on the sea wall, pounding the sand until it looked like granite. Slanting onto the porch, the rain was splashing and forming puddles, and the rocking chairs creaked in the wind. Then the murky daylight was swallowed by dusk all at once and the rain glimmered like silver threads being spun from the mist.

Malone followed her upstairs.

She could see herself in the bedroom, the rain coming down in sheets beyond the glass doors that led to the widow's walk. There was an old iron fireplace. Malone made a fire and left her alone. She undressed and curled up on a chaise, naked, alternately reading and staring out at the rain, as if she were waiting for something. After a while, Malone came back, carrying a bottle and a glass and a camera; he began taking pictures of her.

"*My mother was a full-blooded Comanche,*" Malone was saying. Stooping, he aimed the camera at her. "*The Comanches believed your guardian spirit arrived in the form of a vision."* He was clicking the camera, relentlessly. She thought about Tate. Malone had always frightened her. Malone had always fascinated her. *"You had to court the vision,"* Malone was saying, *"with fasting and isolation—self-torture, if necessary. If you didn't get one after that, you had to buy one."* More flash-bulbs went off. Malone stood up and poured himself another drink. *"My father sold visions,"* he said.

Carrying his drink, Malone opened the french doors. He was standing with his back to her. The wind had shifted. The rain was beating straight down on the balustrades outside, and Malone was talking, in a lilting tone, the cadence of scotch and the pounding rain.

"In 1938," Malone was saying, *"my father was managing a border radio station in Villa Acuña . . . did you ever hear of Villa Acuña? Did you ever hear of Dr. R. D. Singleton—pirate of the air waves and medical miracle maker?*

"Among my earliest memories," Malone was saying, *"was Singleton's Del Rio estate: pet penguins in the Texas heat, Galapagos tortoises sleeping around a tri-colored swimming pool, eight thousand blooming rosebushes which were lit at night by neon, and Mrs. Singleton practicing scales on Norma Talmadge's old rosewood piano."*

He sent her a lopsided smile. Then he whirled abruptly and darted outside, and bounded onto the parapet where, knees bent, he started to catwalk in the lashing rain.

She heard Malone's glass drop and crash three stories below. Rising, arms outflung and listing dangerously in the wind, he moved out of sight.

She pursued him, shouting at him as he plunged sideways, caught the slippery balustrade and swung himself up. He doffed an invisible cap at her and kept going. Then he disappeared into nowhere.

Head bowed in the pouring rain, she cursed him.

She found him downstairs, sitting beside Allison on the sofa, soaking wet, reciting his father's old radio advertisements for rupture cures, electric bow-ties, autographed pictures of Jesus and *". . . prayer cloths guaranteed-to-heal warts, wounds, burns, boils, fractures, stomach cramps and leprosy."*

"You're insane—" she shouted.

She was weeping when he came upstairs.

"If I knew *why*, I'd *know*, wouldn't I?" he said.

He went into the bathroom and came out carrying a couple of

towels. He led her in front of the fire and began to dry her hair and towel her body, slowly and tenderly. When he finished, he undressed and dried himself in the same manner, as if both of them were children of some other wiser self that had taken up habitation within him.

Then he pulled her down in front of the fire and made love to her with the same curious tenderness, without hunger or need, with more reverence than passion, creating a languor, like birds gliding on a southbound wind. Tate was forgotten, a creature from a former world, earthbound. She felt herself becoming Malone, and she felt Malone becoming her, as if they were exchanging natures in some profound and irrevocable way that would leave them both altered. Then she started to shake, visibly, and for a fraction of an instant, she *knew* Malone and, with no idea of what it meant she heard herself crooning to him, *"Bater . . . bater . . ."*

Now she was in a Holiday Inn.

He wasn't Malone.

He was nothing like Malone.

He was big and bearlike, with copper hairs on his chest.

He was looking at her with a puzzled look. She knew he wanted to ask: Was it all right?

She got out of bed and began to get dressed.

"Will I see you again?"

"No," she said.

He looked relieved.

The stewardess had set a tray in front of him. On it was a scarlet lobster tail, a pile of neon-bright string beans; the food looked plastic. Next to him, the executive had pushed his glasses onto his forehead and was eating methodically the numbers still clacking in his head; Malone could hear them.

Fog licked at the glass. He remembered that was the way fog looked in Galveston.

It had quit raining. He remembered that, too. It had quit raining. He remembered waking to find Joanna gone. He'd gone out looking for her and found her walking on the beach, wearing an old gray sweatshirt and faded jeans.

The wind had turned gentle, a sea breeze, light as the breath of children. The sun was coming up. She was walking slowly along the water's edge, hands locked behind her back, watching her own footprints appear, like a hunter tracking herself.

Then she stopped, and he saw she was watching a small crowd that had gathered for a wedding on the beach. The bride was barefoot, dressed in flowing gauze, daisies braided in her hair. The groom wore chinos, a rope belt, a pale blue shirt. The sunrise glittered on the Gulf and he could smell the scent of talcum and cologne, the closet smell of last year's chiffon; women were clutching wide-brimmed hats and teetering on high heels across the sand. He came up behind her.

"No," he said.

"Black swans," she said. It was the image that had come to her, she said: they were like a pair of black swans on a pond. She remembered them from her childhood as amazing creatures with vermillion beaks and thundercloud feathers—devil swans—fenced off from the others, from the mundane and the pristine.

"No," he repeated.

Her eyes traveled over him and he knew she had fallen in love with him in the old way, in all the ways she had sworn to leave behind.

He felt it as a threat, something that might happen to him, a force pulling at him, threatening to ground him.

He was carrying the camera around his neck. "Try to understand."

She shook her head. She didn't understand.

She was weeping.

He was connected to Copernicus, he said—and to Galileo and Newton—and to the planets and to the mysteries that governed them. He was connected to Planck and to Einstein—to the possibility that gravity curved space and, at the speed of light, there was no passage of time.

He was connected to flight; that was his strongest connection.

"The others," he said, "want to go into space to beat the Russians. They want to go because NASA made a promise to Kennedy, and now Kennedy's dead so the promise is holy. Or they want to go because they're driven, the way Tate's driven. For me, it's different," he said. "I'm being pulled. There's a magnet—out there—and whatever it's composed of, the matching particles are in my cells."

She quit weeping. She turned and stared at the water for a long time. Watching her, he felt numb. The pain would come later, he understood that. Then she turned and a shudder passed through her.

Silently, she took the camera from him and focused it and studied him through the lens before she clicked the shutter. *"What are you going to do with my photographs?"* Her voice sounded odd, clear and pure as the ring of crystal.

"Take them to the moon," he said.

50

He'd started thinking about Malone in the afternoon. No reason. He'd been thinking about Isabel Howard—the thing that had been initiated in Mexico City, one of those packages from Fate that had been marked: *Return to Sender*. Somehow it made him remember that June, fourteen years ago, when Malone and Joanna came back from Galveston and it had all blown up—he had seized Malone by the throat and slung him from bed, raining irate blows on his naked body. Malone had let him. Malone had stood there, unprotected, taking the blows, refusing to fight back, blood streaming from his nostrils as his body swayed and bowed and dissolved under the thud of fists against his flesh.

Tate pulled out of the hospital parking lot. It was half-past ten. Mist hugged the streets and blurred the moon and turned the green neon letters on top of the Shamrock Hotel into an indecipherable signpost from another time.

He remembered going down to New Orleans. Joanna had followed him there. He'd registered in a small hotel, less than a dozen rooms; wooden shutters had closed off the laughter of tourists. Across the street, a French Quarter jazz band had wailed and throbbed. The month in ICU had drained him. Exhausted, he'd slept and wakened and slept again. Then, at midnight, he'd got up and dressed and left his room, crawling the bars in search of a catharsis.

She'd come searching for him. It was after two in the morning when he looked up and saw her in the mirror over the marble counter in the French Market; he was wolfing down doughnuts.

She slid onto a stool next to him.

"I needed a stranger," he told her. He knew she'd know he meant a woman.

"I loved Malone," she answered. *"If I hadn't, it would just have been a dirty game."*

"And now?"

"He's agreed to a divorce. He's gone."

"None of the Calders have ever been doctors," he said. *"I wanted to go back to the strength of Ben Calder. I wanted to have an impact. I wanted to beat Lep. Thirty days in ICU and you can't walk out on any of them—and you can't not care. Lep came up there. He didn't belong there, but he came anyway, to show me he could—and he stayed a long time, watching me, and finally he said: 'You're the nineteenth-century humanist and I'm the modern man.'"*

She took his coffee from him and sipped it. *"What kind of stranger?"*

"I bought her," he said. *"I paid for her."* He met her eyes in the mirror. *"Do you want to get married?"*

"Every good Jewish girl marries a doctor."

"I don't want that kind of life."

Her response had been, *"Neither do I."*

On Westheimer Boulevard, he stopped at a Thrift-i-mart and went in, moving under the glaring lights past shelves of toothpaste and mouthwash, bags of charcoal and cartons of lightbulbs to the rear of the store where he picked up a tape recorder for Manuel.

The check-out girl was chewing gum. She rang up the tape recorder, then suggested he might need tapes. "Aisle six," she said. He acquiesced and went back for the tapes.

Outside, he locked the package in the trunk. Then he climbed back behind the wheel and pulled out into the street, hesitating only a second before he headed in the direction he had known he would take—knowing he was bringing his memories with him, and the married man, and the flawed *patrón*, and the surgeon—carrying the beeper in his shirt pocket, symbol of that atavistic urge which had once been as primitive as the carving out of the heart of the enemy—transformed—

savage into surgeon. He didn't know whether the memory of Malone or Isabel Howard had set thoughts like that going in his head.

At the Houston Oaks, he didn't drive up to the entrance and give the Porsche to the attendant. Instead, he parked in a far corner of the deserted lot which, by day, served *The Galleria,* a vast underground maze of shops through which thousands moved daily, buying and spending. It struck him that he had seen patients move through the hospital routine in the same manner. The thought implied that, like shoppers, they had chosen their disease—and doctors and merchants, from that perspective, might be indistinguishable.

The thought didn't please him.

He walked quickly past *Lubeck's* windows. From inside massive pastel Easter eggs, live rabbits looked back at him, each quivering pink-eyed creature wearing a priceless necklace—in contrast to his own raw libidinous urge, as yet unendowed, as pure as the rutting impulse of the he-goat—he was a male animal following the scent of musk and tea roses.

Thick and humid, the air enveloped him. Overhead, an unseen hand rolled a bowling ball across the sky and a flash of lightning split the haze like a crack between two worlds. Then the rain came down, sending him sprinting for the revolving door.

Under the sheet Allison could see the outline of Guero's body. His ribs had been taped. Below the tape, the sheet lay flat over his abdomen until the rise of his groin.

A lamp burned on the nightstand behind his head. His skin was the color of honey. His eyes were blue. There was a bruise on his cheek. The police had beaten him.

"It was the thirties," he said. "The emigrant agents got ten dollars a head for farm labor. Every spring, they'd sign up thousands of workers for the sugar-beet fields in Michigan—" He reached out and laid his hand on her breast. Outside it was raining. Allison could hear the rain. "Why do you want to know this?"

"I want to—"

"They'd pack them into the back of a truck and fasten a tarpaulin over them to make them look like a load of potatoes. Then they'd drive forty-eight hours straight from Texas to Michigan. One of the trucks was hit by a train. It was carrying forty-four workers. Twenty-nine were killed. One of Manuel's sons was killed. There was a child in the truck, but somehow he survived." He took his hand away. He moved the straps of her gown down her shoulders, exposing her breasts. He looked at them for a long time. *"Que linda eres,"* he said; beautiful.

She didn't respond. She didn't move. The rain beat against the window.

"Manuel raised the boy," he said. "When he was seventeen, he was out organizing the farm workers. They were still paying the *braceros* fifty cents an hour to chop Texas cotton. He was knifed in an uprising in the fields outside of Beaumont." He leaned over and kissed her nipple, running his tongue around the edge of it. *"Que dulce."* Bending her head, she pressed her mouth to the back of his neck. Then he pulled away, slowly.

"Lupe—my mother—was Manuel's last daughter," he said. "She wanted to live in Mexico. He let her go when she was fifteen. When she was eighteen, she came back—then—maybe six months later—she turned up pregnant. It was a *gringo,* she told Manuel that. It wasn't rape, she told him that, too. She refused to say any more than that.

"I'm glad you were born," Allison whispered. "I'm glad you exist."

Guero shook his head. "For a long time, I didn't feel that way. I used to look at every *gringo* on the street and hate every one of them. Then one day, Manuel said to me: 'Half of you is a *gringo.* You can't use up your life hating half of yourself.'"

A cold bitter smile crossed Guero's face. He fell silent a moment. The light struck his profile. Allison caught a glimpse of the boy he had buried under the angry man.

"Lep put me to work in the chemical plant," he said. "I made trouble there, too. Then, three years ago, Lep came to me. He was training a team of *Chicanos* to send into Mexico. It was right after the big Mexican oil strike. The Mexican *campecinos* were getting no royalties, nothing. It was Lep's way of trying to break the nationalization of Mexican oil. If the poor could be provoked into enough violence, then Washington could move in to save Mexico from a rigged revolution." He stopped talking. He leaned over and took hold of her nightgown and removed it slowly. His eyes scanned her body. *"Eres una encantadora,"* he said softly. He didn't touch her.

"I want to know the rest," she said.

"That's when Lep became all *gringos* to me. That's when Lep became everything I hated. I reached back into Mexican history, and I claimed all the revolutionaries as my fathers. I kept inciting Lep's chemical workers. Lep had me fired. Then he started having me picked up like a cockroach by the cops. What I was after was DOM. It's like benzene. It accumulates in the organs and in the bone marrow. You bleed from the skin. It affects the chromosomes and the white blood cells. Rodriguez was going to file suit. He was killed and dumped in the channel."

Allison turned her head away. Her eyes filled with tears.

"You wanted to know," Guero reached out and traced a path with his fingertips from the hollow of her neck to her pubic mound. He let his hand rest there.

She took his head gently between her hands and pulled him to her breasts. *"Dame tu amor,"* she whispered, rising to meet the pressure of his hand.

"Has there been somebody else?"

She leaned over, close to his face, and spoke against his lips. "Why, does it matter?"

"Has there?"

"He wasn't like you. He didn't look like you. He didn't feel like you."

"I never wanted to be the first."

"Why?"

"I could never be sure—"

"What?"

"—that it wouldn't be an act of anger," Guero said.

He left Morrison behind.

He left the hospital behind.

Tate left behind all the bodies of the day, those in various stages of disease or decay, disrepair. He left behind that relationship to the body, everything catalogued and defined in terms of function or malfunction. What he was asking for, without asking, was to take pleasure in a body that was whole, unflawed, unfamiliar—not to be healed—to be explored so that he could rediscover his original attraction to flesh, the mysteries of flesh.

Isabel was wearing a white robe, flowing, like spilled milk. Underneath, her skin had the scent and texture of a newly peeled almond. In bed, her hair brushed against him like a dark wind.

He meant for it to be a contained experience, an isolated act, unconnected to his daily existence—need meeting need, the release of tension in the spasms of passion. He knew the body, he understood the manipulation of the body; he took pleasure in his own skill, in the authority of his own skill.

Not having to think about those things left him free to know her.

He had known women who responded only to anger, a pounding hostility; she was not one of those. He had known girl-women who liked to be titillated, cajoled; she was not one of those. He had known earth-mothers who had reduced him to adolescent investigation meant to reassure himself that the vagina had no teeth; she was not one of those either. There was a frankness about her body, a response to his touch so unpremeditated that it seemed accidental. Her face was grave, unamazed. In the dark, her eyes were like quicksilver, some quality of soul peering through, without sorrow, ineffable, summoning him to join her in that center of darkness where all light blazed.

He prowled over her, listening to her body as it swayed, humming soundlessly in waves. He remembered her body as sculpture; he remembered his own hands bringing it to life. Now he saw her solidity had been an illusion. He saw that only a thin invisible membrane gave shape to a pulsing and chaotic profusion of life; it kept her body from being fluid, from escaping from him. He ceased thrusting. Letting go of all need for assertion, he had the sensation of swimming, of being carried by the current of a swollen river that was rushing to its own destination. He felt an immersion of self, a return to something less evolved than animal; some creature he had been when the organs of brain and heart and groin had been closer together, functioning as one, unaware that they were separate from the ocean which was their home.

He was bathed in sweat.

He was holding her. In the darkness, her flesh gleamed, salty, perishable. He was watching the rising and falling of her breasts, engrossed in the enigma of her breathing. It crossed his mind that as long as they held each other neither of them could die.

51

"*I'll offer you a one-time trade,*" Isabel Howard was saying on tape. "*One piece of information in exchange for my child.*" A special antenna on the limousine, raised by Lep's chauffeur, had captured the exchange at NASA.

It was late, nearly midnight—rain beat against the glass, audible over the sound of the tape. The glass elevator was rising. Looking up from his desk, Lep saw Merritt Lockwood inside, wearing her coat slung over her shoulders—a brown tweed coat, hand-woven, expensive. He watched her emerge, noting she'd washed her face and applied fresh makeup, like putting on the face of a stranger. Behind the mask, he recognized the familiar signs: at least twice a year, she was struck by an urge to fill the back of her pickup truck with camping gear and strike out for the cabin in the Big Bend country, growing as baked and hard-muscled as a pioneer woman, returning only after an inch of dark roots started to show in her strawberry-blond permanent and his own image began to take shape in the evening campfire. He'd always drawn her back. She'd gone to New York. She'd gone to Los Angeles. He had allowed her those aborted attempts to live her own life, whatever that meant. He'd made her rich enough to do as she pleased so that she could find out what pleased her had been to please him.

"*. . . Partly out of conviction,*" Isabel Howard's voice continued,

"... *partly out of a political response to the American feeling of diminishing power, and partly to assert his authority over the multi-national corporations—the President's going to come out for public ownership of solar energy . . .*"

Lep frowned. "That's the crucial part," he said. "Public ownership of solar energy."

"... *He's going to make the announcement to the nation at the Energy Fair. . . . He'll call for a freeze on private exploration . . .*"

"That's the kicker," he said. "It sets us in direct opposition to the President."

He rewound the tape and set it going again, aware of Merritt watching him, aware of his own reflection in the rain-washed glass— like one of those God-descended creatures who had ridden to earth on twisters and blue northers to tame the devil-inhabited plains of Texas. Now, he was out to tame more than that.

"The President's got a full-scale press campaign ready to go," he said. "Every citizen of the United States as a shareholder in the sun." Lep's eyes strayed over Merritt. She was still beautiful. She still had the power to stir him. "It's an act of evangelism." He switched off the tape. "The people as proprietors of their own salvation. Solar energy owned and operated like Amtrak or the post office."

"*If* he can get Congressional approval," she answered. "*If* he can get through the challenges in the Supreme Court. *If* he can get a budget appropriation. Those are big *ifs.*" She smiled without feeling. "The pie in the sky is the sun."

"He can freeze private exploration without any of those things—a presidential decree's a bitch to circumvent." He paused. Something was wrong. "What is it?"

"I was remembering Warren," she said.

He had a swift memory of her first husband from Indiana who had started as a roustabout and worked his way up to pipe gang, installing equipment—and became a plant man, tending the big pumps that pushed the oil through the line. It had been the line patrolman's job to walk the line and check for leaks. The line patrolman drank. Somebody had lit a forbidden cigarette and set off an undetected leak. Warren Lockwood had died in the explosion.

"Why Warren?"

"I don't know." She spoke carefully. "Maybe it suddenly occurred to me that I lived twenty-two years before I met you. I was born. I had a childhood. I lived with my grandmother." She hesitated. "I had a pony. Did you know that?"

"No."

"Do you remember the first time we made love?"

"Yes."

"I've always loved that cabin," she said. "I love the Big Bend country. I even love the sound of the coyotes howling." She shook her head. "I considered myself lucky. You were one of the most desirable men in Texas."

"In the Southwest—" he corrected. He rose and came toward her.

"I'm going away."

He shook his head. "It's the wrong time."

"Your tapes are transcribed. I left instructions for Allison. Everything's in order."

He rose and started to pace, talking, staccato—about the dream of flight being brought into its ultimate form, vision made carnate, computers and circuits and complex electronic systems serving as adjuncts to his will. Consciousness soared, he said. Matter was dense. Matter could be lightened with power; density could be blasted into weightlessness. In that place where everything was lighter than air, worlds could be constructed in seconds and man could move toward the status of gods through his own inventions. He saw she was growing uneasy listening to him, as if an intuitive warning bell had sounded in her, a wariness.

"I'm forty-seven years old," she said.

He smiled. "Try to imagine what it would be like to make love in zero gravity."

"No." She wrapped her coat closer around her shoulders.

"Can you imagine how it would feel to fuck and fly at the same time?"

"No." She walked slowly toward the glass elevator.

"If I were twenty years younger, I'd try it," he said.

She entered the elevator. She turned to face him. "With me?"

"Yes."

"What about Sugar?"

'She's my wife."

"And the others?"

"They don't count," he said. "You're the one I'd want to fuck in the universe."

"No," she said. She pressed the button. The glass elevator descended.

He watched her through the telescope. He watched the pickup truck come out of the underground parking lot, and he followed her with the telescope until the fog swallowed her up. Then he went back to his desk and called Anson Pearce and ordered a tail on Merritt Lockwood.

A vein in his neck began to throb.

He stilled it.

He played Isabel Howard's tape again.

The Energy Fair was the first of May. May Day.

A coldness overtook him, a dry imperturbability that removed him from all emotional encumbrances. He felt the texture of his skin change. He felt his heartbeat slow. Willfully, he shed everything personal; he shed every previous plan and every attachment. He sat like that, motionless, until he began to feel buoyant, until he felt his mind float beyond the confines of his own limited knowledge and experience, reaching out toward the moment he'd defeat the President at his own game.

52

The clock on the Porsche dashboard said twenty past two.

The rain had quit. The rain had washed the city. Tate's headlights cast gleaming yellow ribbons on streets that shone like black mirrors.

Isabel sat next to him, wrapped in silence. The silence, too, seemed washed, glistening.

He heard himself talking. He was listening to himself, like listening to the voice of a stranger.

He was talking about his marriage. Fourteen years. The *Houston Chronicle* had called it the merging of empires—oil and mercantile, Calder and Lubeck, Gentile and Jew—calculating it in figures: What was love worth? One plus one equals how many millions?

His marriage had no heart.

He was talking about Lep and the distortion of his heritage. Ghosts from the past. He'd heard voices when he was a kid. He'd seen visions. Then they'd vanished. He'd cut himself off from the glory and the passion of those Calders who'd loved life.

Lep had no heart.

He remembered the first time he'd ever seen the human heart. It had looked smaller than he'd expected, more vulnerable than he'd expected. It had made him aware of his own heart, its atavistic beat, sending the message through his veins that life was involuntary, a mystery. Humility had swept him. He had wept. Then he'd had his last vision—like the visions of his childhood—a vision of destiny and a vision of time.

He wasn't sure he could explain it.

He'd suddenly understood that in the nucleus of his cells where the genetic code was stored, was also stored a knowledge of who man had been and who man would become. He'd understood that he was part of a biological chain that went back to the origin of man and forward to a future that wasn't entirely unknown. He had understood that time and the clock were not one and the same—that the clock didn't measure time; it reduced eternity to minutes and hours and years—that the past wasn't dead at all, but alive, pulsing and vital, still present; and the future was already born, only waiting to be recognized.

Now, his life had no heart.

And Morrison had said, "The country has no heart."

The streets of the Medical Center were deserted. Only a scattering of lights burned in the hospitals, fewer in the medical schools and the research labs; the silhouettes rose in harsh relief against a star-strewn sky.

"It's the modern-day equivalent of Lourdes, isn't it?" she said.

"Specialist as Saviour," he answered.

He took her in the rear entrance of Calvary, leading her through the labyrinth of corridors. A porter was mopping the floor. An intern passed, bleary-eyed, suffering from battle fatigue. In a hospital, pain waited for sundown. Pain crept in at night, and death's shadow took inventory. Between flurries of emergency activity, a peculiar hush reigned; part reverence, part fear.

Illness produced martyrs and tyrants, he told her. Illness produced strange mutations in the personality. Some patients got trapped in the whirlpools of self-pity. Others yielded to trancelike states that severed all connection to the processes of the body. Others turned into children, deferring even to orderlies.

Faced with the facts, the Vice-President would go through a period of pretense, elaborate strategies of denial. After that would come a long hard look at the reality.

He ushered her into the lab, reclaimed the can of X-ray film from the files and put the reality on the projector. Then he switched off the lights and started the film. "This is the result of Morrison's cardiac catheterization."

He saw her nod in the darkness, her eyes fixed on the images that flickered on the screen.

"We puncture an artery near the groin," he said, "and then a catheter is threaded over a guide wire and manipulated through the artery to the heart. That snakelike shadow is the contrast medium that has been injected—its path through the coronary arteries is being filmed at sixty frames a second." He stopped the film and pointed at a white coagulation. "Do you see that?"

"Yes."

"The heart's supplied with blood by two coronary arteries. This is the artery that supplies blood to the left ventricle. You can see there's an occlusion there—a blockage. It's a serious blockage because it's the main artery to the left ventricle." He switched the film on again. "There are also critical occlusions here—in the circumflex artery, which supplies the back of the heart. He's also got a left ventricular aneurysm—as a result of the destruction of the muscle. There's thrombus there. The heart's weak enough for him to go into heart failure. Do you see this area?"

"Yes."

"This part of the heart that's not moving—is dead. When an area of the muscle is deprived of oxygen, it dies. It becomes whitish scar tissue. In Washington, after his first attack, they put him on digitalis to strengthen the remaining live heart muscle—but the portion of the heart muscle that's dead isn't reversible."

"What does that mean?"

"Even if you increase the blood supply to the deprived area, it won't help the dead tissue. But it will help if we cut it out."

The machine crackled as the film ended. Tate switched on the light.

"So there's a problem with the system that pumps the blood to the heart?"

"Because of damage to the heart muscle."

"You're telling me he could die?"

"Yes." He watched her wrestle with it. He was struck by the strength in her.

When she spoke, there was no trace of panic or hysteria. "How will you proceed then?"

"He's not improving."

"Surgery?"

"Yes."

"What kind of surgery?"

"Repairs may buy him a bit of time, but not much. He couldn't return to anything near normal activity, and he couldn't be exposed to any stress." He spoke slowly, carefully. "Morrison doesn't strike me as the kind of man who'd be crazy about a passive existence." He paused to remove the film from the machine. He snapped a can around it and crossed the room to return it to the file. He was aware of her waiting for the rest of it.

With his back to her, he said, "There's another way. It's high risk, enormous problems and a low rate of success—but when it does work, what you've got is a human being who can return to functioning at full capacity."

"What other way?"

Tate turned around. "Remove the entire heart," he said, "and give him a new one."

Isabel crossed her hands over her chest. Her shoulders twitched slightly, as if in protest.

"A transplant," he said.

53

He opened his eyes to a dull gray dawn. There would be no sun. He could tell that by the haze coming through the shutters. It was one of those mornings when the clouds stacked up, one on top of the other, turning what had been a horizon into a ceiling—the way life did that, turned horizons into ceilings, transparent ceilings that made their presence known only when you struck your head against them.

The wind was blowing. The trees were whipping their branches against the house and the hunting dogs had set up a low wail, which meant Manuel hadn't fed them yet. A low throb of thunder announced the prelude to another burst of spring rain. Out of the gloom would come a blanket of new green to cover everything fleetingly before it withered and burned in the summer sun.

He rolled over. Joanna wasn't there.

Then he realized Joanna was standing at the foot of the bed, holding a rifle on him.

It crossed his mind that in the southern states, it was a common occurrence for a woman to shoot her husband and be acquitted; in Texas, it was the other way around. He had had four hours' sleep, he had three operations scheduled before noon, and he could smell coffee; a wife who meant to kill her husband wouldn't make coffee. That crossed his mind, too.

"What are you doing?"

"Emergency," she said. That's what he'd said last night. The clock in the library had been chiming 3 A.M. *"Gunshot wound in the chest,"* he'd said. He'd gone into the bathroom and closed the door, making subversive noises, like a thief rifling through his own emotions.

"Is that loaded?"

"Yes." She squinted at him through the sight, deadeye, like the crack shot she was. "Where were you last night?"

"At the hospital."

"Fidelity's out of the question. Honesty's not."

"The Houston Oaks."

"Anyone I know?"

"Put the gun away."

"Do you remember when we went back to New Orleans last January —to that same hotel? We were going to save the marriage, remember? Then the off-duty loneliness set in. I saw it in your eyes. In restaurants, you started to pull out my chair, take my elbow—all those courtesies that take place between lovers who are about to become strangers—"

He rolled out of bed and pulled on a bathrobe. He opened the shutters. Outside, the oleander bushes glistened, leaves washed clean by last night's rain, spindly branches bent under the morning wind. When he turned around, she still had the rifle leveled at him. "Put it away."

"I'm trying to get your attention. I don't like strange beds. I don't like strangers."

He didn't say anything.

"There was a geologist," she said. "It was a splendid affair. Like a Christmas toy. It lasted until the battery ran down—"

He came across the room and took the shotgun out of her hands.

"There was a physicist," she said. "I went to his apartment. I listened to a recording of Eric Satie on the piano. He was impotent with his wife. He explained Heisenberg to me. Did you know the same experiment performed by different people comes out differently?"

"I don't want to hear anymore," he said.

"There was a pilot," she said. "He flew rock groups around the world. Did you know in Bombay, the Parsis feed the corpses of loved ones to vultures?"

"Why put yourself through this? Or me?"

She had started to shake. He couldn't tell if it was anger or fear.

"And a real-estate developer," she said. "I picked him up on the Loop, and I didn't even ask his name."

He turned and left her. He went downstairs to the library. Rosewood-paneled, the room was dark and musty, seldom used, filled with photographs, oil maps, books on Texas history and family albums. It smelled of Lep. It smelled of old leather and power. One of the glass guncases was hanging open, the keys dangling. He put the rifle back in the rack, locked the case and returned the keys to the top drawer. When he came back to the bedroom, Joanna hadn't moved.

"Sugar wants to have the children baptized. On Easter Sunday," she said.

"For Christ's sake—"

"That's what Sugar said. For Christ's sake." She attempted a laugh. It cracked in the middle.

He started toward her. He could feel the jealousy. He wanted to shake her. He wanted to hold her.

"She's from out of town," Joanna said. "You don't know her name and you're never going to see her again." It came out clipped. It stopped him. "Are you?"

"Yes."

"Malone's coming back."

"How do you know?"

"I *know*. My bones know."

"You don't owe me—"

"What's her name?"

"Isabel Howard."

"I won't see Malone if you don't see her again."

"Could you do that?"

"No."

"Neither could I."

He crossed the room and looked out again. The hounds had quit barking. Manuel was feeding them. The dogs were penned at the rear of the property, between the guesthouse and servant's quarters, a hundred yards from what had once been stables. The stables weren't used anymore. The horses were boarded out. The servant's quarters were buried in a garden which, against all laws of nature, produced a bright confusion of year-round blooms. He could see the tulips. Mist veiled the poppies. The Easter lilies were threatening to bloom. Overhead, the clouds hung low, blanketing the earth with a fine drizzle. A few erratic raindrops, big as nickels, sparkled in the gloom. Then the clouds cracked and a thin sheet of light illuminated the estate, as brief and reticent as a nun's smile. It might have been a hundred years ago except for the sound of Manuel's transistor radio. The whine of steel guitars and country fiddles split the dawn: Texas Bob Wills and his Texas Playboys.

He turned around.

She was staring at him. "How did we get here?"

"I don't know," he said.

54

Midmorning sun suffused Merritt Lockwood's office. Allison watched it cast a golden glow on the pale carved nineteenth-century armoire, and sparkle on the crystal accessories and trail across the nest of white chamois furniture before it filtered through the greenhouse garden of blooming tiger orchids to shimmer across Merritt's desk.

She sat behind the desk. She had coveted the room. She had imagined herself only once removed from the center of power. She had imagined herself surrounded by orchids and bottled sunlight. Now—last night—Guero had disrupted that.

Her flesh prickled with the memory: *Yo te amo . . . te quiero . . . dame tu amor . . .*

Then she realized Lep was scowling at her from the doorway.

"Dinner for the international press delegates is at eight o'clock," she said, turning suddenly brisk. "It'll be served in the private wine cellar at *Tony's*. After that, a tour of Houston's night life—"

Lep crossed the threshold, still glowering.

She rose, came around the desk and perched on the edge, crossing her legs. In the same brisk tone, she read from her clipboard,

"Tomorrow night, the floating banquet starts at nine. Merritt said you wanted a late departure so all the refinery lights will be blazing when you go through the Ship Channel. The slides are ready. Your speech is prepared. There'll be radio equipment on board available to the journalists so the story of META can break instantly around the world." She looked up from the clipboard. "The band's arranged. The menu's barbequed ribs—except for the Iranian caviar and champagne." Her voice broke, slightly.

"You've been busy."

"Merritt taught me to be organized."

"Does that include the order to have Guero released?"

She didn't flinch. She opened a crystal box, took out a cigarette and lit it with a matching lighter. "I was sure it was something you'd overlooked."

"So you told Dixon Amory I authorized it?"

"No." She inhaled deeply.

"How'd you pull it off?"

"The way they train models to go down the runway at *Lubeck's.* They tell them to think: *I'm beautiful, I'm loved and I've got a secret.* It's the female equivalent of *'balls.'* If Dixon Amory chose to believe I was acting for you—" She made a helpless gesture.

A glint of amusement rippled Lep's eyes. "You've got all the earmarks of becoming a great bitch."

"They beat him up," Allison said quietly.

Lep's amusement vanished. She heard him curse under his breath.

Crushing out her cigarette, she crossed to the window to look out over the Houston skyline. "Very few women get a close look at power," she said, "much less a crack at it." Her voice had turned firm and quiet. "I know it's a ruthless game. I'm not looking for a rule book because I know there're no rules. That much I understand." She shook her head. "But I don't understand what you're doing with Guero."

"I'm not Guero's enemy."

"What are you to him? What's he to you?"

Lep joined her at the window. A wave of his hand encompassed the North-Central area. "The oppression of the *Chicano* is an obsolete issue. The Calders have always been beyond that—now, history's catching up with the Calders. There's a place for Guero at the top level of power." Lep's face creased into a wry half-smile. "That's not unrealistic. It's the path most radicals take."

"Then why tyrannize him?"

"He needs toughening up. If he stays angry, then let him be tough— he'll live longer. If he shifts and comes in—then his toughness will serve him." Lep made a fist and pressed it under her chin, tilting her face. "You want everything—and I'm going to teach you how to get it. Would you like to know why?"

"Yes."

"Do you believe God created the world in seven days?"

"I don't know."

"Do you know the lesson in that?"

"No."

"Never create a world without a witness," he said.

She didn't smile. She forced herself to meet Lep's eyes. "Guero's your son, isn't he?"

"No."

"I don't know why I never saw it. It's so obvious. He has the Calder eyes. He has your eyes."

"No."

"I've watched you. You control people by telling them how to interpret what they see."

"If you can ask the question, then I assume you can tolerate the answer." Lep's face hardened. "So you should be careful what questions you ask."

"Are you Guero's father?"

"No."

"Do you know who his father is?"

"Yes."

"Who?"

"He's Tate's son," Lep said.

55

The crickets paused. A desultory breeze rustled the oleanders, scattering petals from the potted azaleas about the brick terrace and filling the air with the scent of night-blooming jasmine. When the breeze quit, the night turned still and humid, preview to a long hot summer.

For nearly a half-hour, Tate had been cutting back and forth across the olympic-sized pool with slow deliberate strokes. Now he pulled himself out and got into a terry-cloth robe.

Joanna came out, wearing a peach-colored gauze blouse over her minimal bikini and carrying a tray with liquor and glasses. She poured a brandy and offered it to him.

Frowning, he took it. He swallowed a slug of brandy. Around the terrace, scented candles burned in hurricane lamps, casting a romantic light that drove away insects. Past the lamps, the night was stone-gray, a moon dimmed by clouds. He picked up a towel and attacked his hair —attacking the moment when they had bound themselves, miniaturizing the marriage the way aristocratic Chinese bound the feet of newborn females. It had become a contract of cruelty and license—two people taking lovers like prescriptions for a disease that nobody had diagnosed. Thinking these thoughts, he watched her shed the blouse and swim the pool twice.

When she came out, she said, "Do you want me?"

"I'm not crazy about charity."

She flinched. He felt a sting of triumph. He watched her dry off and get back into the blouse and walk to the edge of the terrace. After a moment, he set his glass down and followed her. She was looking out over the masses of roses. She was pinning up her hair. He found his eyes scanning the nape of her neck. He felt like a man treading a mine field. He had a sense of a detonation about to take place.

She turned slightly. "When are you taking Antonio to Mexico City?"

"The end of April."

"I want you to take my father."

"For hyperthermia?"

"Yes."

"You know I can't take that responsibility."

"I'll take the responsibility."

"You can't."

"Then take it for me."

"For a liberated woman, you make a lot of demands."

"Free—" she corrected.

"Are you?"

She turned fully and faced him. "You're a sonofabitch to ask."

"Sometimes I feel like one of those gorillas in the Hermann Park Zoo—do you remember when we took the kids?"

"That was six years ago."

"What were the gorillas' names?"

"Ji Ji and Vanilla."

"I knew you'd remember." The cords in his neck were taut. He could feel them throbbing. He heard the crickets start up. The dampness bruised him. He wrapped his arms around her and cupped her breasts. He could feel her heart beating, mysteriously, as if he'd never seen or touched a heart. "That's where it broke—at the zoo. We stood there looking at those damned monkeys in their diorama—their quarter-of-a-million-dollar split-level town house complete with tropical landscaping and heated swimming pool—" he didn't finish it.

"You broke it first."

"You counted on that."

He let her go. He crossed the terrace and picked up his brandy and drained it. He was pouring another when she came back.

"How long will she be in Houston?"

He knew she meant Isabel Howard. "Until the first of May." He saw a flash of pain in Joanna's eyes. It pleased him. "Haven't you found that there's a point—after you've slept with someone—when you're no longer strangers and you're not necessarily friends?"

She bent over the hurricane lamp and blew out the candle. He watched her move around the terrace blowing out the rest of the lamps. Then she came back carrying the last one to light their way to the house. The candlelight made her look anachronistic, from a past century.

For the first time in years an old memory of Vietnam broke through. He remembered Krong-Kuang. Krong had been a Montagnard. Krong had been a *njau,* a witch doctor. Krong had been a mercenary, trained by the Green Berets. *"Every man has many souls,"* Krong had said. *"Some of yours are lost."*

He took the candle from her. He blew it out. He became aware of having smashed the lamp when he heard it shatter against the brick.

The moon drifted. Joanna's eyes caught his in a moment of passing light.

He lifted her into his arms and carried her inside and up the stairs.

The bedroom was dark. He left it in darkness. He carried her across the room to the four-poster bed and threw himself on her, pulling at the gauze blouse and tearing away the fragile bikini.

Her flesh shimmered. He felt its power; he felt the imperative that had compelled him to make his commitment to flesh, to the magic and the terrors of its endurance and its perishability. Mortality resided in the flesh; so did life.

Did it? And if it did—why did he have to keep proving it to himself, over and over?

He took her harshly, inviting her to thrash and flail, wanting to use all of his strength to subdue her, to claim his power over her, driven by a need to erase the imprint of any other man and leave only his own.

It hit him hard. It wasn't Isabel. It wasn't medicine. It wasn't Vietnam. It went back—long before.

He felt the veneer of self-constriction being stripped away. He heard Joanna cry out, a strange primeval cry that sent spasms of pain through his groin. He rocked on the edge of some perverse salvation. There was a roaring in his head. Then his groin burst and a series of convulsions passed through him, the letting go of hope and self-pity and buried rage.

The silence rang.

He couldn't bring himself to look at her. He couldn't move.

He heard her get up and go into the bathroom and close the door. He heard the shower go on.

His eyes were closed.

Krong had performed a ceremony for him before he left Vietnam. Krong had called on the spirit of the mountain, which had been destroyed, and the spirit of the rice, which no longer grew, and the spirits of the rain and the rivers and the water buffalo. Then Krong had hung an amulet around his neck and had recalled his multiple souls.

He rose. He tied the arms of the terry-cloth bathrobe around his waist and turned on the light. The bedroom looked strange to him. Crossing to the dresser, he pulled open a seldom-used drawer and retrieved the amulet he had buried there. He stared at the engravings on the stone—four animals: the unicorn, the turtle, the dragon and the phoenix.

It wasn't medicine. It wasn't Isabel Howard. It went back to Lep. He remembered the stallion, *Graf*. He remembered the child in Mexico.

The penalty for nonfeeling was violence.

He heard the thought. He knew it was important. He willed himself to remember it, knowing it meant more than he could absorb at this moment.

He turned the amulet over in his hand. The meaning of it came to him. Malone was the unicorn. Lep was the dragon. Joanna was the phoenix. He saw himself as the turtle, carrying his hiding place on his back.

It wasn't Lep.

He had done it himself.

He dropped the amulet over his head. He got into his clothes. Then he pulled a suitcase from the closet shelf and set about packing.

He was finished when she came out.

She was wearing a Chinese wrapper and she smelled faintly of lilac.

"It's over—" he said.

He picked up the suitcase and went down the stairs.

Outside, the clouds had clustered over the moon. It was threatening to rain.

He took the Porsche out of the garage and down the driveway. The street was empty. He headed into it.

56

"I don't *want* to be baptized," Cissy said. Her real name was Victoria. Nobody had ever called her Victoria. "Ugh! They stick you in the water like you're a slimy fish or something—"

"And I don't want a *bar-mitzvah*." Benjy's face was grave. In the summer, his ribs showed. Summer was three months off. Joanna could already count the ribs under his T-shirt.

"It's all dumb," Cissy said.

Cissy wasn't good-natured, Joanna thought. Neither was Benjy. It came from too much insulation, too many wishes voiced and instantly granted. "Sometimes we have to do things we don't want to—for the sake of other people," she said. It wasn't what she had meant to say. She had no idea what she'd meant to say. She was practicing spiritual blackmail, she thought.

"When's Daddy coming back?" Cissy pouted. She had brought a hairbrush to the breakfast table and was brushing vehemently at her hair.

"I don't know," Joanna spread butter on a blueberry muffin. Ferns filtered the southwestern glare, turning the gallery into an oasis—glass and faded chintz and Mexican tile—a soft rainwashed light streaming in to burnish Benjy's tousled hair and graze Cissy's cameo profile. She had always endowed them, purred over them like a cat with a golden litter. Truth would be hard for them.

"Look," she said. "Everybody has his own version of God. Because nobody really knows who God is. So there're different traditions. Christian, Jewish—you have to respect both of them because they're yours."

"Will he come and see us?" Benjy asked.

"Of course not," Cissy said. "God's in a box. That's where God is. They call it a church or a temple, but it's really a box—and then they say that's where God is. But that's not where He is at all." Cissy laid a hand on her rib cage. "He's in here—"

"I meant *Daddy*—Benjy threw out both arms and sent his milk toppling.

"Clumsy!" Cissy giggled.

"I'm not."

"God knows you are—"

"I hate God!"

"He'll *get* you for that."

How many angels could dance on the head of a pin?

"Billions.

"Viewed from far out in the universe, wouldn't the planet gleam no bigger than the head of a pin? And wouldn't humans be angels?"

Had Malone said that?

"What Papa needs is a miracle," her mother was saying.

The sun was streaming past Swiss batiste curtains embroidered with strawberries. On the kitchen windowsill, an Italian ceramic swan rose from a sea of scarlet pots brimming with grape ivy. Her mother was trotting from sink to stove, releasing clouds of steam and the reassuring smell of chicken soup.

"I'm ashamed," her mother said. "Papa's dying," she said. "I make soup and I take it to him and I watch him eat it, and I know in my bones that he's dying." Her mother started to cry. "Do you see what I do? Every day, I weep, and I weep for him—but under the tears, I'm glad to be alive. I try not to be glad. But I can't, and it shames me." Her mother dabbed at her tear-stained cheeks with a corner of her apron. "Moses crossed the Red Sea, didn't he? Malone walked on the moon. Those were miracles, weren't they?"

"I don't know." Joanna occupied a stool. Her mother was moving around again, setting a kettle on to boil.

"Only the Jews think you can bargain with God for a miracle," her mother said. She was loading the dishwasher. "If you baptize those children, you'll break your father's heart—but sometimes I think the Christians are right. What do they call it—an act of grace. That's style, isn't it? And God knows your papa's always had style."

"I spoke to Tate. He'll take Papa to Mexico City." Joanna hesitated. In the pause, she could hear the kitchen clock ticking. "The hyperthermia's not a miracle."

Her mother turned. "They pump the blood through a machine, isn't that right? The machine heats the blood? The heat kills the cancer cells?"

"It's not that simple."

"What is? Living? Dying? Believing?" She peered at Joanna. "Marriage? No—marriage, least of all."

"Tate's gone. Last night, he packed a bag—"

Ida turned her attention back to the dishwater.

"When your papa and I got married, marriage was still an institution. Your generation rebelled at that. You didn't want to be fed into an institution. Maybe you were right. But your papa and I—we were committed to each other—even through the mistakes and the betrayals. If you have a root, the branches can grow wild in any direction and the leaves can fly with the wind—but the root has to be there, deep." She looked up. "I'm sorry." The kettle started to whistle. Ida reached for a teapot. It crashed to the floor. Clutching at her heart, Ida stared at the broken pieces. "Oh, my God—"

"It's all right—"

Her mother continued to stare at it, stricken. "When I came from Russia, I lived at my cousin Rabinowich's house. In Brooklyn. Behind the grocery store. The bedroom was so small, you had to lie down to make the bed. And the trains went past. In the kitchen, if I broke anything, Rabinowich would call me terrible names in Yiddish." She was trembling. "For years afterward, even after I married your papa, every time I broke a dish, my heart would hurt—"

"Papa's going to be all right—"

"Damn Rabinowich!" Her mother took a plate from the open dishwasher and slammed it to the floor. "Damn him—" she cried, sending another plate crashing. "Damn his soul!" she shouted, slinging dishes, defying Rabinowich in Yiddish and crying out in triumph as the china shattered.

The teakettle was still whistling. Her mother picked her way across the broken china and turned it off. Then she reached into the cupboard and held out a platter. "Here—maybe you need to break something yourself."

On Westheimer Road, bulldozers rumbled like yellow dinosaurs, generating clouds of dust and dozens of new shopping centers. Joanna stopped for a light near a newly erected billboard which read: LLOYD'S OF LONDON PREDICTS HOUSTON WILL BE THE WORLD'S LARGEST CITY BY THE TWENTY-FIRST CENTURY.

She frowned at it. Houston kept annexing adjacent communities spreading like an ink blot, piling up new tax revenues and new obligations for community services while the older agencies in the inner city —like the *Casa de Vida*—were being slowly squeezed out.

She kept her mind on that; it was easier to keep her mind on that.

Picking up speed, she joined the stream of traffic heading downtown. The board meeting started at eleven. She felt obliged to attend. She'd been the one to get the *Casa de Vida* financed for another year, using her name and influence to do battle for funds; she remained the only *Anglo* involved. Now, as well as the threat of financial cut-backs, they were facing an onslaught of problems from the *Chicano* community itself. She kept her mind on that; it kept her from feeling an overwhelming fear, a sudden sense of her soul being stolen, a feeling of skating on cellophane.

Near the hub of the city, she veered off into the Montrose area and headed down the familiar streets. The house she and Tate and Malone had once shared now served as the *Casa de Vida*—only mildly refurbished by a coat of slate-gray paint and a dozen red flower boxes filled with wilting geraniums, and tilting slightly, like a ship in a northern gale. Under the direction of a *Chicana* social worker, it was run as a clearing house. Volunteers took case histories, dispensed reassurance, then sent most of the women on to other agencies for medical services, dental repairs, legal advice, abortions and child-care counseling. On the upper floors of the premises, only two classes were taught: English and birth control.

Joanna parked in a gravel bed at the rear. The old side porch, now glass-enclosed, served as reception room and outer office. Maria Lopez, a volunteer receptionist not much older than Allison, handed her an agenda as she entered. "They're waiting for you in the sun-room upstairs," Maria said.

"Has my husband called?"

"No."

"Is there a telephone free?"

"The front office is empty—"

She went down the hall. Furnished in leftovers and hand-me-downs from other agencies, the office was redeemed by three large windows that faced the street. She sat at the scarred desk, dialed the hospital and glanced at the agenda while she waited for the line to connect.

The first issue, as always, was jobs—the median income of the *Chicana* was still less than three thousand a year.

She tried to make herself think about that.

The second was political power—LULAC, the League of the United Latin American Citizens had provided new guidelines for the education of the *Chicana* woman in order to exercise the power of the vote.

Her mind refused to address itself to the vote.

The issue of birth control, always inflammatory, had now been labeled *genocide* by the militants—what they wanted taught instead was "reproductive freedom." At the other end of the scale, a handful of feminists were protesting "special oppression": *machismo,* the double standard and the role of the Catholic Church.

The issues seemed suddenly complicated, inextricably tangled.

She got Ellie on the line. Ellie told her Tate was in surgery.

"Ask him to call me at the *Casa de Vida.*" The call felt desperate. What would she say to him?

She hung up and forced herself to focus on the last two items on the schedule:

Diminishing Participation: The women are being told the Casa de Vida represents Anglo brainwashing; their husbands have a fear of being turned into pochos, defined as "a Mexican who has pretensions of becoming a gringo sonofabitch."

And:

Bureaucratic Blackmail: We are facing retaliatory cutbacks in finan-

cial aid because of the participation of our volunteers in radical activities such as the Rodriguez protest march.

Then she laid her head on the desk and let the fear wash through her. It came out in tears that flowed swiftly and lasted only a few moments.

When she raised her head, she felt dizzy, like a needle of a compass attached to a roller coaster, erratic from being pulled in too many directions at once.

Something had happened to her hearing. There was a roaring in her ears, like the engines of a plane in flight. Then, when it ceased, the slightest sound seemed louder and sharper, as if she were tuned in too loud in order to listen for directions which might come at any moment in the timbre of a whisper.

She heard the car pull up to the curb before she saw it. She heard the sound of the car door opening and closing. She heard the footsteps come up the walk before she focused on the figure with only a detached curiosity, hardly taking note of the lean agility, the thinning dark hair and the prominent cheekbones. Not until he was out of sight did his identity register.

It was fourteen years.

She wasn't surprised—as if she had extended an incautious invitation to the fates and it had been accepted.

The hallway was in shadow. A square of light from the porch framed his silhouette. For a split second she felt herself being pushed backward, into an old dream, like falling off a cliff. Then she heard her own voice, absolutely calm, as if it originated in some serene part of her being that had been waiting to say his name.

"Hello, Malone."

He stopped where he was. His voice echoed. "You're still beautiful."

"I have a meeting. Upstairs—"

He came toward her, then. He looked down at her. He didn't touch her. The creases around his eyes had deepened. His eyes were black, sparks burning in them, like fire at the end of a tunnel. "I'll wait."

"Where've you been?"

"Hanging out in the fifth dimension."

"What happened to the fourth?"

"It turned out to be a truck stop."

"I knew you were coming back."

"Did you?"

"*Why?*"

"I'm going to pilot Lep's sky rig." He smiled. His teeth were white, like the sand in Galveston. "It's an irresistable venture," he said. "The bastard's going to steal the sun."

57

On the upper deck, waiters were pouring Dom Pérignon.

Zev asked for scotch. Then he moved through the crowd, looking for Allison.

On three sides of the deck, breathtaking slides were being cast against the night on angled screens, positioned so that the components of META appeared to glide in a slow-motion ballet beyond the planet Earth as though Lep Calder's space factories were already being constructed in the Texas sky. As stirring as march music, Lep's voice filled the air with conviction. *"Man has always survived by expanding . . . Man has always expanded by moving into the unknown . . ."*

Zev passed a security guard on his way to the stairwell. A waiter thrust a glass of champagne into his hand. Carrying it, he descended to the lower deck where he leaned over the railing and emptied it into the sludge below. The brackish waters of the Houston Ship Channel parted sluggishly; the ship moved without grace. Then he looked up and thought: Hell will blaze with less brilliance.

Along the shore, the network of refineries and chemical plants had been etched with a flaming pen. Light ricocheted from metal towers and mosquelike storage tanks, creating a spiraling inferno that rose and fell, burning with an ominous beauty. Watching the spectacle move past, he felt a wave of resentment for those who—unlike the Israelis— had never experienced modern warfare on their own soil, and so arrogantly displayed fifty miles of resources and industry like jewels on black velvet. Frowning, he dropped the glass into the channel and headed for the bar.

It was tucked under the stairs, intended for use during inclement weather. A single bartender was polishing glasses. Facing the line-up of red-leather stools was a full-color photograph of Campbell Malone taken after the moon shot. Malone was wearing the look of a man who, clear-eyed, had already read the inscription on his gravestone, and it had made him laugh.

The only occupant at the bar was Allison, holding onto a glass of champagne and staring at the photograph.

Zev slid onto an adjacent stool. "Had enough of the high frontier?"

She nodded. She was wearing something bare and shimmery under an antique shawl, an embroidered silver dragon guarding a field of poppies. She looked beautiful and troubled.

He ordered scotch. The ice tinkled over the sound of Lep's voice which filtered down from the upper deck.

"*. . . a third industrial revolution in space is as close as the shuttle. The new frontier, out there, is only two hundred miles from every person on earth . . .*"

"—and now ladies and cowboys, for a bit of space rapture," Zev said. He sipped at his scotch. Allison didn't respond. She continued to stare at the photograph. "Interesting man—Campbell Malone?"

"Yes."

"Have you met him?"

"A long time ago."

"They say the Israeli press is tough—but it's your press who buried him. Half-Indian, double-Irish, they said. They loved him. Then they turned on him. The old news clippings said he sold stamp books, moon rocks and an undershirt that had made it halfway to Venus." He raised his glass to the photograph. "NASA only paid their heroes thirteen grand a year. Then they were dumped in the backlash—when the public started crying they should quit producing garbage in space and clean up the cities."

Allison turned to look at him. The shawl slipped from her shoulders. He caught it and wrapped it around her.

"Why aren't you upstairs?" he asked.

"Why aren't you?"

"At the sound of God's voice, we Jews become refugees."

She smiled. The smile didn't make it to her eyes.

Lep's voice continued, ". . . *Imagine the first creature that crawled from the sea five billion years ago. To that creature, earth—with its oxygen and its gravity—was a hostile environment. Yet, they ventured beyond the limitations of the sea to master this alien world. We are their descendants—we who populate this planet—and now we dare to master the world of space . . ."*

"It's the opposite of what he's selling, you know," Zev said. "Earth mastered the sea creatures. Earth changed their form, their nature, everything—in the same way that space'll change ours." He spoke gently. "At first, we'll carry oxygen. We'll re-create gravity. After a few billion years, we'll adapt. Man as we know him won't exist." He grinned. "Maybe he'll even develop a conscience."

"Where'd you learn so much about space?"

"A journalist picks up a little bit about everything."

"You don't like Lep, do you?"

"Do you?"

Her face clouded slightly. "He's not an ordinary person. When you're around him, you never think about whether you *like* him or not. He's brilliant and powerful and exciting, and it *carries* you. Only"— she paused to trace a watermark on the bar with her finger—"he's always looking out—past the horizon. He never looks back."

"At what?"

"People."

He reached out and took her hand. "Has anybody told you how beautiful you look tonight?"

"No."

"Can I help?" he asked softly.

She shook her head. Her eyes strayed to the photograph again. His gaze followed hers. He remembered the old rumors—bouts of recklessness, hallucinations in space—too much drinking afterward, a flaw in Campbell Malone's psyche, which refused to stay quiet and hidden away.

"I was fourteen when he walked on the moon," he said. "I was picking plantains on a kibbutz near the Galilee. That was the distance he covered—from the Galilee to the moon. The old people couldn't span it. To them, the heavens belonged to God. I remember the amazement

I felt. I remember looking up at the night and wondering how it would feel to watch the earth rise over the moon—" something in her face stopped him.

"Malone's my father," she said.

"That wasn't in the press clippings—"

"I haven't seen him since I was four." She smiled. "He doesn't look back either."

"Then he's a fool," Zev said.

She motioned to the bartender to refill her champagne. The bartender popped a new cork, poured with a flourish, then retreated to the end of the bar to answer the phone. She studied the bubbles swirling in her glass. "He was like lightning," she said. "That's the way I remember him. He made everything a little scary and wonderful."

"And now?"

She shook her head. "It's like this shawl I'm wearing. It came down through the Calder family and there's a story that goes with it, but everybody's forgotten it. If something's a hundred and fifty years old, maybe it's all right to wipe out its origins. But I'm eighteen, and whenever I think about Malone, it feels"—she made a helpless gesture— "incomplete."

"Maybe it's time to complete it?"

"I'm afraid to."

He let go of her hand. Her gaze was fixed on him. She looked open, vulnerable. His eyes flicked to the end of the bar where the bartender was hanging up the phone.

"That was Mr. Calder." The bartender addressed Allison. "He wants you on the top deck. Right away."

She hesitated. Zev drained his glass and pushed it across the bar. "Scotch." He brushed Allison's cheek with his lips. "I'll wait—"

He watched her go.

The bartender filled his glass. "It's none of my business," the bartender frowned, "but if I were you—"

"What?"

"—I'd stay away from Lep Calder's private stock."

Guero drove. The car, a four-year-old Mustang, belonged to Carlos. A badly dented rear fender rattled. Carlos chain-smoked.

On Loop 610, the traffic had thinned to a trickle. The moon looked cold, unfriendly. Past downtown, Carlos checked his watch. "Twenty minutes before midnight." The freeway began its ascent.

Guero looked down. Below was the old Dickson gun plant. Ahead, the Loop rose, becoming a high-rise bridge that spanned the Ship Channel. Checking the rearview mirror for patrol cars, he kept his speed inside the limit. Halfway across the bridge, he pulled up alongside the railing and stopped. He left the parking lights blinking. Carlos got out and raised the hood to make it look like car trouble.

Guero emerged carrying binoculars. A dark T-shirt, jeans and sneakers rendered him all but invisible against the night. Crossing to the railing, he took in the harbor. Lights from the waterfront bars blazed amid darkened flophouses. The massive trucks were parked, the tugs were moored, the forklifts were silent; crates of stacked cargo waiting to be loaded towered over the transit sheds. Carlos appeared next to him and pointed downstream. "Is that the ship?"

Guero peered through the binoculars and nodded. "Maybe twenty minutes, maybe a half-hour before it reaches the bridge."

He went around to the rear of the car and checked the Loop for signs of police again before he opened the trunk. The knapsack was stashed under a blanket. He harnessed himself into it. Then he retrieved an iron crowbar from a rusted toolbox and met Carlos in front. At the first lag in traffic, they stooped swiftly, in silence, and pried open the manhole cover. Quickly, Guero lowered himself through the gaping hole. He clung to the rim, legs swinging out like a pendulum over the Channel, aware if he missed the drop, he'd plunge more than a hundred feet to the waters below. He took a deep breath and let go. The catwalk caught him.

"*Ramona's*," Carlos hissed. The manhole shut.

Crouching motionless, Guero gave himself a moment for his eyes to grow accustomed to the shadows. Overhead, a spasm of traffic rumbled past. From below, the vapor from raw sewage and chemicals assailed his nostrils with a stench like a septic tank. He could hear the dark lap of the water, forty feet deep, and the gurgling of pools of mire. He thought about Rodriguez, his organs racked by poisoned chemicals, floating in the Channel.

He stood up—he was on one of the main catwalks. From there, he could see the three others that ran parallel, used by repair crews, crossing from one side of the bridge to the other and interconnected by lateral catwalks every fifty feet. At each end of the bridge, a network of

steel beams dipped down into a cat's cradle which was based on a concrete slab thirty feet above the water's edge. He walked quickly to the
end and took a look at it, going over it again: afterward, he'd climb
down the diagonal steel trusses, then up the V-shaped structure again
to the place where it met the first ground support—from there, he'd
shimmy down to safe territory. He figured five minutes, no more than
that.

Returning to the center of the bridge, he chose a midway spot on one
of the lateral catwalks, relieved himself of the knapsack and checked
the position of the ship again. Then he surveyed the Channel. The Gulf
Freeway, it was called; sailors called it the most treacherous channel in
the world. Narrow and shallow, the forty-five miles from Houston to
the open Gulf was crammed with barges and tugboats, dredges and
yachts and sailboats and fishing vessels. Ninety percent of the most poi-
sonous cargo in the country—lethal gases and toxic bromides and viru-
lent herbicides—went past the refineries and chemical plants that
blazed with light all the way to the San Jacinto Monument. From one
fire, or one accident—or one judiciously placed bomb, Carlos had
argued—a chain-reaction explosion could send it all to Kingdom
Come.

"No bombs," he had said.

He opened the knapsack. The packets were neatly tied. Each contained reproductions of a photograph, an occupational history and the
hospital records of a dozen men whose deaths were directly related to
the hazards of working in one of Lep's chemical plants:

Julio Martinez: *Consistent exposure to DOM—substitute for Chloro-
Methyl-MethylEther—an intermediate product used in the fabrication
of nuclear power and fuel for power plants. At thirty-five, Julio, a
non-smoker, had died of oat-cell lung cancer.*

Juan Diaz: *Exposure to benzene—used in petroleum refining and
pesticides—a proven carcinogenic. At twenty-eight, Juan was dead from
acute myelogenous leukemia.*

Pepe Jiminez: *Thirty years of exposure to vinyl chloride had killed
him at fifty-one from cancer of the liver.*

There were others.

The cancer statistics of three-quarters of a million chemical workers
were represented in a dozen personal obituaries. More effective than
bombs, he had told Carlos.

He watched the ship move closer. It was strung like a Christmas tree with glittering lights. Through the binoculars, he could see a full-dress orchestra and couples dancing on the upper deck. A burst of envy stirred in him, and anger; the ancient envy of the outcast child collided with the anger of the outlaw. His binoculars searched for Allison—even as another part of him remembered the revolutionaries he'd claimed as his models: the fighting priest Hidalgo and his *grito,* the shout for freedom that had rallied a Mexican rabble army in 1800; Pavon's guerillas, and Morales whose *campecino* armies had paved the way to Mexican independence from Spain—and Benito Juarez, a shepherd from Oaxaca who had deposed Maximilian—and Zapata and Villa who, with their peasant armies, had instigated the Mexican revolution of 1910. He had filled himself with the pain of those who had lived before him, their cries and their longings, their power of endurance and dignity of soul. The dead were alive in him. They had ordered him to affirm the life of the oppressed by remembering death; then had ordered him to demand the death of oppression by remembering life.

The ship's horn blasted. As it approached the bridge, he cut the string on the packets and crouched, poised, waiting for the ship to pass underneath. When it was directly below him, he emptied the knapsack into the night. The death notices fluttered down, papering the deck like macabre confetti.

He was already running when the commotion started below and a hail of bullets suddenly peppered the catwalk where he had been. He didn't look back. He kept going, dodging pistol shots as he ran.

The first response was laughter—as though it were a game.

Allison knew it wasn't.

Before the hands reached up to capture the fluttering leaflets—as if they were Lep's confetti; another piece of Lep's drama—before the reality penetrated and a cold fear spread like a common chill, she knew it was Guero.

Zev found her. She didn't have to find him. He appeared and took her arm and began to move her efficiently through the crowd.

"It's Guero—" she said.

He didn't stop to ask questions. He steered her across the deck, through dancers frozen under the twinkling lights; they looked like insects pinned to Lep's board with diamond stickpins.

Then the crack of pistol shots scattered them like marbles.

Over the loudspeaker, Lep ordered the band to keep playing. Lep ordered everyone to keep dancing.

Briefly, the boat touched the nearest wharf to eject the security guards. Moving directly behind them, Zev hurried her ashore and into the shadows.

"Where do we start looking?"

Ramona's ceiling was strung with wilted papier-mâché animals. Across the rear wall, somebody had painted an acrylic mural of Mayan warriors and feathered serpents; it was lit with red bulbs. A Mexican wearing sunglasses was playing a bombastic piano.

Hanging onto Zev's hand, she scanned the tables. Guero hadn't been at *The Harbor Lights* or *The Athens*. "He's not here, either."

"Maybe it wasn't—"

"It was. I *know* him—"

Over the clatter of glasses and beer bottles, an old longshoreman was telling stories; nobody was listening. A waterfront hooker, wearing gold sandals and purple shorts, was arguing with a Bangladesh sailor. Two Russian seamen were holding up a third who was threatening to pass out.

Ramona was behind the bar, a big raw-boned woman in her early thirties, wearing a black tank-top and men's trousers.

Allison spoke in Spanish. "Where's Guero? Have you seen him?"

Ramona's eyebrows had been shaved and penciled high on her forehead. She raised them higher and cocked her head in Zev's direction.

"Police have cordoned off the area," Zev said curtly. "All we want to do is get him out of here."

"Please—" Allison leaned across the bar and whispered to Ramona in Spanish.

Ramona's eyes narrowed. Her lids twitched. She crossed herself and took a swift inventory of the bar. "He's being passed from place to place by friendly hands."

"Has he been hurt?"

Ramona shook her head. "Go to McCarty and Clinton. Take a right and go two blocks. Go around to the rear entrance of the Hong Kong. Talk to the mama-san who's cook in the kitchen. She'll take you to him." She jerked her head in the direction of a curtained doorway. "Use the storeroom—there's an exit to the alley."

Zev parted the curtains for her. Red light from the bar gleamed in the darkness, then went out as the curtains fell together, like a fire being extinguished. He led her past haphazardly piled cartons, past a cluster of garbage cans; she could hear rats scurrying. A match flared for a moment in his hand. The back door creaked as he opened it. He looked up and down the alley before he motioned for her to come out.

She moved behind him down the length of the alley where he made a quick surveillance of the street. "We'd better take an indirect route."

"Why?"

"Just a feeling. It's not impossible we're being followed, is it?"

Allison shivered. She pulled the shawl closer around her.

Taking her arm, Zev trotted her across the street and through a series of alleys, winding and backtracking. Then he halted abruptly and listened. Allison heard nothing. He wrapped his arm around her and moved her at a steady pace through the shadows. "What'd you tell Ramona?"

"I said Guero was my lover."

"Is he?"

She turned her face up, meeting his eyes. "You were the first. He was the second."

"You didn't lose any time, did you?"

"I've been in love with him since I was seven." She began to weep silently.

Zev pulled her into a doorway and held her. He gave her a handkerchief. She blew her nose.

"A small case of *machismo*," he said. "I have to remind myself it's a product of slave cultures." His head turned quickly at a rustling sound. From somewhere, a kitten mewed softly.

"I wouldn't have known what I felt—without you."

He sent her a grim smile. "That'll warm my old age."

"I love both of you."

"You can't do that."

"Why not?"

"Maybe, at eighteen, you can." He cupped her face in his hands. Then he took his hands away and her cheeks burned, as though he'd left his prints on her. "But not with me."

She raised her eyes. His face was half-concealed in shadow. She had a sudden sense of foreboding. "There's something deeply wrong with it, isn't there? With META—and Lep? Even Malone?"

Again, something rustled in the alley nearby.

He pulled her behind him. Cautiously, he crept from the alcove into the alley. From a nearby bar, the twang of an electric guitar began to throb down the narrow passage. Then a sudden noise split the air, like a whip cracking.

Zev reeled backward before he crumpled.

She threw herself over him, screaming.

58

A murder had taken place . . .

What had triggered the thought? From the dressing room, Joanna glanced at the bedroom clock. Twenty-four hours had passed since Tate's departure; she hadn't slept. She could feel the effects of that.

Why had it suddenly struck her now?—that it had been murder, the deliberate killing of a marriage, conceived and executed by both of them; they had been accomplices in the need to end it violently after years of polite and futile blows.

Crossing the bedroom, she looked past the shutters. She could see the light on in the guesthouse. She could feel Malone's presence, moving around there, waiting for her. Hope promised Malone would restore her to herself. Fear said he might not.

She put on a shirt the color of marigolds. Not a new shirt, well-worn, like what she was bringing to Malone and what she was after.

The children were asleep. She paused in each room to bend over each of them, tucking in the covers. She thought about Allison. She felt a strange burst of anxiety for Allison.

There was a story of Kafka's that began: *"The evidence shows that this is how the murder was committed . . ."* She couldn't remember the story, only the opening. The phrase kept running like an irrational leitmotif through her mind.

Downstairs in the kitchen, she dialed Allison's number. Nobody answered.

Carrying a flashlight, she let herself out the back door. The moon was in hiding. Malone had walked on it. Now he was going out there again because Lep had plans for the universe. The thought engendered another wave of uneasiness. *"It's what I do,"* Malone had said. *"Space flight costs billions—you can only do it for the devil."*

When had he said that—and what did it mean?

She walked quickly, following the beam of the flashlight, oddly disoriented, as if the path were strange to her and so was the man who waited at the end of it.

Two years ago, she had redone the guesthouse in unbleached muslin and wicker. A lamp made from an antique Chinese picnic basket cast a diffuse glow. The light creased Malone's face. He looked older—that was her first thought as she let herself in.

His eyebrows shot up as if he heard the thought. Shirtless and barefoot, he was wearing white duck trousers. He had inherited the Indian's hairless chest—his flesh had always had the hue and texture of desert rock, "—and you're thinner."

"It's stylish—"

"You were always stylish."

"Now I work at it."

"Don't," he said. He had champagne icing in a copper bucket. The cork popped like a gunshot. In a fleeting trick of eyesight, she saw an odd luster around him, as though he were casting a silhouette of light instead of a shadow. It vanished as he handed her the glass. "What shall we drink to?"

"Fate, hope and charity," she said, making him smile.

He sloshed soda-water into his own glass. "In nineteen sixty-nine, I passed out at a cocktail party in Lausanne. When I came to, it was nineteen seventy-five. My space suit had been stuffed and sent to the Washington Museum of Science, and the moon had turned back into a piece of green cheese." He grimaced. "Ex-hero, embalmed in alcohol and interred in history, gets another chance at self-respect."

"You're working at it," she said.

"Sorry—"

She wanted to say: *"We don't have time."* The thought floated, unspoken. She knew he heard it and dismissed it. For Malone, time had no meaning. A moment could be expanded, blown up like a dirigible, big enough for a journey. In between the moments were cracks. Malone only visited the moments; he lived in the cracks.

He came toward her. He took the glass out of her hand. "You're not drinking your champagne."

"It doesn't seem necessary."

His eyes drew her. It was like entering a cavern and moving toward a lighted exit that turned out to exist in the iris of another hidden eye. "What keeps pulling us together?"

It struck her that her mind had held it in place. She wondered if the only fixed point in nature was the prerogative of the human mind—if what seemed man's most mercurial organ was capable of the most rigidity? She wondered what would happen if her mind let him go. She felt the thought begin to make it happen. It made her slightly dizzy. Then she saw it had never existed in her mind at all.

"The soul makes choices," she said quietly.

"Soul's choice?"

"You're one of those. So is Tate." The words seemed curious to her, unexpected. "I don't understand how it works. All I know is—it doesn't matter whether those choices can be lived out or not. They exist. And they last a lifetime. They may appear to be in conflict, but somewhere they're not. Somewhere else, they represent a deeper wisdom—"

He took her in his arms. He held her. Against her ear, he whispered, "You're the only thing on this earth that's ever felt like home to me."

The night turned still. All rustling ceased. Only the crickets rent the air, relentlessly singing the blues.

She felt her flesh go searching for her old self, slightly afraid, not of Malone, but of what she might find.

Malone's hands were cautious, tentative, like a man poaching on another man's territory, like a man out of touch with his own need.

Then she felt it begin to happen, a meeting of need, both of them seeking regeneration—the lighting of old fires, a passage backward—making love in remembrance. She could feel them both reaching to recapture the old selves which had been able to experience new passions before the tracks in the brain had become worn and the heart had been numbed by self-betrayal.

The true meaning of decadence is the inability to love.

Malone didn't say it aloud. She heard it anyway.

His mouth brushed her flesh, back and forth, stirring his hunger and hers. He was whispering against her flesh. She heard him through her flesh.

Her body followed his. He held her, without holding on, boldly and easily, entering her and leaving her, in an erotic trapezelike rhythm, perfectly synchronized. He had no need to own her. She could feel the knowledge in her body that he would always let her go. For that, she loved him. For that, she hated him.

He cradled her and rocked her. Slowly, he drew her to that place where fear met desire, where her form threatened to shatter and all sound vibrated through her cells; she heard him through her cells. Then silence claimed her and the end of all erotic ceremony.

His rhythm changed. An urgency took him over, a boundless hunger that broke through in tears—she wept with him—tears of shared grief for the past they had lost and the promise of future loneliness. Then a terrible cry emanated from him—filling her—the wail of a man in exile from his own nature, the love-cry of a man utterly lost.

"Tell me about her," Malone said softly.

"She's a magnificent creature . . ."

"Beautiful?"

"Yes."

"Searching?"

"There's a wild gene in her." Joanna watched a shaft of moonlight strike the curtains and outline Malone's profile against the pillow.

"I knew Tate had adopted her. I knew she'd taken the Calder name. It seemed better to leave it alone." Malone frowned. Conflicting emotions passed over his face. "That's not entirely true. Whatever the impulse is—fatherhood—I didn't have it. It always seemed to me the only gift to give someone you love is to let them go." He turned to face her. "You gave it to me."

"You took it," she said.

He smiled. "Does she have your fierce honesty?"

"In her own way."

"She's the future, isn't she? That never struck me—until I knew I was going into space again. Then I thought—Allison's your immortality. Whatever there is that's decent in you, she'll carry on—" he frowned again. "In some way, that's being a father, isn't it?"

"It's done," Joanna said quietly. A chill threatened to grasp her. She willed it to pass.

"Not the future—"

"That's not in our hands."

"If we don't claim it, Lep will grab it," he said grimly. He reached out and drew her close. She could feel the pulse beating in Malone's throat. Weeks of irrational and isolated fears rose in a wave that washed over her. "I'm not Lep's tool," he said. "Whatever happens—I want you to know that."

"What are you saying?"

His expression hardened. He had turned inward. "Think of it as a Faustian pact. I get to escape the planet, and he gets to control it." He closed his eyes. "It's what I do. Space flight costs billions—you can only do it for the devil."

Her ears rang. She remembered she had heard him say it before he said it. She remembered Malone had always done that, engendered chaos, divine accidents. That was finished. This was bigger and darker, a shadow that extended beyond her own private world.

The phone was ringing. It seemed to her it had been ringing for a long time before she recognized it as an outer summons.

Malone's eyes were closed. She could see the pulse beating in his throat.

Reluctantly, she rose to a sitting position. Reluctantly, she picked up the phone.

On the other end, a man identified himself as a reporter for the *Houston Post*.

It took her a moment to register his words.

Malone opened his eyes, watching her.

The reporter spoke quickly, urgently: They had obtained a bloodstained shawl, he said—a Chinese dragon, silver and red flowers. The shawl had been found on the waterfront. An Israeli correspondent had been shot. Her daughter, Allison Calder, had reputedly been witness to the shooting. Could she verify this? Did the shawl belong to her daughter? Did she have any comment?

She dropped the receiver. "It's Allison—"

Malone was already getting into his trousers.

59

The bullet swam in a glass receptacle; the liquid had turned pink and cloudy from Zev Malachi's blood.

The damaged aorta had been patched; that had taken nearly an hour.

Peering through telescopic spectacles and wielding a pair of fine metal tweezers, Tate removed the tiny splinters of metal, one by one, cleaning away the ravaged tissue as he went; that ate up another twenty-two minutes on the heart-lung machine.

Then a pool of blood formed abruptly in the chest cavity. Tate searched for the leak, found it, and sewed it up. Almost immediately, another pool formed elsewhere. He located the trouble spot and mended it. Now a third leak sprang. He was still searching for it when the anesthesiologist said quietly, "Malachi's dead."

The ringing of the phone split the darkness.

Isabel switched on the lamp. The clock said three-fifteen. A male voice crackled over the wire, brisk and familiar. "Your line's tapped. We'll wait."

She dressed and took the elevator down to the empty mezzanine. The coffee shop was closed; a night porter was mopping. A stray drunk went by, tie askew, holding an empty highball glass. A young couple passed, carrying a sleeping child.

A cluster of pay phones in metal shields overlooked *The Galleria*. Glass elevators rose, three stories high, arrested in flight over a maze of terraced shops and tiled walks and vacuum-packed seasons: near a frost-bound skating rink, a patch of astro turf was filled with umbrellas and tables in a facsimile of a summer sidewalk cafe. The President had called Houston a schizophrenic city, split down the middle: on one side was exaggerated affluence; on the other was more substandard housing than Detroit and the highest homicide rate in the nation.

The phone rang twice before the same brisk voice answered and told her to hold. Then the President picked up. "How soon can you get to Calvary Hospital?"

"Ten minutes."

"A foreign reporter's been shot. Israeli. He was in Houston at Lep Calder's invitation. He was also with Lep Calder's granddaughter when the shot was fired. The reporter's in surgery. His name is Zev Malachi. Can you get to the girl?"

"I think so."

"It's Texas," the President said. "Too many echoes. It could be PLO —but it's too close to the Vice-President for my taste. Vinnie Anderson will meet you in the waiting room of the Heart Institute. I want him to debrief the girl before the FBI, the CIA and the Houston police move in. Can you manage that?"

"I'll try."

"One more thing. How are you?"

She smiled. "Fine."

"Your phone's tapped, your room's bugged and Lep Calder's watch-dogs have got you covered. The word's out," he said.

"What word?"

"You're a tiger in bed."

The line buzzed.

Lep ushered Anson Pearce to the glass elevator and watched him descend—Pearce poised like an acid-tipped arrow. He'd gotten nothing from him. It wasn't his own Security Force.

The clock on his desk said half-past three. He switched on the microfilm of Zev Malachi's record and studied it: date of birth, military service, career record, foreign assignments. On the playback machine, film insets flickered past: Malachi in the streets of Jerusalem; Malachi with a girlfriend; Malachi manning a machine gun; Malachi with a group of friends, an arrow pointing to one of them, singling him out as a member of MOSSAD, Israeli Intelligence. Malachi in Pakistan—an article on hunger. Malachi in East Africa. He stopped the machine.

He rose and crossed to the window and stared out at the darkened skyline. He stood there a moment, his hands clasped behind his back. Then he came back to his desk, swiveled in his chair, picked up the phone, put a call through to Dixon Amory.

The phone rang once. The voice that answered wasn't the voice of a man awakened from sleep.

"How'd Malachi get hit?"

"It was a rookie. An accident."

"What the hell are you doing?"

"Trying to run a Police Force," Amory said.

The surgeon's creed was: the body was a complex machine; death was a mechanical failure. The axiom failed Tate. This one was personal; Allison had made it personal.

Death, when it was personal, was a firing pin. It triggered an explosive desire to live. It triggered a desire to run.

Surgeons didn't run.

Last night, when he'd left Joanna, he'd known—for the first time in years—he'd quit running.

He shed his surgical clothes. He took a back route to Foley's office where he'd left Allison with a night nurse and a sedative. In the outside corridor, he'd stationed a hospital guard to stave off any reporters or police who knew the hospital well enough to sleuth for Allison among the daytime offices: His orders were only Isabel Howard was to be allowed through.

He knew he should have called Joanna; he hadn't.

Joanna's eyes accused him of that as he came through the door.

"A reporter called—" She looked pale and tired, as if she hadn't slept. She looked frightened. "The guard let us in."

"Where's the nurse?"

"Allison didn't want her."

Malone's back was turned. He knew it was Malone. Malone was making coffee—as though he hadn't been gone for fourteen years. Looking at Joanna, Tate knew they hadn't been here more than a few minutes and they'd been rousted from the same bed.

He put it away.

Malone turned. "I'm taking META up for Lep," he said. For an instant, Tate felt his eyes lock with Malone's. There was something old in it, older than either of them, as primitive as Cain and Abel or Jacob and Esau; it struck him that he loved and hated Malone in some way that had nothing to do with Joanna.

He put that away, too.

Allison was dry-eyed. The sedative hadn't knocked her out. It had glazed her. She was teetering on the edge of a hyperactive reaction. He wondered what kind of greeting had taken place between Allison and Malone. He had an impulse to say: *"I raised her. She's mine."* That, too, he filed. All of it took place in the same instant that he saw somebody had turned on Foley's monitoring system and Allison's eyes were fixed on the screen where an assistant was sewing up Zev Malachi's chest.

"He's dead, isn't he?" Allison's cheeks were streaked with tears, mascara-smudges around her eyes; there were bloodstains on her dress.

He turned off the monitor.

A dry sob escaped Allison. "Why bother to sew him up?"

"It's an act of respect."

Allison started to tremble and take in small gulps of air. "The bullet was meant for Guero—"

Joanna handed him a leaflet. "Lep took the international press on a cruise down the Channel." She had her voice under control. "Guero dropped hundreds of these—"

He looked at the leaflet. His blood turned cold. The death of a stranger—an unforeseen assault, a meaningless pistol shot. Old war senses stirred. He had no way to put it together and no time to work on it, and he knew it involved questions he had silenced for years; but he felt a door blow open in his mind, wide enough to tell him it was time to go through.

He watched Malone pour coffee and carry it over to the couch. He checked an impulse to move forward and intercede as Malone laid his hand gently on Allison's shoulder. Allison looked up at Malone and burst into tears. Joanna wrapped her arms around Allison and held her while she wept. Malone turned and came across the room and held out the coffee.

Tate took it from him. "Thanks."

"The Israeli was her lover," Malone said.

Tate's eyes searched Malone's. Malone looked older, austere. The years had brought out the Indian in him. In Malone's eyes, time had once splintered: Tate had seen himself as a boy on a search for the twin who'd died—he had seen the other half of himself as Malone.

Behind Malone, the door to the corridor opened and Isabel came through the reception room.

"The floor's filled with police and reporters," she said. There was a man with her, light-haired, in his early thirties, wearing rimless spectacles and a dark brown suit. "Vinnie Anderson," she said.

Joanna held Allison closer. Tate watched a swift appraisal take place between the two women.

Quickly, Isabel explained the political ramifications of the shooting. Zev Malachi was Israeli. Lep Calder's guest. It was Texas. "We want to avoid an international incident." Quietly, she described the value of an official debriefing that could save Allison from the bureaucratic pack.

"I'm taking her home," Joanna said.

Allison pulled away from Joanna. She stood up. She was shaky on her feet and her eyes were bright. Tate moved toward her. He watched her eyes travel around the room, asking for wisdom, or knowledge at least, some sign from any of them that the world could be explained. He saw himself through her eyes. He felt the despair that made her sweep the room with an angry gesture.

"Don't you understand?" she cried. "It's coming apart! It's all coming apart!"

60

Malone drove. She held onto Allison.

Tate followed in the Porsche.

She put Allison to bed. Tate administered a shot. Malone stretched out on top of the covers and took Allison in his arms, cradling her, soothing her.

She left them alone.

She went down to the kitchen and boiled water for tea, sitting alone to drink it, feeling slightly in shock, floating in that surrealistic state which dissolved reality, which heightened and diluted all feeling at the same time. Questions bobbed in her mind like corks on a turbulent sea, promising to lead her into that precarious territory where truth bordered aberration. There were hairline cracks in her psyche; they would part for her.

Tonight, there had been loss.

Out there, waiting to happen, was more loss; something whispered that to her. They were on a journey of tears, something whispered.

It was almost dawn.

She found Tate in the library.

The room was a shambles. He'd pulled dozens of books off the shelves and he was seated at Lep's desk, going through all of them, old books and photograph albums, looking for something she knew he couldn't name, a history he'd failed to understand. Exhausted, overwrought—he seemed caught in a bout of madness—he was pawing through masses of old records and papers and photographs as though he'd been possessed by the belief that they contained an answer.

He took no notice of her. Like a man chasing ghosts, he seemed consumed by a need to affirm some continuity, the sense of one generation affecting another, changing the shape of another, in some inexorable and immeasurable fashion.

She knew it was more than that. She'd always known—it was more than that.

Looking up suddenly, he stared at her as if he'd never seen her before and when he spoke, his voice was hoarse with emotion. "I was born with Ben Calder inside of me—"

"So was I," she said quietly. "So was Malone."

He continued to stare at her. "When did you put it together?"

"I didn't."

"How did you *know?*"

"I don't know." She shook her head. "Maybe"—she hesitated—"maybe, always—"

"All these years," he said, "I've been trying to kill him."

He got up. He went past her without touching her.

Without touching her, he went through the door.

61

He slept on the couch in his office. Three hours' sleep—fraught with dreams he couldn't recall. He had surgery at seven: a Marfan—two defective valves; the congenital disease that would have killed Lincoln if Booth hadn't. He had surgery at ten. A gypsy chief: heart failure. The waiting room overflowed with gypsies; they'd slept on the couches and on pallets and on chairs pushed together, performing their ablutions in the public restrooms—men in pinstriped suits flashing gold cuff links and pomaded hair, women teetering on stiletto heels, laden with bracelets and rings. The waiting room smelled of garlic—the remnants of the gypsies' supper was still spread on a table: sausage and pigs' feet and hogshead cheese. *"Eat—"* the old woman said, stabbing a piece of sausage on a knife and holding it out to him.

He had surgery at noon: a bypass. Another at four. He was in the middle of it when Foley sent word the Vice-President had gone into cardiac arrest.

The radio was going. Nobody spoke. Nobody said Lyle Morrison might not survive the surgery. Foley's eyes told him. Tate didn't need Foley's eyes to tell him.

They had performed three bypasses around the diseased area. Precision grafting. The grafts had to swing around the pulmonary artery and the left atrium. It was major arterial reconstruction. The clock kept moving. A quarter past six.

"Take him off slowly," Foley said.

The heart stopped.

"Apply fibrillation."

Electrical paddles shocked Morrison's heart. The organ leaped briefly to life, then quit. "Put him back on," Foley ordered. The cardiopulmonary bypass machine began to pump Morrison's blood again. Foley checked the monitors—arterial pressure, brain waves—and looked at the clock. "One more time."

"He's not going to wean," Tate said.

Tate heard his own voice—the surgeon's voice, crisp and reassuring —the tone of the select with the uninitiated.

Fran Morrison dabbed at her eyes with a tissue. Her hand shook.

"I'll have to call the President," Isabel said. While she put in the call from Foley's office, he went through the file and found a copy of the consent form. Isabel held out the receiver. "The President wants an official report."

He took the phone. The voice that came through had the familiar hearty ring. *"Can you give me a picture?"*

"The device is called an ALVAD," Tate said. "Technically, the initials stand for Abdominal Left Ventricle Assist Device. In effect, it's an alternative heart. We implant it in the stomach and connect it to the natural organ. It's powered externally by a clinical drive console equipped with a pneumatic pump monitor. It relieves the heart of eighty percent of its work—"

"Isabel tells me it's still experimental. Does Foley consider it absolutely necessary—?"

"We can't wean him from the heart-lung machine. Without a heart-support system—" Tate left the death sentence unspoken.

"And if you can't wean him from that?"

Tate hesitated. "We'll have to find a donor."

He listened to the pause on the line. Behind him, he heard Fran Morrison emit something between a cry and a whimper.

"You understand we're talking about the Vice-President of the United States?" Another silence took place. Tate didn't fill it. *"Of*

course, you do." The President cleared his throat. *"You're Lep Calder's son, is that right?"*

"I'm a surgeon."

"I hope to God you're as efficient in your arena as he is in his."

"It's the same arena," Tate said. "It just depends on whether you're rooting for the Christians or the lions."

"A premature death interrupts the soul's journey," Joanna's father was saying. Released on a twenty-four-hour pass from the hospital, he occupied the head of the Passover table. "Zev Malachi was a Jew," he was saying. "An Israeli—a stranger killed in our midst on the eve of Passover."

The newspapers had been filled with it, and the television newscasts —Zev Malachi's shooting, the police hunt for Guero.

Joanna cast an anxious glance at Allison. Allison's face was pale. Aftershock had followed last night's terrors, a mute acquiescence to sedatives and sleep, a bit of soup, tonight's obligatory attendance at what would probably be her grandfather's last seder. Allison wore a simple blouse and dark skirt, her hair pulled back with a ribbon at the nape of her neck, making her look like a Victorian schoolgirl, like someone who'd taken temporary refuge in another time.

"Every life is interrupted. Every journey is left for others to finish." Her father was talking about Passover. Feast and wake. Jews didn't forget. Identity in remembering, her father was saying. Remember the slavery and the flight from Egypt—and the holocaust—and the assassination of an Israeli correspondent on the Houston waterfront.

It was raining again, one of those spring deluges that could come and go all night. Cissy and Benjy were noisy and impatient. Like the rain, the children's voices seemed to be drumming inside her head.

Her mother brought in a crystal plate arranged with unleavened bread and bitter herbs and the roasted shankbone of a lamb, symbols of despair and deliverance. Her mother had asked for a miracle. Moses had crossed the Red Sea. Malone had walked on the moon. Tate would take her father to Mexico City. She heard her own thoughts. Scattered, they refused to come together. Like a dislocated swimmer in a swift current, she felt herself clinging to whatever floated past.

Her father refilled the wine. He said the prayer to the fruit of the vine and to the blessings of the earth and to the angel of death who had spared the first-born of the families of Israel. Then he poured the wine for the Messiah. "The Messiah comes in many forms," he said.

The wine sparkled, waiting for the Messiah. Cissy was sent to open the door. Outside, the rain pounded, slanting off the roof of the porch.

Her father raised his glass. "Next year, in Jerusalem," he said as Cissy shrieked.

Framed suddenly in the doorway was a young stranger—halted, like a wilted bird arrested in flight and staring at them—hands stuffed into the pockets of a leather jacket, dark hair plastered to his skull by the rain.

"It's Guero's friend. Carlos—" Allison cried, already up and running toward him.

They disappeared onto the porch.

Joanna went after them.

The porch was empty. Rain and fog obscured the night. She saw a set of blinking taillights pull away from the curb. Calling Allison's name, she ran down the steps, but the taillights vanished in the pouring rain.

Tate held the tape recorder.

"I, Fran Morrison, closest living relative and spouse of Lyle Morrison, authorize Dr. Tate Calder to install in my husband, Lyle Morrison, a mechanical cardiac-assist device known as the ALVAD . . .

"I understand that the temporary left ventricular assist pumping device has been extensively tested in the laboratory and in animals, and has been used in humans on a limited basis . . ."

The priest was standing near the door, hanging onto his rosary and mumbling unintelligible prayers.

"I understand that the positioning and nature of the ALVAD requires abdominal surgery and, because it is temporary, a second operation will be necessary for its removal . . .

"The risks and the complications associated with the surgery and the use of this device have been explained to me. I acknowledge that no guarantees have been made to me concerning the results of surgery or the performance of this device. I further understand it is the only alternative that affords any possibility of preserving my husband's life . . ."

The consent form rustled in Fran Morrison's hands. Her hands were still shaking but her tears had ceased.

"I hereby consent to the surgery and the implantation of this device . . ."

He shut off the tape recorder and handed Fran Morrison a pen.

From the doorway, the priest murmured something that sounded like, "*Amen.*"

The guesthouse was dark. She turned on the lights and went through it. Malone's duffel bag was still in the closet. Two shirts and a pair of trousers were on hangers. Malone wasn't there.

She picked up the phone and called Calvary. Tate was in surgery. Tate was unavailable. "Tell him it's urgent."

She turned off the lights. It was drizzling outside. The moon cast an eerie numinous light through the mist. She made her way through the garden toward the servants' quarters. Moonlight shimmered on the roses. Next month there would be hyacinths. The crocuses would bloom. The rain had battered the Easter lilies. She remembered dawn was Good Friday.

The light went on as soon as she knocked. Lupe came to the door. She was wearing a cotton wrapper printed with cabbage roses. Lupe motioned for her to come inside.

"I have to find Guero." The kitchen light hurt her eyes.

Lupe turned her back and started a flame under a chipped enamel pot.

"Allison's with Guero." *I have a child,* she was saying. *You have a child.*

She watched Lupe turn around. She felt a rush of something like love, or guilt, an inkling of the mystery of blood connection and the penalty of disavowal. Lep had provided Lupe with money for Guero's education. Lep had taken care of Guero's physical needs. Tate had watched his son grow up, every day, without touching him, or holding him.

Lupe poured coffee. It was black and bitter. Joanna drank it standing up.

"You know where he is. You're his mother—"

"He's not a son."

"What?"

"I wanted him to be strong and brave and powerful. He became those things." She spoke quietly, choosing her words. "I wanted him to have a place in the world. Instead, he chose to fight for men who are weaker—" she hesitated. "He became a father, not a son."

"If the police find him first—"

"Don't bring me fear."

"*Love—*"

Lupe shook her head.

He changed into sterile garments. His own clothes were hanging on a hook; the amulet from Krong dangled. He hung it inside his smock.

In the operating room, the console was already in place. The ALVAD was waiting for insertion. No bigger than a man's hand, it was constructed of plastic and shaped much like the vessels used for intravenous feeding.

Morrison had been temporarily reduced to partial bypass support. Now he was returned to full support. All pharmacological agents had been stopped except for the heparin which had been increased to prevent clotting. The chest incision had been extended below the navel. Morrison's stomach area was exposed. Foley was connecting a low porosity woven graft—preclotted with fresh donor blood—to the abdominal aorta.

Moving in, Tate fashioned a small aperture to receive the inlet tube of the pump. Plastic tubing and artery joined. Man and machine joined.

Foley elevated the heart. Foley removed a circular piece from the left ventricle. Tate sutured the sewing ring which would hold the pump in place. Stabilizing the heart with his index and third finger inside of the ventricle, he applied fourteen Tycron sutures reinforced with Teflon patches.

Foley attached the pump-outlet graft to the ALVAD. Tate positioned the pump in the left side of Morrison's abdomen. Foley checked it, then activated the pump, evacuating residual air from the aorta and left ventricle.

Tate looked at the clock. Foley eyes flicked to his. Whether the ALVAD worked or not involved as much engineering as medicine. Whether it worked or not would be evident in the next few minutes.

"Take him off bypass," Foley said.

The scrub nurse bowed her head. The anesthesiologist stiffened with tension. One of the technicians cracked a half-hearted joke as the process began of releasing Morrison from the heart-lung machine.

Foley's face remained impassive. Tragedy was often a companion to risk, Foley accepted that. Death was sometimes the price extracted—Foley calculated his losses before combat. Out of combat came progress—progress that went beyond the preservation of one man and endowed death with meaning by transforming it into a tribute to life. Tate knew the code. He had learned it from Foley.

A dead silence fell.

The scrub nurse looked up and smiled.

"It's working," Tate said.

Joanna wandered through the house. The wind was blowing the oleanders against the house. She'd left Benjy and Cissy with her mother. They wouldn't be back tonight. Tate wouldn't be back either. Or Malone. It struck her that's what alone was—not expecting anyone.

In the library, the books were still out, strewn around. Lying open on the desk was Anna Calder's yellowed diary, kept intermittently, gaps in it, years that passed without entry. *A premature death interrupts the soul's journey* . . . her father had said. What else had he said? Trying to remember, she felt fear grip her again. Fear for Allison. She imagined the police finding Guero. She imagined shooting.

She used the phone on the desk. Sugar answered. "I have to talk to Lep—" Lep was one man in Houston who could call off the police.

"He's not here," Sugar said. *"I don't know when he'll be back. Tomorrow, I think. He came in about six . . ."* Sugar's voice wandered. There were holes in it. Joanna could hear the loneliness escaping through the holes like steam through a collander. *". . . and then they left . . . They took the plane. The big plane. I heard Lep call the pilot . . . There were eight men. They were speaking German. Maybe it wasn't German. You know how that technical language always sounds?"*

"It's important," Joanna said. "Where did they go?"

"Go?" Sugar drifted again. *". . . the most powerful man in Texas. I never ask . . . I discovered by accident the Lockwood woman's gone. She's left him before, you know—but she was young then. So was I . . . I heard him ask the pilot if the plane was overloaded. He might be at the ranch. You can try the ranch. I wouldn't. One must be pru-*

dent. *Isn't that so? For women, I mean. Men can do anything. It's a matter of national pride."*

"If you hear from him—"

"I tried to hate her. I never could. There's no spite in me. There's too much spiritual certainty." Sugar's voice faltered. *"Do you ever have that feeling—"*

"—ask him to call me. *Please—"*

"—*that something terrible is about to happen?"*

Joanna hung up.

62

The clay tile roof of the ranch sprawled below the small plane. There were no jeeps in the driveway; Tate saw no signs of life. In the encroaching dawn, the pool glittered, shaped like the Calder logo, a five-pointed crown. There was nobody around. Past the tennis courts, the semicircular amphitheater rose, used for concerts and rodeos—every Easter Sunday, it became an open-air cathedral. It, too, was deserted—nobody working there. Tate used the mike to speak to the pilot. The wings dipped and turned. The plane soared over patches of cactus and wildflower blooms, bursts of fuschia and almond and day-glo yellow, springing from land as rough and wrinkled as elephant hide. On the limestone hills, gasoline-powered windmills gleamed in the shifting dawn. He looked down on the cemetery where three gener-ations of Calders were buried. Then the fenced hunting preserve began —buffalo grazing with ibex, giraffe and blackbuck antelope. Lions roamed. Panthers. Last year, too many hunting parties had depleted the big game—Lep had closed off the preserve and had recently re-stocked it with shipments of wild animals from East Africa.

There were binoculars in the chair pocket. Tate used them. Lep's plane was parked on the airstrip. It looked empty. Nobody on the air-strip. Nobody around the hangar.

"The police are still on a hunt for Guero," Joanna had said. He'd re-

turned her call from the hospital. Morrison was resting in Intensive Care—arterial pressure was being maintained; the ALVAD was supporting the heart. On the phone, Joanna had been weeping. *"Allison's with Guero"*—he had heard her fear. *"Somebody's got to find Lep and get him to call off his dogs."*

Directing the pilot to circle once more, he scanned the land through the binoculars. No cowhands on the range. Nothing. Nobody. Animals roaming the hunting preserve. Then he realized he was looking at something odd. More wildflowers. It took him a moment. Unless you knew every foot of the ranch, you wouldn't know there were no wildflowers there.

He was looking down at a compound. An electrical fence, newly constructed. He could make out a power plant. A water tank. Two metal quonset huts. Men wearing earth-colored garments were setting up some kind of apparatus; it looked like a receiving antenna, massive, maybe a quarter-mile in diameter. Everything had been painted, camouflaged, to look like another spring profusion of bluebonnets and cactus blooms.

He spoke into the mike again. "Bring it down."

Before time began, the world had looked like this: the sun breaking through clouds with an eerie light, stirring the pulse of a sleeping earth, the rattling of stiff brush in the wind and the endless white desert broken only by boulders formed of pulverized dinosaur bones. Spirals of dust rose from the wheels of the jeep. He might have been a restless animal, stalking. He passed a herd of zebras. A baboon screamed. Beyond the gaunt cliffs of the granite mountains, leopards prowled the gorges. It might have been the dawn of time—before Ben Calder or those who came afterward, before Jacob Lubeck or Malone's Comanche ancestor—before man even walked upright, when the sky was still ruled by the beating of wings and the earth was yet the dominion of beasts.

A hawk circled, charred by the sunrise. He heard an elephant's trumpet call, primitive, majestic.

He drove automatically, not bound by the motions, aware of some creature inside of him, looking out at the landscape through his eyes, like truth trapped against the window of time. He had a sudden knowledge that this creature had made itself known, centuries ago, peering out through the eyes of the ape he had been, and it had peered out through the eyes of the boy he had been, and it would peer out again through the eyes of the old man he would become; it could never be harmed and it would not die. Changeless and imperturbable, it stirred within him like the eye of eternity waiting to perceive the will of God.

Up ahead, a cloud of dust appeared. A jeep was coming toward him, miniaturized by distance—he knew it was Lep—he had a sense of the two of them traveling across the borders of time: like men driving chariots, armored by breastplates and armed with arrows—like men driving tanks and wielding machine guns—like all men who had ever engaged in the combat of the ages, fathers killing sons and sons killing fathers, and this filial murder had been called civilization.

He told himself he had gone past that.

He halted the jeep. He turned off the motor and sat there, waiting. The wind rattled the windows. There was a rifle beside him—every jeep was equipped with a loaded rifle—Lep had one, too.

It wasn't Lep's responsibility; it was his.

Lep's jeep was closer, coming from the direction of the compound he'd seen from the air. What was Lep building there? Lep was sending Malone back into space to lay the foundation for factories on the high frontier. Lep had arranged worldwide press coverage. So why the secrecy? And why a ground antenna? Why on the ranch?—and not at NASA? Why the camouflage?

It had nothing to do with him. It was Lep's—and Malone's.

The thought seized on Malone—the first time he'd met Malone. Malone had loved Joanna first. Malone hadn't lost, Malone had defaulted. Afterward, Lep had said about his own marriage to Joanna: *"The rich, like certain species of Texas cattle, are expected to crossbreed."* Afterward, he had defaulted.

The sun was climbing, a fiery orb, the eye of heaven. How many generations of murder had it witnessed?—waiting for man to look inward?

He picked up the rifle. He unloaded it.

He got out of the jeep. A lizard scuttled across his boots. Antelope tracks led west, toward a man-made watering hole, out of sight; he could hear a rhino bellowing.

He stood in the open and waited for the jeep to screech to a halt beside him. He saw Lep's hair was silver in the morning sun; he saw Lep's eyes were cobalt, impenetrable as stones. Lep's window came down. "What's the trouble?"

"Allison's with Guero," he said. "That makes her a fugitive." He heard the anger present in his voice, older than words, deeper than words; it had a beginning and ending that had nothing to do with what he was saying. "The cops mistook Malachi for Guero," he said. "Allison could be hurt—"

The antenna rose on the jeep. Lep made a radio call. Tate heard him say, "The Garras incident. Consider it closed. I want every patrol car notified. Immediately." Tate heard him say, "If anything happens to Guero or anyone with him, I'll hold you personally responsible." Lep shut off the radio and lowered the antenna. Tate watched him hesitate. "Is that why you came?"

"Not entirely." He watched Lep's eyes travel over him, appraising him. Then Lep opened the jeep door and reached for the rifle. "Leave the rifle," Tate said.

"There're rattlers this time of year. The pumas are loose. So are the lions."

"The most dangerous animal in nature is man."

Lep's eyes narrowed suddenly. "Of course, you're right." Lep smiled. "Particularly if those animals are father and son—?"

"Something like that."

He watched Lep climb out of the jeep. Lep stood facing him, with his back to the sun. Wind hissed through the brush. Tate could feel the sun's heat—a man's spit would dry before it struck earth; a man's bones would soon bleach and add chalk to the earth. It was true of all men. The creature inside of him peered out through his eyes to permit him an intolerable glimpse of an infinite past and an infinite future.

"I was lucky—my father killed himself." The wind captured Lep's voice and sent it blowing across the desert. "At the time, I hated him for dying—" Lep left the sentence unfinished. Tate watched him cup his hand around a lighter's flame and light a long brown cheroot. "How's the Vice-President?"

"I want you out of my life." Tate spoke quietly, as if the words came from that place within him where the creature resided, from an odd limitless patience, beyond anger and pain.

"I haven't done that, have I?" Lep sucked at the cheroot. A cloud crossed the sun. "You went into medicine," Lep said. "I became the Heart Institute's biggest donor—I called it charity . . . You married a Jew. While you were in Vietnam, I moved your wife and child into my territory, into the Calder estate—already occupied by Manuel and Lupe and Guero—a library already filled with Calder history and Nazi lugers . . . You were in the jungle performing surgery on Vietnamese peasants—I was manufacturing defoliants and white phosphorus." Lep paused to grind the cheroot under his boot. "And your cancer research —the link with chemicals—chemophobia, I called it. No matter where you went or what you touched—"

"That's over," Tate said.

"You couldn't ever be simply a doctor, or a husband—or even a humanitarian. The Calder drive is too big for that—"

"Ben Calder ran from men like you." He was standing in Lep's shadow. He moved out of it. "Men who owned everything and gave nothing—"

Lep scowled. "That's the legend, isn't it? Ben Calder, revolutionary and lover—the heart of Texas?" Lep shook his head. "These are different times, harsh times. Frontiers are no longer conquered by one man on horseback. Man's destiny is out there"—his gesture took in the heavens—"in space. To conquer it requires men and millions of dollars and machines. The time of the heart is over."

A cheetah shrieked in the distance. The cry echoed. Tate felt the wind shift. He heard a voice in the wind: *"To abandon the heart is to remain in this desert forever . . ."*

Lep had heard nothing. "The world's in crisis. It's a watershed time. After META goes up—nothing will be the same."

"The heart's always the same."

"Vision," Lep said. "Daring," Lep said. "Greed. Power. Those aren't dirty words. The heart's obsolete. The heart's impotent."

"Whatever you're doing—whatever you're building in that compound out there—whatever you're sending into space—"

"It'll be *yours*."

For an instant, Lep's figure blotted out the sun. Tate experienced a moment of blindness, a world thrown into darkness. "I want no part of it."

"You're a holy fool."

"Maybe."

"Blind—"

He was shaking, suddenly, as though the sun had turned cold; he was freezing. *"I want you out of my life."*

63

Malone came in through the back door. Sun flooded the kitchen. Old silver lined the sink, newly and vigorously polished explosions of light. Lupe was kneading bread. Malone could smell the yeast. He felt a pang of nostalgia, a fleeting yearning for a life he hadn't chosen, had never lived.

He poured himself a cup of coffee. "Tell her I'm out by the pool—"

He chose a spot in the sun. A hummingbird whirred among the pots of flamingo-pink azaleas. He could smell the perfume of roses. A lizard darted across the brick, flashing its flame-colored throat, agitated. The sun had dried the air. It was clear and brilliant. The sky was an unholy blue. The morning seemed filled with small miracles, ordinary, nothing grand or compelling; it brought a constriction to his throat.

He sipped at the coffee. It tasted faintly of chocolate. He committed the taste to memory. He could smell the citrus from the orchard. He committed that, too. From the limb of a pepper tree, a mockingbird cawed and cackled and called out insistently. Another responded, high-pitched and shrill. Quills of golden light struck the twisting branches of a fig tree; he remembered the taste of figs, felt a sudden craving for the taste of figs. He could hear Manuel digging, singing in Spanish, unintelligible.

A slight wind rustled the grass. The grass was a pale spring green, new-born green, short and thick, bursting. A hound barked. He sat motionless, still as a lone animal, aware of the awesome might of the earth, older than a man could remember. There was no memory in him and no sorrow. He had never been a rooted man. Yet the morning's beauty seemed suddenly unbearable. It threatened him with feelings of severance, the wrench of parting, stabs of regret experienced by an abolished self. Within him, some homeless creature was taking leave of what was ancestral and primal.

Then he looked up and saw Joanna outlined above him. Sunlight glinted in her hair. She was wearing a gold-colored caftan, winged sleeves patterned with the markings of a monarch butterfly. Watching her move toward him, he had to tell himself again he had arranged his priorities according to his convictions. For a fraction of an instant, his convictions failed him. For that fraction, he felt a longing for kinship with the upright savage who had cut a jungle path or pulled himself toward the peak of a snow-encrusted mountain, whose world extended no more than a few feet around him—the world he could manage with his primitive tools, the world he could defend with his primitive weapons. He felt the loss of hearth and flesh and woman. Then—his eyes fixed on her—he saw Joanna's form shimmer and splinter into millions of fragments, reaffirming the dance of atoms engaged in continuous reconfiguration, and the commitment of his spirit toward something changeless and eternal.

She sat on the edge of the chaise. Her face was scrubbed, without make-up; its nakedness touched him. Her eyes darted over him. He could feel himself trying to freeze the moment, trying to stamp it in memory.

"You're leaving—?"

He nodded.

She laid her head on his chest. "When?"

He wrapped his arms around her and squinted at the sky. "Not until the sun's straight up."

"A noon flight?"

"To Cape Kennedy. We blast off tomorrow." He felt a tremor pass through her. "Don't—" he whispered. Underneath the thin veil of silk, he could feel the warmth of her flesh. He wanted to make love to her. He knew he wouldn't. They had traveled through that country. There was no more urgency, no more danger. He knew he'd carry the wanting of her until the end of his life; he'd carry her touch and her scent and the night-curves of her body and the sharp blinding glimpse she had given him of the mystery of her soul.

"I know. I drove Allison and Guero to Galveston last night," he said.

"She's safe?"

He nodded. A nervous laugh escaped her. He heard the relief in it. "She loves him," he said.

"She's only eighteen—"

"So were you."

"That was different—" she stopped. He could feel a struggle going on inside of her. She moved out of his arms and looked toward the orchard. He knew she wasn't seeing the orchard. "Do you remember that Palm Sunday the three of us marched in downtown Houston?—after Martin Luther King was killed?"

"Yes."

"The fault line—the crack in the golden egg—it had only started to split back then." She spoke haltingly, finding her way. "We heard it break—you and Tate and I. You took flight. We tried to build a life on it. In our own way . . . we tried to mend it. But the break kept widening and after a while—I'm not sure exactly when—we started to pretend it wasn't there. Back then, we knew it ran through the country. We didn't know it ran through ourselves."

"Nobody knows that at eighteen."

"I'm twice eighteen. I'm through with blind feelings. They're better than nothing—there is no nothing, only the emptiness that leaves room for cruelty. But if you stay blind, all the feelings become dread." She searched his face. "I keep having the feeling that we're moving toward the end of something, and the most I can do is be a witness to it—"

He took her hands. "The world's not coming to an end," he said quietly, "only the world as we know it, as we imagined it. Man exists first in his own imagination—then he becomes what he's imagined. The world exists first in man's imagination—we have to be able to conceive a new one."

"I never knew whether I loved you because you were truly free or truly mad."

"Both," he said.

He took her in his arms again. Holding her, he could feel the warmth

of the sun, and he could hear the humming of the bees and the current
of the desert wind and—reaching out, without moving—he touched the
pulse of eternity, beating, with a fierce love for everything that began
and ended with a man and a woman, for everything that was alive.

"Take care of the earth," he whispered.

64

"Hyperthermia," Tate said. Rufino Sanchez's eyes filled with tears. "Mexico City," Tate said. Sanchez clasped his hands. "You'll have time to think about it. In the meantime, if we could keep this between us?"

Sanchez nodded. Sanchez could have been a candidate for one of Guero's leaflets. Sanchez had worked for Calder Chemicals for eighteen years. Cancer of the bladder. Anarchy of the cells. Nothing had restored order.

Sanchez was the fourth terminal patient this morning who had asked to be taken to Mexico City; Antonio had spread the word.

The word hadn't reached Donna Luigi—Tate went through the explanation again for Donna Luigi. Donna Luigi didn't weep. Donna Luigi closed her eyes and crossed herself. Then she laughed, an Italian chortle of combat and triumph.

Striding down the corridor, he held a conference with himself. What was he doing? He knew what he was doing—throwing himself back into the world of medicine.

The corridor opened into an octagonal-shaped nurses' station. Loretta wasn't there. Somebody had left a pot of chrysanthemums on her desk, the leaves gone limp, the petals turning brown. He carried the flowers to the sink and gave them a drink. Then he went through his charts.

Pedro Torres. Cancer of the colon. Three chest tumors, inoperable; he had opened the chest cavity and closed it up again. Direct exposure to chemical fumes without adequate protection for fourteen years. Torres had almost paid off the mortgage on a small rancho outside of Taxco; Torres' dream was to retire there—if he lived.

Tony Cabrera. Ex-boxer. A tattoo on his right bicep: a snake swallowing its own tail. Member of a *cholos*, a *Chicano* street gang. Vietnam veteran—consistent exposure to the defoliant Agent Orange. The tumors had invaded his spinal column.

Something made him look up. Malone was standing beside him.

Malone was wearing a khaki open-necked shirt and olive-colored trousers and he was carrying a duffel bag slung over his shoulder. "I came to say good-bye."

Tate laid the charts down. Behind Malone was a bulletin board. It had been covered with hand-written prayers and supplications and colored post-card photographs of Mexican-Catholic saints. "Why?"

Malone shrugged. "I like to leave a clean house."

"In case you come back?"

"That's the risk, isn't it? Coming back?" Malone's face was grave. It looked lined and chalky, like a fresco. "Joanna loves you," he said.

Tate held up his hand. "Don't—"

"I didn't come to discharge an obligation—"

"There is none."

"We're friends."

"Are we?"

Malone grinned, without insolence. "Fellow explorers—" Tate felt him groping. "We pushed at the frontiers—the three of us. Space. Healing. *Eros*. There was integrity in it."

"I'll leave that to you."

"I love you. That's what I came to say."

Tate looked into Malone's eyes. He saw his own reflected there—ancient cobalt, glistening—stars swimming in them. He felt his neck tense. He felt every nerve in his body jangle in resistance. Then a tremor shot through him, something harsh and powerful that demanded acknowledgment of a kinship beyond understanding, of an unbreakable bond that had already stretched across time and space.

Reaching out, he embraced Malone. Then he dug inside his shirt and pulled Krong's amulet over his head and hung it around Malone's neck.

"*Vaya con Dios*," he said. Go with God.

65

The television was on.

"*. . . Calder Enterprises has confirmed the launching of the shuttle yesterday afternoon, carrying the components of META in its sixty-five-thousand-pound cargo hold. Now, orbiting at seventeen thousand miles an hour, it has released its cargo and the four-man crew into geosynchronous orbit. Estimated to cost eight billion dollars, META has been called the first step toward the industrialization of space . . .*"

"I don't believe in God," Benjy said.

From the window of the upstairs bedroom, Joanna looked out over the spreading sea of guests. Hundreds had started arriving at sunrise—paying Texas deference to the Easter sunrise—spilling over the ranch grounds in raucous exchanges, carrying plates of ostrich-egg omelets and *menudo* and chile, and balancing margaritas and long-stemmed glasses of champagne. She had started to drink at sunrise herself; it had given everything a slight glaze.

"Don't be silly—" Sugar was on her knees, tying Benjy's bow tie.

On the television, the newscaster continued to report the launching of META. "*. . . stabs of horizontal flame . . . the engines consumed more than a hundred thousand pounds of fuel before the rocket left the pad . . .*" Joanna imagined Malone in the ocean of space in his silver canoe. The thought made her head swim.

A hawk was spinning in circles overhead. The clouds hung low like a washline of dirty linen. The sun was cold. Below, minks and sables covered flowing garden dresses reminiscent of the old south. The younger women wore the hard-headed *chic* of the Wild West—cropped leopard jackets and twenty-four carat jeans and diamond-banded Stetsons. The total effect was oddly of vagrants dressed in glittering castoffs, the symbolic vestments of ill-formed fantasies, the splendid waste of idle hands spinning gold into straw.

"Don't you *remember*—" Benjy was arguing with Sugar. "Well *show* me God then."

Cissy giggled, "God's in a bottle, dummy."

"What bottle?"

"That's what Sugar said. Didn't you, Sugar? I heard you. No bottle spirits today, you said. I'm high on *God's* spirit—"

"*Godspeed* . . ." the newscaster was saying, ". . . *it was the final message from the launch crew to the META astronauts as the shuttle blasted from earth* . . ."

Tate's eyes closed. He'd showed up at Isabel's suite at 2 A.M. Exhausted, he'd fallen into a dead sleep. They'd made love as the first pale rays of daylight flung streaks against the linen drapes. Easter sunrise. He remembered he was expected at the ranch for the baptism. There was a seat on a plane with his name on it waiting at the hangar.

"*. . . the shuttle launched without incident. After forty-five minutes and fifty seconds, the second Orbital Maneuvering Subsystem burn over Africa thrust the spacecraft into a two-hundred mile circular orbit. The payload bay doors of the shuttle opened on schedule. The manned META satellite was removed from the cargo bay by remote manipulator arms and released into orbit* . . ."

Spasms of fatigue gripped his muscles. Isabel was murmuring in a low husky voice, still thick with lovemaking. He realized she was addressing herself to his unspoken question: *Who are you?*—as if she recognized the fact that he had known her and had already forgotten her and what he had felt was not to be trusted without a translation.

"Francesca—" Isabel had taken a photograph from the drawer in the table beside the bed.

He glanced at it. The child was Cissy's age, dark-haired, eyes like copper pennies. "Yours?"

"She's in Mexico City. Mexican law gives custody to the father. She was two when I left. I go back once or twice a year, whenever I can get the time—" she lowered her eyes. "It's difficult when you do what I do . . ." She took the photograph back and laid it on the table. "Lep offered to buy her for me from my ex-husband."

"That's not my business."

"I know what you're thinking. Is my daughter for sale?—Probably. Do I want her?—I don't know. Why would Lep make such an offer?— What did I trade? What was my price?"

"I don't want Lep in my bed," he said. "I don't want Lep in my life."

He watched her get up and go into the bathroom. She had left the television on. ". . . *the expansion of META into a habitat and construction base in space will be completed in the next forty-eight hours . . .*" He switched off the television. He asked himself what he was doing here. As if in response—from across the room—the beeper in his jacket pocket started to shriek. By giving orders to his body, he made himself roll out of bed, shut the beeper off and call in.

The service connected him to Foley. It took him a moment to realize what Foley was saying. He felt his body resist. He heard himself answer, "I'll be right there."

She was coming out of the bathroom when he hung up. Her body looked statuesque, patrician, as if he'd never touched it.

"They've found a donor for the Vice-President. Forty miles outside of Houston. The heart has to be harvested there."

"Harvested?"

"Removed from the chest—" he was pulling on his trousers.

"I'll be ready in three minutes."

He started to protest. He remembered it was her job. "You've got sixty seconds," he said.

"Chilly for ten in the morning, isn't it? Feels like a norther—"
"I knew I should have worn the lynx—"
Joanna smiled.

Impervious to the wind, she moved through the heat of the crowd, body heat, furs brushing at her, jewels winking in the sunlight. Caterers were at work under a dozen canopies, preparing lunch for twelve hundred to be served after the baptism. She could smell the *cabrito* cooking over the sand pits of open coals. A whole Longhorn steer rotated on a spit, dripping juices onto smoking mesquite.

"By God, Joanna, you ought to be proud of your kids—"

"Thank you, Senator." She smiled.

"Over here, Joanna—I want you to meet . . ."

Sugar was sober. It was she who was holding a glass. Was she drinking for Sugar—as if the alcohol had a quota to fill and had reached out and grasped the wrong Calder? She wasn't a Calder. At the moment, she wasn't even Tate's wife.

"Damned if Lep didn't get that bastard off the ground. Cost me ten thousand dollars in bets—"

"Hell—it was always clear as a diamond in a goat's ass hole—"

Joanna smiled.

Two country western bands were vying with a black gospel choir. The baptism wasn't until noon. Under the tents, chefs were laying out Corsican ram with mint, venison-stuffed dolmas, Sika deer with plum sauce. Fried rattlesnake. Tacos al carbon—flour tortillas stuffed with pieces of stewed white-tailed deer.

Something bright caught the sun—a pendant. She recognized the pendant. She had fastened it around the neck of an Easter bunny for *Lubeck's* window. A single perfect pear-shaped stone weighing twenty-three carats, it dangled like a chunk of ice from the flawless neck of a wildcatter's wife. The woman was hanging onto his Sulka necktie. He was pushing her past in a wheelchair.

"Where's that sonofabitch husband of yours? You know what they say about Calvary?—go in with a cold and they'll cut your heart out—"

He left a surgical resident sewing up the chest.

He came back in a patrol car, with the siren blaring.

Isabel was waiting in the helicopter. The pilot had the blades going.

He climbed in, carrying the heart in a covered stainless-steel bucket filled with cooled saline. The helicopter lifted off immediately. It started to rain, the sun shining through the rain. He watched Isabel trying not to look at the bucket.

"Who was he?"

"She," he said.

"A woman?"

"A girl. Homicide. Nineteen years old. Itinerant. Up from Laredo—Boy's Town—it's a red-light district."

"What happened to her?"

"Somebody knifed her and split. A brawl in a bar. She died at five A.M. She was carrying an organ-donation card. The coroner called as soon as he got the body."

A nervous giggle escaped Isabel.

"What's funny?"

"The Vice-President, with the heart of a Mexican whore."

"She wasn't Mexican. She was Vietnamese."

He closed his eyes. The blades roared. He thought about Krong. He thought about rain beating on the helicopter while they picked up the dead and wounded. The monsoon season was called *Nyam Fon.* Rain crashed without surcease. At night, black bats flew about in the rain, screaming.

"I'm sorry," she said.

He opened his eyes and looked at her. "It's not ideal," he said. "The ideal donor is young, vigorous and the heart's still beating, except that the EKG fulfills the definition of brain death. In Morrison's case, if the donor's death takes place less than three hours before the transplant and the tissue match is decent, and we're pressed."

"Pressed?"

"Nobody's stayed alive on the ALVAD for more than twelve days."

The radio was playing at the nurses' station. A newscaster was saying, ". . . *no visitors were allowed beyond the passgate to the eighty-eight-thousand acres occupied by Kennedy Spacecraft Center. Newsmen viewed the blast-off of META from a boat on the Banana River. Lep Calder has been unavailable for comment. Here, in the Satellite Lounge on Atlantic Avenue, this reporter is talking to citizens of Cocoa Beach . . ."*

Inside Morrison's room, the machine was compact. Yet, it took up space, usurped the space of the man, not the physical man, the spirit of Lyle Morrison.

"How long can I live on this machine?"

"One day at a time." Tate checked the monitors, silent, less noise than a toaster. Silently, the machine powered the ALVAD which, in turn, empowered Morrison's heart.

"I have the politician's nightmare of dying surrounded by my compromises—" Morrison's smile was feeble. "In Colorado—in my father and my grandfather's day—*compromise* was a dirty word. They were miners. The old man died of silicosis. If you asked a bunch of IWW coal miners to compromise, they'd blast you away."

"Take it easy."

"I made myself a promise. Before I died, there'd be one clear important issue where I wouldn't compromise . . . not to let the greedy bastards have everything. They took the coal and the gas and the oil— that's enough. The power of the sun belongs to the people. Do you understand?" An angry light blazed briefly in Morrison's eyes. "All the polls tell me I've got the odds of a dark horse."

"That's what they said about Lincoln and Roosevelt," Tate said.

Isabel was in his office.

"Don't call Washington," he said.

"What happened?"

"It's the tissue match. We rate it from A to D. You can only get an A-match with identical twins. A B-match is sound. We don't do less than a C—"

"You're not going to operate?"

He took off his white coat and got into his jacket. "That's right." There was a necktie on the hanger. He wrapped it under his collar and started to knot it.

"I could use a bit more explanation."

"The body's immunity system goes into instant combat with anything it interprets as foreign. The alien heart is an invader." He was aware of the surgeon's voice—brisk and removed. "We've developed drugs to suppress the immunological system—they leave the patient vulnerable to infection and they're not infallible. What we've got is a D-match. The odds are the heart would start to reject within seventy-two hours."

She was silent a moment. "That wasn't the explanation I meant," she said quietly. She rose. "Do you have a cigarette?"

"Sorry."

"Happy Easter—"

"My children are being baptized today."

Her eyes strayed over his face. "You're more like him than you think, you know."

"Who?"

"Lep," she said.

Lep's security guards served as ushers.

Organ chords rose. Hundreds climbed the aisles of the open-air cathedral. The organ played *"Christ's Entry Into Jerusalem"*—a rousing march tempo—Christ's procession toward death and transfiguration.

Joanna faced the pulpit. The lectern was shrouded in white satin. Behind it, light filtered through a free-standing mural of stained glass depicting a lion and two lambs. The gospel choir was singing, *"There's Room at the Cross for You."*

She felt strange. She felt not herself.

The choir began singing, *"Were You There?"*

A man slipped into the seat beside her. For an instant, she didn't know who he was. For an instant, Tate looked at her with the glassy stare of a blind man. A hard bright indifference had enameled his features; he looked like a man who had put out his own eyes.

She stared at her fingers twisting on the creamy crepe de chine of her lap. The organ was playing again. She felt the sound grip her, sweet moving strains that swelled and filled her, promising to carry her over the heads of the crowd like a figure by Chagall, the mystic Jew who had painted the ascension of man. She had the feeling she might touch Malone out there.

She quieted her hands.

The organ faded. The minister rose from his seat and climbed the pulpit. He towered, impressive, prematurely gray—laconic gestures like a western hero—his robes billowed in the wind. The loudspeaker magnified his voice and distorted his words. *". . . the Devil as outlaw . . . the high noon of the soul . . ."* rolled off toward the hills accompanied by an echo that sounded faintly like a woman's laughter.

Something made her turn. Lep had arrived and was taking his seat. In the instant before he averted his eyes, she *saw* him. She saw his face stripped naked—hunger and hollowness exposed and shining—an insatiable need that meant to swallow everything it touched.

She dropped her eyes.

"He's after the sun," Malone had said. How could a man swallow the sun? And if that could be—what kind of creatures could live in a cold, dark world?

The thought bewildered her.

Bewilderment was a choice—she knew Sugar had made that choice —the ultimate refuge; it left Sugar free of responsibility. It left Sugar endless time to wander through the inner wasteland that accompanied a life where nothing was beyond her grasp and everything was past her reach.

The sun dimmed. A huge cloud darkened the horizon. The air snapped with sudden cold.

"*Dearly Beloved,*" the minister was saying, "*forasmuch as all men have sinned and fallen short of the glory of God . . .*"

Somehow, she had risen. The minister had beckoned and she had obeyed. Somehow, she was standing with Tate and the children before the baptismal font.

"*. . . Almighty and everlasting God, we call upon Thee that these Thy Servants, coming to Thy holy baptism, may receive remission of their sins . . .*"

She could feel Lep's eyes on her back.

"*. . . Grant that all sinful affections may die in these Thy Servants. Grant they may have the power and the strength to triumph over evil . . .*"

Every idea scattered. Everything clear and sacred vanished. She relinquished all certainties. The constrictions of perception ceased. On a faraway hill, a buzzard perched on a dead armadillo; she saw it clearly. She heard the shriek of a distant ground cuckoo, the bird the Mexicans called *paisano*. She heard the clop of hoofbeats, horses in pursuit, hooves tattooing the granite surface of the earth—men pursuing land, dividing up the future. She saw a woman, wind whipping at a woolen cloak, standing in the sunlight on a dusty road, weeping. She heard the thin wail of history like the cry of an abandoned child.

"*I baptize you in the name of the Father, and of the Son, and of the Holy Spirit. Amen.*"

She felt Lep's eyes, and knew what they were saying. They were saying, *Nothing is enough.*

"*. . . this moment of grace . . .*" she heard herself saying.

Her heart was hammering. The microphone was in front of her. How had she come to be here? Overhead, the noon was sunless. Clouds had swallowed the light. She could hear her voice, echoing. It didn't sound like her voice, echoing.

"*. . . you belong to a new generation, capable of embracing more than one faith . . .*"

She was grasping the microphone. She was talking to Cissy and Benjy. It wasn't her voice. The words weren't her words. The sound of them blew through her like wind through a reed.

"*. . . See us clearly . . .*" she heard herself say. "*We are the children who've lost our way. We've forgotten why we're here . . . on this lovely, lovely earth . . . We once knew. We once knew how to love . . .*"

She stopped, suddenly cold, shivering in an icy blast of wind.

It started to snow.

BOOK SIX

66

The plane took off at dawn, heading southwest, toward Mexico City.

Around it, the sunrise exploded.

Tate watched his passengers crowd together at the windows, hands and faces pressed against the glass—eight cancer patients and relatives —to give themselves up to the spectacle of a new day being hurled forth from the pit of the sky.

He had explained everything to them. Everything was the fact that some might die.

A nimbus of fire ripped at the tattered darkness. Before the imminent birth of a molten sun, the dull scrim of night disintegrated. Then the day's first breath swept the sky clean of ashes and rays of light touched the wings. Behind him, he heard a moment of silence fall, like a common prayer, and in that moment, what he saw was a miracle—he saw what they saw—the shadow of death being burned away.

Antonio shouted, "Bravo!"—and then another, and another. A chorus of cheers and applause filled the plane. They were applauding the sunrise.

Rufino Sanchez raised his accordion and started to play. His wife, Rosalita, six-months pregnant, hands lifted high above her head, was clapping—Tate saw Ida Lubeck join her. Then Sol started to clap, and Pedro Torres and his wife, and Donna Luigi and her fifteen-year-old granddaughter, Sophia, who was dressed in red. Loretta Tibbs, big-boned and homely as a stork in her nurse's uniform, was clapping with the others—the Mexicans called her *tia;* she broke into laughter as Antonio grabbed Tony Cabrero's mother, whirling in and around the swivel chairs in a fierce wild rhythm of his own invention.

Tate watched a broad grin break Tony Cabrero's jaw. He had seen Juana Cabrero, no bigger than a sparrow, reach out and hold her son —ex-boxer and street gangster—as the plane took off. He had seen them, mother and son, as a traveling *pieta;* he had seen the others as innocents and wards, afflicted voyagers on a flying pilgrimage. Now, watching them, he wondered what indomitable quality of the human spirit had generated a joyous festival instead? A celebration of life?

He suspected the answer lay beyond the boundaries of medicine.

Turning away, he looked through the window again. Below, the Gulf of Mexico receded, looking like a small flat patch of blue in a child's paintbox. He listened to the laughter. He heard the accordion rise jubilant. Ahead, were the Sierra Madre Mountains, the gleam of snow lingering on the topmost peaks. For a moment, he had a swift image of the plane being forced down in some forgotten place in the mountains. He imagined a new tribe, formed from the joy of living. He imagined the nucleus of a new world—children and music and poetry—springing from the riches of varying cultures. Under such circumstances, would ambition and stress and malice survive? What would it be like without socialized cruelty? Would the cancer vanish?

Turning, he strode into the party, stern-faced, moving with the bearing of a surgeon carrying reality, mutely demanding dues and deference to reality.

The accordion quit. Antonio halted his dance, frowning. Then suddenly, Antonio broke into laughter.

"Don't worry, I won't die—" Antonio roared. "I'll tell you why I won't die. When my eyes close forever, they'll be the last eyes that ever saw a holy goat with seven eyes and turquoise horns. It's true I saw it in a dream. But I saw it, nevertheless—and until someone else on earth sees such a creature, Antonio Orestes Carranza will *live*—" Spinning, Antonio gestured to the others. "And what have you seen? A green monkey? A cow with nine tails? What? *What?*"

"I saw a bird with golden feathers and a man riding on its back," Sol Lubeck answered softly.

"Me, too—" Pedro Torres called out. "I saw it, too—"

Laughter rippled through the crowd and rose, triumphant. The clapping began again. The chords of the accordion rang in Tate's ears. The moment gripped him like the fingers of a dream—as if these men and women were the creatures of his own dream—demanding he recognize something important, demanding a response to an urgent message he had failed to decipher again and again. The thought promised to lead him into absurdity. He banished it. He had a sense of something imperative being lost. There was a fraction of a second when he might have called it back. He let it go. The urgency faded. All that was left was an odd throbbing in his chest, as if his heart had closed like a fist around the lost message, and now was telling him there would be consequences.

The owner wore a spattered apron. He was opening oysters with swift deft motions and tossing the shells into a plastic-lined garbage can. A dozen customers lined the oyster bar, swallowing oysters as fast as they were opened and washing them down with Lone Star beer. Overhead, on a small color television screen, a local newscaster was summarizing advance reports on the Energy Fair and the President's scheduled arrival in Houston.

At one of the four small tables, Joanna sat across from Vinnie Anderson over plates of boiled crabs, charcoal grilled shrimp and okrastudded Creole rice. Anderson spoke softly. She had to strain to hear him over the cracking of oysters and the banter at the bar, and the television competing with the sounds of traffic on Westheimer Boulevard.

". . . Naturally, we've established a security force at the Astrodome for the President. Police along the route and around the Warwick Hotel—"

"I don't understand." She watched Anderson take off his glasses and wipe them. Bespectacled, he had a studied earnestness. Without his glasses, his eyes had a shrewdness, an educated tolerance, the look of a man who wouldn't be surprised by anything.

"The word is there's going to be another big *Chicano* demonstration." He put the glasses back on. "Mostly chemical workers. The carcinogenic issue. The demonstration is scheduled for Friday night, right after the President arrives. The Warwick faces Hermann Park— that's where they'll hold it. The word we've gotten is—Guero's at the center and it might be dangerous. I thought you'd want to know that."

Her heart stopped. "Allison's with him."

"I know." Anderson shrugged. "Graft, corruption, bribery, murder—who's sleeping with whom—it's my job to know."

"Are they back here—in Houston?"

He shook his head. "I was hoping you'd know. The police files call him an urban guerilla. It's an exaggeration—but he does keep changing his base. The last we heard he'd left Galveston. The police have been ordered by your father-in-law to keep their hands off. Either Guero doesn't know that, or he doesn't trust it. Houston cops don't like being told what to do—even by Lep Calder. If Guero leads the demonstration and it turned into a riot—they'll have an excuse to go after him. If your daughter's with him—"

Her heart had started again, galloping. "I haven't heard from her."

"Will you let me know if you do?"

"I'm not very good at this. Cloak and dagger, isn't that what they call it? But it doesn't make sense. You invite me to dinner. You fuel my concern for Allison, all my anxieties. You know everything about everything except where she is—"

"Not everything." He applied himself to the grilled shrimp. "I have two children of my own. Two boys," he said. "My wife and I are apart. I miss the boys. This job has its own lonesome aspects." He smiled, warily. "In my end of government, we're supposed to develop a knowledge of human nature and an immunity to our own. Every now and then, something breaks through the shell." He met her eyes. "I was at the ranch for the baptism."

She lowered her eyes. When she looked up again, she saw he had set his fork down; he was waiting. "Was it your file or your radar that told you I might be available?"

"I didn't mean to be blatant."

"You weren't." For an instant, it crossed her mind that she might sleep with him, draw comfort from him, in the old way. "I can't," she said. "I've gone past that. I don't know where I'm going, but—" she halted. "I'm looking for another way to experience the world."

"Are you always so direct?"

"No."

He removed his glasses again. He looked at her, without the wariness, a clear open gaze that lasted only a moment. "Maybe if I'm lucky," he said quietly, "I'll run into somebody else like you. And maybe she'll be where you used to be. And maybe my life won't change. But I might."

Antonio died.

Thursday, the twenty-ninth of April, 7:21 P.M. Official cause: Respiratory Complications.

Alone in the public rest room, Tate retched into the toilet.

Malignant Melanoma: Inoperable Stage Three tumors. The projection had been three to six months. Given any approved medical therapy, long-term survival would have been out of the question.

Long-term survival was out of the question.

He turned on the faucet. He cupped his hands and gargled, throwing his head back vigorously and spewing bile into the sink. It was the old wing of the hospital. Everything had old Spanish arches. The lights were too bright. The plaster was thick with paint. He splashed water on his face. The scar on his cheek had healed, a thin slightly pink halfmoon; the scar had been his last gift from Antonio.

Antonio had roused from the anesthetic, still connected to the machine, his blood still circulating from the shunt in his thigh through clear plastic tubing. *"Promise me. Change the sign in the bar."*

"To what?"

The technicians were Mexicans. Among themselves, they spoke a secret language, hidden inflections, concealed meanings in the Spanish phrases.

The mortality rate was one in seven.

Antonio Orestes Carranza: Patient No. 54 in the annals of Systemic Hyperthermia by Extracorporeal Circulation in the treatment of Advanced Malignant Disease. *Antonio Orestes Carranza:* Fatality No. 8.

Never count the dead. Doctors forgot the dead. He told himself it was a meaningful death, in the service of medicine, the future, patients who would come afterward.

He had promised to change the sign at *Rosa's. To what?*

He came out into the corridor. Thirty feet wide, the corridor looked like a church, an eccentric waste of space, Gothic ceiling and tall windows flanked by shutters. A statue of the Virgin of Guadalupe stood watch over a faded tile mural of an Aztec sun ritual. Loretta Tibbs was waiting for him. He knew she had followed him, watchful, concerned.

He wondered if she was remembering Antonio's laughter. How could a man dance to his death? He wanted to ask her that.

"You picked a fine way to spend your vacation—" he said.

"Your father-in-law wants to see you."

"If you had twenty-four hours to live, how would you spend them?"

"With Robert Redford," she answered.

He took the elevator from a crowded twentieth-century lobby. His father-in-law had been moved from Intensive Care to a private room in the modern wing. There were no signs of respiratory problems. After treatment, Sol's system had been sloughing off the dead cancer cells at a rate his body seemed able to tolerate. Sol Lubeck was ten years older than Antonio. What kept the spark of life burning in one man—and abruptly extinguished it in another?

Forbidden questions. Questions for monks and theosophists. He felt the loss. He didn't know what to do with the loss.

The elevator thrust him into a maze of corridors, narrow and gleaming, devoid of arches and statues and age-darkened paintings; the smell of wood-polish was markedly absent, but the same army of maids had been transplanted intact, now rubbing industriously at stainless steel and formica.

Sol's bed had been raised. Ida had buttoned him into rose-colored pajamas. At the moment, Ida wasn't around. Sol's eyes were closed. Tate crossed to the window and looked out through the dusk toward the mountains where the snow-capped peaks of the twin volcanoes— *"The Sleeping Lady"* and *"The Warrior,"* ancient guardians—rose east of the city. Under the Mexican affinity for romantic names, he knew the harsh shadow of bravado and fatalism stalked three-quarters of the country's population who were outside the cash-earning labor force. In the poorest subdivisions, christened with names like *Hope* and *Light* and *Miracle,* the most repeated word was an old Mexican dare. *Salsipuedes.* Get out if you can.

Salsipuedes. The word had echoes. *Get out.* He stared out over the city, lights beginning to go on. *Run away.* Was that his Anglo way of reading it?—his own personal reading? How would Antonio have read it? Or Guero? Why was he thinking about Guero now? From below came the constant echo of car horns honking. Inadvertently, his hand strayed to his scar. His fingers rested there. He had always suspected he had once blurted it out—too drunk to remember—and Antonio had never raised it again. Had that happened? How many times had Antonio blessed his brawls? Why? Why had he gone to *Rosa's* to be beaten up by a *Chicano*—any *Chicano?* Had Antonio understood his need for penance when he hadn't?

Salsipuedes. He understood what it meant. It was a word that told a man to run when there was nowhere to run.

He turned around. His father-in-law's eyes were open. He saw Sol had been watching him. He saw Sol had felt his heart racing. "Antonio's dead," he said. The cruelty slipped out. Berating himself, he watched Sol react.

"It's like a war, isn't it?" Sol said. "Your companion dies and you feel a terrible grief. Then a moment later, the feeling that sneaks in is relief it wasn't you—"

He crossed to the bed and took Sol's pulse. "You're doing fine." There was a crucifix over the bed, mass-produced, the same kind of crucifix that had hung over Antonio's bed.

"I've been going over my accounts." Sol smiled. The smile was weak but there was strength behind it. "Keeping books on my life—" Sol hesitated. "My relationship with you, for instance. You're a good doctor. You're extending my life. How can I not love you for that? On the other hand, you're my son-in-law and you've left my daughter—" Sol paused, leaving the sentence unfinished.

"It's your bookkeeping." A breeze stirred the air. Tate could smell night jasmine.

"When I add it up, it comes to only one thing. What's yours, you must love. Sometimes you don't want to. Sometimes your heart is like stone. But you have to find a way. Picasso painted the truth, you know. He understood life. His eye was like a hammer that shattered everything—so it could come together in its own way." Sol's eyes closed. "Love what's yours, and when your death arrives, you'll love it too . . ."

"You're going to live."

Sol smiled. "I love it, you know."

"What?"

"Life," he said.

67

Hermann Park is a war zone—

Nobody was sure how it had started, how it had turned suddenly, exploding—*without provocation,* the radio report said; speeding through traffic lights, Joanna listened to the car radio. *Garras,* they said, known as Guero . . . a *racial outburst*—it was the weekend before *Cinco de Mayo.* According to a presidential spokesman, the President was *grieved* by it; police had cordoned off the Warwick Hotel. It had started with three hundred demonstrators. Then more than a thousand had converged on the park, brandishing weapons, bricks, broken beer bottles. It had started with singing and shouting and passing out leaflets—

She had to park three blocks away. Police helicopters roared overhead. Sirens shrieked in her ears. A car had been set afire, gasoline flames licking at the night. She passed a first-aid center set up by ambulance attendants; stretchers were being carried through the streets. A woman was hurrying, clutching her child—protecting her child. People were fleeing past her.

At the north entrance, through a police car loudspeaker, someone was shouting commands. Nobody obeyed. A policeman tried to stop her; she pulled away. In the park, fire bombs were exploding. A woman rushed past her, wielding a knife. Police were knocking heads with clubs and pistol butts. The loudspeaker was threatening tear gas.

She flinched at the sight of a man running, hunched over, a savage abrasion on his forehead, tears pouring down a dirt-stained face. A shot ricocheted off Sam Houston's statue. A woman screamed for her child. Men crawled for cover, hiding behind boulders: *a newsman's been stabbed*—in the parking lot, a car exploded; flames crackled, blazing.

The grass sloped. She crossed a low hill, her heart hammering, breathing hoarsely, searching the faces for Allison and Guero. She passed a television camera. She imagined news clips: picnickers on the slopes, riders trotting leisurely along the horse trails, children spilling through the zoo—Guero shouting from the open shell of the outdoor theater, his voice being drowned out, the crowd swelling into a mob—

A man moaned, bruised and bleeding. Another, holding his head, face gaunt, was bellowing in pain. A brick struck a television camera, smashing the lens. Members of the SWAT team were dragging two young boys, cursing in Spanish. Gunfire flashed. In the splattering light, she thought she saw Allison—

It wasn't.

She tried to stop people, asking for Guero, asking for Allison. Nobody listened. The lake was a black mirror, leaflets floating. She ran along the edge of it, calling out, her voice lost. A covey of spotlights came on suddenly, bleaching the trees; wherever she looked, a white sun blinded her. A warning came over the loudspeaker, followed by a strange twittering, like insects. A blast of white fog floated toward her. Her throat closed, acrid; her eyes burned. Around her, people were coughing and sputtering, staggering. Somebody took her arm—a woman, a scarf tied over the lower half of her face—leading her, briskly. Another shot rang out, a single shot, as if it had someone's name on it.

"Are you all right, Mrs. Calder?"

There were cameras. She was facing the cameras. The woman had pulled off the scarf. The face was familiar, a newscaster's face, the same face that had covered the unveiling of *Lubeck's* Easter windows.

"I'm looking for my daughter. Allison. And Garras. Guero Garras." She blurted it out. Somebody listened. She had to fight not to weep. One of the men gave her a Kleenex, offered her eyedrops. The cameras were rolling. She heard the newswoman say the police were holding Allison; the police were taking Allison to the north entrance.

She started to run again, stumbling and tripping, her heart hammering in her throat. The path was lighted; some of the lights had been shot out. She could hear the animals roaring and screaming from the zoo. Ahead, the dome of the Planetarium rose, bulky and ominous.

They were dragging Allison down the steps, hands under her armpits and pulling her along. Allison was raging and screaming, trying vainly to flail at them. There were three of them. She heard herself shout, shrill, imperious. One of them heard her. One of them turned.

A light blazed. The cameras had followed her.

She stood frozen a moment, disheveled, her dress torn, tears streaming down her cheeks. Then her legs started to move. She was aware of an aching ankle. She refused to hobble. Her legs carried her, an odd authoritative stride, an assertion of dignity, order, maternal and savage; her voice sounded cold and threatening.

"I'll take my daughter now," she said.

The cab was locked into traffic on the Paseo de la Reforma. Tate paid the fare and got out. The Reforma was jammed. Mexico City came alive after dark. Exhaust fumes rose. Horns honked, raucous and impatient. On foot, he moved faster than the maze of cars.

Flower stalls blazed with gladioli and dahlias. Illegal venders were out, accosting tourists and pleasure-seekers, offering serapes, straw donkeys and angels, tin-plate masks of the Aztec sun god. Child beggars roamed, thrust from the squalor of shantytowns, the lost cities on the outskirts where thousands existed in makeshift shelters. Two young boys were taking in mouthfuls of gasoline and blowing it out in bursts of flame for pesos.

His feet moved mechanically. His eyes flitted over a pair of carved serpents, a bit of grillwork, an old man, decrepit and joyous, eyes brimming under a ragged sombrero. His eyes saw these things, but all day his thoughts had been spinning around him, outside of him, forming another being who disproved his existence. He had only one certainty: Medicine wouldn't save him. He wasn't sure from what.

He stopped at a tamale cart. Somebody shoved him. He whirled, poised to fight. A young hoodlum raised his fists, face turned boldly toward him, filled with the memory of past insults. The face looked like Guero's. The face vanished.

He left the Reforma. On the side street, he passed gated walls, stone houses with balconies, a pharmacy. He could hear music and laughter.

He could hear the disconsolate squawking of caged tropical birds. The crowd thinned. Instinct led him to the hotel. Away from the fashionable shopping and business district, blank exterior walls faced the streets of a slightly seedy neighborhood—brick walls protecting five stories of luxury. Inside was a maze of courtyards, walls, ramps and levels. The restaurants were filling up, so were the bars. In the lobby, he asked for his key. Classical guitar music was coming from stereo speakers. He asked for his messages. He had none. Houston seemed another life, lived by a stranger.

It was a long way to his room. Traffic was going in the opposite direction, groups of businessmen and couples heading out for the theaters and nightclubs. When he reached his door, he hesitated, reeling, as if from a blow, as if when Antonio died, Picasso's hammer had struck him and he had been vainly trying to keep the pieces from flying apart.

He put the key in the door. He sensed a presence before he entered. Then he caught a whiff of tea roses.

Isabel was standing at the window, motionless, looking down into the courtyard garden. He saw she had ordered ice and set-ups, whiskey and scotch. He saw she was holding a glass and a cigarette. Her outlines were sharp. She looked lost under the soaring ceiling, isolated against the extravagant white-washed space of the duplex suite. She turned, wearing something garnet-colored, like a knife slash, or a sudden wound.

"I have a reservation on a midnight plane—" she hesitated. Something had cracked her self-assurance. "I bribed the maid to let me in."

"Why?"

"I saw my daughter—"

"And—?"

She shook her head. "I can't take her. I thought I could, but I can't."

He wanted to lash out at her. He could feel the urge for violence rising in him, offering him a refuge. He poured whiskey over ice. "Farewell, Francesca—" He saw tears spring to her eyes.

She set her glass down. "I'll go."

He watched her put out her cigarette and pick up her handbag. He let her get to the door before he said, "Don't—"

It took her a moment to turn around. "I didn't want to be alone . . ."

"Neither do I."

"I haven't eaten—all day."

He crossed to the phone, dialed Room Service, and ordered club sandwiches. He heard a shaky note in his voice. "Beer or milk?"

"Milk."

He relayed the order. When he hung up, he saw her handbag lying on the sofa; she had crossed to the window again.

"This place has always made me hate myself." She was rubbing her hands together as though they were cold. "I used to blame it on the altitude. I blamed the life I led here. I couldn't go out into the streets. I suffered from patrician queasiness when confronted with poverty"—she sent him a wry smile—"you know the kind. It strikes women who used to be poor."

He picked up her glass and brought it over.

She glanced at it as though it were a strange object. "I don't drink." She went back to the couch, opened her bag and took out a cigarette. She brought him the matches. He lit it for her. "I don't smoke, either." She flashed another ironic smile.

He took a swallow of her drink. It turned out to be scotch. Going down, it clashed with the whiskey.

"She smokes," Isabel said. "The other Isabel. The fearless confident Isabel. She's the one who carried me out of my marriage. She took charge of my fears. She gave up Francesca. I didn't know how much she had taken over until—" she made a helpless gesture. "Why am I running on like this?"

"Blame the altitude."

Isabel shook her head. "Francesca's a complicated child . . . angry. I put my life before hers. She'd like to punish me for that." She was staring down into the garden again. "How can I take that on? I've worked too hard—fought too hard—for a *place* . . . Francesca's the price . . . Whatever's left of who I used to be is ashamed of that." She looked up, stricken. "Why is nothing hidden here? What makes it all come out?—every lie we ever told ourselves?"

"It's that foliage down there. The tropics. Everything grows and dies so fast—"

"Everyone runs from mortality."

"Doctors run faster."

"If you don't want to talk—"

"A patient died. He was a friend. He—" he searched for the words. "Antonio Orestes Carranza. He helped me carry my lie." He finished off her scotch. His hand was shaking. He watched her pretend not to notice.

She answered the knock. He hadn't heard it. When he turned around, the waiter had whipped up a cloth-covered table fit for a banquet. He paid the waiter to leave them alone; in Mexico, you had to pay to be left alone.

She ate voraciously, like a starved child. He found it touching. She didn't press him. She let him be. She had her own pain—she left him with the pain of being himself.

He told her about Guero.

She stroked his arm, a slight tremulous gesture. She looked young, unprotected. The moment passed. She reached for a cigarette. "It's all back there, waiting for us, isn't it?"

"What?"

"All the choices. That's what Houston's about. Anything you want . . ."

He wasn't listening. He was thinking about the young Lupe and the fourteen-year-old he had been. Lep had called it a seduction. He had known it was something else; the meaning had been lost in the terror and the evasion. Lep had absolved him. He had given Lep the power to absolve him. The lie had started there. After that, he had built other lies on it. Everything else had been built on it.

". . . the Vice-President," she was saying, "will watch it on television . . . the Energy Fair. The President . . ."

He heard Sol's voice: *"What's yours, you must love."*

Sol had echoed Joanna: *"We once knew . . . We once knew how to love."*

Had he loved Joanna? He didn't know. Had he loved his children? He wasn't sure. Was love the antidote to pain? By whose diagnosis? Who dispensed treatment? Why was he thinking about the lies in his life the way he thought about cancer? He had once cast a shadow. Then—somehow, somewhere—the shadow began to cast him. If he could undo the first lie, would the others reveal themselves?—right themselves?

Isabel had fallen silent. She extinguished her cigarette. He watched her get up from the table and go back to the window. He felt a brief surge of sexual desire that crested and passed like a wave breaking. Had he loved her? For even a moment? Sixty seconds? An hour? When had he shut off his feelings? Had it started with the disowning of

Guero? What if he had claimed Guero? What if he could claim Guero now? It struck him Isabel could be one of a long line of women with whom he might spend years of lonely hours sharing what-ifs.

She turned around. "What time is it?"

He knew what she was asking. "Ten o'clock." There was time. Supper and bed. He shook his head.

She smiled. He recognized the ironic smile. He saw the self-protection in it. She crossed to the couch and picked up her purse. "If somebody assassinated the President tomorrow," she said quietly, "and the Vice-President died on that machine, and a bomb killed every member of Congress—and they had to start all over again—I'd hang in there."

He let her go.

He heard the door close.

A terrible loneliness engulfed him. Pain threatened to wipe out the conviction of what he had to do. Hanging onto the conviction, he endured the pain: He had to go back and claim Guero.

It looks like a twister hit Hermann Park—

The kettle whistled. Joanna turned it off, poured boiling water into a teapot and carried it to the table.

The back door creaked. Allison came through the back door, looking both fragile and sturdy—wearing an old jacket, hands thrust deep into the pockets. "Manuel hasn't seen Guero or heard from him," she said. She sat down, elbows propped on the table, closed fists pressed against her mouth; she was dry-eyed—eyes like blue celluloid.

—under control . . . The radio was on the windowsill; grape-ivy trailed along the windowsill . . . *twenty-two casualties*—as if they were talking about a war—*four dead* . . . *thirty-six arrests* . . . *Garras, known as Guero, appears to have evaded the police*—

"Turn it off," Allison said.

Joanna obeyed her. She poured tea. Allison stared into the tea. There was an odd strength in Allison's face, a stubbornness, an absence of fear.

"I don't know whether they shot him . . . I think they clubbed him . . . I didn't tell that to Manuel. Manuel's old. Lupe was crying." Allison looked up. "He just—dropped. It happened right after they sprayed the tear gas. His head was bleeding. I couldn't see . . . he was hanging onto my hands when they pulled me away from him. Two policemen picked him up and carried him off."

"On a stretcher?"

"No. He could walk. I guess he could run. The radio said"— Allison's eyes flicked closed for an instant—"he's gone into hiding," she said. "Carlos will take care of him. He'll send word. He'll send Carlos."

"By morning," Joanna said gently.

"You don't think we should call the hospitals, do you?"

"I had Tate's service check—Guero's not at any of them." Joanna smiled, reassuringly, sipping at her tea, pretending everything was normal. Nothing was normal. The service had told her Tate was in Mexico City. She hadn't known he was gone; now she knew he was gone. Her shoulder bag was on the table. She dug into it, found a handkerchief and blew her nose. "It's the tear gas," she said. Allison patted her hand as though she were the child; it felt wrong.

"Manuel gave me a cassette—for Tate." Allison pulled the tape from her pocket and dropped it into the handbag. "He's been tape recording Ben Calder's ghost. He believes that—" she hesitated. "Guero knows Tate's his father." Allison bit her lip. "You knew he was, didn't you?"

"Yes." She tried to remember what it was to be eighteen, when everything pulsated, when everything held the possibility for love or betrayal. She couldn't. The failure made her afraid for Allison; the failure pushed her into becoming the mother again—it felt as wrong as being the child. She realized that was over. They were two women. "I'm sorry . . ." It was the wrong thing to say. There was no right thing to say.

"Guero doesn't care. It doesn't matter to him." Allison shook her head. "It matters—but he doesn't know that. He doesn't want to know. Not yet. Manuel says there's a pig in everyone—he says the pig in the Calders got out of control. He says that's why Guero has to fight. Guero's wonderful. He's brave and he *cares*—" Allison's eyes glowed. "I love him."

"I know."

"I'm not the same person I was. You can see that, can't you?"

"Yes."

Allison got up and crossed to the back door and looked up at the sky. "Do you think about Malone—up there?"

"Yes."

"Malone took us to Galveston. He told me he loved me . . . he said he was proud to be my father . . ." She turned. "I hear myself. I'm all scattered. Talking about everything except—" her voice broke. "I'm afraid. I keep telling myself not to be. I keep telling myself nothing terrible has happened to Guero. But I don't believe it—" She halted. "I'm pregnant," she said.

Joanna rose. She felt a weakness in her limbs. It came back to her—she remembered being eighteen. She remembered love was a mystery into which you plunged deeper and deeper until you ceased to exist. She held Allison. She stroked her hair. "Guero's all right . . ." she whispered, "Guero's fine . . ."

"Manuel says it's always been in the Garras blood. Ever since Ben Calder's time. He says our child will inherit it . . ."

"What?"

"*Un corazon que ama,*" Allison said. "*The heart that loves the unloved.*"

In Tate's dream, it was summer.

The sun dissolved.

He woke, startled, as if someone were shaking him. He was sweating. He looked at the clock. It was almost dawn. He could feel something hovering in the hotel room—some fear or some knowledge. Then he dropped into sleep again, like a stone falling weightlessly through a labyrinth of caverns, through a cold dark monastic silence where faces appeared like cave markings, not quite decipherable. He was being carried past them by the current of a blood-red river: He was amoebic and shapeless, moving toward a strange and awesome sound, like an African drumbeat, rhythmic, thumping. Dread seized him. An impress told him, without question, that he had entered the mainstream of his own veins and was traveling toward the center of his own heart . . .

A shrill sound woke him, like the ringing of the telephone.

The telephone was silent.

He had a distinct feeling of having been summoned. By whom? He dialed the switchboard. No calls had come through.

All day, the feeling bobbed like a cork in his consciousness. In the afternoon, from the hospital, he put in a call to Joanna, then canceled it before it rang. The feeling persisted.

The call didn't come until six that evening. He was still at the hospital.

It wasn't Joanna.

"We've got a heart for Morrison," Foley said.

68

Klieg lights blazed.

Light streamed upward, striking glass, sweeping across the banner of glass that spanned the top floor of the Astrodome Suite where Lep stood, poised, like a bullet waiting to fire—

The spotlights revolved, catching the shine of red plastic boots and polished thighs, usherettes climbing the aisles of the Astrodome, the prettiest girls in Texas flashing the briefest of cobalt skirts and tipping Stetsons banded in Old Glory's stars.

Motionless, spare as steel, aware of the seconds ticking off electronically on the neon board, Lep watched from above, eyes narrowed, intent.

Television cameras were clogging the aisles; a march band was blasting through loudspeakers, at odds with the congestion: families from Astroworld, spectators from the sixteen acres of Energy Exhibits displayed in the Astrohall, Texans and tourists and energy scouts, solar enthusiasts and antinuke groups, the committed and the curious and those who were drawn to a crowd, any crowd—he could pick out the Secret Service men milling through, alert, anonymous—

His gaze shifted to the raised platform, waiting to be occupied, vacant red velvet seats, the lectern flanked by the Presidential seal and the American flag, rippling in the air conditioning. He checked his watch against the board: two minutes and thirty-six seconds past seven. At a quarter to eight, he'd take his place on the President's platform. The Governor would speak first. The Senator would do a version of his usual routine. Then the seconds on the clock would tell him how much to compress or expand what was supposed to be his introduction of the President. Timing was critical.

He looked up toward the soaring overhead dome which provided a window to the darkening sky, his mind racing past it, out into space—

. . . Malone moved steadily, swimming through space.

Moving through silence, steeped in the absolute silence, his ears rang. In the vacuum of space, nothing had ever or could ever be heard; he knew he was moving through millions of years of soundlessness, never broken—

Around Lep, voices rose, glasses clinked. People were climbing the stairs, peering down into the Astrodome and leaving again. *"What about the rumors?"*—clapping him heartily on the back. *"The word's out the President's Address to the Nation's going to be a bombshell,"* —buzzing with speculation. *"—landmark speech?"* The neon seconds kept moving.

Lep spotted Jan Pavlik. The chauffeur was making his way toward him. Pavlik was alone—

He had sent Pavlik by plane to El Paso and, from there, by four-wheel drive to the Big Bend cabin. For the past three weeks, Merritt Lockwood had been in seclusion in the Big Bend cabin. He had kept her under surveillance. Merritt had gone nowhere, seen no one. Alternately, he had missed her and damned her. Then, this morning, he had sent Pavlik to summon her.

He had to extricate himself from the Energy Commissioner before he could take Pavlik aside. "Where is she?"

Pavlik's head swiveled on his burly shoulders. "She wouldn't come. She sent a note."

He accepted the envelope with a curt nod that dismissed Pavlik. Unread, he slipped it into his inside jacket pocket. He was accosted again by a man whose name he couldn't remember. Tuning him out,

Lep's gaze swept the Astrodome. The huge bowl of seats rose, packed with spectators and, above them, the tiers of stadium boxes were filled, all witnesses.

Merritt had been his one true witness.

Loss vied with anger.

Merritt had borne witness to every step—

Inside his pressurized suit, Malone could feel the weight of Tate's amulet against his chest, like a primal connection to earth, his one connection to earth.

He glided, effortlessly, his physical being extended by life-support systems. The oxygen tanks on his back would sustain him for six hours. Strapped into a maneuvering unit, he moved independently; gas jets propelled him. A symbiotic cord attached him to the satellite, like a lifeline at sea.

Above him, he could see the reassuring glint of the oxygen tanks mounted outside the satellite—liquid oxygen being transformed by automatic heaters into gas and piped as precious breathable air inside. The satellite had become his floating world: two simple cannisterlike structures attached to a power module—one serving as crew lodgings, the other as assembly facility. Lep's plan for the future was to expand that world, to add more modules, more living quarters and work quarters; future components would be carried in the shuttle's cargo bay as these had been and assembled in space. Lep's plan for the future was to—

"A slight change," Lep had said. "A minor adaptation." Over cold lobster and aquavit. A final briefing for the crew of four on the Calder Grumman Jetstream en route to Cape Kennedy. "A hundred thousand dollars a day," Lep had said. "Two million apiece in bonuses." For meeting the deadline. The deadline was crucial.

Lep hurried down the stairs. The lower floor of the Calder suite was packed. He moved briskly through the crowded complex of rooms, heading toward a small private office, locked, accessible to no one but himself. From there, undetected by the Secret Service, a private line ran directly to the compound in the wildlife preserve on the ranch. If any problems arose, there'd be a report on the quarter hour. If the hot line remained silent, everything was proceeding—

Voices hummed. Men in dark suits were playing billiards, firing at plaster ducks in the shooting gallery, striking balls on the putting green, waiting for the President—

Greeted at every step, he managed to keep moving, aware of each second, responding without breaking his stride. In the Western-style saloon, men called out to him from bar stools, leaned against suede walls and waved, spilled toward him from cowhide sofas; a pair of shapely legs gleamed here and there punctuating the intermittent sound of a female voice—he recognized Isabel Howard's voice. *"—besieged by the press,"* she was saying. Vinnie Anderson's response was impatient. *"Hell—nobody's seen the President's speech—"*

He locked himself in his office. He sat at his desk and swiveled in the chair, unlocking the drawer that held the hot line.

The seconds went by.

He removed Merritt's note from his inside pocket and stared at it. He hesitated. Without opening it, he dropped it into an ashtray and set it afire with his cigarette lighter. With a grim lucidity, he watched it burn, letting the flames devour the special place she had occupied, watching the connection that had bound Merritt to his own destiny turn to ash. A feeling of emptiness swept him. He reminded himself he had reached the brink of tonight's triumph because he had never experienced a failure of vision or an absence of nerve. He had never experienced loneliness—

Malone floated free, the only one floating free.

Looking back, he could see the others enclosed in separate work stations, completely pressurized, clear plastic domes mounted on cranes that swung out from the satellite.

He waved at Bones Fairchild—black, a construction engineer with an exotic repertoire of scatology. Bones was operating the beam builder from controls inside his plastic dome. The last beams, thin as paper, strong as steel, were being extruded, rolling forth from the machine which turned compact rolls of graphite-bonded fiberglass into ten-millimeter trusses.

A remote manipulator system was assembling the final trusses as they rolled from the beam builder.

Inside another work station, nicknamed a cherry picker, Hollis Monroe—ex-test pilot, space engineer and amateur broncobuster—was using remote manipulator arms to spot-weld the beams with electrode current.

Below, Lep's godchild gleamed.

Malone swam toward it.

He swam through darkness. The vacuum of space was experienced as darkness. He knew it wasn't. He knew concealed within the darkness of space, invisible to the eye, was streaming sunlight.

He could see the machinery and the satellite, the planets and the stars, and even specks as small as grains of sand, micrometeorites, flying past at thirty miles a second. Sunlight was a mystery that could be observed only by reflection; sunlight made its presence known only when it encountered form. Science had proven what his Comanche grandfather had always known: the sun god inhabited every darkness and emerged from darkness only to reveal the blindness of man.

Science had a name for it: Sundark . . .

He quit swimming. He floated, looking down.

The silver web of support beams formed two rectangular panels covered by alternating panels of tilted mirrors and grids of silicone cells. The mirrors collected the sunlight. The silicone cells stored the sunlight. Mounted between the panels was Lep's slight adaptation: a microwave antenna. Originally designed to serve the needs of the satellite, the solar platform had become a utility plant—the antenna was converting the sun's energy into microwaves and transmitting them to earth.

"A beachhead." Lep had called it—while no laws yet existed to challenge the rights of piracy.

Lep's eyes had glowed—

In the near future, Lep saw five hundred Calder astronauts, a hundred thousand tons of material, ten flights a day by the shuttle, enough solar power to light the city of Houston. Past that, past his own lifetime —sprinkled like stars in the heavens—Calder solar platforms would service the planet.

Malone hovered, remembering.

Then he checked his watch and swam through the Sundark toward his own deadline—

At 7:30 the line didn't ring—

Sugar was halfway through her third julep—Sugar was playing cards with Cissy and Benjy as Lep strode through the Victorian dining room. "Joanna's looking for you—"

"Later," Lep snapped.

It was 7:32 and 45 seconds—

He halted a moment at a far table where the President's wife was nursing a cup of coffee. She was redheaded—like Merritt—smaller, compact ambition. He read her as afraid of only two things: pain and obscurity. "Do you have everything you need?"

She nodded, courteously. He had offered them the stadium suite last night during the peak of the riot in Hermann Park. She and the President had traveled in an unmarked staff car followed by a White House coterie and Secret Service. The President was resting in the sleeping quarters below. Except for a brief tour of the Energy Fair, the President had remained in seclusion. "Hospitality, Texas style," she said.

"My pleasure." It was 7:33.

"The President spoke with the Vice-President just before they took him into surgery." She lowered her eyes. "The President's grateful to you for the press blackout on that." When she looked up, he saw a guarded mistrust, an instinct for danger. She misplaced it. "I understand one of the surgeons is your son?—Dr. Tate Calder?"

"Yes."

"The President's in the chapel—"

It was 7:33 and 56 seconds.

The chapel was tucked away in an alcove. He had converted one of the powder rooms after a number of bullfighters had refused to perform in a place without a chapel. The door was closed. Two Secret Service men waited outside. Vinnie Anderson went past, engaged in last-minute check-out operations. He imagined the President, kneeling, in front of flickering candles. It was 7:34.

He turned. Joanna was standing in his path. He saw her flinch, as if the expression on his face were a blow, as if something about him—the cells in his body charged like batteries—were emanating a force that threatened to flay her.

"Guero's disappeared—" She was tense, chalk-white. "The Police tear-gassed him in Hermann Park last night. They took him away. He was hurt. He wasn't taken to jail. He's not listed in any of the hospitals—"

"Not now." He brushed past her.

She grabbed his arm. He glared at her. He pulled away.

It was 7:34 and 8 seconds.

Malone pressed the gas jets.

He glanced back at the satellite. Like a lost harbor, it beckoned in the interstellar void. Inside the workshop, the machinery had been stowed and bolted; in the living quarters, the crew was shutting down and repacking all housekeeping hardware and systems.

He checked his watch. He approached the antenna again, with an odd absence of urgency, knowing what he had to do and how much time there was to do it. Gliding, weightless, he looked up at the sun. Momentarily, it blinded him. In a gesture that had come down in his genes through his Comanche grandfather, he bowed his head to the god of the sun. It was a gesture that defied Lep's parting words,

"Harvest the Sundark."

The chapel was silent.

Lep stood. He had no urge to kneel. The impulse that had made him turn and enter as the President emerged had not sprung from devotion.

He had entered the chapel as a man about to reach out into what had once been God's domain. He had entered the chapel as a man to whom technology had given the extensions of power that had once been God's prerogatives. Now he stood quietly—a man who had chosen not to re-create God or to expand His image into One he might worship.

He had no need to bow his head. He had no need of petition. Knowing that he traveled toward death, he had set his intent to meet God as an equal. Now, he used the moment to reaffirm his goal.

Then he turned and left.

It was 7:43 and 12 seconds.

69

The operating room was closed. No observers. Upstairs, the dome theater was empty, locked.

Two attendants rolled in the donor, moved him onto the operating table and attached the monitors.

Tate glanced at the chart. No relatives, the chart said. Early twenties. A motorcycle accident—too many donors came from motorcycle accidents. A crushed skull. X rays had showed fractures at the base, ear to ear. A smashed pineal. Destruction of the midbrain. No reaction to painful stimuli and no reflexes.

The skull was wrapped. Except for the mouth and the nostrils where tubes from a respirator had been attached, the face was covered by a light green surgical sheet. The same kind of sheets covered the body except for the chest area. The chest rose and fell. The young man was breathing. The heart was pumping. On the monitor, the brain waves were sluggish, all but flat: The young man had entered the twilight of the medically dead.

"The brain is master of the household"—Foley had argued in his push for legal acceptance of brain death. *"All the other organs are servants. When the master dies, why should healthy servants exhaust themselves in useless tasks? Why not put them to work for another master?"* Why not—

The liver would be sent to Sam Houston Memorial. The corneas would be frozen and stored in an eye bank.

Something felt wrong.

Nothing overt. Everything had been checked out before his plane landed. Blood type. Tissue type. *"Simpler than a bypass,"* he had assured Morrison before he left for Mexico City. He hadn't said a third of all transplant patients died on the operating table and another third suffered a stroke or brain damage. He hadn't told Morrison his body might reject the new heart; he hadn't told Morrison if he made it through the first six months, what he'd have was a fifty-fifty chance of making it through another six months. He assumed Foley had said these things.

What felt wrong? Why had he argued with Foley from Mexico City? What instinct had urged him not to come back?

"I need you." Unlikely words from Foley. No explanation. He hadn't needed one. *"You'll have to do the harvesting and assist with the implant."* Thirty operations a day, seventy-five-hundred operations a year, six million in fees—now, Foley's eye was failing.

Was it something as naïve and shortsighted as the duplicity involved in substituting his own eyes and hands for Foley's? Was it—?

A nurse came in to tell him Foley had Morrison on the table in the adjacent operating room. They were opening Morrison's chest. Ten or fifteen minutes, no more. Foley would send word when to start.

Tate nodded. The nurse left.

"Start the IV," he ordered.

The needle went in. Consciousness resided in the part of the spinal cord that extended into the midbrain. The donor's master switch was crushed. The donor's brain no longer sent messages of pain through his nervous system. Tate ordered anesthetic anyway. He always did. He had ceased, long ago, pursuing the contradiction in it; he had trained his mind to stay away from contradictions. He seldom had the luxury of an anonymous donor; he had trained his mind to stick to the living, not the dead.

Somebody had turned on the radio. He wasn't listening. He was remembering the first time he'd seen Morrison, recalling the fierce pain that had struck his own chest. Had it been a warning? What kind of warning?

He reminded himself heart surgery was a chronicle of failures—sur-

geons who'd tried and failed—discoveries that had come about by accident, solutions bought at the price of individual lives. Among the gods
of Surgery—a journalist had once written—there were no failures, only
the inexorable march of Medicine. The journalist had accused surgeons
of being addicted to the sweep and the power, to the risks and the privileges. The journalist had wondered if men who were afraid of the mystery of life chose to devote themselves to the mastery of death?

Why was he remembering that now?

He looked at the clock. Seven minutes had passed. He heard the
radio. *"Thousands are still milling about the Astrohall, viewing the
technology of the future . . . The President is expected on the platform
in the Astrodome any minute. Rumors are flying concerning his . . ."*

"Turn it down." Tate's voice was sharp. He checked an impulse to
lift the sheet, to take a look at the face of the young man whose heart
would beat in Morrison's chest.

Piracy, the journalist had called it.

"Magic," Krong had said. *"Only a shaman can touch the human
heart . . ."*

*On the coast of central Vietnam, in a village on a destroyed plateau
of the Chaine Annamipique Mountains, Krong had instructed him in
the magic of voyaging into the Beyond to contend with the spirits for
troubled souls . . .*

The nurse reappeared. "Dr. Foley's ready for you to start." She
spoke briskly, uniform rustling as she left.

The radio was still going. Tate blocked it out. One of the technicians
was describing his Saturday night date. He blocked that, too.

"Shut off the respirator." He heard his own voice, reluctant, something trying to hold him back.

He watched the young man's chest until the breathing quit. The chest
heaved, quaking violently, before it fell silent, inert. A bolt of lightning
cleaved his own chest, passing as swiftly as it had come. The nurse
held out the scalpel.

He shook his head. "Not until the heart stops—"

It would take a few minutes before the heart realized it was deprived
of oxygen. On the monitor, the heart continued to beat, boldly.

*The Vietnamese woman had been in labor for two days. With each
contraction, the woman squatted and, holding onto a rope, rocked back
and forth with the patience of one who had never known anything but*

a time of danger. Krong had been wearing a musical harness of necklaces and bracelets and metal bells; each time he moved, there was a harsh cacophony of sound . . .

A minute had gone by. Another minute passed. He knew Foley was removing the ALVAD from Morrison's abdomen and transferring his blood circulation to the heart-lung machine. He watched the heart on the monitor, seeing the shadow of Krong's magic offerings: *a small bowl filled with rice beer, a raw egg floating on top, a miniature machete cut from a strip of bamboo and three pieces of magic quartz.* He heard Krong whisper that the child might be the reincarnation of the woman's brother who had been killed in a bombing raid. He heard Krong say, *"The past creates the future . . ."* On the monitor, the heart continued to beat steadily.

He was standing over the donor. The chest was flat. One hand protruded from under the sheet over the side of the table; the hand was waxen. Again, he had to check the urge to uncover the face, as if the young man's face held a meaning for him—it occurred to him there might be something profoundly wrong with taking a man's heart without paying his respects to what had once been a personal identity. Then his eyes were drawn to the monitor again, where the heart had started to struggle, valiantly, the ventricular peaks beginning to jerk erratically, as if in disbelief.

"The past creates the future," Krong had said.

He had seen that.

He had seen, in some way, the dead had decreed the destiny of the Vietnamese child who had not yet been born. He had seen the present sorrow would invoke tears a hundred years hence, and an act of kindness would provoke another at a future date. He had seen that even if the devastated land could be returned to rice fields, the whine of the bombs would remain, and the death cries, and the grief of the survivors, to permeate the atmosphere and affect the mind and spirit of those who came afterward; and these unseen elements would have the power to bring forth a new time of cruelty.

Watching the heart on the monitor, watching the line go wild in an erratic jagged struggle—watching it falter—he wondered why, at this moment, he saw those truths again.

The line became a saw tooth. Then it fell, snaking out in a final losing wave.

He heard himself say, "Harvest the heart—"

He made the incision. He was aware of a slight tremor in his hand, like a final sign of inner resistance.

The breastbone was cut with an electrical saw. A retractor opened the rib cage.

He stared at the heart. It fluttered slightly, no more than a leaf, in a memory of contraction.

He waited a moment.

He had performed an episiotomy. Krong, draped in a blanket, had chanted, riding into the Beyond on an invisible water buffalo, in quest of the gift of birth. Then the infant had been born, erupting, as if thrust from the very center of Hell—a monstrous mutation of a boy-child, elongated head and wasted limbs, its sexual organ no more than a rudiment. Firmly, he had pressed his fingers around the tiny windpipe. Krong had ceased chanting. In the silence, the woman had taken the child and held it to her sagging breasts, humming softly, as if she had not seen its monstrousness and had not noticed it was dead.

He cut open the pericardial sac with a scissors.

The heart was bloodless, blue and still.

His hands moved efficiently, automatically. He snipped the blood vessels. He cut the aorta. He had to lift up the heart to cut the four pulmonary veins that entered the left atrium from the lungs.

The organ came free. Holding the heart in his hands, he stared at it. He was aware of an assistant, waiting, with a basin filled with saline. Cupped in his palms, the heart trembled.

Something made him look up. The sheet was slipping slowly from the donor's face. Nobody caught it. He watched it slip.

Disbelieving, he stared at the donor's face. Stunned, he felt his vision blur in a last attempt to blind him to the recognition.

His son . . . not his son—

Lightning struck his chest again, fierce, unbearable.

The thing he was holding in his hand was Guero's heart.

70

The sun was the heart of life . . .

Through deep space, through solitude and utter silence, Malone heard the buzzing of bees, birdcalls, human voices—

Life had been born from the sun's energy . . . Life survived by the sun's radiance . . .

On his watch, the seconds beat steadily. From moment to moment, time stretched and contracted. He had returned to the satellite to retrieve the one laser tool which had the power to sever the antenna. Now, directed by gas jets which propelled him toward the solar platform, he felt time carrying him—

The umbilical cord trailed out behind him.

Earth spun slowly, a marbleized sphere, veined and luminous.

The loneliness of exile threatened him briefly, then passed.

Man had once had fins—man yearned for wings. Man's destiny was flight. Was it—?

Freed from an earthbound eye, wouldn't future generations see the solar system was nothing more than a small family in the universe?— and Earth as only an aberrant child? Wouldn't Allison's children find it amazing that billions of people, crowded together on that tiny sphere, had perceived themselves as the whole of Creation? Wouldn't Joanna's grandchildren come to see they inhabited only one of many worlds— and learn to revere the passing miracle of life in a boundless universe?

He had a moment of doubt. Then he pressed the gas jets.

Ahead in the Sundark, Lep's antenna sparkled, rising from a sea of dazzling light—

"More light—" Foley ordered.

Somebody pushed a button. The lights descended, beaming down on Morrison's open chest.

Tate stared, sightless, invoking numbness, trying to hold off the despair that threatened to crash over him, intolerable, battering at the dam constructed of duty; weakened, flawed, the dam wouldn't hold—

Foley was waiting—

Morrison was on bypass. Morrison's body temperature had been cooled. Some calculation of Tate's brain noted these things. Whose brain? Who was he? Take from the dead and give to the living. How had it come to be *Guero*—?

Foley's hands were deep in Morrison's chest. Foley was cutting the thin pericardial sac, exposing the heart. Tate saw the chamber was enlarged, the walls irretrievably scarred. What force had kept Morrison alive through multiple coronary attacks? By what tenacity had Morrison survived on the ALVAD beyond all time projections? What unholy God had arranged the moments of three lives to converge in *this*—

His head pounded. The nerves at the back of his skull crackled, like power lines about to explode.

Somebody said, "—a decent man." They were talking about Morrison, high-pitched, like a screaming in his ears.

He watched deft hands clamping the aorta and cutting it close to the heart. Whose hands? His own? Gloved hands—efficient, the hands of a technician. No longer connected to his brain, free-floating, moving automatically, like severed hands in a dream.

He knew the barrier that separated him from hell was as thin as the pericardial membrane—

He cut the major arteries, skillfully—mute skill—disconnected, feeling he might black out; something supported him, mercilessly, demanding consciousness, sight, pain—

The veins and vessels dangled. The chambers were open. He cut through the septum. Foley caught Morrison's heart before it fell back into the cavity. Foley dropped Morrison's heart in a basin.

An assistant drained the pericardium. The tube sucked up the liquid; the sound sucked up everything treasured, beloved, sucked up all meaning—

The chest cavity gaped: Morrison was waiting for a heart—

—*Guero's heart.* What crimes had decreed the hearts of the young were to be sacrificed? To what? *Who was responsible?* His throat tightened. The room threatened to spin—

Foley had trimmed the organ. Foley was handing him the organ.

His hands sewed the left atrium first. His hands made the right atrial connection. Six vessels. Then the large arteries—the pulmonary and the aorta. Pain stabbed at his neck. Pain gripped his shoulder blades, fierce demanding—

From a long way off, he heard Foley say, "*Apply fibrillation.*"

Metal discs touched each side of Guero's heart. A charge shot through Morrison's body. Guero's heart contracted suddenly, roused back into life, and slowly . . . slowly . . . began to beat.

Tate raised his eyes. The lights burned his eyes. His lids refused to close. He heard a whimper. The sound filled him, rising, like the guttural howl of a wounded creature, like a cry from the soul's wilderness. The lights seared his pupils, pulling him into a whirling vortex, unending—

Past the klieg lights, the audience blurred; shapes swayed and merged, becoming a single form filling the stadium, a collective beast waiting to be stirred or tamed.

Lep stood in front of them, a streak of white, gaunt strength, distilled, like a beaker of liquid silver. ". . . *plasma torches to recycle garbage . . . amphibian cars powered by battery cells . . . fuel briquettes from sawdust . . . what would our forefathers think of these solutions?*"

He watched the clock. Contempt empowered his voice, like a rolling thunderhead, bearing down on the audience with the force of a twister. "*. . . men like my grandfather, Ben Calder—who pushed west into land no white man had ever seen before . . . who extended the Texas frontier, opened the cattle trails, built the Houston Ship Channel . . . paved the way for the new frontiers of oil and chemicals and industry. What would those pioneers have thought of the concept of limited growth?—of a philosophy that asks us to be managers of scarcity?—of* *solutions that tell us to dole out pittances of energy that will grow smaller and smaller until the lights go out in the world—?"*

The beast roared in response.

Lep watched the clock—

The parking lot was badly lit. Cars filled the shadows, packed together, sleek as porpoises. Joanna's heels rang on the concrete.

The door of the Mercedes wagon resisted. She pulled at it. When it came open, it sent her staggering backward. She wanted to weep. It was an indulgence to weep.

Then she heard somebody call her.

Vinnie Anderson was making his way through the cars, sprinting, without a sound, soft-soled shoes, necktie flapping, spectacles glinting in the shadows.

He halted in front of her. "They clubbed him," he said. No preamble. "When they got him out of Hermann Park, they pistol-whipped him." Staccato. Like a recital. "They crushed his skull. They thought he was dead. They panicked. They gave him a fake I-D, listed him as a motorcycle accident and took him to the morgue. When they got there, it turned out he wasn't dead. They dumped him in Emergency at Calvary."

She got into the car, slammed the door and started the ignition.

He leaned through the window. "They added an extra touch."

She turned to look at him. "What?"

"They put a donor card on him."

Particles swirled around him, small clouds of micrometeorites, cast from a star that had exploded long before his birth . . . particles racing swift as bullets through the void.

In the silence, Malone heard Japanese flutes, unearthly . . . then a majestic melody rose and swelled, a multitude of organs . . . a children's choir, high, melodic . . . deeply moving.

In the silence, he heard—

Malone felt time stop—

He felt himself split—felt the time-space continuum rupture—felt himself being hurled forward into the future through space, and backward into the past through time—

*He felt his Comanche grandfather's presence . . . returning him to
an Eden where no distinction existed between Heaven and Earth . . .
where a man dreamed of a buffalo herd and, on the plains, found the
buffalo, waiting . . . where a man spent his life in pursuit of a vision
and that vision decreed his journey on earth . . . where the first law of
life was not survival, but Oneness; some form of God connected everything . . .*

*. . . and he saw that, like his grandfather, he was no more and no
less than a ceremonial runner.*

*In the same instant, he was hurtling toward a future where ten bil-
lion people occupied the earth . . . and a band of ten thousand set out
into space . . . traveling in a generation ship for a hundred years to
reach another planet . . . to colonize that planet according to their
dreams, increasing their numbers to ten billion . . . when another generation ship would set out again to voyage for another hundred years
into the universe: in quest of Eden . . .*

*. . . and he saw that, like those future voyagers, he was a participant
in the death of one world and the birth of a new one, already taking
place—*

His eyes were drawn to Earth again.

He felt the pull of Earth. He turned away.

Below him, the solar platform sparkled like a sea of fire—

"Life is a burning, a fire reaching for fuel—"

The car radio was on. Joanna had only a dim awareness that it was
on, only a dim recognition of Lep's voice—

*". . . How did human life develop from molecules? Through the
process of metabolism. Through the burning of fuel—"*

The windshield was streaked.

The moon was gray, behind clouds. The streetlights glared. She
pressed the accelerator, weaving through traffic, speeding through
streamers of light.

*"—the quality of any civilization can be measured by the energy it
consumes. When man consumed primitive energy—plants and animals
—man built a primitive society. When man learned to consume the energy of wood and steam and wind and water, the level of civilization
rose. In our lifetime, as man burned the energy of coal and gas and pe-*

troleum, civilization soared to new heights—carrying man to new heights—carrying man into space—"

Traffic thinned in the Medical Center.

She entered the parking lot at the rear of Calvary, looking for Tate's car.

Her headlights picked up the Porsche.

"Progress demands the consumption of fuel, the burning of energy. Progress, like fire, appropriates—it seizes and devours—it claims energies other than its own—"

She pulled in next to the Porsche and got out, already running—

71

Lep could feel the President's eyes on him; he could feel the wariness, the President's growing suspicion the political momentum he had gathered was being pirated—

"*I say there is no energy crisis—*"

"*I say today's prophets of doom are like the whalers who set up an outcry when kerosene replaced whale oil, and like the miners who predicted disaster when petroleum replaced coal—*"

The television cameras were blinking, aimed at him—

Lep felt the audience respond. Palms outstretched, he had the sensation of holding the crowd in his hands as—five years ago—he had held a model of the solar platform and explained it to Merritt. He felt himself hold the crowd firmly, with authority, grasping the packed stadium in his hands as his grandchildren and their grandchildren and the Calders who came afterward would grasp the planet—

"*The doomsayers tell us we're on the verge of using up the entire energy output of this planet—*

"*What they say is so . . .*

"*They tell us our civilization is voracious—*

"*What they say is so . . .*

"*They offer us defeatism. They offer to take us back to the seventeenth century—*

"*I say no—I say that abundance and wealth is the natural state of life. I say that metabolism—the burning of energy—is the natural mechanism of evolution—"*

He paused. He felt the audience waiting. He saw the television cameras blinking. He could feel the President's uneasiness, the dawning realization that a scrupulously guarded speech, a carefully sculptured populism, might somehow be eroded before it was unveiled—

"We are moving into a new time—"

He heard his voice come back through the loudspeakers, quiet force, the voice of a prophet—

"A time for a new kind of pioneer. A time that demands that we open the world, not close it—"

He heard his voice deepen, rolling like thunder, godhood speaking—

"I say we reach out beyond the planet. I say we create the highest form of civilization ever known to man. I say we set as a goal the consumption of the energy output of the entire solar system—and move toward a future that harnesses the energy of the galaxy—"

She was told, *"Dr. Calder's in surgery—"*

She tried the main reception desk. She didn't know under what name Guero had been registered; all she had was a description. She was told the Registration Offices were closed, what she was asking was impossible—

She was told, *"I'm sorry, Mrs. Calder. Dr. Calder can't be reached in surgery—"*

The elevator carried her upstairs. If she could reach the dome—rap on the glass, catch Tate's attention—the idea carried her through the maze of corridors. The door to Foley's office was locked. She took the back route, the same route she had taken with Malone the night Zev Malachi was killed; she heard an echo of Allison's voice, *"It's all coming apart."* Allison had *known.* What? She, too, had *known.* What?

A light burned in the empty reception room. She went through it, past Tate's office, hurrying down the short hallway that led to the entrance to the observation dome. That door, too, was locked. She went back and retrieved the keys. Then she unlocked the door and mounted the stairs.

A hush pervaded the dome. Red carpet absorbed her footsteps. White formica counters, sterile, were cold to her touch in the freezing air conditioning. There were eight observation rooms, eight operating rooms below. The first two she passed were dark and empty. In the third, she saw light strike the viewing window from below. Entering, she looked down.

A patient occupied the operating table, surrounded, bound by tubing to machines, something vaguely familiar about him. She searched the squad of green caps and masks. She could see Foley, snapping orders like a General. She didn't see Tate. The patient looked bleached, skeletal—a shadow of someone she had seen before—she recognized the Vice-President.

She drew away. A stool toppled. It thudded against the carpet, leaving a dull echo in the silence. She set it upright and left.

Outside the observation room, she halted, suddenly seized by confusion. She had an urge to run. Something beyond herself carried her into the adjacent viewing room.

Tate was down there.

Tate was alone.

He was bent over the operating table, obscuring her view of the patient's face. Intent, hunched over, hands rising and falling, he was suturing the chest. She could see the open chest cavity, gaping, immense, something odd about it, something grotesque and ominous. She could feel the same ominous quality in the monochromatic stillness of the operating room, in the absence of attendants and machines. She saw Tate pause. She saw a spasm pass through him. Then she realized he wore no cap, no mask, he wore no gloves; and another swift memory of the night of Zev Malachi's death flashed before her: Allison's voice, *"He's dead, isn't he? Why are they sewing him up?"*—and Tate, answering . . . *"A mark of respect."*

The chest cavity gaped, a bottomless chasm. Why did it gape so? What was she seeing? Then she *saw*—

The cavern held no heart. She was staring into the deep abyss of a human chest without a heart.

Recognition broke through, like her own heart cracking—

Shock turned her rigid. A cry stuck in her throat, unutterable. Pain refused to be discharged; pain welded her to the sight of the violation, demanding she be an accomplice. She was riveted to the motions of Tate's hands, sewing; she was connected to the convulsions that gripped him—she waited for each one, shuddering with each one—even as she resisted the recognition of what he was doing: Restoring Guero's outer form.

Tate looked up and saw her.

His face was stricken, wet with tears; his face told her he had been making a lost attempt to repair—not Guero, but himself.

Grief shone from his eyes—

She saw the blindness had been stripped away, leaving the world naked; stripping him naked. In the bleakness of his face, she saw everything he was and had ever been, exposed—she saw he was more naked than he had been at birth or would ever be again except, perhaps, at the moment of death. She saw it as a moment of death; the death of everything that had gone before.

She tried to pull her eyes away.

His anguish held her.

For an instant that seemed an eternity, their eyes locked and she felt the moment of death she had seen in him being passed to her; she felt death split her consciousness, felt it split her psyche, felt it blast her inner world apart. The look bound them. Quivering, it bound them as fourteen years of marriage had never bound them, as no sexual union had ever bound them, as no knowledge of flesh and no earthly contracts could ever bind them.

A sob escaped her. Tears released her, rivers of tears streaming down her face.

Wrenching away, Tate fled—

Lep paused. Not a sound could be heard in the Astrodome. The red lights of the television cameras blinked steadfastly—

"*Here, tonight*—"

He watched the neon board—

"*—in honor of the President of the United States*—"

He made a sweeping gesture of respect in the President's direction—

"*—in the name of Calder Enterprises*—"

He kept his eyes on the board—

"*—in the great American pioneering spirit of private endeavor—man will step into the twenty-first century*—"

From the corner of his eye, he saw the President scowl. He saw the President lean over and whisper to Isabel—

The board ticked off the seconds—

He saw Isabel shake her head—

Malone hovered over the solar platform, holding the laser, gauging his distance from the antenna.

Something made him look up.

Three hundred billion stars were his companions, indifferent witnesses to his ballet in the heavens . . .

He stared at the configuration of the stars.

He felt time stop—

He heard a heartbeat in the silence. His own? Or God's? Did everything alive share the same heartbeat?

His eyes were drawn to Earth.

He saw the earth was breathing.

He could read its thoughts, feel its passions and its pain, glimpse its dreams. He could feel the longing and the discord of the human heart which, like the Sundark, permeated every inch of void.

The instant passed. The vision vanished.

Turning from the sight of Earth, he aimed the laser—

PRIVATE PARKING: A crossguard blocked the entrance. In a lighted booth, two Astrodome guards were wearing pistols.

"Calder—"

The gate lifted. A parking space appeared. The Porsche slid in. Tate had no memory of having driven it here.

The parking lot was filled with shadows. He made his way through the cars like a man in a dream discovering himself on a speeding train with no memory of having purchased a ticket or boarding, and no certainty of his destination; only a sense of being propelled by an incoherent need—

There were more guards at the door. "Calder—" He managed to show identification. His hand shook. In the outer vestibule, he could hear Lep's voice booming through the loudspeakers.

"*—the sun as an endless source of teeming energy. . . . With America's intelligence, and its creativity, and the powers of its technology, why have we intercepted only minuscule amounts of that energy?*"

Lep's voice produced chaos in him. Like a wary drunk, he walked a straight line through the chaos. He could feel pieces of himself break-

ing off, like an avalanche cracking. He had a fear of his mind cracking—

The elevator rose. Flashes of clarity assaulted him, fierce, unforgiving—

He had remembered it as a seduction. It hadn't been a seduction.
The boy had persisted, dogged Lupe's footsteps, spied on her—even at
fourteen, hadn't the boy set out to exercise the rights of a Calder?
Dove hunting—in Mexico—hadn't Lep demonstrated that sex was
plunder and, afterward, a secret between men?

The Stadium Suite was locked. He let himself in with his key. There
was nobody in the suite. Nobody playing billiards. Nobody in the
shooting gallery. There was nobody in the nightmare but himself—

Lupe had been a virgin . . . Lupe had worn a silver cross around
her neck. The whole time the boy was making love to her, she had
clutched at the crucifix and, at the end, she had cried out, *Madre de
Dios*—

An inner witness, stone-eyed, told him he was pleading guilty to the
lesser crime—

—in search of deliverance—

In the saloon, he went behind the bar and filled a glass with scotch.
He turned on the television set. Lep filled the television set. Behind
Lep, on a platform, Isabel was sitting between the President and the
Governor. He left the sound off, watching Lep, studying Lep—

Madre de Dios . . . the boy had hated himself, had hated the raw
sexual drive that had been stirred. Obsessed, he had transposed guilt
and shame into a sexual tyranny—he had threatened her with exposure, exile to Mexico—forcing himself on her, as though the boy had
been commandeered by Lep's demon.

The scotch burned his throat, constricted his chest.

Her pregnancy had appalled him.

He had taken his secret to Lep. Lep had accepted it, without remon-
strations, with a tribal pride, as though he'd passed through some necessary rite like a chieftain's son sent out with one arrow to bring back
the heart of a deer.

The bar was mirrored. He stared at the mirror, like peering through
fog at a stranger. The image fractured, telling him his psyche was frac-
turing—

—under the guilt and the pain and the anger, he could feel something struggling to break through.

He turned off the set. He left the bar and climbed the stairway. The door to the viewing room was locked. He remembered, in nightmares all doors were locked. He used his key. Inside, the lights were out. The lounge had been cleared. The loudspeakers were turned off. A crew was working in the dark, suspending a large filigreed platform from the ceiling. Somebody growled, "Nobody's allowed up here—"

"*Calder*—" he answered.

Guero had been a Calder—

In his mind, he heard Lep say, "*There're Calder half-breeds all over Texas—*"

He looked down. Struck suddenly by dizziness, he watched the Astrodome spin around Lep's figure—white suit, silver hair—like a Roman candle, exploding. For an instant, he could feel the power of absolute power, the madness and splendor of absolute will, the ruthlessness that had attracted and repelled, shadow as light, darkness as fire, the seduction that had been a rape, Lep's rape—

His mind threatened to snap—

Rage offered to hurl him into a maelstrom of ancient hatreds. Rage offered him deliverance, primal, a frightening image: *Graf,* the wild stallion that couldn't be tamed, seduced, exploited, was to be killed. Was to be killed—

Guero—

He saw Lep's as a monstrous force. He saw himself destroying it—

The image shattered. Another surfaced, struggling to be form—

In Lep's face, he *saw*—

The Astrodome plunged suddenly into darkness.

He was staring into a black pit. The loudspeakers were on. The pit was filled with Lep's voice, rolling through the darkness, reassuring the Secret Service . . . over his head, the eerie construction suddenly glowed, iridescent—

"*What you see is a model . . . What you see is a miracle . . . What you see is the first connection ever made by man between Earth and the sun—*"

He bolted.

The rooms below were dark. Outside, the corridor was pitch-black. Some faculty other than sight thrust him toward the stairs. He plunged down them.

"*At this very moment, two hundred and fifty miles from Earth, panels of photovoltic cells are collecting sunlight—*"

Lep's voice filled the dark stairwell.

"At this very moment, an antenna is converting the sunlight to microwave energy, like a radio beam, and transmitting it to a ground receiver—"

Tate struck the ground floor, his breath coming in short bursts, running.

"In fifteen seconds, electricity converted from sunlight will reach the Astrodome . . . In ten seconds, the Astrodome lights will go on again—"

He pushed his way inside the darkened stadium, shoving his way through the crowd.

"Five seconds from now, Calder Enterprises will lead this great nation into a new frontier of energy . . . three seconds from now, the Astrodome will be lit for six minutes from the power of the sun—"

The lights blazed—

The crowd cheered.

Lep stood above him, arms outstretched, triumphant. *"America has plugged into the sun!"*

Trapped in the crowd, no more than twenty feet from the platform, Tate stared—

Lep's face glowed with victory.

Tate saw what he had seen from above: Rage was not deliverance.

Lep's face creased with pride.

Tate saw what he had seen from above: The face of a man who was going to die.

The lights flickered, like a warning.

Then they blew—

Plunged again into the darkness, the crowd started to roar. Around Tate, pandemonium broke—

Malone hesitated.

Something warned him. Something made him stop and look back.

He saw the fire—

He saw the fire as another vision; a dark vision to be banished by disbelief: flames springing from one of the oxygen tanks on the satellite. Then, stunned, he saw the flames were real—noiseless in the vacuum of space, rising without a crackle—sparks flying, threatening to ignite the other tanks.

He jerked forward. His body tensed, trying to push through zero gravity. His mind racing, he pressed furiously at the gas jets, forcing motion, unwieldy, like the jumps of a grasshopper. How had it happened? A flaw in one of the heaters? A puncture by a flying micrometeorite? God's hand—or man's flaw?

Were they the same?

Inside his pressurized suit, he felt his body soak with sweat. What was happening to the others inside the satellite? He knew. Pushing toward it, he could feel the heat of the fire. He knew. Eerily silent, the flames leaped, shooting off sparks—then the other tanks caught, bursting into silent flames against the glossy darkness.

The cord still bound him to the satellite—to his companions inside the satellite. How long before it blew apart? And if he reached it before then, what could be done?

The silence rang. Nothing. He kept going. Nothing. Overwhelmed by helplessness, he released his pressure on the gas jets—

Nothing.

Time ceased—

He saw he had been given an instant in time, as all men were given an instant in time . . .

He saw he had been given a vision, as all men were given a vision . . .

He saw he had been given a choice, as all men were given a choice . . .

He understood his final choice.

He saw his life had been a burning. He saw his life had been a flight. How would he take his leave? In flames—or flight?

In a single motion, he raised his hand and bid farewell to his companions, and cut the cord.

Floating, weightless, he soared free, falling upward—choosing the ascent of man—the right of man to take his place among the stars.

He saw the satellite explode. Silent. Soundless. A rainbow aureole of flames. Debris swirling from a flaming comet. He saw the flaming debris strike the solar platform. Stored sunlight blazed, incandescent, like a floating city of light. Spinning, falling free into the void of unknown worlds, his eyes kept returning to the light. He saw it as the mystery of life . . . and by the light that burned in the heavens, he saw that mystery triumphed over loss, as life went spiraling through time and space to seek its resolution in another form.

72

"Guero's dead . . ."

Allison wept. Joanna held her.

"I knew—"

Joanna held her.

After a while, Allison rose, leaving Joanna sitting on the edge of the bed—the bed Allison had slept in since she was a child—Joanna could see the old dolls on top of the armoire; a breeze ruffled the curtains, mourning the passing of childhood.

Allison stared out of the window.

A clock was ticking, like time's heart, beating. Death always stopped time. Life started it again.

Allison turned. "It's not Zev's child. I know that. I know it's Guero's—"

"You're carrying the child that was meant to be born," Joanna answered gently.

"Do you believe that?"

"If you want it. If you love it—"

"And if I don't—"

"Nobody can make that choice for you."

Fear winged across Allison's eyes. "Why do they kill *everything*—?"

She wanted to answer: There is no *they;* only *we.* She was silent.

Allison hadn't asked how he died. Later, Allison would ask how he died. Truth would wait. Truth would wait until they could all bear it.

"You used to tell me tears washed the windows—but I can't *see* anything. Only the cruelty. I can't *feel*—"

Joanna rose. Slowly, she moved across the room and took Allison in her arms again. Holding Allison, she had a sense of two of them, poised on the earth.

"You will," she said softly. "You'll feel again . . ." She took Allison's face in her hands and looked into her eyes. They told her fear would yield to wonder. They told her grief would yield to life. "I promise you . . ."

Gently, she released her.

Quietly, she turned and left.

She went through the house, turning on lights. She went into the kitchen and lit a fire under the kettle and set out a teapot. Her motions were strained, mechanical, designed to keep her moving. She told herself wisdom was grace. She told herself grace was trust. She could remember not knowing these things—not believing them. She knew Allison had called forth a wisdom that was not yet hers.

When she turned, Allison was standing behind her.

Allison had washed her face. She had combed her hair. Allison's eyes filled with tears again. She brushed them away. "I have to go—"

"Where?"

"Tonight . . . I have to stay with Lupe."

The teakettle whistled. Through her own tears, she watched Allison go.

The sky was black, blistered by stars. The wheels of the Porsche skimmed the streak of highway, like traveling over ice. Tate pushed the speedometer needle toward the hundred mark. Clumps of scrub oak whipped by and silhouettes of timber trembled in the open space. Oblivion beckoned, easy on a Texas road: You pressed your foot down on the accelerator and went straight to Hell.

He had passed through Hell—seared, he could feel the wounds that might never become scars, unhealed, to be borne—and now he had entered that cold and barren land that stretched beneath the pitiless eye of Judgment.

Guilt offered to make him sovereign of isolation. Guilt offered to crown him emperor of no-man's land.

Something resisted—some small awakening of a wish to live, tenuous and fragile—the protest of another voice, halting and uncertain, to ask if he presumed himself to be the center of the universe?—so powerful that one early anguished act of sexual exploitation had determined the entire journey of another creature?

How could that be?

Vietnam . . . his marriage to Joanna . . . medicine—he could see the distortions—choice without commitment, the objectifying of flesh, the substitution of mastery for feeling, of experiment for love. Yet, was he so powerful that he, Tate Calder, had not been subject to life's shaping forces? Did he believe that destiny could be preempted by the secret orders of an abolished self?

It could not be.

The road blurred. A fire blazed at the base of his skull, sparks danced across the windshield, and through a roaring wind he heard the voice of life—

Within every distortion was its penalty; within every cruelty was its consequence; from the seeds of lovelessness sprang the man-made jungles that flowered into violence—

—guilt was not repentance—

—and every evil came from fear of loving—

A night owl screeched. Tires struck gravel. The Porsche spun twice around the road. The night stood still. He heard the crickets' song. On the side of the road, he sat behind the steering wheel, shaking.

From the terrace, Joanna could still hear snatches of the radio broadcast. "*. . . cause has not yet been determined . . . Lep Calder remains unavailable for comment . . .*" Looking up, she stared at the stars. They looked cold and rigid. The sky looked forbidding. It drew her and, at the same time, it turned her away; it refused her access. She could hear the phone ringing; it took effort to become aware of the phone, ringing.

She came back into the bedroom. On the radio, the announcer was saying, "*. . . NASA was in ground contact with three of the crewmen when the satellite explosion occurred. At that time, the fourth member* *of the crew, Campbell Malone, was engaged in extra-vehicular activities . . ."*

She turned the sound down and answered the phone. She heard Tate's voice. It took her a moment to register it as Tate's voice.

"I'm calling from a gas station in Waelder," he said.

It took her another moment to answer. "It's on the radio—"

"I thought I'd better call. I thought you might need—" he didn't finish. "It blew up," he said.

"I know." She had an image of the town of Waelder. Highway 90, an hour and a half away. Patches of fields. Quiet, shady streets. A town of church steeples and red barns and silos, like something she had once known and lost.

"I'm sorry about Malone."

"I haven't been able to think about Malone—"

"Everything blew up."

"Yes."

"I was there, at the Astrodome. When the lights went on again, Lep was gone. At the hangar, they told me he took the plane to El Paso. That means he's going to the Big Ben cabin." He hesitated. "I think he's gone there to die."

She was silent. She was trying to understand what he was telling her.

"I never loved Guero," he said. "That's how it happened."

She started to tremble.

"Do you understand?"

"I don't know," she said.

"I have to see Lep. Before he dies, I have to *see* him."

She could hear his struggle. He was telling her his struggle wasn't over. He was telling her he knew pardon was something he had to grant himself.

"I can't," she said. "It's too much—"

"That's not why I called. I called to say something else. I wanted to tell you"—his voice broke—"I loved Malone."

She washed her face.

She could hear the radio, *". . . he may have elected to reenter the earth's atmosphere by turning his gas jets full-thrust to depletion. This would abruptly alter his impulse vector and cause a long spiral-like trajectory descent . . ."*

She brushed her hair.

She could hear the radio, ". . . *at about four-hundred-thousand-feet altitude, friction with the atmosphere would produce enough heat to disintegrate his pressure suit. Death would be caused by pressure drop, air embolisms in the heart and brain, followed by asphyxiation and burning . . .*"

She came back into the bedroom.

"*. . . it is, of course, also possible that he elected to remain in space. In that case, he would continue to orbit the earth for the next four or five hundred years . . .*"

She turned the radio off.

She picked up her handbag and went down the stairs and out the front door. A breeze stirred the air, soft, like a caress; she could smell the Gulf in it. She looked up. The stars seemed nearer, less inaccessible, Comanche-like fires warming the endless prairie of the sky. The loss of Malone filled her, reaching out—first love, lost love, love that had never been meant to be lived—the brightness of it shone in Allison; he had given her that. She tried to see Malone up there. She couldn't. He had gone too far. She imagined him waiting four or five hundred years—for his great-grandchildren's grandchildren to catch up, and even go beyond him. She imagined him waiting for another generation to take the divine primeval spark of life and resist the urge for conflagration. She imagined him hoping that even in her own lifetime men might learn to tread with tenderness upon the earth and soar with awe into the universe. The thought was the closest she could come to *kaddish*.

The breeze shifted. She could smell the desert in it, suddenly.

She crossed the grass and got into her car and pulled out of the driveway, heading west toward Highway 90.

73

Darkness rushed past. The air smelled dry, like ashes and the bleached bones of animals, corroding for centuries. Lep felt the mountains swallow him up and then thrust him out again, the way they swallowed the moonlight—carnivores of time . . . he was covered by a thin film of sweat . . . Pavlik was driving. He hadn't driven himself in years; he had occupied the back seats of limousines, dictating, making telephone calls, creating international corporations, or ordering the demise of companies that had outlived their usefulness . . . now, the jeep climbed, careened, curved downward again, as if it might hurl him out and downward, rendering him helpless.

The air bristled. Gorges leaped and opened, then vanished. The headlights swept the stark chiseled rock, rising sharp and steep, dizzying. He felt clammy. He had a fear of dissolving, a fear of disappearing into quicksand . . . his ears split from the altitude. Creatures darted across the road. The road had once been the Comanche War Trail. Every May, at the time of the Mexican Moon, Comanche war parties had come through the Chisos Mountains to raid Mexican villages. These were the Ghost Mountains, still haunted by the spirits of dead Indian warriors. *Despoblado,* the Mexicans had called the Big Bend country. Desolate.

The jeep had left the campgrounds behind, backpackers and trailers and tents, speeding beyond the boundaries of the National Park. High up, he could smell the fir and the ponderosa pine; he could hear the rattle of aspen leaves. Then the canyon veered and dipped, past bedrock, heading inward toward the desert again, off the main road and into the back country. The Basin dropped. He felt it drop away. He couldn't see it, but he could hear the sound of the wheels, echoing off into nothing . . . and more nothing . . . he could smell ancient rock and pulverized bone. The wind was fierce. Cold. The road followed the contour of the canyon, winding and twisting. The desert smelled brittle. The air tingled, too clear to breathe, heady as opium and filled with a pulsing nearness to death that aroused convictions of destiny and fears of oblivion . . . the fear made him smile; he meant to mock fear as the desert mocked him, but the smile froze, half-formed, coiling inward and snaking down his throat to the pit of his stomach, searching for a cavern in which to hide. The jeep found the clearing. He could see the cabin, primitive, a light burning inside; kerosene—Merritt's pickup truck was parked in front. Pavlik brought the jeep to a halt. A pack of coyotes set up a wail.

"Leave me here."

Pavlik turned. "Do you want me to come back for you?"

"No," he said.

Except for a butane cookstove, the cabin remained as it had been . . . *built by Ben Calder, logs hewn with a hand-ax . . . an Indian wife, buried here; so was Anna Calder . . . Ben Calder had gone back to the ranch to die, but they had buried him here, outside of Eden where, like the Indian warriors, he was sometimes seen, roaming—*

Lep shivered.

The furnishings were spartan—a scarred oak table, a few rawhide chairs—simple necessities. The only source of heat was the stone fireplace. The fire had gone to embers. There was a last log. Merritt saw he was shivering and put it on. He saw she had been packing. There was a battery-powered radio on the oak table, he knew she had been listening to the radio reports.

He hadn't spoken.

"Are you hungry?"

He shook his head.

"I had hoped—" she didn't finish. She went into the bedroom and came back with a blanket, as if he were an old man. He dismissed the blanket with a gesture. He stood with his back to the fire, chilled; the log failed to catch, one log never burned. She was scrutinizing him. "When I heard on the radio that it had blown up out there, I went outside and I looked up. There was no fire in the heavens. There wasn't anything."

He didn't reply.

She was wearing faded jeans, a bronze-colored sweater, her hair was dark at the roots. She brought a duffel bag in from the bedroom and set it by the door. "Why did you put me under surveillance? Did you think I'd betray you? Didn't you know the only person I ever betrayed was myself?" The words spilled out of her. "Are all women fascinated by power? How long did it take Allison? A week? Two weeks? It took me twenty-seven years." She caught herself. Her voice dropped to a whisper. "Why did you come here?"

He didn't answer. He knew there was an answer she wanted. He didn't know what it was. She bit her lip. She shook her head. He watched her go back into the bedroom. She came out wearing a windbreaker, her hands shoved into the pockets. She stopped at the table. She pulled a cassette out of her pocket, made an adjustment on the radio and inserted the cassette in the tape deck. He heard his own voice,

"*She was a dancer. She called herself Acacia . . . I was told when Acacia raised her hand and found a pistol in it, she froze . . . until they took her away . . . I was told these things by Ernst . . . I made no comment . . .*" Merritt wound the tape forward. "*I instructed that a horse be sent to Muncie, Indiana . . . a blaze-faced sorrel mare, gentle enough for her two-year-old daughter. I also sent a saddle and a split-fringed buckskin riding skirt . . .*"

She shut the tape off. "When I first heard it—I thought—that child and I, we're the same age. I wondered where she was, what had happened to her. Then I realized"—she returned the cassette to her pocket —"when I was two years old, you were already . . . heartless."

"It's not important." They were the first words he'd spoken.

She was staring at him. "I had hoped—" again, she didn't finish. "The note I sent with Pavlik—?"

He shook his head. "I didn't read it. I destroyed it."

He watched her go to the door and pick up the duffel bag. She looked back once. "It said—I never loved you."

He knew she was lying. It wasn't important.

He heard the door shut. He heard the pickup truck start. He heard the sound of the motor vanish into the silence of the mountains.

The wind was cold. He could smell rain. He went past the Indian graves. The bluff sloped down and a stratum of rock cropped out. On the ledge, against the face of the rock, stones had been piled—the women had been buried there, with their cooking implements, flat stones used for grinding corn and flint scrapers, which had been used to dress deer skins, and bone needles. The men were buried higher, always in the most prominent spot.

Lep carried a flashlight. He had come for firewood, but the night had drawn him, higher; impelling him to climb the bank.

Ben Calder had taken the Comanche War Trail back from the Mexican-American War . . . He had brought Garras back, a child, purchased for seven dollars. They had camped here . . . hunting for deer—

He climbed the slope which the Indians had long ago terraced in a semicircle, using rising walls of rock—a dozen terraces. Years ago, he had found Comanche bones here and a number of arrow points. The beam of his flashlight struck the crevices in the broken hills. He had once found hand mills here, hollowed out of rock, tools used to grind corn; he had found spearheads and beads made of mussel shells. He had never disturbed these things. He had always left them where he found them in commemoration of the savage within him.

He heard the rumble of thunder. He heard a coyote scream.

Turning, he swept the beam of the flashlight across the mescal pits below. Circular mounds, some of them twenty-five feet in diameter, had been built with a rim of rocks that was always higher on the northwest because of the wind. The Indians had roasted their *peyote* on heated rocks and put it away to ferment until the time of the mescal feast when, sitting in a circle, each warrior was given the portion that would grant him an interview with the spirits who brought guidance.

There had been an apple orchard on a bench of rich loam which washed down from the mountains. Between the mountains and the orchard was a series of broken hills and, at the foot, there had been a spring that dried up in summer. Garras had fashioned a bow and arrow. Then Ben Calder and Garras had climbed to this spot—

He turned away. A mountain meadow spread out before him, like an oasis in the desert. The wind blew through his white suit. The wind chilled his bones. Lightning flashed.

Garras had taken aim. The arrow had zinged, piercing the buck's haunch—

The electrical storm broke. The moon vanished behind thunderclouds and the sky boiled like a furnace, lighting the landscape with streaks of blood. The wind churned. The sky split into jagged patterns of phosphorescent light, but no rain came, only handfuls of hail that struck him as he ran.

He fell. He felt rock strike bone. He felt blood trickle down his shin. The leg was pinned under rock. He couldn't move.

The night fell silent. The storm had cleared the sky. The stars shone.

He heard a rustling. He heard the soft pad of creatures. A pair of red eyes gleamed in the darkness. In the gleam of the flashlight, watching the coyotes creep from the bush, the word that came to him was *loveless—*

74

Tate saw the door to the cabin, open, blowing in the wind. He saw the kerosene lamp burning inside, a dead log on a pile of embers in the fireplace. Outside, he had looked up past the ridge of the Indian burial grounds and seen the light burning; he saw himself climbing, following the light—

He saw these things again—

The flashlight cast its beam into the open pit. His shovel rang against the earth.

He had wrapped what was left of his father in a blanket. He had set a lantern beside him. He had taken a rifle from the cabin but the coyotes were gone—

He saw these things again through tears that wouldn't cease, as if the course of an inner river had been changed and the banks overflowed—

He saw these things again as if he were a stranger, happened by accident to have been father to his son and son to his father—

His shovel rang against the earth. The wind howled its dirge of predator and prey.

He could hear the eternal murmur of the desert, crucible of saints and prophets, landscape of visions and miracles, starlit sunburned place impervious to those who came seeking an answer to the false and foolish question that asked whether man was a higher form of beast or a lower form of God. He could feel the menace in this land

where coyotes had foraged through centuries of wind and drought—
where man had always grappled with the devils of his mind—where the
stone-eyed vulture perched upon abiding rock, waiting for man to
unshackle God and return Him to infinity.

There were lesser worlds. He had lived in lesser worlds.

The mountains pulsed and glowed in the distance, a trick of smoky
light. He could smell the sweet fermented scent of cactus. A spark of
joy sprang from forbidden depths, traveling through despair, wrested
from darkness. As it sometimes happened in dreams, he caught a
glimpse of something permanent and untouchable—he recognized the
truth of dreams and what had been his waking state as sleep—he saw
he was in transit, and men were fallen angels, all.

The grave was dug. In this lost and barren place, others had been
buried—

He looked up. He saw Joanna. He saw her tears—

He knelt beside the gaunt giant of a man who had been his father,
pieces now, a lump of blanket. He slipped his arms beneath it and
raised his father to his breast and cradled him before he laid him in the
earth.

Stooping beside him, Joanna cast the first handful of dirt—

75

She had boiled up coffee in an old enamel pot and left it for the grounds to settle. She had found flour and yeast in the larder and mixed up a pan of dough. There were eggs and dried beef in the cupboard. He watched her set out an iron skillet and left the beef to soften in hot water so it could be fried like bacon.

He had brought water from the well.

A fire roared in the fireplace. He had built it.

Her purse was open on the table. Manuel's cassette of Ben Calder's ghost was running in the radio's tape deck; he had left it running, whirring soundlessly, nothing on it beyond the passing of time.

They had moved beyond time.

He went outside. There was a snap in the air, but the wind was still and the mountains looked frozen against the fading night. He walked for a long time. Then he came back and began splitting firewood. She stood in the open doorway, watching him wield the ax in an ancient rhythm. She stood motionless, holding a mug of coffee, her eyes telling him that all things had been torn asunder and in their place was nothing, the blessed nothing of a new beginning, uncreated, waiting to be born.

His eyes met hers. Then he laid down the ax and came toward her, taking the coffee from her, his hand brushing hers, his hand shaped by sorrow.

"I found Selinda's grave," he said. There was a finality in his voice.

From inside the cabin, he heard the tape whirr silently; he heard it quit.

Holding the coffee, he looked out toward the mountains. The silhouette of a live oak crowned the bluff, beginning to cast a faint shadow westward. Then he saw her eyes scan the sky and rest on the last fading star. His gaze followed hers. "Do you think that's Malone up there?"

"He'd like that . . ."

He watched a glow suffuse the sky. Dawn cast forth streamers of light, as if behind the mountain lay another world, waiting, not yet ready to be revealed. The night had been a tunnel. It had not passed—instead, they had gone through it, into infinite chaos—and now, returning, he was amazed to find life still there, still engaged in its familiar tasks, as if it had not been profoundly altered. Joanna took his hand. The gesture told him it was they who had been altered.

"Look—" she said.

The sky turned coral. Light streaked the clouds to rain an opulence on the earth. Through tears, he saw the harshness and the glory of this untamed land—he saw the miracle of sunrise, the renewal of soul, the break in the wilderness through which every man and woman traveled; he saw the cycle of birth and death and birth again.

Then the sun peered over the rim of the mountains, like the eye of heaven opening, and as the sunlight struck the earth, he heard Ben Calder's voice.

The tape was still. How had he heard it? Had it been a human voice? Or the wind?

"You will go from the bowels of the earth to the stars . . . You will change the nature of those you sire and those who come afterward . . . You will sow a wild seed . . ."

DATE DUE

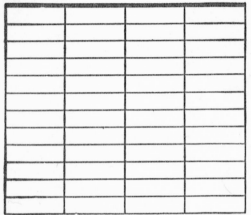